Shadow Valley

A Novel

by Nik Xandir Wolf

Copyright © 2022 Kelp Books, LLC All rights reserved

The characters and events portrayed in this book are fictitious. Any similarity to real persons, living or dead, is coincidental and not intended by the author.

No part of this book may be reproduced, or stored in a retrieval system, or transmitted in any form or by any means, electronic, mechanical, photocopying, recording, or otherwise, without express written permission of the publisher.

ISBN-13: 978-1-964880-02-0

Cover design by: Jaya Nicely
Library of Congress Control Number: 2022941494
Printed in the United States of America

Kelp Books, LLC

For Nick

Gulf of Humedales, Panama
Thursday, March 21, 1968
Hector

Small waves lapped at the white-gray sand in front of Hector Montoya's secluded—and fortified—villa on the Pacific coast of Panama. He stood on his second-floor bedroom balcony overlooking their small private bay, a Pearson thirty-five sailboat tethered to his dock, dense jungle all around. He sipped an espresso from a small enamel cup and heard a soft rustle of fabric behind him.

"You'll never be able to sneak up on me, you realize that?" he said, and even though English was the third of his four languages, it was spoken almost without accent. Hector, Peruvian born, was five ten, muscular, with short black hair, and wore a black robe lashed loosely around the waist.

"Who said I was trying to sneak?" said Lindsay Sheldon, Hector's wife. She slipped behind him and put her arms around his waist, kissing him on his unshaven cheek. "He's still sleeping."

Hector guided Lindsay around so they stood face-to-face. "God, you're beautiful," he said. He kissed the top of her head and slid his fingers through her shoulder-length, sandy-blonde hair. He held her face in his hands. "I can never look away from your blue eyes. And you gave them to our boy."

"More gray than blue," she said. "Dark hair and blue eyes. The girls are going to go crazy for him."

"I still cannot believe I am a father." Hector laughed. "Family and love, the Achilles' heel for people who do what I do."

"Used to do," she said.

"Used to do. Correct. But memories live on in the minds of many. Unless they are stopped, of course."

"I love him so much," Lindsay said.

"I did not know that a love like this existed until I saw his face in the hospital. And every day since. Heath has rocked my whole existence." As a hired killer who never knew his own father, Hector had hardened himself against love and all of its variations. Then, in his mid thirties, he met this girl, Lindsay, and she cracked that shell wide open. And then they had their son, Heath. And it was as though Hector's entire understanding of the universe had been violently ripped away. This girl and this boy left an imprint on his soul so deep, and so complete, Hector was transformed.

For the last twenty years, Hector had traded currency for people's lives to the highest bidder. Fascists, communists, drug runners, and of course, the US government, but all that had changed. It started during his affair with Lindsay, his CIA handler, but it came full circle the moment his son's purple, wrinkled body was pressed, skin-to-skin, against his chest in that hospital in Belize. Holding that child while standing by Lindsay's side in the hospital caused a profound shift in the way he viewed life, and existence. Suddenly this boy and Lindsay were all that mattered. And all that would ever matter.

Lindsay borrowed Hector's cup and took a sip from his espresso. She turned to look out the window at the calm, cerulean ocean that stretched endlessly past the bright sand. "I know he has. I also see everything differently because of him," Lindsay said. "That's why we're here."

Lindsay had been Hector's handler. The person who had managed to track him down in the bloody periphery of the Cuban Revolution nearly a decade before. Then his involvement with heroin smugglers during Vietnam. He was a gun for hire, a mercenary. A very good mercenary, and thus far an impossible one to kill. Lindsay Sheldon of the Central Intelligence Agency had been able to make contact and convince him to work as a secret agent by selling information on his employers to the US government. If this were found out, it would make him very unpopular with some of his old customers. And then he dropped off the grid. But, Hector knew you couldn't just disappear with no questions asked. The fascists didn't like it, and certainly the CIA didn't.

Hector and Lindsay had to pivot quickly when they decided to keep the child. It wasn't all that difficult to buy new identities and build a discreet villa in Panama. It didn't guarantee safety, but the villa was fortified on all sides by natural barriers deep in the Gulf of Humedales. Four-foot-thick cement walls, a panic room, escape tunnel. This was the only way they could think of to stay together safely, as a family. And after two years, Hector had started to believe it might actually work.

A child's tiny whimper came through the intercom, and it filled Hector's heart with joy. He wanted to hold his son every chance he could.

"I'll go get him," Lindsay said. She turned to leave, and Hector grabbed her. He felt the sensation of the air being sucked from his lungs—a breathless feeling he only got when something terrible was coming. It sounded silly to most people, but it was like his sixth sense. A split second later he heard the blast out on the dock, and the sailboat exploded into a burning fireball of slick black smoke. He remained calm, and even though her whole body was tense, Lindsay stayed calm, too. They both stared out at the scene. He turned her to him again and looked into her eyes.

"We both knew this might happen." He pulled her into a hug. "We have to execute Project Exodus."

Lindsay's head dropped to his shoulder. "No…*no!*" She pulled away. "I would rather die fighting them as a family than give him up now." She looked out, scanning the blue horizon marred with flames and the acrid scent of burning oil. "We could hide him in the panic room."

Hector didn't know who "they" were. It could be any number of organizations that had tracked them down. In the end, it didn't matter who; they had to move. Two Zodiacs with twin outboards came cutting around opposite sides of the bay, four armed men in fatigues in each.

"Project Exodus," Hector said.

"There has to be another way." She stared back at him, pleading in her eyes.

"Our son deserves a life better than what we can provide," Hector said, and even though his words were firm, he felt like his heart was being torn from his chest. "Better than on the run with us. Or dead. He will be with kids his own age. Without the threat of death every day." Hector wasn't sure if he was saying it to reassure himself or Lindsay. As much as he hated the idea of it, the kid shouldn't have to grow up marked for death. That was why they had developed Project Exodus in the first place. It was a contingency plan to get Heath into the United States safely should anything go wrong. He was set to be adopted by a couple that Lindsay had met during her time at the Defense Language Institute in Monterey, California.

"Execute Project Exodus," she said.

The boats were nearly beached in front of the villa now. Hector kissed Lindsay, and she nodded. They sprinted into the house. Hector pulled a pistol from behind a mock Manet painting, and Lindsay kicked a stool at the breakfast bar. A Luger dropped from beneath the counter. Moving quickly but methodically through the villa, they slipped down the hall and into the child's room. The child stood at the edge of his crib in blue onesie pajamas, crying.

The child, not quite two years old, held his hands to his cheeks, tears streaming through his tiny fingers. "Momma, ouch. Loud. *No me gusta.*" The child had been practicing Spanish and English together, and his words were mumbled and broken through the tears.

"I'm sorry, sweetie. We'll get you someplace quieter." Lindsay picked him up, kissed his shock of black hair, and held him close to her chest.

Hector, picking up a phone receiver from beside the crib, used the rotary to dial a local number. It rang. "Exodus," he said clearly, and hung up.

A small explosion detonated at the front door, and Hector led the way downstairs with his pistol at a ninety-degree angle, Lindsay trailing with the crying child. At the back of a large walk-in closet, Hector opened a hatch and helped his wife and son into a large panic room and sealed the door. At the back of the room, he led them down a set of stairs into a dimly lit corridor. He closed it and turned the wheel hatch behind them. They hurried through the damp, narrow hallway for nearly a quarter mile before they finally reached the end.

"*Dios por diez,*" Hector said. A little charm he'd invented for luck. He turned the wheel hatch and pushed the steel door up, then peeked through the jungle canopy. It was clear.

Climbing the ladder, he stepped out and helped Lindsay up. They struggled through the foliage to a small bike path and heard the high whine of a motorcycle engine. Moments later, a minibike sputtered to a stop in front of them, a teenage boy wearing battered clothing, rope sandals, and a mop of messy brown hair looked up at Hector, eyes like pools of fear.

"*Donde esta* Dona?" Lindsay asked.

"*Dios mio. Es verdad, Angel de la mureta.*" The kid's voice was shaky, and so were his hands.

"*Quien es? Donde esta* Dona?" Hector shouted. The kid looked terrified and shrank back.

"She is in surgery," the boy managed to strangle out in broken English.

"Shit." Hector looked at Lindsay; his eyes felt heavy, his sinuses clouded like he might cry at any moment. "Give him to the driver."

She tried to give the child to the teenager, but the tiny limbs clung to her, and the child wailed. "No. Mami. No. Mami. I love youuu." The *I love you* sounded like one sweet, passionate word with a singsong at the end that shattered Hector's heart all over again.

"*Dar a este niño a* Dona Diaz. *Entender?*" Hector said.

Their plan had been set for the two years they'd lived here. Dona Diaz was a doctor at the local hospital and worked with the couple that Lindsay had met in Monterey—Grant and Eydie Hastings. They were physicians with Doctors Without Borders and spent months each year in Panama volunteering. Dona was supposed to make the pickup, get the kid to Grant and Eydie, and the new family would fly back to California together. If Hector and Lindsay were able to kill a few people or buy a few people off, they planned to locate their son and find a new place for their family to hide together. They both knew that was a long shot.

"*Sí.* Immediately, señor," the boy said.

Hector turned back and reached for the child. Lindsay resisted.

"We'll be together again, I promise," Hector said, looking into her eyes and wanting it to be true as badly as she did.

She kissed the child's head again and handed him to Hector, and at that moment, gunfire ripped through the tree canopy overhead. Hector recognized the sound of Kalashnikov rifles.

"It is time. We have to," he said.

Hector hugged the child and felt the small, warm body against this chest. The tiny arms around his neck, the hot tears on his collar. He realized the tears were his own mixed with the boy's, and he wanted to collapse in grief right there in the jungle. He kissed the boy's cheek and tucked him gently into a child seat attached to the rear of the scooter. Taking a thin chain from around his own neck, Hector removed his onyx ring and strung it through, then placed it around the child's neck. More gunfire ripped leaves and slammed into tree trunks around them.

"Go!" Hector shouted, and the teenager hit the gas while the child pleaded, cried, and begged.

"Papi. Papi. Mami. *Por favor.* I love youuuu."

Hector turned to Lindsay, and they both dropped to the jungle floor and crawled until they were sheltered from the bullets by the bunker door. They caught their breaths.

"Ready?" Lindsay asked.

Hector tried to smile. This was what he had loved most his entire life before Lindsay, and before Heath: being underestimated and correcting that in blood. Here especially he had the benefit of being on his own land. Hector had a preternatural ability to survive dangerous situations. And to kill. He just hoped that after two years retired, he still had it.

"They want the Angel of Death," he said. "I guess we should go back and give them what they came for." Hector looked through the foliage toward his home. Lines of smoke drifted up in hot, gray clouds. He helped Lindsay down the steel ladder and closed the hatch. They moved methodically back toward their house. Their mousetrap. They were prepared for phase two of Project Exodus. Project Exterminate.

Part I

They call them cold-blooded killers—
They say they are heartless and mean—
But I say this with pride,
That I once knew Clyde
When he was honest and upright and clean.

But the law fooled around,
Kept taking him down
and locking him up in a cell,
Till he said to me,
"I'll never be free,
So I'll meet a few of them in hell."

—Bonnie Parker, 1934

Chapter One
Thursday, June 14, 1988
Heath

1

I cracked my bronze Zippo and snapped the flame to life, lighting my cigarette. The heat fanned my sweat-beaded forehead. Stepping out of my black Crown Victoria, I felt the blast of the Central Valley dry heat. It somehow felt hotter than the flame had. I inhaled and draped an arm over my open door. I exhaled and watched the smoke drift up toward the low, burning late-summer sun. My childhood home in the outskirts of Shadow Valley looked sun parched with cracked white paint along its weathered trim and clapboard siding. And beyond the house, weeds lined the fifteen acres of dead orange trees. It looked like an abandoned property.

Inside I could hear muted gunfire, so the TV was still on. I could also hear the rattle of the old swamp cooler. It meant Mom was doing okay. But I still felt guilty leaving her out here alone in her condition. She deserved better.

Coming up the bowed steps, I noticed something tacked to the door. A final foreclosure notice. Opening it, I scanned to the bottom line. We owed thirteen thousand by September 15, or the ranch was going to auction. If it weren't for Mom inside, I would let the capitalist pigs take the place. But she wanted to live here until she passed, and I was determined to let her. I tore the notice apart, letting the scraps blow off the porch and scatter out toward the empty fields.

I sat in an old rocking chair, which had been my dad's, to finish my cigarette and counted my tips from the afternoon shift at the Blue Cue. I had eighteen dollars. I would need a thousand shifts in three months to save the place at this rate. I hadn't always been so broke. After high school, I'd made a decent wage framing houses with a local contractor, but the building industry crashed after Black Monday the year before. And worse than that, my weed supply had dried up. The only reason I took the job bartending without pay was for the tips and the ability to move a few ounces a week under the radar. My go-to guy, Victor Munoz, had gotten pinched by the Shadow Valley PD a week ago. The bastards had beaten him within an inch of his life and locked him up. Word was they were trying to deport what was left of him. I needed to be careful, but I needed money worse. And without a lot of weed fast, I had no idea how to save this place. I was glad Dad was gone. He didn't have to see me ruin this place.

Robert and Linda Walker had adopted me out of a group home at age twelve shortly after they had bought this ranch. They couldn't have kids on their own, and this place was some sort of retirement dream they had conjured up. They had wanted a simpler, more peaceful existence away from the hustle of downtown Shadow Valley, where they worked in social services—Robert as a family court judge and Linda a social worker. I guessed this ranch twenty minutes out of town was the idyllic, Western-style living they wanted after watching *The Duke* all these years. Shadow Valley's slogan was "A Town with True Western Hospitality." That might have been the case in the 1800s, but now, in the 1980s, it was a cesspool of crime and poverty with one of the highest murder rates in the world.

2

Inside the house, the air was stale and smelled faintly of urine, which meant I needed to check Mom's bedpan. I peeked into the living room. She was sleeping in her elevated hospital bed in front of the blaring TV. She looked peaceful. Mom used the bathroom normally most of the time, except when she slept. She had never really recovered from her stroke a year before, and besides occasional flashes of memory and basic functionality, she was largely vegetative. I turned on an oscillating fan in the kitchen and sat in front of it. As soon as I started to cool off, the phone rang. I went to the living room and muted a rerun of *Dukes of Hazard*, then went back and answered it.

"Walker Ranch," I said.

"May I please speak with Robert Walker?" the voice said. Sleazy, formal. A suit.

I fought the urge to scream at the guy. We'd been getting debt collectors calling the house since Dad died three years ago. He had been only seventy-eight when he'd passed, and even though he'd been a judge and made decent money, he'd also had a gambling problem. He used to go to Vegas once a month to "visit his money."

His death had been sudden and tragic. Never a man to be idle, he worked out on the ranch every day. Always out there mending barbed wire or herding cattle with his gray mare, Stormy. All it took though was a damn rattlesnake. One early summer afternoon, there was one coiled up in the tall grass, right at the edge of our property. It leapt up and spooked Stormy. She was a good horse, too, but she was never quite broken all the way. But some horses, like people, weren't meant to be broken, so I never faulted the horse. Dad fell off her when she reared, and broke his hip. The doctors at Yokut Delta Hospital fixed him, but Dad died shortly after surgery.

"Robert Walker is dead. He's been dead. Stop fucking calling," I shouted into the receiver.

The voice persisted. "Then can I speak with Linda Walker?"

I exhaled, gripped the phone, and pressed the phone hard against my forehead. "She's sick and can't speak. Anyone else on your list?"

Silence.

"Look, I'll make your job easier. Everyone's dead. Okay? Send your bills to J.G. Watts and Associates in Shadow Valley."

"Are you the head of the household—"

I slammed the receiver down. Mom groaned from the living room.

"*Shit.*"

I filled a mason jar with water and went to her side in the living room, then tipped the brim to her lips. They were dry and cracked, and her breath smelled sour, but she took some water and licked her lips. Her eyes opened and searched the room before finding me.

"Bobby. Where's Bobby?" Her withered hand brushed my cheek.

"Dad is gone, Mom." I placed her hand on her lap. "Are you hungry?"

"Where's Bobby?" she said with a whimper. Mom was eighty-one years young now, and it made me sick I couldn't give her better care than this. She and Robert had adopted me when I was twelve years old. When no one would consider housing me. After I'd killed two men in cold blood.

"How about some applesauce?"

I stood and brushed her thinning gray hair back, and she looked up with a rare clarity in her gaze. "Heath, my boy." She smiled, her stained, crooked teeth showing. It was a lucid moment, and even though I loved when I got these flashes of her, it made me sad too. I missed the days when she would take me hunting, fishing, and horseback riding up through Shank's Hollow. Stormy and Shasta in a dead run, dust kicking up from the pounding hoofbeats. "I have something to give you before I forget." I patted her hand. She'd said this before, and every time I asked her what it was, she asked me who I was.

I brought a tin cup of applesauce over and helped her grip the spoon. She fed herself, and a glob of sauce dribbled down her chin. I changed her bedpan, liquids only thankfully. After the stroke, a hospice nurse would come by every day. But once I stopped paying, she stopped coming. I'd sold off the cattle, equipment, everything I could to try and buy us more time, but there was nothing left. Needless to say, I needed a miracle. I wiped the sauce from Mom's chin. Then the phone rang again. My stomach knotted up. I marched to the phone and picked it up.

3

"I *said* to call the goddamn attorney's office—"

"Heath?"

"Who the hell is this?"

"Bro, it's Avery."

"Holy shit, man. How are you?"

"Better than ever. You okay?"

"Sorry, yeah, I've had these bastards calling every ten minutes looking for my dad."

"Still trying to save the family farm, huh? California's last true cowboy." Avery chuckled. He'd been trying to get me to move to Santa Cruz since we graduated high school almost five years ago. He checked in every few months to tell me how amazing his misadventures were in petty crime and beautiful surfer girls.

"I'm no cowboy. This place just keeps sucking me back in." Avery and I had met at a group home, Hotel Dog Shit, and we'd bonded instantly. He was there the night of the killings, too. After everything cleared up, he got placed in a home nearby, with the Angler family. They used to live in a double-wide right on a bend in the St. James River, where the water pooled nice and deep for swimming, and a band of feral peacocks made their soft, lovely call into the hot summer nights. We had good times there as kids, and I was sad when he left. He was like a brother to me. A brother who always got himself into trouble, which I always got him out of.

"How many times do I have to invite you out here, man? I'm telling you, stress-free communal life, all the weed you can smoke. And we make some cheddar on the side."

"I want to, buddy. You know I do, but—"

"But you have to save the ranch. I know, I know. Always duty first with you. You're going to die young out there from all the stress, man. You need to at least come surf. Find a nice girl. Or a not so nice one." He chuckled again.

"My mom needs me. Otherwise, I'd be there, you know that."

"I know, man. I know. But you could do a lot more for her with money."

I paused, waiting for him to follow up on that with an idea, but he didn't. "So it's going well up there? Are you sure you're good?"

"I'm perfect, man. You don't have to worry about me anymore."

"I'll always worry," I said. And I did. Avery was always planning a minor crime or two, and about to fail miserably until I stepped in. I either helped him or watched him get caught. I learned that early on, when he got busted for stealing test answers from Ms. Ken's desk. After that, I became his barely willing accomplice so I could ensure his safety more than anything. After the Ms. Ken incident, I helped him change our grades in Mr. Donald's math class, change his attendance records in Vice President Pomelo's office, and later, I would drive him to Shadow Valley Save Mart to jack handles of liquor. Among many other moronic schemes he couldn't pull off on his own. I could never really tell if he was simple or brave. But it didn't matter. We had survived Hotel Dog Shit together, and that was everything.

"You always had my back, man. Which is why you need to check your mail. Did you get a package?"

"I just got home. What is it?" I stretched the phone cord across the kitchen and checked the mail slot beside the front door. There were several letters and a bulging, padded manilla envelope. "Bill, bill, past due, and an envelope from Hideaway Enterprises. That you? You starting a legit business?"

"We're not registered with the state, if that's what you mean. But check it out. I think it's the answer to your troubles, man."

I tore open the packaging, and inside was a bag of ground Santa Cruz Coffee.

"Coffee?" I said.

"Inside, man. Come on."

I opened the bag and poured the coffee grounds into the porcelain sink, and it reminded me of sifting through cereal for the prize as a kid. A Ziploc fell into the sink. I stopped, picked it up, and tore it open. Inside were golden-green, compressed nuggets that filled the air with the sweet, skunky smell of high-quality weed. I pulled the baggie to my nose and inhaled deeply, feeling my shoulders and body relax. The scent was pure happiness, like the pleasant, early-morning promise of a warm spring day.

"Holy shit," I said.

"I told you, man. That shit is the best hash I have ever smoked. There's, like, five hundred bucks worth there. You sell that, send me two hundy, I'll send you more. As much as you want. Pay some bills, whatever."

"Dude, seriously, this couldn't have come at a better time." I smelled it again. "Where did you find shit this good anyway?"

"I've moved up since Shadow Valley, man. I've got a network, partners. I'm big-time." I could practically hear him smiling.

"Is there a *lot* more where this came from?"

"Fuck. Serious? How much do you need?"

"A pound or two? This batch will help me keep the power on, but I need thirteen grand by September, or this place goes to auction."

Silence.

"Avery?"

"Yeah. Hold on. You need *how* much?"

"Thirteen thousand worth or I lose the ranch." I wondered if I should reread my book on alchemy, since that might be easier than pushing thirteen grand's worth of anything on the broken-down day drinkers at the Blue Cue. But I could always up my hustle, find a new spot or two. Something.

"I can't get that much hash this short of notice." He paused, and I heard him clicking his tongue. "But you know what? I probably shouldn't—" His voice lowered to a whisper. "I probably shouldn't even offer this gig, but I might have another way for you to score twenty, twenty-five Gs in one week. But you'd have to come to Santa Cruz—and maybe spend a couple days at sea."

"At sea? Doing what?"

"Come on, you know you can't ask me that."

"Okay, what about my mom?" My heart started to race with adrenaline and fear. I had no idea what he was up to, but as long as I lived through it, it would be worth it. If it meant I could actually save this place. If I could really get Mom the care she needs and let her live here until she passed, I would do anything.

"Use the cash from that shit I mailed you and hire someone to watch her, or whatever."

"And it's twenty-five Gs in one week? But you can't tell me anything about the gig?"

"If you're serious about making some money, let me make some arrangements. But even if I get you hooked up, especially if you get the gig, you can't go asking questions like that."

"Got it, so just show up in Santa Cruz and bam, twenty-five grand."

Avery laughed. "Exactly. If you're serious, I'll set it up. Just don't tell me you'll come and fucking bail on me. I'll be vouching for you. With my partners."

"When do you need me? Can I at least ask that?"

"It will take a couple of weeks to set up, minimum. I'll call you when it's ready. When you get the call, you'll need to get here in twenty-four hours."

"Or what? They'll kill you?" I laughed, Avery didn't.

"I'll call you. Make sure you're home."

"I'll be here. I promise you that. And, thank you. Seriously."

"Yeah, yeah. Capitan. No worries. This is going to be good for both of us." Capitan had been my nickname on the high school baseball team. I played first base, he played left field.

"Oh, right. The *Dodger*."

"Hey, hey, never mind the nicknames." Avery hated his nickname. He'd had been so skinny that he'd been called Skeletor, or Dodger because he was impossible to hit with a dodgeball, or a baseball, or anything, really. "Go save the day, huh?"

"Yeah, yeah," I said.

"Peace and love, motherfucker. Talk soon."

"Talk soon," I said, and Avery hung up.

In the living room, Mom turned the TV back up so loud the windows panes buzzed in their worn wooden frames. I needed to make her some dinner and get back to the Blue Cue. I could unload this hash pretty fast if the right crowd came around. I would find out one way or another.

Chapter Two
Thursday, June 14, 1988
Heath

1

"You always short pour your most loyal customers?" I said, and shook the ice in my empty tumbler. Beads of condensation fell from the glass and were absorbed into the coaster. The old jukebox droned some Johnny Cash while the local unemployed, veterans, and drunks taking a sick day sipped their warm beers.

"You always drink like this when you're on duty?" said Ray Mendoza. Like Avery, I'd known Ray since middle school. Not from foster care, but when I started at Oak Hills, the rural school district outside of Shadow Valley. He worked most nights at the Blue Cue.

"I'm six two, two hundred. I can handle more than three of your weak-ass Jack and Cokes."

"Weak-ass? Always talking shit." He smiled and I laughed.

"Hit me with another shot in there," I said, and slid the glass toward him.

"Hey, it's your show, bro. But I just thought you might take it easy because of them." Ray nodded toward the rear entrance, where four Vagos rolled in looking gaunt and scraggly and mean. The apparent leader of the group, Yeezus, looked like some kind of Alice Cooper knock-off with long black hair and eyeliner. They walked through the bar, and a few of the regulars nodded to them. They took position on the elevated area of the bar around a pool table and began to rack the balls.

"*Shit*," I said. "Last fucker I wanted to see."

"How much do you have left?" Ray was the one who had gotten me the job bartending during the day. In exchange, I gave him ten percent of what I sold to the bar clientele.

"I've only sold about half." I felt the hash through my jeans pocket. "Probably two forty in cash."

"Why don't you just keep my cut, come back tomorrow. They never come two nights in a row."

I patted my pocket and looked around. The electric bill was past due, and I needed to pay that, plus get food and some medical supplies. I needed the full five hundred. Across the room, Yeezus laughed, and all four bikers looked in my direction, two over their shoulders. They whispered, and I stood, slugging down the much stronger drink Ray had finally poured.

"Maybe you're right," I said. I'd run into Yeezus before, and he'd warned me not to push my weed here, even though I'd been the one pouring their beers that day. It wasn't in my nature to let anyone tell me what to do, but I didn't want to cause Ray any trouble. Not to mention the fact that I was outnumbered.

"It's the right call," Ray said. "Come back tomorrow. And don't forget my cut."

"Thanks, brother." I turned to leave, and at that moment, she walked in. Rori, the most beautiful person I had ever seen in real life. The kind of girl that charged a room with lightning energy, like how I would imagine it would feel in a room with a huge celebrity. It was like you just knew that everyone in the room couldn't take their minds off this one person, and neither could you. They consumed your thoughts and the room with just their presence.

Yeezus catcalled as soon as he saw her, and she flashed him a smile that looked more like a warning. I'd seen her come in with these Vagos the past month or so, and the way they treated her bothered me. It was none of my business, but it got to me. The catcalls, the rough grabbing of her ass, the pet names like wench and biker bitch. I thought maybe I was pedestaling her because she was so goddamn beautiful, and that maybe she was as terrible as these Vagos on the inside. Unlike her though, they looked the same inside and out.

2

"On second thought," I said, "I'll take another Jack and Coke. And a Screwdriver with a cherry." It was the only thing she ever ordered here, and I rarely charged her.

"Heath, bro. Come on, man, I don't want a body count on a Tuesday night. Especially not yours." Ray's voice was pleading. He pulled the glass away and cleared the coaster.

I sat back down.

Ray had played baseball with me and had seen me at my worst. Even though I had gone to years of therapy for what happened in the group home, it didn't stop the nightmares. You couldn't kill two monsters and have it just gone away despite what the cop, Domino, had tried to tell me afterward.

I would lash out sometimes, even when I didn't want to. Becoming a Walker was the first good thing that had ever happened to me, and even though I didn't want to fuck that up, I sure came close. I couldn't control it sometimes though. I would just get into a blind rage and throw a bowl or smash some kid at school. Mom and Dad would try and help me focus my anger. They taught me to belly breathe and count to ten. They even had me reading poetry to take my mind off it.

I had nearly killed a guy during a baseball game sophomore year. The Oak Hills Aztecs were down 11–1 to a larger school, Shadow Valley High, when a senior ace pitcher had dropped a fastball into my left thigh. I rushed the mound and clocked him clean with a right hook, then mounted him like a goddamn bull rider and whaled away until two of his teammates tore me off. I knocked both of them on their asses and was going to work my way through the whole team until my catcher got me calmed down. The pitcher, James something, almost lost his scholarship because he couldn't play for ten games with a cracked jaw and broken nose. In the aftermath, Mom and Dad started with the poetry. They also got me into martial arts to teach me "discipline" since they train you to be defensive, not offensive. At least that's how it was in the Tae Kwon Do I took. But to be honest, it just made me a better fighter. I could throw leg kicks like Bruce Lee and really end someone's night. Or life.

"Rori doesn't belong to that scraggly fuck," I said. "She doesn't belong to anyone."

"Heath, you promised. There's only one rule." I could see the fear in Ray's eyes. He knew what I could do, and he knew I wouldn't back down. And I very badly wanted to help Ray out and just leave. But he and I both knew that it wasn't going to happen.

"It's my rule, too. Always stay low-key," I said, my words falling to a whisper when Rori approached. She sat on the stool beside me and cleared her throat.

"Barkeep," she said, holding up a finger, an upward lilt in her voice. She was in a playful mood.

"Heath ordered for you," Ray said. He finished pouring her Screwdriver and plucked a cherry from the garnish dish, setting it on top of the ice in her tumbler.

"You just assume you know what I want, Heath?" Rori said.

"It was a hunch, since you've never ordered anything else," I said.

Rori glanced my way and smiled. It was something I looked forward to every time I came to work. When her focus narrowed on me, the world went away in a sort of tunnel where the smell of stale beer and flickering neon sign around us disappeared. I thought about all the wrong things, and my words came out in a jumbled mess every time. My focus shifted between the slight crease above the soft arch of her upper lip, the contours of her high cheekbones, and the silvery glint off the glitter in her eye shadow. She said something else, but I was caught inside the gold flecks of her green eyes and missed it.

"What?" I said.

She laughed. "I said, how's my favorite bartender?" She took a sip from her drink, then made a face and sucked at her teeth. "Christ, that's strong."

"I'm great," Ray said, leaning over the bar. "Day shift over here just called my drinks 'weak-ass,' I believe were the words."

"Some people can handle their liquor better than others," Rori said. "Heath can handle it." She nudged me with her elbow.

Rori had seen me taking shots and chasing them with beer just about every weekday. I liked to keep a steady buzz to forget about how depressing this bar was. Rori usually only ordered a couple drinks and sipped them. Sometimes she came in alone, and I liked to pretend it was to see me. The truth was she rode around with these biker assholes most days.

She turned her stool so her body opened up to mine. "How's your mom?" she asked, meeting my eyes and striking a nervous prickle down my neck.

When the bar was slow, she would crack me open and investigate me. I felt like she knew she had a power over me, probably because she had this effect on most people. I told her everything she asked about, mostly. I didn't tell her about my life before getting adopted. I never told anyone about that part of my life.

"She's pretty much the same. She had a lucid moment, called me Heath earlier." The memory of that beautiful moment reminded me of why I was here. I needed to sell the rest of this hash, and these bikers were fucking that up.

"That must have been nice. You think she'll come around?"

I shrugged. "The doctors said that most of her recovery would have happened in the first three or four months. She might get better, but at her age, it's not likely."

"I'd like to meet her," she said very matter-of-fact, her green eyes still fixed on me. Yeezus barked something at her from the other side of the room. She waved him off.

"Are you serious?" I asked, the comment catching me off guard.

"I'm always serious." She sipped her drink and cringed again. Then she took a long gulp and shook it off. "I lost my mom when I was eleven to pancreatic cancer. I just think it would be cool to meet her. Not like any of these assholes take care of their mothers. From your stories, she sounds like an amazing lady." She finished her drink and raised her glass to signal for another.

I hadn't known about her mom dying when she was so young, and it was the first insight I really had into her childhood, since she usually avoided questions about herself. It made me wonder what that would be like—having a mom your whole life and watching her die. It sounded worse than never knowing her. It sounded like a goddamn tragedy. And then I saw Rori, maybe for the first time. There was pain behind her eyes. And the skull quarter note tattooed behind her ear suddenly made sense. I had asked her about it once, and she said she'd grown up singing with her mom, but she had left it at that. I wanted to ask about her dad, but I wanted her to offer that up when she was ready.

I tapped at an ice cube in my glass. "I can't guarantee she'll even remember *me*."

"It could help her though, right? Someone else talking to her?"

"It could. The nurses used to talk to her when they were doing her physical therapy."

"Hey, sugar, bring us a pitcher, huh?" Yeezus stood at the edge of the elevated platform, arms spread like Rori's behavior was wearing thin on him. The focus of every liquored up, half-functioning small-town cowboy in the bar turned to me. The person holding her up.

"You don't have to go up there," I said. Ray filled a pitcher with MGD and slid it over to her.

"Heath, come on," Ray said, begging now. "I could lose my job if anything happens."

"I broke it off with Yeezus two days ago," Rori said. "He's just doing this to get under my skin, you know?" She stood and grabbed the pitcher with both hands. "Don't worry. I'll be back for my drink."

3

She marched confidently across the room, clutching the pitcher of beer in her right hand. Chalk-white skin gleamed through rips in her stone-washed jeans. I had a hard time reconciling this girl with the one who had lost her mom and wanted to meet mine. The one who rode with bikers that had recently carved up a couple of Puerto Rican dealers over at Red Banks bar in Lemon Cove for selling them some low-grade heroin.

When she got to them, one of the lanky henchmen took the beer and poured it into dirty glasses. She whispered something to Yeezus, then came back to grab her drink.

"Ready for a show? This asshole is about to lose fifty dollars." She winked and went back to the pool table.

They re-racked, and Rori broke with surprising force, sending the balls scattering around the table. Everything seemed like it was going smoothly at first. Everyone in the bar paid close attention even though they pretended not to. Once the two were underway, I was shocked to see how good Rori was. Making bank shots, spinning the cue ball with some English. I couldn't help but wonder where she had gotten all that practice in. I watched Yeezus closely. He was becoming increasingly agitated with every shot Rori made. It was like watching a bad movie play out. One where you knew the outcome but were powerless to stop it. I pushed my drink away and poured myself a water to clear my head.

Yeezus was good, too, and the game went back and forth until it came down to the eight ball. Yeezus missed his first shot at the corner pocket. Rori stepped up, leaned over, and took careful aim. Then called her pocket. Without hesitation she knocked the eight ball straight into the corner pocket, the cue ball left spinning on the table.

Rori straightened herself and took a stack of rumpled cash from the table. Yeezus glanced around with a rare timid look. His buddies chuckled and mumbled something. Yeezus's face flashed with anger. Rori started toward the bar, but Yeezus grabbed her roughly by the arm and yanked her toward him. He paused, then leaned in and kissed her hard on the mouth. His crew laughed even harder. When he released, she stayed still for a moment, smiling. Then she reached back and slapped him hard across the face.

The murmuring in the room fell away, and all three bikers around Yeezus looked stunned. Even Ray was frozen behind the bar. Then Ray's hand instinctively shot out and gripped my shoulder. To calm me, to hold me in place. I stayed on my stool and watched, but my chest felt like a guitar string tightened one turn too far. I remembered the trick that worked the best when I felt the seduction of violence ring out inside me. Pull me toward it. It was a poem I had found in one of Dad's books. I recited it from memory to distract me. To pull me out of the vortex of anger I was staring into. *"Buffalo Bill's / defunct / who used to / ride a watersmooth-sliver / stallion / and break onetwothreefourfive pigeonsjustlikethat."*

All the testosterone in the building was focused on powder-keg about to blow, but Rori just spun and bounced on the balls of her feet. She approached the pool rack to put the cue up. Yeezus followed her. She glanced over her shoulder, and her hand moved slowly back to the pool cue.

She pulled the cue down quickly and turned to swing on Yeezus, but the bastard saw it coming and grabbed the stick firmly down by where her hands gripped it. He tore the cue away and gathered a fistful of her hair in his hand, snapping her head back. I leapt to my feet and breathed. I recited the next line of the poem, *"Jesus / he was a handsome man."*

Rori's liquid eyes, wandering the room, shimmered in a stratum of light that filtered in from the blinds. I took a short step forward, a glass tumbler in hand. *"'And what I want to know is.'"* My body was in movement. Muscle memory. Calm nerves. Words flying through my mind and out of my mouth. I was winding up; then my pitching arm was fully extended. The glass tumbler whistled through the air. It found its mark, and the heavy glass exploded against the back of Yeezus's skull.

He released her and grabbed at the wound, falling to his knees. Blood sprang from the wound and leaked through his interlaced fingers.

Rori slipped away and the other bikers rushed me. I tagged the first one with two jabs and a right cross that made him slip onto his ass—out cold. I turned to face the other two, but it was too late. I got clipped on the chin with a strong haymaker from the third biker. I fell to my knees and felt a pool stick crack hard against my back. The world spun bright, and I felt like I was sinking through the floor while my body dragged across it. Then I was through the back door and into the alley.

The last two bikers propped me up against a brick wall, and I caught an elbow to the face. My left eye started to swell shut. I did a bob and weave while they both swung erratically, landing glancing blows. Then I caught a knee to the stomach and doubled over, trying to heave breath. I wanted to let loose, really tear into these guys, but I couldn't find my moment. I dropped to my knees in hopes they would show some mercy. Instead, it seemed to encourage them. The taller one to my right picked his foot up, which had a steel-toe boot attached, and was about to come down on my head with it when Rori sprung from the back door, holding a brick.

"Leave him alone," she said, her face reddened and fierce.

The first biker shot her a death stare. "You saw what this bastard fuck did to Yeezus. No way we let him walk out of here."

"Fuck off, bitch," the other one said.

She charged them, and they turned to defend themselves, but she stopped a few feet away. Her face hardened, her eyes vacant. She looked murderous with the brick held high over her head. They started to laugh and then moved toward her, ready to tear her apart, too. That wasn't going to happen. With their focus on the brick, I quietly stood behind them.

I whispered the last line of the poem, "'How do you like your blue-eyed boy, Mister Death.'" They turned, and I divided my quick succession of jabs and right crosses between them.

They quickly recalibrated and fought back. The taller one connected to my cheek with a straight left. Then he suddenly yelped and fell to his knees. He slumped over, unconscious. Rori stood behind him, holding the brick.

The shorter biker spun and caught her with a backhand that rocked her head back and split her bottom lip. She cried out and stumbled back. I gathered what energy I had left and connected with a roundhouse to his head so hard, I felt like my shin cracked. He went down, and I moved to help Rori back inside, but instead, she jumped on top of the guy with that same vacant look. Sitting on his chest, she raised the brick but hesitated. She could put him out of his misery, but I didn't want that for her. I didn't want her to go through what I had gone through all these years. Death on my hands. It haunted you.

4

I stumbled over to her and held my hand out for the brick. She didn't look up. Then the back door swung open, and Ray came out holding a rusty six-shooter that he kept behind the bar.

"You guys better roll out," he said. "I called the cops. I'll make sure these assholes don't follow you."

"Thanks," I said.

"I better not get fired over this," he said. He went back inside and closed the door.

Rori dropped the brick and I helped her up. The first guy she'd hit groaned and puked, which meant he wasn't dead. She helped me hobble out of the alley and back to my Crown Vic in the parking lot.

In the parking lot, I tossed Rori the keys to my Crown Vic.

"I don't have a license," she said.

"What about your bike?"

"I used to ride with Yeezus."

"Christ, I can barely see," I said, tilting my head back to see her through the swelling.

"*Fuck*." She sounded both excited and scared. "Where are we going?"

I heard sirens in the distance. "Just drive," I said.

The tires chirped when she pulled onto the road, and she hit the gas. "Where do you live?" she asked.

"Out next to Easton Veterinary."

"I know it," she said. "They cremated my pit bull, Sally, out there when I was eleven." She seemed to be fine behind the wheel despite not having a driver's license, so I leaned my head back to try and stop the pulsating blood that trickled out of my nose. She turned the radio up, and "Folsom Prison Blues" came on.

We drove without speaking for a few miles, and once we were out on the country roads, she turned the radio down. "I had that handled, by the way," she said. "Those middle-aged, fake-ass bikers weren't going to do anything."

I let out an angry laugh, and it hurt. "I know those guys, and they are anything but fake. What the hell did you see in that guy? Can I at least ask you that, since my face looks like I got gored by a fucking bull?"

"He was interesting. And connected," she said.

"Christ. Connected to murderers. What are the chances he's going to come after us?"

"He won't. He's too smart to look for me."

I had no idea what that meant, but I let it slide. "What's the plan, then? He won't follow you home?"

"He doesn't know where I am anymore. I'm…recently between places," she said, her voice softening slightly. The first sign of vulnerability since I met her. But it also struck something inside me, a survival instinct. A gut reaction. Had she used me because she needed a crash pad?

"And you need a place to stay. Right? Seems convenient, doesn't it?" It came off harsher than I wanted. The thought of Rori staying at Mom's thrilled me, but if she was just using me, fuck. I wanted off this train.

"Hey, I didn't plan for Yeezus to pull that temper tantrum."

"Had no idea he would show up, right? You remember I live with my mom?"

She glanced at me quickly, her face tightened. Dark orchards raced past our windows. "That's not how I operate. Maybe I had some idea Yeezus would react that way, but I had no idea you would. Christ, you're kind of coming at me hard with this shit. I just saved your ass."

She did have a point. There was no way she could have known it would shake out like this when she showed up tonight. But she must have known *something* would happen coming to a bar Yeezus would be drinking at. And it didn't mean she hadn't had me lined up as a place to stay.

"All right. All right," I said, breathing to calm down. "Thank you for driving. And you're welcome for saving *your* life back there."

Her face softened again. "You did fuck those guys up. That was kind of awesome."

I wanted to smile, but it hurt too badly. "So, what's the plan, then? *Do* you need a place to stay?"

"Honestly, I can find a place. I do have friends."

"Are you going to stay or not?" I said, wondering how she had somehow flipped the whole script on the conversation, and I was now on the defensive.

"I mean, if I can help, sure. Maybe for a day or two. I can talk to her, your mom, and the worst case would be that when I leave, she doesn't remember meeting me."

I knew I should push back and focus on unloading the rest of the hash. But my face was busted up, and I needed a day or two to heal anyway. And almost like she could read my mind, she put her hand on my thigh and added, "I can also help clean you up." Then she smiled at me. "The least I can do."

It was all she had to say, and she knew it. It wasn't even fair.

"Oh, and you're welcome for saving *your* life. You know, with a brick, *and* the driving," she added, and hit the accelerator.

Chapter Three
Thursday, June 14, 1988
Heath

1

"Shit. Shit, shit, *shit*," I said, leaning back on my bed in the converted garage. Rori sat beside me with a bottle of vodka and some cotton balls.

"Eddie really opened you up," Rori said, swabbing a cut over my right eye. I hated that she knew these creeps by name. I hadn't gotten knocked around this bad since sparring with Victor Jimenez, a guy twice my size at Jung's USA Tae Kwon Do in high school. The place that had taught me how to take a roundhouse. And land a few.

"You should have used the brick on that bastard," I said, and winced when she taped the butterfly stitch over my eyebrow.

She laughed lightly, then blew on the wound, and it felt both hot and cold. "Seriously though, I'm sorry I dragged you into this." Rori dabbed at a few more spots on my head, then down my neck at some scratches.

"Mom used to say, people meet on purpose, even if they don't mean to," I said.

"Ha. So I was supposed to ride with Yeezus just so I could meet you?" She blew on my neck. "I saw you watching me as soon as I first walked in."

"It wasn't just me," I said. Her breath smelled sweet and hot from sipping the vodka, and I felt dizzy and excited at once. Rori was actually here in my bedroom, blowing on my skin, her pursed lips inches from my skin.

"Maybe I noticed you watching for a reason."

Her fingers grazed my earlobe, and I got chills. "It was either fate or dumb luck we both ended up there tonight, I guess. I wasn't even supposed to be there."

"Or bad luck," she said, and smiled. "Fate knew you would need me tonight."

"Fate knew you would try and crack a biker with a pool cue and start a riot?"

"Fate's a bitch. I can be too."

I smiled at that, then winced from the pain. "How did you know I would clock those guys?"

"I didn't. But I knew you could handle yourself."

She was right about that. It was like death and destruction were always on my horizon, all around me, and for some reason, I was preternaturally good at surviving.

She touched my cheek with a cotton swab, and I pulled back. "So tonight was either fate or a plan to humiliate your psycho ex with me as backup? I look that easy to manipulate?"

Rori laughed. "I wasn't trying to manipulate you." She held my face and looked into my eyes.

"Everybody wants something," I said. And it was true. There were only three people I had ever met who put other people's needs ahead of their own. Officer Domino, and my parents.

"Don't you think some people just say and do what they mean to?" she asked.

"No. Everybody always has an angle."

She moved her hands to my chest and applied slight pressure while she slid them down my sides.

"*Ouch*." I grabbed her wrists; my right side felt broken.

Rori's eyes narrowed, and I released her hands. They fell softly to my chest, and she kept them there. "Yeah? What's my angle, then?" She sounded wounded.

"Easy. Everything in the world is about sex. Except for sex. Sex is about power."

"You just come up with that?"

"Oscar Wilde said that."

"That's easy to say for a man. But I didn't save *you* back there for sex. I can have sex with just about anyone." She said it in a weary way. Like she'd had enough male attention to last her a lifetime.

"First—" I sat up and winced, and she leaned in to help me. "I saved *you*. Second, maybe you helped me for power." The words had come tumbling out. I wanted to stop them, but Rori was actually here with me, and I couldn't reconcile the desire for her to want to be here with the nagging voice in the back of my mind that she was here because she had nowhere else to go. "Third—"

"If I wanted power, I could ride with a bigger biker gang than those four mangy Vagos. I'm here because I like you, stupid."

"Third—wait, haven't you been trying to get me into bed this whole time?" The bruising on my face felt bulky and numb and hurt when I smiled. My argument with myself was cut short when she said she liked me. Maybe she actually did. She pushed gently on my ribs, and I flinched.

"Don't move, you'll open up the cut." She laughed and kissed around my swollen right eye. "And no, I wasn't trying to go to bed with you back at the bar." She let her fingers graze down my arm; her face looked calm, even kind. Like she had when we just talked all those times at the bar.

"Oh, good. Then I don't have to worry about you making a move on me." I touched her chin with my fingertips. Pain shot through my shoulder, but it was worth it.

"Do you always kill the mood like this?" she asked, and kissed me on my neck.

I leaned my head back and felt her breath when she kissed me again. "Wait. Just out of curiosity, when did you actually decide you wanted to sleep with me? Was it before or after I saved your life?" I smiled and winced again.

"Shhh." She held her finger to my lips. "I'm about to lose my girl boner."

She helped me out of my bloody T-shirt, then kissed down my chest. When she got to my waistline, she unclasped my belt.

"Can I say one more thing?" I asked.

"No."

She unsnapped my button and pulled my zipper down. Her small hands reached inside and grabbed me, and I responded by getting hard instantly.

"Okay," I said. "I won't say that Oscar Wilde was kind of right."

Rori looked up at me with her head over my crotch. My cock in her hand. "Maybe." She giggled at herself. "Since now I have all the power in the palm of my hand."

She teased me with her tongue, then stood and walked to the end of the bed. She pulled off her vest, then her Van Halen tank top. Her black bra juxtaposed the nearly translucent pallor of her skin except her neck and arms. A girl with a farmer's tan. She pulled her ripped jeans off and crawled onto the bed until she straddled me. I helped her unclasp her bra, and she placed my hands over her small, wide-set breasts. Her hip bones jutted forward, creating space where her black panties didn't touch the skin of her stomach. I kissed her chest, and she pushed me gently back, then peeled her panties away. Then she worked her hips over mine, teasing me with a back-and-forth motion.

"Is this the power you were talking about?" she asked.

I groaned. "It has to be. I would literally do anything you told me to right now."

She moved her hips so I was partially inside of her, then stopped and took my hands, bringing them up and placing them on her throat. She squeezed my fingers and moaned.

"You can take the power back. If you want."

I'd never choked anyone, and the softness of the skin under her throat felt vulnerable and raw. My first thought was that this was a trick she'd picked up from the bikers. I pulled my hand away, my dick starting to shrink. I tried to refocus; I kissed her chest, then her breasts.

She moved again, back and forth. Then, with a quick movement, I was fully inside of her. She pushed my hands over my head and held them there, and my ribs and shoulder ached, but I didn't care. Her long hair cascaded down around my face, creating a tunnel. A tunnel with only us inside. The walls, the room, the bed, all of it floated away. It was only the two of us in the entire universe, in a celestial rhythm together.

After, we lay there spooning, resting on my good side. A tacky moisture between our bodies. I looped my hand under her arm and cupped her breast. I kissed the back of her head, and the scent of her hair smelled salty, familiar, and inevitable.

"Are you feeling better?" she asked.

"I might need another drink and some Advil. But I'll be okay."

"Do we need to check on your mom?" she asked.

"I can check on her in a bit," I said, feeling like I might drift off but knowing that I probably shouldn't with the blow I'd taken to the head.

"No. I'll check," Rori said. "I want to. Just tell me what to   do."

I explained how to check Mom's vitals and bedpan and to shut the TV off. A few minutes later, she returned and slipped into a big spoon behind me.

2

The next morning, I woke up at close to 10:00 a.m., and the bed was empty. I reached across to feel for warmth, to make sure I hadn't invented my incredible night with Rori in some erotic novel of my dreams. I sat up and winced in pain from my cracked rib, then knew it was real. For better or worse.

I prodded my eye, and the swelling had gone down, but it hurt. I slipped on an old cotton robe and sniffed at the air coming through the laundry room. It was the honey-sweet scent of my dad's old waffle iron—like funnel cakes at the fair. I cinched the belt closed and slipped through the laundry room into the house.

Inside, Mom had an old John Wayne film on that she'd seen a million times, *Hondo*. Rori stood over the kitchen island in a pair of my boxers and T-shirt. She flipped the waffle iron open and pried a waffle onto a stack of about a half dozen. She glanced at me over her shoulder and smiled, her wavy hair pulled back into a ponytail.

"Take a seat in there, I'll bring you some breakfast," Rori said.

Mom looked peaceful and intent on her show, so I stepped past her and sat on the love seat beside her elevated bed. Rori came in a moment later with a waffle and a cup of coffee arranged on a TV tray.

"Your mom told me she was hungry," she whispered.

"Mom told you that, huh?" I forced a chuckle in case she was trying to make some sort of off-color joke.

"Yes, she said that they were your favorite."

"Hey, not funny." My father had made waffles almost every Saturday and Sunday since the first week of my adoption. They were a favorite of mine, and the smell of the caramelized batter, melted butter, and maple reminded me of all those mornings growing up. And how, later, in high school, I had been annoyed by his wake-up calls with the scent of pancakes wafting behind him. My chest tightened remembering him. He woke me up one morning when I had a vicious hangover, and I yelled at him, and he never made them for me again.

Rori's eyes widened like I had stunned her. "Did I do something wrong?"

I opened my mouth to respond when the TV froze, and the sound stopped. We both looked at Mom, who had her eyes trained on us.

"Heath, my boy," Mom said, "you walked past without even a good morning, you don't thank this lovely girl from the hospital for the breakfast, and now you're talking over my show. What's gotten into you?"

Her words were so simple, her voice calm, and yet it struck me, like getting bucked in the chest by a Clydesdale. Mom was having her clearest moment in months. And it had something to do with Rori and the pancakes. I felt momentarily stupid for not thinking about a trigger like the waffle iron to jog her memory. "Mom." I grinned and it hurt. "I'm sorry."

I walked to her and hugged her. She kissed the top of my head. "Why don't you and the nice girl here go in the kitchen and finish your breakfast. I'd like to finish my show."

I stood, grabbed the TV tray, and mouthed an apology to Rori. She followed me into the kitchen and sat across from me at our old, scarred pine dining table.

"That was incredible," I whispered, my whole body buzzing with excitement. I knew it wouldn't last, but moments like these were why I had to save this place. We needed as many of these as we could squeeze out of this old ranch.

"She was completely out when I first came in. The only food in the house was expired waffle mix, so I thought I would make a few and see if they were edible. Once they started cooking, she perked right up and asked for one. Told me where to find the TV trays."

"Should we bring her one?" I asked.

"She ate two!" Rori said, beaming.

"That's a goddamn miracle." I wanted to kiss Rori right then for this moment. I wanted to laugh and to cry. I wanted it to last forever.

Rori paused, then said, "What are you going to do?"

"Keep feeding her waffles, I guess."

Rori pulled a fresh foreclosure notice from the elastic waist of my boxer shorts that she had on. "It says you have, like, two months left here?"

3

I took a bite of my waffle, then a sip of the coffee. It was strong and bitter and blended perfectly with the corn syrup sweetness of the waffle. "I have a big score coming up in Santa Cruz in two weeks."

"Big score? I thought you just sold dime bags to drunks."

"First, ouch. Second, my best friend has something bigger lined up. I'm probably not supposed to talk about it. But it's enough to save this place and hire a nurse back on."

"Then what? You stay here and go back to hustling Red Banks, or Blue Cue?"

"You got any better ideas?" I asked.

Rori moved her face in close, a quiet, excited tone in her voice. "Yeah. Let's get the hell out of the valley altogether. It feels like the mountains and the pollution are closing in on me. I can't hide from it. Not anywhere." It was the first I'd heard of her plans, and I thought it was odd how quickly she wanted to leave, and the thought that first crossed my mind was she wanted to get away from the mess we had made with Yeezus and the Blue Cue. But she hadn't seemed worried about that the night before. Maybe there was something else that worried her. Something she wasn't ready to reveal.

"You can hide here for a while," I said. "Maybe I can pay you to watch Mom while I run my deal up in Santa Cruz."

"I would rather tag along to Santa Cruz. Get the hell out of here." She paused, maybe realizing she may have seemed too eager, and recalibrated. "I just have too many bad memories in Shadow Valley. There's a ghost every time I pass a place where something terrible happened. An old house, a bar, a whole town."

"Young lady, can I have some more juice?" Mom asked from the living room.

I grinned. "She really likes you. You did something. I don't know what. You really should consider staying."

"I like her too. I like her son even more." Rori slipped her hand over and interlaced her fingers with mine. Rori's soft, lightly tanned skin drew a sharp contrast to my bronze color. Rori noticed too.

"What are you anyway, nationality wise? I mean, it doesn't matter to me, of course, just curious because your dark hair and complexion make your eyes so much bluer."

I took another long drink of coffee. "I honestly don't know. I guess I never told you this, but I never met my bio parents. No idea who they are, where they're from, or if they're even alive."

"Huh. Would be kind of nice to know, I mean, instead of not knowing. Who your parents were. Biological parents, I mean." She was stumbling on her words, cautious, second-guessing.

"Yeah. It's not like I didn't ever wonder, you know. I wish I could sometimes. But then, I'm kind of afraid to. What if they're awful people?"

"They gave you that hair, and those eyes. Your eyes *are* beautiful," Rori said.

"You know, I knew it. You do just want me for the sex," I said.

She reached over with a fork and took a bite from my waffle. "I just wanted your waffle." She winked and sipped her steaming black coffee.

"I'll bring Mom the juice," I said.

"Oh, yeah. Okay." She smiled.

I slipped into the living room and set the orange juice on Mom's tray. When I started to leave, she grabbed my hand. "Heath, my boy, I have something for you," Mom said, her voice clear and lucid, reminding me of all those years growing up. It made me miss her the way she was, which wasn't fair to her. But I did.

"I know, Mom. It's okay," I said, just wanting to savor the moment.

"I love you, son." Mom let my hand go and switched her gaze to the TV.

"You and Dad are my real parents, forever," I whispered. I kissed her on the forehead.

"I'll get it from the safe later. Go have fun with your little friend. She's quite a handsome girl." She whispered, "Don't screw it up." I laughed lightly. Mom was always trying to set me up with any eligible girl she could find. It had been annoying as a teenager, but also endearing. She just didn't want me to be alone when she and Dad finally passed.

I patted her hand and went back into the kitchen and sat at the table across from Rori, lost in my thoughts. She seemed to sense that and sipped her coffee quietly.

"Are you going to get it?" she asked.

"Get what?"

"I heard what she said. You have something in the safe?"

"Oh, that. Yeah, it's nothing very valuable. It's just... It's a ring from when I was a kid."

"From what part of your childhood?"

"Before the Walkers. Look, there's something about me. Something I did when I was a kid that I should tell you."

"You can tell me when you're ready. I know enough." She smiled and patted my hand.

"I didn't want it. That's why it's in there. I told them to throw it away," I said after minutes of silence.

She looked up at me from her coffee blankly.

"The ring. It's from my bio parents."

"I can't even begin to understand what that feels like."

"You know what, I do want it. Let's get it. Tonight."

"Whatever you want. I'm here to support you."

4

Later that night, we slipped out of the garage and walked quietly into the house and found the key where Mom had left it on the table beside her bed. Rori followed me inside Mom and Dad's old room, and we opened the closet that smelled faintly of mildew and expired mothballs. I slid the key into the safe, then dialed the combination taped to the top. I opened the latch. The safe was empty except for a small envelope that looked faded and finger worn. Printed on the outside in Sharpie, it said, *Heath*.

I opened it, and long-buried memories of foster homes and cigarette burns and terrible bio kids came flooding back to me. I'd worn the old silver and black ring around my neck for twelve years, since it was too big for my fingers. I slid it onto my ring finger on my right hand, and it fit snugly.

A black onyx stone sat in the center with initials carved into either side: *AO*. I wondered if those were my father's initials. They must have been. Anthony? Andrew? Antonio? Wearing something of his made having bio parents feel more real than it had in a long time. And the fact that it fit so perfectly meant that I was probably more like him than I could ever imagine. I got a chill, and Rori rubbed my back.

"Was that his?" she said.

"It was. I know it."

"What does it say?"

"AO? I don't know. I never knew."

"Is that it?"

We searched the safe and found nothing else. Wearing the ring now did exactly what I feared most, which was why I had wanted to throw it away all those years ago. It was a constant reminder that I had another set of parents who had abandoned me. And all the possible scenarios of who they were and why they would do that would start to run through my mind again, and I didn't want them to. Not now, not ever. I kept the ring on and followed Rori back to the converted garage, where she held me again while we drifted off to sleep.

5

Two weeks slipped by in a blur of cicada songs, heat mirages on the blacktops of the road, and dust devils in the foothills. After I sold the hash I had, we kept busy by hunting with Mom's shotgun and riding my old dirt bike way back into Shank's Hollow, searching for Native American potholes in the granite slabs in the mountains. At home, the three of us did just about everything that we used to do as a family, with a few extras for just Rori and me.

Since Avery never called back, I called him. His phone line was dead, and I wasn't sure what to make of it. All I could do was wait. But what we didn't know was that our time was running out, fast.

Chapter Four
Friday, August 19, 1988
Heath

1

Rori curled her body around mine, our legs intertwined, pressing her head softly against my chest. The afternoon was hot, and we blasted the swamp cooler. Our humidity formed over the glass window in my room, creating a barrier from the dry, cracked landscape outside. I traced my fingers down her arm and stopped on a circle of raised scar tissue on her forearm.

"Burn?" I asked.

"One of my father's cigars," Rori said.

"Christ."

"That's nothing." She took my fingers and ran them over her wrists. The skin was welted with small scars so fair, they blended in. Underneath, the bone felt pitted.

"What the hell is that from?"

"He handcuffed me to the sink in my bathroom. That was nothing either." She placed my hand on her scalp. Just behind her right ear, I felt another lump of scar tissue. "Cracked me with his nightstick."

"Jesus, your father did this to you?" I didn't know why she chose this morning to finally open up, but I wanted to say just the right thing to let her keep talking. To be a safe place to confide, though I had no idea how to do that.

"He gets drunk, and it's lights out. A different personality. I used to call him Mr. Hyde in my head. He would become an unpredictable, living, breathing nightmare, where just setting a beer down in front of him might set him into a tailspin. Then he's in your face, screaming, ripping your hair out," Rori said, her body tense, her eyes focused on the ceiling and slightly misty.

I turned toward her and pulled her into my arms. Somehow, I wanted to reassure her that not only would I never hurt her, nobody else would ever again. "I've seen my share of shit in foster care and group homes," I said, and showed her a few burns and cuts from bad foster homes. "Kids that have shit like that happen to them have a hard time getting past it." I didn't like sounding doomed, so I rephrased. "We can get past it, though. You and me. We found each other on purpose, to make it through together."

She pulled away and sat cross-legged on the bed, facing me. Her eyes fixed on mine. "Wait a minute. You never told me about other foster homes or group homes."

"I have never told anybody about that. The Walkers were my parents. And some really bad shit happened that even ten years of therapy didn't help."

"Heath, you can tell me. You can tell me anything."

"You won't think differently about me, about us?"

"God no. We're in this together. And we're getting out together."

"You'll never see me the same."

"Heath"—she placed her hand on my leg—"I'm a safe place."

I nodded and drew in a deep breath. My heart raced slightly, bringing the memories back. I exhaled slowly and started. "We called it the Hotel Dog Shit. Well, that's what the kids that lived there called it when I got there. I'd just turned twelve. But let me back up."

2

I was born into foster care. That's what my social worker, Debra Price, used to tell me. Some nice family adopted me when I was a baby, but things didn't work out with the couple, and when they split, I got sent back.

At around three or four years old is when my memories start, when I can begin the count of all the homes I lived in. Probably about twenty by the time I was five. I try and count them up like sheep sometimes when I get that empty feeling in my chest that makes me feel like I'm floating out into space all alone. I try and count up all the faces I've seen over the years.

It's *fuzzy* though. Foster home after foster home. It was hard to trust anyone after a while, and so I stopped trying to play nice. I just kept to myself and tried to survive. Most parents didn't like that; they wanted you to play along with their little family role-playing. "Come have dinner with the family." Blah, blah. But I already knew the outcome, and so it was really hard to pretend. It's like memorizing all the lines to a movie that you hated the first time around.

Eventually I would fuck up and punch someone's bio kid, piss my bed, or break something and get bounced. Nobody ever looks at their sterling little bio kid when a window is broken; they look at the "troubled" foster kid. Someone once told me, when your real bio kid fucks up even really bad, tortures the cat to death—real serial killer stuff—you just punish them and move on. The foster kid fucks up, he's gone. And that's how it was for me. That is, until I was about eleven, almost twelve.

The last foster home I got kicked out of was Rodney and Linda Diaz's. All I had done this time was steal twenty bucks from Rodney's money clip so I could buy some food for the three other kids living there. Sammy, Michelle, and Pedro. Didn't matter that I went straight down to 7-Eleven and bought us all hot dogs, sodas, and a case of water because the refrigerator and pantry were completely empty. Except for condiments. And I had already puked twice eating ketchup off a used plastic spoon. None of that mattered. Not even that I knew all the money the state gave that family was supposed to provide us something to eat. I stole. I was gone.

That same day I got sent straight to my first group home. I guess they had run out of foster homes that take repeat offenders like me. Plus, I'd just hit a growth spurt. I was taller than my last foster mom now. Maybe five six. Nobody likes troubled teens. Once they hit growth spurts, they get big enough to cause real damage. It scares these suburban do-gooders.

A cop picked me up and drove me to the group home, which is a fancy name for an orphanage. Debra couldn't bear driving me out here, I guess. The first thing the cop said to me was that his pals call him Domino, and that I was his pal now, and that I could call him Domino, too, if I wanted. I liked the name, and so I called him that, and I could see him smile in the rearview.

He had kind eyes. Also, he looked middle-aged, about the same age as most of my foster parents, which just seemed old, but not old like grandparents old. I wondered if I had grandparents still alive and what they looked like. Not that it mattered, I'd never meet them. Still, I couldn't help wondering about them, too.

Most kids I met in the system knew their bio parents and had stories. Good ones, and terrible ones. One time, Sammy, the nine-year-old from Rodney and Michelle's house, told me his dad was a cop, but his dad's girlfriend was a mean asshole of a drunk. She would get trashed on Kessler whiskey and crack him in the head with the ironing board. He went to school for an entire semester with a new welt or bruise on his head or neck every day before his teacher called CPS. That same morning, when we were starving and alone in the empty kitchen before I stole the money, he said if he ever saw that "bitch" again, he'd kill her. "Set the word out! I'll fucking kill her." I always thought that was a hell of a thing for a nine-year-old to say. But he'd gotten it bad, a lot worse than I ever had. And plus, he had to sit by and watch his dad choose a violent, drunk asshole of a woman over him. His own son.

This cop, though, Domino, he seemed all right. Well-groomed and thin. His hair looked like it used to be black, but now it was partly gray, and his trimmed mustache was, too. When we parked in front of Sal's Market, Domino got out and opened my door. I stepped out and grabbed my trash bag filled with clothes. A short, balding, wiry-haired dude came out looking kind of like Richard Simmons with the short shorts and everything. He was holding a nice, shiny, green duffel bag with a wide, kind of gruesome smile. Like a clown, I thought. His crooked teeth made me shiver, but I also didn't want to be rude to this man, who was kind enough to volunteer for someone like me.

"Welcome home, Heath. I'm Sal and brought you this," he said, referring to the bag. He switched his focus and looked at Domino. "I just hate when they arrive with their belongings in a trash bag. But I had a feeling." He turned back to me. "No, you will have a real bag to carry your real clothes into your new home."

He handed me the duffel, and I shoved the trash bag into it. It wouldn't close, but I liked the sentiment. It was the first kind gesture I'd experienced in a long time. Still, something about the guy set alarm bells off in my head. The run-down little market, way out there, on the Northwest side of Shadow Valley, past the ganglands, and into the industrial area. It was all storage facilities, dairies, and plain brick manufacturing plants this far out.

"Where is the home?" I said, looking at the little grocery store.

Sal glanced back and, as if seeing the property fresh through my eyes, said, "Oh, this is the storefront where I work. Back behind, we've converted an old motel into our home. Fourteen rooms, twenty-two kids. You'll have to share a room, but we can put you on the wait list for your own."

I shifted and leaned so I could see around the market, and there it was. A green and white, paint-chipped, old motel with an empty pool at the center that was roped off with yellow tape.

"Come on through the store and grab a snack. I'll take you back and introduce you to Mouse. He'll be your roommate."

I turned to Domino, and he crouched and looked to make sure we were out of earshot from Sal. "Listen, kid. You ever need anything, you give me a call down at the station. I know you don't have a lot of people in your life that have your back, but you have me. Understand?"

I nodded and felt the slight urge to cry. I was so used to people using me for state income, threatening me, or criticizing me, his random kind words hit me kind of different. I choked it back though. No use showing emotion, I'd learned the hard way that people just think you're weak and use it against you when you get sappy all the time. There's always a pecking order in new homes, and I didn't want to start off at the bottom by being a crybaby.

"Thanks, Domino," I said. It felt good to have a cop as a friend. I even knew his nickname. He gave me a fist bump before he left.

I turned and walked through the market, which had an odd collection of food and drinks, a lot imported from Mexico. I grabbed two Jarritos, some chili plums, and some spicy chicharróns.

Sal walked slowly, giving a continuous stream of commands, praise, and encouragement to other kids that we passed. The place was pretty big with kids rambling all over, kicking a worn leather soccer ball, skateboarding in the empty pool, jumping rope, and I had a sudden rush of nerves. All of these new faces, most of them ignoring me or giving me a side-eye, felt overwhelming. I had the urge to make myself small, disappear into a tiny ball, and just watch these kids. See who they were, how they interacted, and find out where, if anywhere, I might fit in. When we got to my room, number eleven, Sal stopped and knocked.

"Mouse, it's Sal. Your new roommate is here." There was a soft grunt from inside. Sal pulled on the master key from his retractable key ring and opened the door.

The room had two twin beds with matching brown comforters, yellowed walls, and a slightly damp smell. I wondered if the place had passed any inspections; it appeared on the verge of being condemned.

I stepped into the room, and Sal, who'd been carrying my bag, handed it to me. "Let me know if you need anything, I'm always in my office. Here's your key." He pulled a key from his back pocket. Then he crouched down slightly—he was only a few inches taller than me—so we were eye to eye. "I'll let you get settled today, but tomorrow you'll need to sign up for a daily chore. Most newcomers work the register. We all do our part around here, and you'll be no different." He turned my shoulders and patted my ass as if to push me into the room but also like we were old college football buddies. It felt like a kind gesture, a friendly gesture. But I hadn't in all these years been touched on the ass by anyone, and I didn't think I liked it.

I put my duffel bag down on the unoccupied bed and realized Mouse was listening to a Walkman. The walls were empty except for a single Van Halen poster up on Mouse's side of the room, a big, permanent mirror along the back wall, the two beds in the center, an old desk in the corner, and a TV that looked half melted.

"You keep to yourself, and we'll get along," Mouse said, and rolled over. I lay back on the bed; the mattress was stiff and smelled slightly of mildew. I stared at the ceiling, getting the hollow, sad feeling again, and I felt like it might swallow me up. I wanted sleep, fast. I needed it to have some sort of escape from this place. I closed my eyes, but my mind raced. The lingering thought I always had before drifting off was why? Why was I born at all if this was how it was going to be? Why were any of these kids born? But we were here, and we deserved better. Eventually, I drifted off.

"Don't make a fucking sound, or I'll cut you wide open," a whispering voice hissed. My eyes shot open, but it was dark. I couldn't move and could barely breath. Someone's weight was crushing my chest, and a hand covered my mouth and nose. My heart throbbed hard against my ribs, and I almost pissed myself—

3

My story was interrupted by the sound of a car roaring up the driveway. Nobody ever visited us, and nobody ever sped up on our uneven dirt road. It made my heart drop, and I felt the familiar suck of air from my lungs. Breathless. Within seconds I heard tires on the gravel in the circular drive out front. I bolted upright and pulled the metal blinds apart. It was a Shadow Valley PD car with two uniforms inside. They skidded to a stop in a cloud of dust. Then hit the siren, which gave a stuttered chirp. Now Rori shot up, her eyes liquid and wide with terror.

"Fuck," I said. I racked my memory, trying to figure out why they would be here. The only thing I could think of was the fight at Blue Cue. But those bikers wouldn't have ratted us out. Unless Ray did, but that didn't add up either. "*Why?*"

Rori slithered out of the bed and crawled to the window, then peeked out. She gasped, put her hand over her mouth, and doubled over, back against the wall. She sobbed softly. In a sweep of anger, I realized she knew exactly why they were here.

"Wait." I looked out again. A fat cop with a cowboy hat got out of the driver's seat, and a thick-neck hillbilly got out of the passenger's seat. The boss and the tough guy. This was how they rolled up on the bars when they wanted to mash a few heads. These testosterone junkies, who worked out and jerked off all day, got to take their angst out on some petty criminals. I'd been one of those criminals before. "You know these bastards?"

She didn't look up.

"Rori? Who the fuck is that? Is this another psycho ex?"

She glanced up from behind her crossed arms. "No… It's my—"

"What? *Who?*"

"My dad."

"You have to be *fucking*—" Things began adding up quickly. Things I'd ignored because, of course, she was twenty-one; she had been drinking with bikers at a bar. Older guys. But I saw it clearly now. Her desire to hide out with me, leave town forever. She was a runaway. A *girl*. I could see it now in the downturned corners of her mouth. "How the fuck old are you, Rori?"

"Heath. No."

"How old?"

She sobbed. "I'm seventeen. I turn eighteen in, like, two weeks though. He's got no right to do this to me. Not anymore."

I felt angry for being lied to. I had been certain she was in her twenties. And I would never, ever fuck around with an underage girl. And that, unfortunately, was the least of my immediate concerns because there were two armed and pissed off cops that had just rolled up to my parent's ranch house like they were about to tear the place apart.

"Which one is he?"

She nodded with a slight whimper. "The older one. Heath, he's the chief."

I reached under my mattress and slipped a loaded .22 pearl-handled pistol into my underwear, firmly against my dick and slightly tacky balls. I had kept it under the mattress since Mom's stroke because she wasn't using it. She used to carry it riding in case she came across rattlesnakes or coyotes and needed to scare them off. I sat next to Rori, back against the wall. I wanted to comfort her, to hold her, to kiss her. But right now, I could barely look at her. This was no small lie. I was fucking livid about this situation, and more than anything, I was furious because I knew it couldn't change how I felt about her.

"We'll get through this. Somehow," I said.

There was a polite knock at the door, followed by a barrage of pounding fists. All quiet in the house, and I wondered if Mom slept through it. I prayed for some sort of miracle that made them just turn out and leave. A call they couldn't refuse.

"This is Police Chief Burke. We have an arrest warrant for Heath Walker. Open the door or we'll break it down."

I peeked through the blinds again, and the fat cop, Rori's dad, stood at the door, hand on his pistol. Thick-neck stood behind him, gun drawn and held upright at a ninety-degree angle. The blinds crinkled, and he shot a glance in my direction. Thick-neck tapped Rori's dad, and they followed each other to the door beside the old garage door that I had disabled when I had converted it. They pounded again. In position, ready to break it down. "Heath Walker, we know you're in there. Don't make this harder than it has to be."

I wondered what B Western he had gotten that line from and what my next move was. I didn't have one, but I couldn't let him take Rori. I knew what would happen to her. "Hide in the bathroom. I'll see if I can get rid of him."

"Don't, Heath. He'll kill you."

"I won't let that happen. Go."

She crawled into the bathroom and shut the door, keeping the light off. I walked up to the door, and they must have heard me approaching, because it got too quiet.

"I'm coming out. I'm unarmed. I have no weapons at all." I said this as clearly as I could. I reached to open the door when the wood splintered and the door swung inward, knocking me on my ass.

"Move and you're fucking dead," the fat man said. He stepped inside, looking around with thick-neck on his six, gun pointed at my face. "Where the fuck is she?"

"Look, I don't know why you're here. But my mom's sick in the other room. I need to check on her."

They signaled an all clear, and thick-neck lowered his gun. Burke stepped closer and leaned down, halitosis and Copenhagen on his breath. "Listen, you little prick. My daughter is seventeen, which makes you a fucking rapist."

"Show me the warrant, or you need to get off my property," I said.

"You must mean this," he said, and stood. He pulled a pair of brass knuckles from his utility belt, slipped them on, and swung on me all in one fluid motion.

I tried to duck, but the blow glanced off my right eye, opening up the recently healed wound there. A thin trickle of hot blood spilled down my face. My vision spun and sparkled; I fell to my side and dry heaved from the pain.

"Leave him the fuck alone," Rori screamed. I rolled my eyes up and saw her standing there in the bathroom door. "I'll come home, just leave him alone, please."

"No!" I screamed. I tried to stand, but Burke kicked me in the solar plexus, and I fell again, gasping for air.

Burke grabbed Rori by the hair on the back of her head and yanked her toward the door. Just before he dragged her outside, she glanced back at me. A look of terror and sadness spread over her face. Tears streamed over her soft cheeks.

Burke handed Rori off to thick-neck, and he dragged her toward the cruiser. Burke grabbed me by my hair next and dragged me out of the garage onto the driveway and stopped. He leaned over, dropping his knee into my chest, and roughly slapped handcuffs on me.

"Get the fuck on your knees," he said, and stood, kicking me in the ribs. Bones cracked with the sharp stab of his cowboy boot. Rolling onto my stomach, I coughed and gagged on blood and dust. He stood over me, the rigid heel of his boot in the small of my back, pushing the air and life out of me, and unholstered his pistol. He aimed it at the back of my head, then crouched down, and I could smell his vomitous breath.

"You touched my daughter. You're gonna die today, fucking spic scum."

In my peripheral vision, I watched thick-neck handcuff Rori and shove her against the back of the car. Then he turned and smiled. The bastard was enjoying this.

"Don't you fucking hurt her," I managed to cough out.

I heard the hammer click on Burke's pistol and realized in a rush of terror what this guy really was. He was going to kill me in my own driveway and probably beat Rori half to death when he got her home.

"Daddy, no!" Rori said, and thick-neck shoved her face into the trunk of the cruiser.

"Don't you bruise her, Johnson," Burke shouted, taking his attention off me for a split second. That was when the boom came, along with the crash of steel on steel. A hole the size of a football ripped into the rear door of the police cruiser.

"Get. Off. My. Property." It was Mom's thin, ragged voice. I turned to see her, and she stood wavering on the rickety front porch, her hospital-style gown loose around her. But she had her tattered San Francisco Giants cap on and the shotgun pointed directly at Johnson's face. "And leave the kids alone."

"Put the gun down, now, ma'am. This is a lawful arrest," Johnson said. Burke leaned his weight into my back; my spine felt like it might snap. He aimed his pistol at Mom.

"Let. Her. Go," Mom said. She racked the pump action and held her stare.

The deputy put his hands in the air, but Burke drew down, sighting a bead on my mom's flank.

"Put the gun down!" Burke shouted.

He stepped off my back, and I breathed; the air burned my lungs. I tried to regain my footing and catch my breath as I got up to one knee. I watched my mom swing the barrel of the shotgun toward Burke, and I grabbed his ankle, altering his aim so the first round missed Mom by a few inches. Johnson lowered his gun at Mom but didn't fire.

There was a still moment when everybody watched. Waited. Then Mom pulled the trigger, aiming for Burke's fat face and pinched head—a cop was trying to kill her son. But the gun just clicked. The double-barrel had only one round, and she'd spent it. Johnson laughed.

"Stupid old cunt." He spit and lowered his gun. Burke didn't. He kicked me again and stood, leveling his gun at Mom. I could see the tendons in his fingers rising, and I leapt at his side just when the pistol bucked. Mom's withered chest burst open, a red mist fanned out behind her, painting the old porch and the swaying stalks of foxtails growing in bunches at the porch line. Burke fired another round before I got to him, and

Mom's body rocked backwards, falling from the porch. She landed on her back, gazing up at the blue summer sky.

"You sick son of a fuck!" I screamed, and every violent act that I had been holding back since high school on account of Mom raged up inside of me. I felt strong and in control. I tagged Burke with two quick jabs and a haymaker to the back of the head before I landed on him. The punch to the back of the head landed so square, it knocked him unconscious.

Quickly I rolled behind his mass, blocking me from Johnson, who would have fired by now if Burke wasn't in the way. I turned Burke on his side so he was facing Johnson, and pulled the .22 from my crotch, slipping the gun discreetly under Burke's neck. A hidden little gun, not much bigger than a wallet.

"Get the fuck up, kid. It's over," Johnson said. I could see him over Burke's ear. He stood by the cruiser, his gun trained on me, his other hand holding Rori against the car. "You got no play left, you dumb shit. Now stand up and take your bullet. Or the girl gets one."

Rori was bent over the trunk, and Johnson stood well away from her. I didn't have time to think, to hesitate. There was no way he wasn't going to put a bullet in me as soon as he had the chance. I fired all five rounds at Johnson. They were quiet little pops, almost like a pellet gun, and I used the first two to calibrate my aim, and the next three hammered home. Two in the neck, one in the arm. He dropped the gun, and his hand jumped to his neck. A look of confusion spread over his face when the blood started to pour down his collar. He dropped to his knees, then to his face.

4

Rori stood, her eyes puffy from crying. I tried to run to her, but everything hurt so badly that I hobbled. I got the keys from Johnson's tool belt and took off Rori's handcuffs. Then she took off mine. We hugged, and she kissed my face, away from the swelling. I cuffed Burke and kicked him once, hard in the ribs. I aimed my .22 at his head and pulled the trigger, but it clicked. Empty.

Rori pulled me away and everything felt distant, like a dream. My mother was dead, I was losing blood, and I had just murdered a cop. Maybe I shouldn't kill another one. Nothing made sense. Inside, the house felt vacant without Mom. It would be empty forever. My family was all dead. I tried not to think about that, tried not to think at all while Rori and I threw food and clothes into trash bags and loaded up the car.

I brought a sheet from inside and two pennies. I quickly covered Mom and recited John 3:16, her favorite verse from the Bible. I placed the pennies over her eyes and heard Burke groan.

Walking over to him, I picked up his revolver, a .357, and cocked the hammer. Taking my time, I sighted town the snub barrel at Burke's fat head and started to squeeze the trigger. That was when we heard the sirens.

"We have to go, Heath. Now." She was right; we had seconds to get the hell out of here, or we were both getting locked away forever. Rori grabbed my arm, and we ran toward my Crown Vic.

Stopping at the passenger's side, I felt the suck of air from my lungs again and turned. Burke was standing now, aiming a small ankle piece at Rori and me. I had no choice but to call his bluff with Rori standing right behind me. He was about twenty yards out, which was the same distance as Mom and Dad's cutout targets I'd grown up shooting out back in the creek bed. Dropping to one knee, I fired two shots that hit perfect center mass. Burke clutched at his chest and dropped to his ass, then fell to his back, writhing in pain. No blood. He'd been wearing his vest, unfortunately. The sirens were getting louder.

We got in the car, Rori behind the wheel, since I was busted up again. She tore down the driveway in a plume of dust. Within a few minutes we were out the driveway, headed in the opposite direction of the sirens. My whole body started to shake with adrenaline-soaked terror. Every cell felt stabbing pain, especially where the boots had cracked my ribs. A numb feeling, one that I'd felt before, when I was twelve, settled over me. Like a knife to the gut, the instant it hit and your body hadn't registered it yet. The comforting numbness of shock. I had killed again, and this time, it was a cop.

Rori followed the meandering road the back way through the foothills. Then we went west, toward Santa Cruz, the only place that seemed to make sense in the moment.

I tried to clear my head, but the thing that kept replaying over and over was Mom's face when the first bullet struck her. Her face was horror stricken. Her lifeless body, the way it fell. After she'd been doing so well. And I had been helpless to stop it. That rage from my childhood filled me, my chest tight with it. I hated, more than anything in the world, the feeling of being helpless. Especially when someone I loved needed help.

Thick-neck Johnson had deserved those bullets. So did Burke. Mom hadn't.

The problem was, it didn't matter how things had gone down. I was a cop killer now. They put out an APB for cop killers. They found cop killers. And there was nowhere to run. But I knew running was our only chance. We had to at least try.

Chapter Five
Friday, August 19, 1988
Art

1

Art Dominguez sat in the farthest barstool from the entrance to Shakers and Shots Gentleman's Club. There were only a few places in the club where he could keep his eye on the bar, the stage, and the door, and this was his favorite. Here he could talk to Tyra.

Art checked his Timex and counted it. It was 8:00 p.m., and in four hours he would be fifty-nine years old, and all he wished for right then was for somebody to turn off "Shake Your Booty" and put on some real music. That, and for business to pick up—it had been nearly dead since the raid.

Art heard the tapping of stilettos approach and a familiar tracing up his spine over his embroidered Western shirt. Lacy Santos leaned against the nearest barstool and stared at Art while the baby powder scent of Chanel No. 5 grew thick enough to chew. When they'd been together, the scent seemed to be everywhere, like a warm Lacy footprint, and he missed it sometimes—all the time, really. Especially on his pillow when he woke up.

"You like poking the beast, don't you?" she asked, her silk robe cinched around her body. She took the shot from Art, tilted her head back, and swallowed it down without a wince. A dark red lipstick marked the edge of the glass.

"Don't miss the whiskey—just miss the smell," he said, realizing the symbolism missed its mark. He turned in his stool to face her, but at that moment, the front door opened, and a face that he'd hoped to God wouldn't show up walked through the door. Art stood and reached for the collapsible baton on his left hip—he was a southpaw, and it always caught people off guard. Lacy grabbed his arm.

"Artsy, please. He'll behave. I promise," Lacy said. She'd been Art's on-again-off-again girlfriend for the past four years, and Art wanted to believe her, but she had a soft spot for customers who fell in love with her—just like it had been with Art years ago. Lacy was thirty-eight now and, Art thought, should be settling down with someone like himself, which was why he'd proposed to her six months ago. Dancing didn't last forever.

"First, don't call me that," Art said. "Second, no boyfriends, no husbands. You know the rules." He made a show out of looking down at his wrist where her fingers gripped him so tightly, the knuckles were white. The kid that just walked in had grabbed another customer by the shirt collar a few days before, and Art had let him go pretty easily, but only because he'd been spending money.

"Artsy, he'll be good, and he pays. Who else am I going to dance for?" Lacy was close to six feet tall with her heels on—a half a head taller than Art when they stood—with a heart-shaped face and dark, glitter-encrusted hair that parted in the middle and fell around her tawny shoulders. Art knew that the reason she'd rejected his proposal was standing in the doorway.

The kid, Armando, glanced around with the rabid passion that only love—and the hormones of a twenty-five-year-old—could generate. The kid had come every goddamn night since she'd taken him home, and he'd been good until a few nights ago. But Art knew the type and knew he'd come back. He also knew the kid would slip up again, regardless of his good intentions. So, Art had done his homework on the little fuck and, of course, found dirt. Art always found dirt. It was a gift from the universe. The only gift, since everything else in his life always seemed to go to shit.

Art softened and sat back down on his stool. He was about five eight and took care of himself by running, boxing, and lifting weights a few times a week. But at fifty-nine, things were starting to ache here and there, and Art was having to rely more and more on his ability to blend in, on disguises, and the element of surprise. "He pays and behaves, he stays."

"He will, I promise," she said.

"He makes a move, you know what happens."

The club, Shakers and Shots Gentleman's Club, was off Mineral King Avenue, a frontage road along the freeway that ran through the center of Shadow Valley. An old hustler, and friend of Art's from his cop days, owned the place. Art was just an investor. When it made money, so did he. To help build and maintain it, he'd cashed out his partial pension from his police work and whatever else he'd made bounty hunting since. But the police had come in and raided the place a few nights before, and business was down. If the cops kept up the pressure and they closed, Art was fucked. He'd be flat broke just in time for retirement. So, even though he wanted to smash the kid to pieces, Tyra and Art needed the money.

"Next up, Lacy Santos," said the DJ while Candi made a quick walk of the stage to pick up the few singles that had been dropped by the construction workers and day laborers in the drop stools. And today, there was one white-collar guy, still in a button-down and tie. Maybe he would bring some friends, Art thought.

"Thanks, Artsy," Lacy said, and pushed his black, felt cowboy hat back to kiss him on the cheek. She turned and hobbled on her tall heels toward the stage.

"Don't call me Artsy," he said, but she couldn't hear him over the pulse of the music. Art pushed his hat down, wiped the lipstick away, and smoothed his black and gray handlebar mustache with his fingertips.

2

"Bartender, another shot," Art said. Tyra finished pouring a drink and gave Art an amused smile. She cashed the guy out, grabbed the bottle of Maker's Mark, and walked toward him. She was closer to Art's age and a former small-time dealer. Art had met her as a beat cop in their twenties, and they'd helped each other out for years: Art had turned a blind eye more than once, and she had fed him information on other pimps, drug dealers, and hustlers.

Art had lost his job after twenty-five years on the force because of a sex-ring bust gone wrong. He'd been working with Burke, a detective he'd trained himself, and the guy was on the level. For nearly a decade Burke had helped Art glean the extras from the job by looking the other way or only logging partial evidence, for his cut of course. The problem with Burke was that once Art had shown him a few tricks, his greed took over. And he wouldn't slow down.

"You ever going to start dating women your own age?" Tyra asked, and she poured him another shot three-quarters full. Tyra was tall, skeletally thin, and her skin a deep amber. She kept her hair clipped short and had a collection of wigs she rotated through, and today's was long, wavy, and red.

"Hey, you turned me down every time I asked you out for the better part of twenty years," Art said.

"Wallace has been dead three and half years now. You ever going to man up and take another shot?" Tyra pushed the shot toward Art, smiling. A game they'd played, a well-worn dance routine where nobody was the loser. Then again, nobody was the winner.

"You were married, then I was with Lacy. Never quite lines up, does it? You sure you're single now?" Art chuckled and sniffed the hot aroma collecting over the shot glass, letting the sting soak into his nose and lungs. It made his brain feel cloudy and effervescent for a brief second; then it would sharpen to a fine point. The room becoming clear to him. Armando took a seat at the main stage, his spine as rigid as rebar.

"I might be, bouncer man," Tyra said. She leaned forward on the counter, one hazel eye trained on him, the other, a glass eye, staring blankly ahead. "You know, some people actually drink this shit?" She was beautiful; Art always thought so. Even though the signs of age were creeping in. Just like they were for Art. The gray she covered with wigs, he covered with hair dye. But he couldn't hide the deepening lines around his eyes and neck. Or the posture that constantly had to be corrected so he didn't become a goddamn hunchback by seventy.

"You know why I stopped. Everyone's safer now," Art said.

"Maybe safe isn't what we need right now. You see that the kid's back in Lacy's section?" She gestured toward Armando.

"Yeah, I saw him. She said he's paying."

"He's breaking the rules by being here."

Art had shared the dirt he had found on the kid with Tyra, and they both agreed that he would eventually have to go, but neither wanted to lose the revenue just yet. "He pays well, and she's our best earner."

"He slips up, you have my permission to do...whatever it is you do," she said, and smiled. Tyra had gotten out of the game after a bad situation with a rival dealer that ended up with her losing an eye. She'd never had much of a disposition toward violence anyway, so they made a good team. Anything physical was Art's department, with her guidance as the temperature gauge.

"Anything I want?" Art asked.

"It's your birthday," Tyra said. "Isn't that right?" She took the shot in front of Art and poured another.

"Getting old," Art said.

"Sixty this year?"

"Easy. Still in my late fifties."

"Watch that kid, old man. We need every customer we can get."

"He won't be back after tonight," Art said.

Tyra paused. "I thought you said he's pay—"

"I have a feeling, that's all. The kid's in love."

"Just, don't kill him. We can't afford any more cops."

3

Art opened his mouth to respond when the office door behind him opened, and Parker, the overweight high school dropout Art had hired to watch the cameras emerged. "Art, phone. It's the cops. You want me to watch Armando?"

Parker was relatively new and not the crack team Art wished he had. He had a faint mustache and a pink, acne-scarred face. Constantly offering unsolicited help when it came to anything potentially violent. But the kid had no finesse. There was something off just a tick, and Art was afraid to let him do anything other than watch cameras.

"Stand at the end of the bar. Cross your arms. That's it," Art said.

Art and Tyra watched the stage. Lacy dropped her robe and stepped up to the pole, her gold sequin bikini shimmering in the overhead light. At the stage, Armando glanced around at the other men like he was ready to pounce. Guys coming in and growing attached to a particular girl were usually harmless, but not always, and Art had dealt with this scenario before. It was why boyfriends were not allowed.

Armando was only here because he made a decent wage as an ace pitcher for the local Shadow Valley High Sierras. The local AAA feeder team. He'd arrived from the Dominican Republic six months ago and apparently had pro potential. He was sturdy, thick shouldered, and had a strong, handsome jawline. But that look of yearning in his eyes was dangerous.

"I'll watch him," Tyra said, and winked. "You sending Parker out?"

"Yes. Make sure to keep Puck off the customers," Art said, referring to Parker by their nickname for him. Tyra gave him a mock salute.

Art walked into the office and closed the door. There were some grainy black-and-white TVs that showed the closed-circuit camera footage, and he could see the mainstage and Armando. Art picked up the receiver, expecting it to be a call from the police chief about the raid a few days before. They'd operated with an implied agreement for years by making significant donations to the local precinct's softball league, which went directly to the police chief, Hugo James. But the police had caught Art and Tyra off guard by booking three of his best girls for "acts of prostitution" and threatening to shut them down. It was all bullshit, and Art had been waiting for this call.

"This is Art."

"Officer Arthur Dominguez?"

The voice was familiar, but not Hugo's. "Who's asking?"

"You don't remember your old partner?"

Art frowned. "Burke? Why the hell are you calling? You haven't sent me work in what, a year, year and a half?"

"It's Police Chief Burke now. Hugo's no longer with the PD," he said, his voice gravelly and muffled.

"You have anything to do with that?" Art asked, a barb to his voice that he hoped came through clearly.

There was always something that bothered Art about that bust that took him down. He and Burke had been working on a human trafficking, underage-sex-ring case, and Art hadn't been able to get enough evidence on the Triad scum that were running it. And Art, after seeing what his own father had done to his mother when he was growing up, wouldn't stand for women being mistreated or abused on his watch. So, he planted a kilo of cocaine from the evidence locker on a massage parlor they were running out on the 198, near the border with Exeter, and bam—the two key suspects were in his custody.

Derek Chow and Peter Wong were two Chinese immigrants who had ties to an organized crime syndicate based in Hong Kong, which had been in operation in the Bay Area since the turn of the century: the Hop Sing Boys. Art had larger concerns, too, about the spread of human trafficking into rural areas like Shadow Valley, where it could go largely unnoticed. He was happy to have the bust, but shortly after they were in custody, Internal Affairs got involved, asking about the missing cocaine. Art lost his job. It was a technique he'd used before, and he'd just wondered, why now? The scumbags were let back onto the street.

Burke had stayed on the force since his statement said that he was "completely unaware" of Art's plans. It worked out for Art though, because for a long time after, Burke had relied on Art to do the stuff the badge couldn't. He would leave some crumbs around for Art to pick up—cash, drugs, guns—if Art took care of some off-duty shit while the blue looked the other way. He broke a few bones, put the fear of God into some bad people, even killed some guys who deserved it, and made it look like an accident. And, of course, he got paid for it. When that business tapered off, Art started to bounty hunt, then invested in Tyra's club.

"He had his turn. It's my department now. But that is not why I'm calling. I need your help with something, and I need it right now," Burke said.

"Who was it that signed off on that raid a few days ago? Was that you?"

"My hands were tied on that one. There've been complaints about the girls and some extra services. I can't have that in my jurisdiction."

"You stopped calling, you raided my club, and you reject my bounties—"

"You've developed a reputation down here for the condition of the bounties you bring in."

"Your fucking guys at intake won't take a bounty if there's a goddamn scratch on them."

"Dead is more than a scratch."

"Lopez? He pulled a fucking gun on me—"

"It was a Civil War replica."

"I'm hanging up now."

"You hang up that phone, and your club is dead, and so's your bounty hunting license."

"What the fuck do you want, then?" Art could feel his blood pumping hard, his cheeks hot. Burke was a loose cannon, and now that he was in charge, the city was screwed.

"It's my daughter. She's been taken."

"Rori?" There was a silence, and Art pictured her when Burke had brought her to work as a towheaded toddler with pigtails and a lisp. Then he remembered her scared, round, little face when he'd tracked her and ex-con Jacoby Shells down in some squatter's cabin a year before. He'd nearly taken the guy's head off with the baton. "Jesus, when?"

"Some lunatic beat the hell out of some Vagos and kidnapped the girl from the Blue Cue—don't ask why she was there. I tracked them to the kid's house, and the little fucker and his mom tried to gun us down. In uniform." Burke's breathing hissed into the receiver. "This is a rundown. I want the girl back yesterday, and the perp she's with buried in an unmarked grave. You're the one I want for this."

Art paused, his heart rate lowering at the thought of going back to doing what he loved best. "How much?"

"Are we negotiating?"

Art envisioned Burke's fat-cheeked, mustached grin and wished he could choke him, but Rori was the man's only child. He was surprised Burke didn't want this kid in one piece; he remembered how Burke liked to find a spot to hole up and torture a criminal off the books. But that was before the chief thing. He needed discretion and plausible deniability. Hence, the call to Art.

"I turn fifty-nine tonight," Art said. "And you've obviously done your homework—I need your boys to lay off the club. Forever. This is my goddamn retirement."

"I can probably arrange for that."

"What is she now anyway, twenty?"

"Seventeen."

"And you're sure she didn't just run away?" Art had never had kids, but he knew Rori had lost her mom, and had to imagine Burke was a shit replacement. Hell, he had girls coming in the club every week with a fake ID and daddy issues.

Burke breathed even harder into the phone.

"This guy, did he know her from before?" Art asked.

"You know what," Burke said, his voice turning venomous, "maybe I should just call the Ramirez brothers?"

"I'm not saying no, but you have to promise to lay the *fuck* off the club."

"I'll have to arrange some things, but I can make that happen."

Art knew there was something Burke wasn't telling him—about his sudden interest in Art's club, and with this rundown. As far as the club went, Art knew the girls did some special favors for a guest here and there, but they were supposed to take that somewhere else. This sudden interest in Art's club was alarming.

Art walked over to his armoire and pulled out a key. He unlocked it. "And then there's my fee."

"Timing is everything in these cut-and-run cases," Burke said. "You know that. I need you here, *now*." And Art did know that. He also knew that if they didn't go to any predictable places, they would be impossible to find. But they would. They always did.

"Five for her, ten for him," Art said.

"Fifteen, are you fuck—"

"I'll bring her back. He'll look like an accident."

"Fine," Burke said, sounding frustrated. "Put him in the fucking ground…I want confirmation."

"I'll bring you a Polaroid."

"Meet me in ten minutes at Easton Veterinary. You'll see the lights."

There was shouting through the door, and Art spun to check the TVs. Armando had a customer in a choke hold while Parker and Tyra tried to pry him off. So predictable.

"Ten minutes, Dominguez," Burke said again.

"I'll be there in fifteen. I've got something here I need to deal with first." Art hung up, pulled his collapsible baton from its sheath, and snapped it open.

4

Art slipped out of the back room and silently behind the small crowd of people watching Armando choking another guy out. The other guy was the middle-aged man in the cheap button-down and Sears tie. When Armando spotted Art, he loosened his grip, and some color returned to the man, but he didn't let go.

"*Le toco el culo*," Armando said, trying to evoke a comradery by speaking Spanish with Art, but Art's Spanish was rusty at best. His mother was second-generation Mexican, and his father was Irish, but neither spoke Spanish. What Art knew, he'd learned in school or on the beat.

"Put him down, Armando," Art said. "It's time to go."

"*Puto!*" he said, and spit.

Tyra stepped in, always the mediator, and grabbed Armando's shoulder. Armando turned and pelted her with a hard backhand. She fell and slid on her ass along the smooth floor. The DJ stopped the music, which made the sharp corners of reality set in. Art leaned down and helped her onto one of the barstools. Kneeling down to check on her, he took a napkin from the bar and dabbed at blood coming from her lip and nose.

"You okay?" Art said.

"Happy birthday, Art," she said, and spit blood on the floor. "He's all yours."

Chapter Six
Friday, August 19, 1988
Heath

1

Once we hit the city limits on the far side of Shadow Valley, I let a deep, tremulous breath escape that I didn't realize I was holding. My lungs burned, and my face, ribs, and whole body throbbed. Rori glanced over, concerned. Rage, fear, and disgust ricocheted around in my chest, and at the center of the hurricane was Rori.

"You need a cigarette?" she asked.

"I need ten," I said. She lit two from the Camel soft pack and handed me one. She cracked her window and blew smoke out in a thin line that disappeared into the deafening void of wind tearing by in a blur of orchards. I inhaled and coughed hard. I spit blood and phlegm out the window and took another drag.

The fuckers had really busted me up. The realization that I'd killed a cop was taking root, and it shook me to my bones. I had needed to do it though, right? Him or us. The next memory was the acid rush of fear and adrenaline when Rori's father had squeezed that trigger, his gun aimed at my head. I should have been dead, and for what? Helping his daughter avoid his sadistic ass. What kind of psychotic, self-possessed asshole would kill a guy and tear into his own progeny with fists and weapons anyway? Then there was Mom. A sob heaved up from my chest, and I clenched my eyes shut to shake it off. But that just made her image clearer. Her limp, withered body, her last ounce of strength she had used to hold that shotgun and save my life. Again. I owed her more than I could ever repay. And I would never be able to do that now.

"The cops—" I said, and stopped because I felt a rage well up from my stomach. I wanted to hate Rori for bringing me into this nightmare of hers. But every time she stole a glance at me, I could see into her wide, terrified eyes. The rage would start to die. She was young, a kid really. I couldn't punish the girl for the sins of her father. Where would that have left me? "Your father. He's going to track me down and kill me. There's probably already a nationwide APB."

Rori put her hand on my knee. "Heath, he won't do that." Her knowing touch shocked me. Not because I wasn't used to her touch, I was by now. But because I'd had no fucking clue who she really was until this morning. She was a stranger, an underaged stranger. I pushed her hand away.

"What? Track us down and kill us?"

"No, he'll do that. He's tried to kill me more than once." Her tone was so cavalier, it came off as hyperbole, but I knew it wasn't.

"Then what?"

"He won't put out an APB. You took me with you. And shot him. It's personal. He just won't."

"There's a dead cop back there. He'll have to do something for the record."

"I know my father, okay? I know exactly what he'll do. He's been doing it for my whole life."

"Then what? What should we do?"

"First, they'll stage it to look like there was a shootout with your mom. Like they were protecting themselves from a crazy old lady."

"Jesus. What the fuck would they even be doing out there 'for the record'?" The thought of them dishonoring Mom's memory with lies pissed me off.

"All they have to say is that they got a tip, or had a call, and when they got there, she fired. The case will be closed."

"Right. They smear Mom's good name. Get off free and clear, and then what? Come for us themselves?"

"He's going to send his bounty hunter. The fucker tracked me down once before. When I was sixteen, he nearly killed the guy I was staying with. Broke his jaw in, like, fifteen places. We'd been hiding out in a cabin up in the Sierras. The guy was an ex-con who liked hunting. I thought I'd be safe with him." Rori's voice shook slightly when she spoke. She sounded truly terrified.

"You're worried about one guy. I—we can handle *one* guy."

"Art Dominguez isn't just one guy. It's hard to explain. He's got some sort of fucked-up gift for tracking people down, sneaking up on them, and crushing their faces in with this wicked little baton he carries." Her hands trembled where they gripped the steering wheel.

"A baton?" I half smiled, and it hurt my bruised face. "What, like the color guard?"

"It's not funny, Heath. The guy is really good. Looks all kind and innocent. Then, whack. You're either dead or a vegetable." She started to cry softly.

I stopped smiling. "This is fucked. How do people like your dad have so much control over our lives? He carries a badge, and he's what? Above the fucking law? He gets to show up on my doorstep with no warrant and beat me until I can't breathe, put two bullets in my mom, and we're the ones on the run? It's fucking horseshit." I pounded my fists against the dash so hard, the glove box popped open.

"Absolute power corrupts absolutely. That's why I wanted to get out of Shadow Valley. It's why I ran away. He could kill me and get away with it. He let me know that every day of my life. You saw the scars."

"He's letting us both know that. I'll have the scars, too."

"We should leave the country," she said.

"He killed my fucking mother." I clenched my eyes again, and my throat seized up. I felt like I might vomit, but instead, tears fell. The salty liquid stung in the cuts and abrasions on my face. "*We* should be hunting *his* fucking ass down."

"We need money."

I cleared my eyes and took another drag. "Avery never called back or returned my calls about that job."

"Well, let's go find out if he still needs help. Twenty-five thousand, and we can head down to Baja, or Zihuatanejo, and be okay for a couple of years."

"Yeah. If we live small. Don't raise too much hell."

"I'm not high maintenance. I'll stay anywhere, even a tent. As long as it's with you."

I looked at her. She was such a juxtaposition. From certain angles I could see her childhood barely fading away, delicate and young. And then in another flash, she was raw, rugged, and ready to smash a biker with a pool cue. Her trauma had changed her into this person, just like mine had when I was twelve. The beatings, the threats, tracking her down—they were not just physical abuses; they were abrasions to the spirit, and they had scarred over. She'd calloused over a dozen times but could still love, hopefully. I still could, I thought. I hoped.

"So you think we should head straight to Hideaway Haze? Try and find Avery?" I asked. We had driven through Lemoore and turned up the 5 freeway. The sun's final orange glare pulsed behind the shallow, rolling, brown foothills to the west.

"If he's home," she said.

Forcing myself to let go of the anger and resentment that filled every part of my body, I tried to focus on what we were doing. We had to survive. That meant we'd be on the run possibly forever. It meant no more California. It also meant we'd never get to do some of the normal shit we used to take for granted, like go to Disneyland or eat In-N-Out.

"I just… If we're going to be on the run for the rest of our lives, is there anything else we should do before we go?" I said. "A last meal? Anything you always wanted to do?"

Rori glanced at me, and her eyes flashed emerald in the light of a passing car. "Can we go to the Boardwalk in Santa Cruz? I've seen the commercials since I was a little girl, and I could never get anyone to take me. I just… It's stupid, I know, but I've always wanted to ride the Giant Dipper."

I laughed, and she looked momentarily wounded, so I backtracked. "It's not stupid," I said. The soft lilt of her voice had driven a sadness deep into my stomach. It was the girlish way she had said it, the puffiness in her cheeks, the way her *s*'s lisped slightly. Not too long ago, Rori was a little girl who never got to be a little girl.

"It's perfect," I said. "We have a head start on anyone who might come for us. We can hit the Boardwalk, find a grocery store, and buy some supplies. Once we get set up for the night, we can dye our hair and change our looks. We'll stay off the radar. Nobody'll be able to find us."

"But first, the Boardwalk?" Rori asked.

"As long as we make it quick," I said.

"I don't want you to cut your hair," she said. "I like it long."

"It'll grow back," I said.

"Fine," she said.

"You want me to drive?"

"Probably should if you're feeling better. I really don't have a license. Don't want to get hauled in on a technicality."

Rori pulled down a darkened dirt road lined with pistachio trees shadowed by moonlight, and we switched.

Within minutes we hummed along at ninety miles an hour, and Rori seemed to quietly pull into herself. The exertion, the violence, it took a toll on us both. No matter how easily the violence came, no matter who came out ahead, it took a toll. She curled her arms around her knees, leaned against the car door, and puffed on a cigarette. A moment later she reclined her chair and closed her eyes.

"Heath, tell me the rest of the story," she said. "Someone pulled a knife on you in your sleep?"

"Right. That was where we left off." The matrix of emotions and adrenaline-soaked muscles in my body were growing weary and shaky. I thought maybe the story would take my mind off the present stream of chaos.

2

"Don't make a fucking sound, or I'll cut you wide open," a whispering voice hissed. My eyes shot open, but it was dark. I couldn't move and could barely breath. Someone's weight was crushing my chest, and a

hand covered my mouth and nose. My heart throbbed hard against my ribs, and I almost pissed myself.

"Stop fucking with him. Look, he's shaking," a girl's voice whispered.

The weight from my chest released, and I reached for the hand over my mouth.

"I'm just fucking with you, kid. I'm going to let you go, but don't scream, okay?"

I nodded and the hand lifted. I shot up in my bed, and there were three people around me. One of them was Mouse with his headphones around his shoulders. I didn't recognize the other two.

"This is Avery and Yessi. Avery's room is the next one over."

"We snuck in through the bathroom cabinet, we burrowed a hole," Yessi said. She was the shortest of the group, about my age, and was thin with a narrow face and a scar over her right cheek. Mouse, I guessed was the oldest, with his short black hair and black shadow mustache coming in.

"Get dressed, we're sneaking out," Avery said. He was taller than me but even skinnier with shaggy, long blonde hair and a tied-dyed shirt.

I nodded again without saying a word. I put my shoes on and pulled a windbreaker from my duffel bag. I followed them into the bathroom, where they opened the cabinet below the sink. We squeezed one by one into the dank, small space and came out into the other bathroom. We continued toward the shower and stopped. They swept the rug aside and pulled up several loose floorboards. We slipped into the dusty crawl space where we weaved through more rotten wood, damp earth, and spider webs which clung to my face, until finally the cold, bright night air rushed into my lungs. We stood and brushed ourselves off in an alleyway behind the hotel.

"That never gets easier," Mouse said. It was one of those ironic nicknames though, because Mouse was taller than I was by several inches, and also had muscular arms and legs. "Let's go," he said.

We followed him down the alleyway until we reached a road beyond which were endless orange groves. We slipped into the dark orchards and walked into that silence, that freedom, that cool, damp night, and it felt good. Very good. I wanted to feel this way again. All the time. Free.

After what felt like a long time, we stopped at a dilapidated red barn with a rotted roof all caved in and covered with moss. Mouse, Avery, and Yessi showed me how to gather up kindling—scraps of wood and branches that were dry enough to catch fire—and we poured our findings into a big oil drum. Mouse took a small water bottle from his backpack and poured it over the kindling. He flicked a match into it, and a quick burst of flames shot up from the cylinder, and I could feel the heat singe my face. It died down to a soft crackling after a second, and I could smell gasoline. That must have been what Mouse had in the bottle.

"All right, it's time for confessions," Mouse said. "You want to go first, new kid?"

"I'm not sure what you mean?" I said.

"We come out here for two reasons. One is to be a support group for each other, since no one else is there for us. The second is to plan the murder."

"Oorah," Avery said softly.

"Oorah," Yessi said, standing stiff and watching Mouse. She relaxed her posture and added for my benefit, "Mouse's dad was in the Marines."

"Goddamn right he was. And it fucked him up bad. But it's not my turn. Heath, what got you here to Hotel Dog Shit?"

"Hotel Dog Shit? Why do you call it that?" I asked.

"Because that's what it is. Dog shit. It's where they send the kids nobody wants and nobody will ask about when they turn up missing."

"It doesn't seem that bad," I said.

"He doesn't know yet," Yessi said, her oily black hair falling over her face. She had on baggy shorts and faded knee-high socks with maroon rings around the top and a ripped Members Only jacket.

"Know what?" I said, and I could feel my pulse quicken. What weren't they telling me? Or were they messing with me? Brought me out here to scare me as some sort of hazing ritual?

"Save it, Yessi. The murder is at the end. First, Heath, tell us your worst moment you have. The shit that eats at you and made you end up here."

"Like, how Mouse's dad shot him," Avery said. Mouse put a finger to his lips to quiet Avery. The firelight danced over his face and close-cropped hair.

"Nothing that interesting," I said. "I never met my parents. They gave me up when I was a baby. I guess, just knowing that is what has bothered me the most all these years."

"Jesus. He's had it easy," Avery said. He was sitting on a big stone now and tucked his shaggy blonde hair behind his ears.

"Hey. No judgements. You know the rules," Mouse said. "Go ahead."

"I have been through at least twenty houses," I said. "I've been kicked, spit on, starved, stabbed with a shish kebab skewer, and cracked in the head with a snow globe. Mostly by bio kids. One was a foster mom."

"God, bio kids can be real dicks," Yessi said.

"I had a couple of good houses, too. One house I wish I got to stay at. But I stole a matchbox car from my bio sister and took it to school. Got bounced just for that. I ended up here for stealing twenty bucks for food. Maybe I regret that the most. Fucking up every chance I had, including my last chance."

Everyone nodded and watched me with careful, caring eyes.

"Thanks for sharing your truth," Mouse said.

They all gathered around and hugged me together. It was the first hug I'd had in years, and I felt the urge to cry again but choked it back.

"I'll go next," Mouse said. "My real dad lit a fire like this one in the backyard after he got laid off at the Jostens factory graveyard shift one night. Late. Like three a.m., and he was wasted. He told me he had a surprise for me. Woke me up out of bed. Once we got out there, he showed me his service revolver he had kept after Vietnam. He told me that if the wind blew to the south, toward Los Angeles, then it meant he would kill me dead and go and get my mom back. The wind swirled for a while. Then the smoke came up thick when the fire faded out. But it blew to the south. I saw the gun coming up from his waist quick though. I was ready. I knew what he was capable of. I ducked right when he fired a round where my head used to be, and I rolled toward him in the dirt and pulled my blade. I stuck him in the thigh, twisted, and took off running. I jumped the back *fence, but he clipped me in the calf with a lucky shot. That was the last time I saw him."*

Mouse pulled up his Dickies pants and showed us a round scar the size of a quarter. "The fucked-up thing is, I kinda miss him now that he's locked up. I mean, I would never tell him that, and I hope he rots in there. But a part of me wants to forgive him. Have him in my life, if that makes sense."

Mouse looked at the fire and hissed, turning his head away. His eyes were teared up, and it was impossible to tell if it was from the story, from the smoke, or the fact that standing in front of this fire right now might be transporting him back to the worst moment in his life. It struck me how a single moment like that, like this, could define your entire existence. How a person could be linked to a moment in time and forever altered by it and have no choice in the matter. We all moved in and hugged Mouse, but he stiffened and pulled away quickly. As if to say he didn't need our sympathy. That he was the strong one here.

Yessi cleared her throat. "For me," Yessi said, "it was my mother's boyfriend. I know it's like everyone says, the boyfriend or the girlfriend come after you. But this sick fucker really did, and my mom was like a goddamn mole in the dirt, blind and stupid and just tunneling away. Ray was his name. He came after me when I was eleven, twelve, thirteen. And one night I videotaped it and sent it in to the cops. He went to prison for thirty years, and my mom was so pissed, she kicked me out. She wants nothing to do with me, blames me for ruining her life. She told me I wanted it to happen so that I could hurt her."

We gathered around Yessi, and she reached wide and hugged us all, her eyes completely dry, her round face tense, her eyes focused on the distance like she had one of those awful memories stuck in her gaze.

Avery cleared his throat. "I guess it's my turn," he said. Avery had such a likeable face, like he belonged in the 1950s, in the movies. Angular, fair, blonde with crystal blue eyes. The bright, almost white-blue eyes that were hard to look away from. "My mom died when I was born. I was told it was a complication of labor. I never knew what that meant. But my dad always blamed me. Every time he would get pissed off at me, he'd yell that he wished I'd died instead of her. But then a couple years ago he starts dating this girl from NA, Gale Swift. And she's a real piece of work. She had a temper that rivaled the devil herself. Once, when I broke some porcelain dove that she had brought home from the flea market over off the 198, she flew off in a rage and stuck me with one of the shards in the neck." He pulled his shirt collar to the side and showed us a pink, jagged scar by his collarbone. "Missed my jugular by less than an inch. She tried to kill me. Anyway, my dad framed it up to look like it was self-defense on her part, and they booted me out here. Fuckin' Hotel Dog Shit."

"Oorah," everyone muttered, and I chimed in toward the end. I felt as though my heart were swelling out of my chest, reaching out to these other souls, these soldiers. These deeply human experiences that had landed good kids in a bad place were all mine. These were my brothers and sisters, and in a rush of emotion, I felt more at home with them than I ever had anywhere else. And yet we were here, in this home of last resort. This run-down orphanage. But from what I could tell, it didn't seem all that bad. Not with these people around me. But the question that had nagged me this whole time was, who were they going to kill and why?

"Are you really going to kill someone?" I asked.

"We're going to kill Sal," Avery said.

"You just got here, so you are probably safe for a couple of days, maybe a week. But you'll get the call eventually," Mouse said. "So we have to kill him soon."

"Get the call?" I asked.

"They come for you at random. Or, depending on the customers. They snag you while you're sleeping. They stick you full of drugs and send you up to the fuck shit suite," Yessi said.

"Why is it called that?" I asked.

"Because, fuck that shit. That's why," Mouse said.

Avery lowered himself to one knee and cried softly, head down. "They got me again last night. I can remember it all. But I remember too goddamn much. They want you awake for the customers. They think we don't know, but there is a whole operation going on. This is a fucking production studio."

My heart began to sprint, my pulse thudding in my ears. This wasn't a prank, these kids were serious, and I was about to be next. They brought me out here to protect me. To protect themselves. "Why don't you just leave? Right now. Why don't we all just go?"

"Everyone has tried that. The cops find you and bring you right back. And you get it ten times worse when they do. It's a hell loop you're stuck in until you die or turn eighteen," Mouse said. "We're not letting them get you. They're not getting anyone ever again."

"You're really going to kill Sal?" I asked, wondering if he could really do it. Actually murder someone.

"Goddamn right we are. We're going to kill Sal and whoever else is in there with him. And we're doing it tomorrow night."

"But, how? With what?" I remembered my conversation with Domino. Maybe he could help us. "Why don't we just tell the police?"

Mouse laughed. "You think they are going to believe any of us? The kids who get bounced out of every foster home. The fuckups. The miscreants. Hell, most of them couldn't care less if it were true anyway, as long as we're off the streets."

"It would get worse for us if he found out we called," Yessi said softly.

I didn't believe that Domino would tell Sal anything; he would believe me. But if what they were saying was true, then Sal not only deserved to die, he deserved to be tortured for the rest of his life. Anyone who would fuck around with helpless kids for sick pleasure, well, they should either be castrated or killed. Probably both. An evil thought wormed its way up, that maybe Mouse and the others were all just mad about something else, inventing a big yarn to scare me into helping. But I could feel the truth in their words. Their voices. Their tears. It was real.

"Why hasn't everyone ganged up on Sal. Stop him in the act?"

"Bigger kids, ones like me—I'm fourteen already—that know what's going on, they lock 'em up at night when shit goes down. Neutralize us so we can't do nothing. They have the game room, where the old hotel lobby used to be: pool tables, projector TV, Pac-Man, all that. Plus all the weed and beer you could want. Sometimes coke. They get you fucked up and distract you so you forget. That's what they did with my primo, Chivo. He was here. They got him good when he was a kid, and when he got bigger, they locked him up in there until curfew. Then he aged out. That's why I keep my head down. Keep quiet. Sal doesn't see me as a threat. This has been in the plans for a while. And tomorrow is D day.

"What's the plan?" I asked.

"Easy. We found a way into their priest studio through the subflooring. There's a whole room back there, behind a big-ass one-way mirror in the suite. We found chairs, video cameras, equipment. All kinds of shit to make VHS tapes and ship them out. And I know the way in."

"But like, how are you going to do it? The killing part," I said.

"Oh, that part." Mouse smiled. "Well, if Chivo came through, then our answer is right over there." Mouse gestured toward the barn with a nod. Then he started toward it, parting the tall grasses with his stride. Stopping at the entrance, he looked back and smiled, then disappeared through a swirl of tulle fog. A moment later he appeared again, out of the darkness. He stopped and held above his head a sawed-off shotgun. Pump action with a duct-taped stock and a duffel bag. My heart started to race again. I was afraid, but I also wasn't. It was hard to explain, but this whole expedition out here, these stories. I realized that these people were me. And I was them. The stories had hooked me into these kids in such a deep and powerful way, I would help them murder the president. If they said Sal needed to die, I was in.

Mouse returned to the fire pit, holding the shotgun across his chest like a soldier. I'd seen plenty of guns in my life. Kids I hung out with from school had older brothers in gangs and showed me their Glocks and Berettas. Plus, I had gone to a couple of Boy Scout camps where we shot clay pigeons with shotguns. I'd never seen a sawed-off except for on TV, but what I knew about them was that the BBs inside the cartridge spread faster when they came out of the barrel. They were made for close-range stopping power. They were really great weapons, too, because you almost couldn't miss. The only problem was, they weren't as deadly. A bunch of little BBs instead of a big slug. But if you were close, it put a hole the size of a basketball in someone's chest. At least, that was on the movies.

"Where's the bullets?" Avery said.

Mouse held up the damp camo duffel bag, then placed it on the ground. He unzipped it, and it was packed with boxes of shells for the gun.

"What kind are they?"

"Buckshot," Mouse said. "Deer killers."

"Shit. That will do it," I said.

"You ever handle one of these?"

"Just a twenty gauge. We shot trap up in Shaver a couple times."

"This ain't no twenty gauge." Mouse pulled the pump back and slipped shells into it until it was full. "Takes five shells. I'll only need one."

"What can I do to help?" I asked.

"*The plan is simple. They pull a kid almost every night. They'll pull someone tomorrow. We'll stay on lookout, and once they are for sure in the fuck shit suite, I'll slip in, blast the fuck out of everyone in there. I'll shoot the glass out and blast the pervert in the suite, wipe the gun, then put Sal's fingerprints on it. Then I'll slip back out through the floorboards. Yessi has the closest room to the suite, so she'll run to the market to use the phone and dial 911. And that's it.*"

"*What about me?*" I said.

"*I just need you to watch my six,*" Mouse said.

I nodded, imagining squeezing through the floorboards and watching Mouse blast a bunch of perverts to pieces. It sounded great in theory, but I knew actually doing it would be terrifying and difficult.

"*Are you sure that thing works?*" Avery said.

Mouse pointed the barrel at Avery's chest, then let out a wry chuckle. He slowly angled it toward the barn. He held it there, the stock against his shoulder, and pulled the trigger. A deafening explosion rang out, and a scattering of holes burst through the barn siding. The sharp scent of gun smoke clung to my nostrils, and my ears rang.

"*I'd say it works. Let's get the hell out of here.*" Mouse tucked the shotgun into the duffel bag, and we ran. Through the dark orchard, back down the alley behind the Hotel Dog Shit, and we squeezed through the floorboards and into our beds. Mouse tucked the duffel bag under his mattress, and we stayed quiet.

I tried to sleep, but my heart raced with my thoughts about tomorrow night. About what was going on here at this group home. About murder. I prayed and prayed that nobody would come for me tonight, even though I didn't believe in prayer. It was the only power I had that night, which was none. I had to beg to a god I was pretty sure didn't exist that I wouldn't get abused by sick, demented men in the middle of the night in a place where I was supposed to be safe. I didn't like this feeling. A totally empty, completely alone feeling. A feeling of utter and complete powerlessness to prevent something terrible from happening to me. And this feeling, this was why Mouse was going to kill Sal. Mouse was protecting all of us. And having that protection, knowing that Mouse was in the room with me with that shotgun just out of reach, well, that felt much better to me than a prayer.

Rori's breathing turned ragged and heavy, so I paused the story and drove in silence while she rested. Traffic was light until I got past Capitola on the 101. I pulled off the freeway after the fishhook toward downtown Santa Cruz. I followed the signs for the Boardwalk.

I parked in a huge, mostly vacant lot across the street from the Beach Boardwalk and just stared for a while at the spectacle. It was bigger than I had expected, and lit up like Christmas with lights flashing and a massive wooden roller coaster booming around corners. I rolled down the window and could hear laughter and screams, and even though I knew we should be hiding somewhere, this also seemed like the last place in the world the Shadow Valley cops would think to look for us. I nudged Rori, and she turned and looked up at me through sleepy eyes.

"We're here," I said.

She stretched and sat up, blinking and rubbing her eyes. "Do you have a cigarette?"

I lit two and handed her one.

She puffed on it in silence for a few seconds, then said, "What time does it close?"

The clock on the dash read 10:31 p.m. "Not sure, but it's open now, let's go."

"But your face. Are you really up for this?"

"I'm more worried about my ribs, but I'll be all right for one ride on the Giant Dipper."

"It'll hurt like hell."

"Fuck it. I was almost dead today, might as well live."

She smiled and changed into tight acid-wash jeans and a loose Black Sabbath T-shirt from the clothes we had grabbed. Stepping out of the warm car, we felt the cold coastal wind pierce our clothes. We both shivered. She leaned into me, and I put my arm over her shoulder while we walked to the entrance. I breathed the briny scent of the Pacific Ocean and smiled. We'd made it out of the sweltering Central Valley and into a new world.

At the ticket kiosk, I noted that the park closed at midnight through the summer, which gave us a little more than an hour. The teenager behind the glass had freckles and a spread of acne across her cheeks. I wondered how close to Rori's age she was.

"Can we get two tickets for the Giant Dipper?" I said.

"Two dollars," the girl said, and I handed her two singles.

The place wasn't all that busy. I figured that made sense because it was a Thursday night in late August—school was back in session. Rori held my hand tightly while we walked the cement path to the coaster's entrance. I could hear the rolling crash of waves through the darkness past the sand to our right. It was hidden by a layer of fog that drifted up the shoreline and circled our bodies like smoke. Rori held me closer for warmth, and my ribs ached. They felt cracked, but not broken. I must have shielded myself to some degree, which was probably why my forearms also felt brutalized. Looking around, I spotted a gift shop. We bought two, thick *Surf City, USA* hoodies and went back out into the night.

There were only a few people in line for the Big Dipper, so we walked right on.

"Let's sit in the back," Rori said. "I've heard it's more fun that way."

The metal arm dropped down on us and held us firmly in our seats, and I wrapped my one arm around my ribs to try and keep them steady and held Rori's hand with the other. Behind a small desk, there was another teenager who pushed a single button, and the train lunged forward. Pain shot through me, and Rori's hand turned damp inside of mine. The coaster clicked slowly to the top, and when we got there, above the fog line, I could see it all. Bright lights that stretched the length of the Boardwalk in both directions, the soft churn of white from the waves crashing over the black, shadowy shore, the arched coastline toward Capitola, making its way toward Monterey. Then farther south, toward Big Sur, SoCal, Baja, and endless freedom.

I looked for the Crown Vic in the parking lot, but the cars were so small from up here, it was hard to tell them apart. Then, the clicking stopped. The train stalled for just a moment right at the top; then the little cars in front of us dropped away, one at a time, down the steep ramp. We suddenly began to race, tearing down the track in a roar of gears and metal.

We yanked around corners at breakneck speed while my ribs felt like they might burst like glass in my chest. Rori screamed, and when I looked over, she was laughing with tears gathering at the corners of her eyes. I squeezed her hand. Soon the turns got slower, and the leaping sensation faded. Our train pulled around a final corner, where the kid stood, his hand over the single button, and there was still nobody in line.

"You guys want to go again?" he said, his newly developed Adam's apple bobbing in his throat.

"Yes!" Rori said, and she leaned into my shoulder while the train clicked back up the incline. She held me tightly, scared and thrilled at once. I bit down, holding my chest and still holding Rori's damp hand. I watched while the cars, once again, dropped away one by one ahead of us.

Chapter Seven
Friday, August 19, 1988
Art

1

When Art approached, Armando clenched tighter. The accountant's eyes rolled back in his head.

"Let him go, Armando," Art said, but the kid was smart enough to know that he was dead without a hostage. Art stepped closer, but Lacy moved between them. If Art waited any longer, the accountant wouldn't make it.

"Don't, Art. He paid. Look, he paid." She pulled a crisp hundred from her gold top.

"Lacy, the kid is twenty-fucking-five."

She looked unfazed by this. "Don't hurt him."

Art glanced at Tyra still sitting, back against the bar. He'd figured this was also why Lacy had come to work bruised lately. This kid was violent, but nobody hit Lacy, or a customer, and got away with it. And if you did it in front of him, you were as good as dead. Tyra flipped Art a thumbs-down. The okay to spill the dirt he'd dug up.

"He's married, Lacy. He has three children back home. Roberto, Maria, and Salvador. All back in the DR. He doesn't love you."

"You jealous fucker," she said, but turned to face Armando. He pled with his eyes, but Art watched a look of resignation flash through them.

"It's not true," Armando said. But he loosened his grip and Art saw the opportunity.

Sidestepping Lacy, Art delivered a quick, vicious left-handed strike that clubbed down on Armando's left collarbone, shattering it. Armando howled and let go of the accountant, then slumped forward, cradling his arm. Art reloaded and came swiftly across Armando's cheek, snapping his beautifully square jaw. The kid collapsed in shock. Watching the blood glide from the kid's mouth, Art remembered why he tried to avoid open wounds. The cleanup. Art helped the accountant from the floor and straightened his tie and collar.

"We're sorry about that, sir. It won't happen again," Art said.

The accountant hobbled straight toward the door, fell, stood, and pushed the doors open. He wouldn't be back.

"Tyra, I've got a meeting with the police," Art said. "Puck will be my replacement for the time being. I'll take care of Armando. Puck, don't do anything stupid."

Tyra and Parker nodded, and Art grabbed Armando by the collar and dragged his limp, bleeding body across the floor, through the parking lot, and lifted him onto the bed of his F-150, torso first, then shifted his legs inside and slammed the tailgate. He covered him with a blue tarp and tucked the edges underneath. Art went back inside the club and took a large, black rollaboard from his locking armoire. He loaded it into the back of his truck, started it, and tore away, speeding into the fading sunlight. In his rearview mirror, he watched the club's neon sign flicker to life.

2

When Art pulled up to Easton Veterinary, the sun's final glare bloomed orange, red, and purple against the pollution haze. There were three police cruisers and an ambulance parked by a ranch house across from the clinic. One of the cruisers had its lights flashing. The ambulance did not. Never a good sign. Scanning the small crowd of uniforms, Art noticed a heavy-framed man push through the small gathering like a goddamn bull. He was thirty pounds heavier with gray spread through his mustache and temples. Burke looked ten years older than the last time Art had seen him, a little over a year before. Art stepped out of the truck to greet him.

"This whole scene is a goddamn shit show," Burke said. "Where the fuck were you?" He moved around to the bed of the truck. His face was scuffed and scratched like he'd face-planted into the gravel, and there was dried blood on his collar. Two body bags were being loaded into the ambulance.

"Who did you shoot?" Art asked. "And what the hell happened to you?"

"Goddamn mess. We have a suspect at large. Armed and dangerous. Killed my goddamn partner and shot me twice in the vest."

"Was he a professional? Ex-military?"

"Shit no. Some kid, Heath Walker, got into a scrape with some bikers over at Blue Cue and kidnapped my underage daughter a few weeks ago. I tracked them down here, and the kid's mom pulled a shotgun on me. Blasted a hole in my goddamn cruiser. I returned fire, and the kid sucker punched me, then put a hole in Johnson's neck."

The name Walker rang a bell, but Art couldn't remember exactly from when or where. "What was Rori doing at the Blue Cue if she's underage?"

Burke turned and grabbed Art's embroidered shirt roughly. He stopped, appeared to collect himself, and released. "Sorry, Art. That kid has more piss in her than her mother ever did. But I want her back. You understand me?"

"If she's almost eighteen—"

Burke's eyes flared with anger, and Art stopped himself.

"Look, you cut the checks, I go get the bounties. What does the kid look like?" Art asked.

"Like I said, his name is Heath Walker. Twenty-two-year-old, Latino-mixed race, six two. Sturdy kid, ex-ball player. Armed and dangerous."

"You mentioned that. You know I've tracked down a lot of armed and dangerous people," Art said, and smiled. He'd missed working these types of cases, the vigilante nature—the hunting of humans—the apex of apex predators. Art had learned to enjoy killing people the law couldn't get to because of bullshit like due process. For the right amount of money. But this didn't seem like the normal case. This was personal for Burke, and there was something Burke wasn't telling him. "Where's the file?"

Burke handed Art a file folder, pages sticking out from the corners. "He's had a couple of possession charges. Fighting. Drunk and disorderly. Nothing serious. Childhood record is sealed by the Feds. Probably just another laundry list of petty crimes. He's a nobody."

Art leafed through the file, and a faint memory pricked up somewhere from back in his police days. But he'd changed a lot from then until now. Back then, he'd wanted to do good. He'd wanted to build better communities and help the people he served. A lot of good that did. He'd been fired and partially stripped of his pension, forcing him to become this. A gun for hire.

"What about the rest of his family?" Art asked. He moved the mug shot clipped to the file into the dim interior truck light.

"I think I just put a bullet in her."

"Christ. No other family? Brother, ex-foster siblings? I need something."

"We found this inside. It's all we've got to go on." Burke handed Art an envelope damp with coffee stains. *Hideaway Enterprises, Scotts Valley, California.* "We made a few calls, looks like some kind of hippy commune up in the Santa Cruz Mountains. Might be a place to start."

"What are they driving?"

"Black Crown Vic. License plate SHDWHI."

The ambulance doors slammed shut, and they started the engine.

"Clever. Anything else?"

"Just don't hurt Rori, I want her back."

"They won't see me coming."

Burke reached into his back pocket and pulled out a zippered leather envelope. Unzipping it, he handed a small stack of bills to Art. "Here's fifteen hundred up front. I'll get the rest when you come back, *with* Rori."

"What if they jump the border?"

Burke paused and looked over his shoulder at the crime scene. His body tensed. "I don't give a fuck if they go to Antarctica. Follow them and finish the job."

"It's illegal to bounty hunt in Mexico. Might be tricky getting back across the border with her."

"I have some connections with the border agents on both sides. I'll make a couple calls."

"Got it. Anything else?"

"Art, I've known you a long time, and you're good." Burke lowered his voice to a growl. "But if you don't come back with my daughter, you won't have a fucking life to come back to. Understand?" Burke was at least six foot two and nearly a head taller than Art, and when he leaned forward, his eyes bulged slightly.

Art met his stare. "Don't fucking threaten me. I'll get the girl. You just better hold up your end of the deal. And don't bother Tyra again while I'm gone."

"Fine. Now get the fuck moving. They're getting away."

Art turned, and when he did, the blue tarp in his truck bed moved, followed by a low, strangled groan.

"What the fuck is that?" Burke asked, his posture tense.

"Reason I was late."

Burke frowned. "Christ. Get rid of that sooner rather than later. I don't want you getting put away in another county."

Art nodded. "I will." He got into his truck and slammed the door.

Burke approached, and Art rolled the window down. "One more thing," Burke said, and leaned in so close to Art that he could smell the Copenhagen on his breath. "My girl, Rori, she's sick. Bipolar, manic-depressive, you name it. Don't listen to anything she says on the way back. Understand?"

"I'll keep her restrained and silenced. I always do."

"Not a word of what she says is true."

"Understood. I'm running down two complete lunatics," Art said, and smiled at his own sarcasm. He started his truck and tipped his hat. "I'll bring you a Polaroid of Heath before I bury him."

Burke nodded, spit again, then disappeared back into the house. A familiar unease about Burke returned, but Art shook it off. His livelihood rested on this rundown. But Burke always paid, and Art always delivered.

3

Art hit the 198 westbound, the direction the suspects had fled. If his experience had taught him anything, it was that people were predictable. The first place they would hit was Santa Cruz—this commune held some potential. The only issue Art saw was all the bystanders. He needed the element of surprise, and that was going to be difficult with a bunch of hippies ambling around all night. So, he'd locate it, case it, and time it just right—timing was everything. Art had an instinct for shit going wrong, which was why Armando was in the back of his truck, sucking oxygen through a broken jaw.

Art passed Acres Road exit when Armando woke up and started thumping in the truck bed. Maybe the dumb shit would stand up, fall onto the 198, and get pinballed into a ditch. But that'd be messy. The thumping got louder. Art might have heard a scream for help.

Art turned north up the 99, took the Goshen exit toward some wide-open farms on the outskirts of town. He headed due east—past rows of roll-up industrial storage that operated during the day. They were all closed up this time of night, usually, though there was a neon light flickering at the back, and it made Art curious. But not curious enough to stop.

A half mile later, he crossed the bridge for the Friant-Kern Canal and turned down a dirt frontage road that followed the cement-sided canal. He stopped when he got to a valve interchange, fifty feet upriver. He backed the bed of his truck flush with the cement bank, killed the engine, pulled a Glock .43 from his ankle holster, and wedged it into his beltline. Stepping out, he lowered the gate and threw the tarp into the water, where it floated like a giant, blue leaf over the slow-moving surface.

Like an insect under an overturned rock, Armando squirmed and tried to catch his footing to stand, grunting through his fractured jaw. His eyes widened when he saw Art's hand resting on the Glock in his waistline.

"You have two choices," Art said. "One, you can promise me that you'll leave town tonight and never come back. Never talk to Lacy again." Art knew from the stubborn fuck's expression he wasn't liking that option. "The second is, you can swim for it. You make it across, you walk away."

Armando groaned, caught his footing, and stood with his good hand in the air. He nodded. Blood dripped down his neck onto his fitted dress shirt. He wobbled. The truck's shocks moved with each step while he walked to the tongue of the bed. He looked at the slow-moving water, then back at Art. It looked like an easy swim. Fifty feet to freedom.

Art checked his Timex, pulled the Glock from his waist, and racked the slide. Round in the chamber, he said, "Just make your decision quickly."

Either he swam, or Art would shoot him. With a gun in his face, Armando seemed to think this was a trap, which was probably true. Art needed to get on the road. Appearing to sense this, Armando took a deep breath, shrugged, and jumped into the canal. Art watched him pull strong overhead strokes with his good arm, easily making it to the far side of the canal. He was in solid shape, seemed to be a good swimmer—mouth-breathing through that busted jaw had to be tough. He grasped at the steep cement embankment on the other side. Too steep. Too slick. Armando slipped into the slow current pulling him closer to the valve interchange.

He tried crawling up the cement again, flattened out against it. Held on long enough for Art to put a bead on him just in case, but that slow, unrelenting current pulled him back down. Art watched him spot the ladder just past the valve, stop swimming, and let the current carry him toward false salvation. Art smiled.

In the glow of the truck's taillights, Art saw the blue tarp ahead of Armando get sucked beneath the surface. Armando panicked and yelped something muffled by the orchards around them. His arms flapped desperately just before slipping under. The surface grew calm like nothing had ever been there. No Armando. No tarp. Just the slow current holding him firmly against the rusted steel fingers of the grate while the brackish water flooded around him like powerful shadows whispering his name.

If the body were ever recovered, it probably wouldn't be worth an autopsy.

Art reached into the back seat of his truck and got out a spray bottle of bleach-and-water mix, a roll of paper towels, and did a quick sweep of the truck bed and interior. He pulled out a zippered dry-cleaning bag and unhooked a pressed, blue pair of trousers and button-down shirt logoed with patches that said *City Utility Line Services*. It was official looking, vague, and worked well on hunts in the past.

He drove back to the road, waiting to flip the lights on when he neared the freeway. Armando's swim lesson had set him back another twenty minutes. No problem. Be better to get to the commune when all the hippies were asleep anyway. Just before dawn was usually the best time to catch somebody off guard. If all went well, he'd be home by midday tomorrow, and there would be a second body seized against that steel grate.

Chapter Eight
Friday, August 19, 1988
Heath

1

After our third trip around the track on the Giant Dipper, the train slowed to a stop, and the kid told us it was time to shut down. I stepped off and felt like my head was still leaning into turns, which made me sidestep slightly. Still clutching my ribs with my left arm, we walked past a long row of carnival games. Rori wanted to pitch softballs at lead milk jugs. I paid the old, gnarled-looking carny three dollars, and Rori knocked a couple off the top. He handed her a keychain-sized banana slug, then pulled a big, garage-type door down. We walked a little farther, and the lights to the whole park started switching off like dominoes down the row. It felt like being forced to go to bed early, only our bed was running from certain death.

"We should get some supplies and head up to Avery's," I said.

She nodded and slipped her cold hand into mine, and we walked toward the car. Out front, a gust of wind kicked up, and it sliced, cold and harsh, through the fabric of our clothes. I shivered.

"He's going to find us," she said softly, watching her feet.

"We need to talk to Avery about that job. Then we can head south."

"I feel like nowhere is safe."

I stopped and pulled her arm gently to turn her toward me. I looked into her eyes; they shimmered in the soft lamplight. "I want that son of a bitch to come for us," I said, and pushed her hand over the butt of the .357 in my waistline. I knew it was bullshit, that we were vulnerable out here, but we had to be safe for the time being.

"Let's go," I said. We walked across the street to Surf City Liquor. There were a few chest-high rows of basic grocery items, a cooler along the back, and a hundred types of hard liquor behind the register. In the home goods section, I grabbed some scissors, hair dye—a blonde and a red hair color kits—a couple tied-dyed shirts from a shelf, and a trucker hat and beanie hanging near the front. The hat had a San Francisco 49ers logo and the beanie, a round Sex Wax logo. Rori met me at the checkout with a bag of potato chips and a gallon of water. I asked for a fifth of Jack Daniel's, and the guy rang up the items.

"Fifty-seven fifty-nine," he said. He was a thin, middle-aged guy with stringy, sun-bleached hair and leathery skin. He looked like he'd surfed and done acid every day of his life since 1960, and I knew how easy it would be to pistol-whip him and walk out with everything, but I wasn't that guy. Not yet at least.

I felt Rori watching me when I pulled out my wallet and counted out everything I had onto the counter—fifty-four dollars even.

"You cash checks?" I asked.

"Sorry, man," he said. "You want to put something back?"

I looked at Rori, then back at the cashier. "Why don't we just swap the Jack for Jim," I said. He did, and the price came down four dollars. The man nodded, bagged the items, and we stepped back into the cold.

2

"We out of money?" Rori said, walking briskly toward the Crown Vic.

"I've got a check from the farm account I can cash. It was the money I was going to use to pay the electric bill. Once we get to Avery's, we'll figure out a plan," I said. It was starting to sound like a mantra—redundant and stupid. Avery hadn't called me back, and if I knew Avery, it was probably because he had screwed up. But I didn't want to worry Rori; she was already shaking beside me while we walked. Hell, I was shaking, too. We didn't have enough money for gas.

We got back into the car and shut the doors, chocking off the wickedly chilly breeze. The chime from the ignition beeped loudly, telling me the keys were in.

"We'll be all right," I said. I pulled the bottle of Jim from the bag, tore the plastic off with my teeth, and yanked the cork out. I took a long pull. When Rori took hers, she seemed to settle into her seat a little more. I figured she'd have a little less to worry about with a buzz.

"Don't cash that check. He'll use it to track us," she said.

I took another pull from the bottle and winced. I replaced the cap and set it behind Rori's seat. I lit two cigarettes and handed her one. "When we're up on that commune with our new clothes, blending in, he won't know who's who. We'll see him coming."

She took a long drag and exhaled. "Okay. Let's go."

"If anything happens, we bounce down to Mexico. Hopefully with some cash to stay gone."

She was quiet another second, then said, "When we get to Mexico, let's learn to surf."

The thought of Rori and I surfing in Mexico, lazing around in hammocks during the day, sipping Tecate in balmy evenings—it warmed me through my chest. I loved when she talked this way. About the future and about things that made her happy. I started the car and turned back toward the 1.

We followed Graham Hill Road up the mountain for about fifteen minutes and came to a turn that led up to Mount Herman, where the camp was. On the corner, before heading up, I found a Quick Stop that had twenty-four-hour service. Being dark out, I could clearly see inside, where an older man with close-cropped hair and spectacles read a thick paperback. I made the turn and floored it up the hill. The road curved left, then right. I made another two turns from a hazy memory, but it worked because a few minutes later we pulled up to the driveway with a hand-painted wooden sign hanging above the entrance: *Hideaway Haze*.

When we got to the end of the dirt road, something didn't seem right. It was dark, and the grass along the road had gone to weeds. There weren't dozens of hippies ambling around high and dancing to acoustic guitar around a campfire. Sitting in the driveway was Avery's faded-green Volkswagen van. I pulled in behind it and killed the ignition but left the lights on.

"This is it?" Rori said. She glared up at the only building we could see: an aging A-frame.

"Something's not right."

I stepped out of the car. Everything was quiet except for the chorus from a surrounding field of crickets. I walked onto the porch, and the planks creaked under my weight. I knocked. Nobody was home. I tried the door, and it was unlocked, so I walked in. I flipped a few switches, but nothing worked. I slipped inside using my lighter like a flashlight and went into the kitchen.

On the refrigerator, there was a card from the Pfeiffer Cliffs and Campground. Sketched on the back in pencil were the initials A.C. Avery Chastain? I walked out to the car and sat in the driver's seat, handing the card to Rori. I took a long, hot pull from the Jim Beam. I lit two cigarettes, and we just sat there for a minute, smoking, with our headlights shining into the little, ramshackle A-frame.

"I guess they shut down. Should we crash here or head south tonight? Crash somewhere like Big Sur?" I asked.

"This place is creeping me out," Rori said. "What about a hotel back in Santa Cruz?"

We were out of money, but I didn't want to belabor the point. "Water's cold, but it's running. I say we cut and dye here, change our clothes, then head down the hill. I've got a tent in the trunk, so we can camp and be all right until morning."

"What about that van? Why's it still here?"

"Not sure. But I know that van, he had it in high school. There's a kill switch that's hard to find. If it runs, I can figure it out."

3

We left the lights of the Crown Vic on and used it to cut, wash, and dye our hair in the kitchen. Somebody had come through and busted what was left of the place up, and it was in no condition to even hole up for even a night. I cut my hair to just below the earlobe, and when the bleach was setting up over my hair cap, I walked out to the VW and flipped the visor down. The registration fell onto my lap. Avery Chastain, registration expired next month.

I poked around the center console, then opened the glove box. Inside sat a small ring of keys. One of them slipped into the ignition. I reached under the dash and up near the odometer. I flipped a tiny fuse switch, and the panel lit up. I said a quick prayer and turned the key. It lunged over once, then stopped, which meant the battery was nearly dead. My previous car had been a '69 Karmann Ghia, so I knew VW engines pretty well, since they had a knack for breaking down. It was almost always the distributor.

I did a quick walk around the van, and the tires seemed good, and there were really no dents either. It was a solid vehicle. I slid the side door open, and it smelled a hint of wet dog and weed. There were some rumpled clothes, blankets, and a ten-foot surfboard inside with a long crack across the middle.

I closed the door and went to the back and lifted the engine cover to check on a few things. I pulled off the spark plug covers and blew into them one by one, spit on the contact points inside the distributor, then hooked up a pair of jumper cables and started the Crown Vic. I left it to charge the battery.

Back inside the A-frame, I found Rori shaping her newly red hair into a pixie cut, using a mirror on the fridge and a handheld mirror she must have found in the bathroom—her light hair had taken the dye quickly. I checked my hair, and it had turned from black to an orangish blonde. I washed the bleach out, dried it with a towel from my backpack, then put on the tied-dyed shirt and the Sex Wax beanie.

I didn't think a single person who knew me back home would even recognize me. Rori put the loose *Surf City, USA* sweater back on and turned the 49ers ball cap around backwards. She looked like a teenage skater boy. In the mirror we barely recognized ourselves. Rori bounced on the balls of her feet and kissed me. Becoming someone else in a new place felt good in a weird way. Maybe because it felt safer. I did a quick sweep of the room for our garbage, putting it in the plastic bag from the liquor store and locking it in the trunk of the Crown Vic.

Back in the van, I said a little prayer to the car gods and turned the ignition again. It chugged a few times, and a puff of black smoke burst from the tail pipes. I went to the back and twisted the distributor a couple centimeters to the right. I tried it again, and it purred with that characteristic high whine of Volkswagen exhaust. We were in business.

I pulled the Crown Vic around the back of the A-frame, then pulled the van around. Working quickly, I loaded it with our two bags, the water, and everything else from the car. I threw the Vic keys into the woods, and Rori hopped into the passenger's seat of the van. I flipped on the lights and checked the fuel gauge and groaned. It was, as I guessed, nearly dry. Then I remembered the gas station at the bottom of the hill. That didn't help though, because we were fresh out of cash. I gripped the steering wheel so hard, my knuckled popped up, white as clay. Maybe we would get lucky, and the old man would cash the check. I'd get gas one way or another. There was no way I would let Rori fall back into Burke's hands. Ever.

4

I coasted into the Quick Stop on fumes and stopped at a pump that looked like it was from the fifties and still self-serve. I started pumping the gas, and inside, the older guy sitting and reading behind the desk glanced at us over his wire-framed glasses. Pumping gas was on the honor system here, it seemed, and I thought about just driving off, but I didn't want an APB out on a green VW after we'd just gotten a clean car. So, I went into the cramped store that smelled of motor oil and sweat, and up the register. In the background, a radio played Pat

Robertson's *The 700 Club*. I did a quick scan and didn't see any cameras.

"Hello, young man," the cashier said without looking up. His thinning gray hair was combed neatly along a part on the left side of his head. He wore a button-down shirt and was reading *This Present Darkness* by Frank Peretti. There was a *Bush-Quayle '88* bumper sticker on top of the cash register. This looked like it was his store, but his eyes were bloodshot and tired. I thought maybe he wasn't the normal guy working the graveyard shift, since it was after 12:30 a.m. now. "You going to fill her up?"

"We are. And hey, Ross," I said, spotting his name tag, "can you do me a favor? Can you cash a check for me?" I tried to sound as polite and Republican as I could, but the outfit and the van certainly weren't scoring me any points.

"We don't cash checks, kid. Try the grocery store in the morning." He didn't make eye contact when he said this, which started to get under my skin. He really needed to cut us a break, and even though he didn't know it yet, it was his best option. I could feel the anger prick up inside my chest, so I started another poem in my head. *"Girlboys may nothing more than boygirls need."*

"Look, sir, or Ross, I ran out of cash, and all I have is this check. It's for sixty-three dollars. How about I sign it over to you, and you cash me out with fifty." I didn't care about leaving a paper trail of a check stub, especially if I signed it over. If Burke was tracking us, it wouldn't help him for days or weeks, and we'd be long gone.

He looked at me now, then out to the car, where Rori placed the handle back on the pump. "I recognize that bus. You part of that camp up the road? You look like one of those Godless hippies I called the cops on."

Goddamn it. The old bastard not only wasn't going to help me, but he sounded like the reason Avery was fucking missing. All of Avery's careful planning, my job—down the drain because of a stodgy, old conservative in the wrong place at the wrong time. The flash of anger tripled in my chest and burned out my arms and up my neck. I double-checked the room for cameras and spotted zero. *"I'd rather learn from one bird how to sing."*

"The pump has stopped," Ross said. "Do you plan on paying me?"

I shifted my weight and balled my fists in my pockets. "Forty dollars back, and I'll sign the check over to you." I was pleading now, not for my sake, but for his.

"I don't cash checks, young man. Now, you owe me the eleven fifty for the gas, and if you don't provide it, I'll have the sheriff down in a matter of minutes. He's a personal friend of mine." The old man shook a little with self-righteous anger.

"Okay. Easy. I'll just borrow it from my friend." I started to walk away, then stopped. "You have a bathroom, by the way?"

"Out back, key's on the register." He dog-eared his book and placed it down over the election bumper sticker, making it clear he was watching me carefully.

I walked out to the van and felt my muscles turn to gelatin with fear and anger, soaked in adrenaline. But he had done this, that man. He had chosen to make this situation life or death, even though I had offered him good, honest money. I couldn't relax my fists if I tried. Rori sat up in the passenger's seat, smoking with the window down.

"What's the deal?" she said.

"Just have to take care of something real quick. Stay in the car."

"Heath," she called after me. "I've got a bad feeling."

"Two minutes." The door to the bathroom was old with chipped paint. I jiggled the key into the door, opened it, and as I'd hoped, it opened outward. Moving around back of the shop, I found a two-by-four with some rusted nails leaning against a dumpster and went back to the bathroom. If I wedged it just right across the frame, it could hold someone inside. I hid the board just out of sight, around the corner, and left the door slightly ajar. I walked back around to the man at the register. *"Than teach ten thousand stars how not to dance."*

"Your friend have the money?" he asked. "I'll call the sheriff. Don't play with me, boy."

"Yeah, he's counting it, but there's a few dollars in change, if that's okay."

"Any American currency is fine," he said.

"Hey, I couldn't get the key to work out back. You mind?"

He seemed to relax when I mentioned that we had the money coming, and he stood for the first time. He was over six feet tall and pretty sturdy and not as old as I had thought, maybe late fifties, early sixties.

"The door is a little tricky," he said. I handed him the key, and he got up and walked around to the back where I followed him. He moved to slip the key into the door, but when he pushed at it, the door bobbed open. Turning to face me, he said, "You playing some kind of goddamn game—"

"You shouldn't have called the cops on Avery," I said.

I shoved him into the bathroom and moved to slam the door, but he was much faster and stronger than I had anticipated. He shoved me back, hanging onto my shirt with his right hand. The fabric tore as he yanked me forward. I tried to ram my weight against the door to close it, but his foot wedged it open. He shouldered the door open with surprising strength and released my shirt, sending me sprawling to my ass.

Reaching into my waistline, I pulled the .357, but before I could aim it at him, he lunged forward and swatted it away, hard enough to send it clattering to the ground twenty feet away. Then he yanked me to my feet, where he landed a quick uppercut to my solar plexus. He gave me space, then landed a quick right to my already swollen cheek, and pain burst through my face and neck.

"I was a Navy prizefighter. First in my battalion, son." He landed a quick jab to my chin, and I saw light crack in my periphery. Moving with what effort I could muster, I ducked a strong right cross.

Taking a step back, I collected myself. The old man was going to fucking kill me. My rage built, now completely unsuppressed by the man's age or physical condition. Avery and

Rori needed me. I willed myself to get it together. The old man reared back for a knockout blow, and I dropped to my ass and rolled to the right, then scrambled toward the .357. The old man was hot on my trail, and just when I got my hand on the grip, he took a firm hold of my hair in his fist. With his free hand, he landed hard, crushing blows to my back and neck. Managing to get to my knees, I gripped the gun tightly. *"How do you like your blue-eyed boy / Mister Death?"*

I came around with the butt of the .357 straight down on the man's forehead. I cracked him harder than I had meant to, and the skin on his forehead split. He slumped over, his weight falling right on top of me. Squirming out from under his mass, I grabbed him under his armpits and dragged him inside the bathroom. I checked myself in the mirror and cleaned up some blood from my face and hands, wiping a smudge from my father's ring.

I used the two-by-four to wedge the bathroom door shut and tossed the key into the dumpster. Inside the station, I pulled the cash drawer open. There looked to be a few hundred, and I shoved it all into my pockets. Making a quick inventory of the place, I grabbed a few maps—California Coast, Southern California, and Baja Mexico—and a twelve-pack of MGD, another pack of cigarettes, and some Slim Jims.

5

Walking to the van, I got hit with fresh waves of pain and adrenaline surging through my body. I just wanted to get the hell away from this place, but at that moment, another truck pulled up and parked at the farthest pump from us. It was an F-150, and there was a dark-complexioned cowboy driving it. I kept my face down and hurried to the van, jumping in and starting it quickly. Throwing the van in gear, I pulled away carefully so it didn't look obvious we were fleeing a crime scene.

"You okay?" I asked. Rori was slumped down in her seat, eyes on the floor.

"I'm okay," Rori said, her voice sounding tense and frightened. "Just feel like we should get the hell out of here. I have the creeps from this weird mountain town."

"Well, we're going to an even weirder one. We're heading to Big Sur in the morning." I handed Rori the postcard I'd taken from Avery's refrigerator.

"Why don't we just go straight to Mexico?" she said, setting it on the dash. "Figure it out from there?"

"I would, but I think Avery's in trouble. Once I know he's safe, we can go."

She didn't say anything else, so I just kept driving down that dark, winding road toward Santa Cruz. After nearly passing out while driving, I decided to pull off in Capitola. It was past 1:00 a.m. when we parked the van at a public lot near Capitola Beach. Rori had fallen asleep. I moved the surfboard onto the roof and used the blankets and clothes to make a little nest. After I helped Rori from the passenger's seat, she folded herself up in the center of the floor. Lying next to her, I felt an exhaustion crash over me that was so heavy, so fraught with pain and burned-up adrenaline, I almost couldn't sleep. All I heard was the hiss of rolling waves a few hundred yards away.

Chapter Nine

Friday, August 19, 1988

Art

1

Art drove up the 99 north and exited onto the 152 through Los Banos without stopping. On the seat beside him, he had the file open with a map to the location that had been roughly sketched by Burke. The directions weren't complicated, and if anything, a hippy commune called Hideaway Haze couldn't be too hard to find.

When he got to Santa Cruz, it was well after midnight. He made the turn off the 1 and headed up Graham Hill Road toward Felton. After about fifteen minutes, he approached a gas station on his right, just before the turn marked on the map had him driving up to Mount Hermon. Art checked his gas gauge, and it was resting on empty, so he decided to fill up here before he went up to get the bounties. Once he had the girl, he didn't want to make any stops or take any chances. He'd go straight home and collect the rest of the money from Burke.

The lights were on inside the mini-mart, and there was a Volkswagen van parked outside with a skinny teenager with red hair in the front seat watching the station. Art parked at the farthest pump from the VW. A surf bum with blonde hair and a beanie walked out of the station, got into the front seat, and pulled away toward Santa Cruz. Art stepped out and started filling his truck. He waited a minute while the numbers ticked up and went into the station, but it was empty. Dead silence. Art wondered if the guy was in the back stocking shelves or something. He reached into his wallet, pulled out twenty bucks, and left it on the counter.

He walked back out to the pump, which had stopped at twenty-two gallons. $18.62. Close enough. Stepping back inside his truck, he opened his luggage and took out his vacuum-sealed disguise, pulled it open, and changed. Then he slipped his Glock into his ankle holster and clipped his baton to his hip, where it looked like some sort of tool or utility. Nobody ever looked twice at it. He started the truck and went up Graham Hill Road.

It was pitch-dark, but the map was accurate, because withing a few minutes, Art's high beams were pointed straight at a sign that read *Hideaway Haze*. The sign was wood and cracked and hung sort of off-center from two round posts over a dirt driveway that let up through some pine trees. He pulled past the sign and shut off the truck on the dirt shoulder, then switched off his headlights. It was quiet and dark, which wasn't what Art had expected. Something in his gut told him this wasn't right. He pulled the truck sideways, blocking the driveway, and turned it off again. From his luggage he pulled a flashlight and went on foot up the pathway with his gun drawn.

It was a couple hundred yards up the narrow driveway before Art came to the clearing where he spotted a dilapidated A-frame cabin. Beyond it to the left was an open field with a dozen yurts all coming apart. The place was gutted and trashed, like the aftermath of Woodstock.

Tucking the gun into his waistline, Art went up the stairs and into the open front door. The place was damp and dark. Art went through each room, looking for signs that somebody had been there recently, but saw nothing. Then he got to the kitchen and walked up to the sink. There was standing water in the basin, and the drain was partially clogged with cut hair. It was draining, but slowly. Red dye was splashed on the side of the discolored porcelain.

Art moved the flashlight and noticed something glint from a window that faced out back. He walked to the rear door and kicked it down. Since the wood was partially rotted, it fell easily. Sitting in the pale starlight was a black Crown Vic. *Fuck.* Art sprinted to his truck, started it, and floored it back toward the gas station.

2

Pulling back up to the Quick Stop, Art slammed his breaks, screeching to a halt. He went back inside the store and called out. He heard a faint grown from behind the store and went back out and around to the back. A partially rotted two-by-four blocked the bathroom door. Art took it down and tossed it aside. He heard another groan from inside. The door was unlocked, and he pulled it open. Inside was exactly what he'd expected: the gas station attendant bleeding out on the tile floor from a head wound.

Art went back to his truck and grabbed an ammonia capsule. These came in handy whenever he needed his bounties looking a little fresher when he brought them to the station. He pulled a cotton-covered glass cylinder from the jar and cracked the glass inside by pinching the cotton. The smell of ammonia and alcohol filled the car. He stepped out and pulled the door open again.

Kneeling beside the man, Art felt for his pulse. It was weak, but still there, so he placed the cotton under the man's nose and compressed his lungs a few times to get him breathing deeply. It took a few breaths, but the old man's eyes fluttered open, and he looked around, confused. His head wound was deep, and he'd lost a lot of blood. Without a hospital, the guy would be dead by morning.

"The kids that did this to you," Art said. "Do you know where they went?"

"Kids?" the old man said through a ragged breath.

Art put the salts under his nose again.

The man perked up a little more. "The blonde kid. He hit me." He reached up to feel the wound on his head, but Art grabbed his hand and put it back.

"I just need to know where they went, and I can get you to a hospital," Art said.

"That Volkswagen, they must have stolen it—it was the doper's." His eyes started to close again, and Art put the smelling salts under his nose, causing his eyes to roll back in his head, then snap forward.

"Where did they go?" Art said.

The man was silent, so Art shook him a little. His body flopped like he was already gone. "Most of the dopers went to Big—Sur," he managed to mumble to stop the shaking.

Art stood and looked around.

The old man groaned and reached for his head again and whimpered, "Help me."

Art thought about shooting him but knew this was going to make the news and didn't want it to be traced to him. The thought of calling the cops crossed his mind, too, but these kids leaving a trail of bodies would help justify any means when Art finally got ahold of this kid, Heath Walker.

Using a pocketknife, Art cut the rolling cloth hand towel attached to the wall and pulled out a three-foot segment. He rolled it up and went back to the old man, who was still breathing and softly groaning. He pushed the towel down over the man's nose and mouth and held it there. Just before he died, the old man's thin arms thrashed around and pushed Art's face away. People's survival instincts always came through, even when it was too late. It was something Art had seen more times than he liked to remember, and it was the images of these contorted, dying faces that woke him up every morning with his pulse buzzing like a hummingbird.

He placed the rag over the wound and put the old man's limp hand over it to make it look like he was trying to address the wound and collapsed. It wasn't perfect, but he didn't care. Burke would make sure the kid got linked to this. Art did a quick cleaning of the room and his hands with the bleach-water mixture in a spray bottle, then wiped down everything he had touched. He pushed the door back in place and replaced the two-by-four.

Back in his truck, Art drove toward Santa Cruz. He would hit the 1 and be in Big Sur in two or three hours. All he had to do was find that green Volkswagen he'd seen earlier, or find Avery. He had to admit, the kids had done a pretty quick and clever costume change; he hadn't expected that so soon. It usually took a bounty a couple of days to get their hair cut and a new wardrobe. And they had even managed a car swap. Maybe these kids were better than his typical rundown. Or that he was getting rusty.

3

It was just after 2:00 a.m. when Art rolled into the sleepy alpine town of Big Sur with its small, cabin-like restaurants and inns. It was a strange sensation to be in such remote areas of California that were so close to bustling little cities like Carmel and Santa Cruz. And the striking juxtaposition from Shadow Valley. These were separate universes. Art had been to Big Sur before on a case, and he remembered the ranger station just before Ventana Inn, and that was where he headed.

There was a single brown Chevy truck parked out in front of the visitor's center, and a small column of smoke on the far side of the building. The living quarters, *bingo*. Art shut off his vehicle and contemplated going in and waking the poor bastard out of REM sleep with a bang on the door and a gun to the face, but decided he'd get a few hours' sleep and wait until the ranger got up to open up the center. Also, he didn't know if the guy was alone or not, and didn't want the situation to get away from him. Art rolled up a sweater from his luggage and propped it against his door, stretched his legs across the bench-style seat, and tipped his hat over his eyes.

4

Art must have been more tired than he had thought, because he woke up to the sharp sound of metal tapping against the glass of his driver's side window. He sat up, groggy and confused, but after a second, the world clarified. The ranger was a she, and she was young and not bad looking with long black hair pulled into a ponytail, an oval face, and a light coating of makeup that made her seem younger than he was by about thirty years. He rolled down the window and adjusted his hat.

"This isn't a campsite, sir. You'll have to get moving, or I'll have to fine you," she said, and tilted back her wide-brimmed, green hat so the dawn light caught her light-brown eyes at an angle.

"I came in late and hoped to stop in for a map, is all. You opening up soon?" Art said in his most sincere and apologetic tone.

"We don't open until eight, but come on in, and I'll pour you some coffee, and we'll see about that map. I might be able to tell you where you need to go."

"Doug," Art said. "Doug Weaver, and I appreciate this." Art stepped down from his truck, and they were about eye level. He extended his hand, and they shook. She turned and started back toward the building that looked to be a sort of duplex with the visitor's center in front and living quarters in back.

"Name's Kate. Come on, Doug. You look like you need caffeine more than I do."

"Right behind you," Art said. It was cool out, so Art pulled on a knitted sweater with a Southwestern pattern. Before he stepped out, he slipped his Glock from its ankle holster and moved it to the small of his back. He also grabbed a set of handcuffs, a gag, and a vial of liquified Quaalude. Art didn't want to hurt her, but he needed to borrow a few things.

5

If it were up to Art, any man who physically overpowered a woman should have his knees shot out and dick removed. If there was one thing Art hated, it was seeing drunk guys getting unnecessarily violent, but especially with women. It caused a surge of rage inside of him that made images flash like old, reel-to-reel, black-and-white movies of his father beating his mother. And of his father bleeding when, just after his sixteenth birthday, Art nearly killed the old man.

Because of his father, Art had sworn he'd never drink. His father's abuse also had something to do with the reason Art had taken the job to protect and serve. He'd wanted the power of the badge to fight evil. The problem was that nobody on the force stayed that starry-eyed for long, and you learned quickly that if you didn't scratch some backs and let the other guys see you get your hands dirty, you ended up a liability. When he'd learned that, he'd started to drink. Slowly at first, with beer and cider. Then later he moved on to vodka and whiskey. He loved the vanilla and dried fruit aromas of good bourbon. The way the alcohol singed your nostrils in a raw panic of pleasure. He needed a shot right then, just to smell, but it was only 6:30 a.m. He needed to get back to the club and clear his head, but first, he needed to get these goddamn kids.

The house was warm with the fire crackling, and Kate remained still except for her chest moving, which meant she'd be fine. The great thing about coffee was that it was strong and bitter and covered up the taste of drugs well. He'd given her a healthy dose of Quaaludes and helped her over to the bed, head resting on the pillow. He hesitated and pulled out a zip tie. He would have roughly five to six hours before she woke up. And since he planned to leave his truck here, he needed to make sure she didn't make any calls, in case his hunt went long. So, he zip-tied her wrists to the bedpost, leaving her head resting comfortably.

Rummaging through her closet, Art found a backup ranger outfit and tried it on. It was snug but fit well enough. He put on the hat and checked himself out in the mirror. The handlebar mustache looked all wrong for the ranger getup, so he found a razor in the shower, a pink disposable one, and brushed at the handlebar portion of the mustache until it was reshaped into a straight line at the corners of his mouth. He found Kate's key ring, flipped to the key with a Chevy logo on it, pulled it free, and tossed the rest at her feet.

Outside, he breathed in the cool, pine-and-ocean-scented air. He went to the ranger truck, unlocked it, and got in. Attached to the dash was a CB radio, and some files and equipment. He pushed everything aside, started the truck, and headed back toward the little town, where he remembered passing a small coffee shop by the only gas station. Art figured that in a town this small, someone there would know where the assholes from Santa Cruz were hiding out.

6

The café was called Big Sur Bakeshop, and it was bustling for being just before 7:00 a.m. The whole room smelled of patchouli oil and BO, and it wasn't hard to tell why when you looked around. Most of the people in the room probably didn't have running water, and they all had a distant gaze to them like they'd been frying out on psychedelics all night. Art ordered a cup of coffee and sat down at a small table next to a couple who both had long, blonde dreadlocks and wore Jamaican-style clothing. Nothing like a white Rastafarian, Art thought. He sipped his coffee and waited for someone to take the bait, and after a few minutes, he wondered if the room was too brain-dead. Then, the guy next to him looked at him; his eyes went down to Art's patches, and he had a revelation.

"Hey, you're not Kate," he said.

"I'm definitely not Kate," Art said. "I'm Doug Weaver. Kate is on family leave for a couple of weeks."

"Far-out, man. Babe, Kate's in some sort of trouble," the man said. His somewhat more focused partner looked up from her coffee and scone.

"I just saw Kate, like, two days ago. She didn't say anything."

"She just had something come up medically. I'm filling in for a couple weeks."

"Wow, I hope she's okay," she said.

"She'll be fine. Should even come back to work here if things go well."

"That's great, man. Really. Great to hear," the man said.

"You two look very"—Art chose his words carefully—"local. Do you happen to know a man named Avery Walker?"

"Avery?" the woman said. "Doesn't ring a bell."

"He might have come down with some people from Santa Cruz."

"Wait, is he a tall, Swedish-looking guy?" the man said.

"That sounds about right."

"What do you want with him, man? You an informer?" she said. This was apparently funny, because the couple laughed, and she placed her thin-fingered hand over the man's forearm and squeezed. Her fingernails had a black layer of grit under them like she'd been digging in the forest, probably hunting for jade which, Art remembered, the guy he'd come out here to find had been doing. It was just lying around out here and pretty valuable, especially if you didn't want to work; it was something.

"I'm not. But his brother came by the station yesterday looking for him. Any help would be appreciated. He said he'd stop by."

"All those Santa Cruz scabs went to work up at Pfeiffer Cliffs, man," the woman said.

"Margo, this guy's a cop," the man said.

"He's helping someone find his brother," she said. There was an obvious tension about helping out any sort of authority between the two, even one who was just a park ranger. Art stood.

"Thank you both. I won't tell anyone about our little chat," Art said, which seemed to calm them both down. He stepped out of the café, and the sun was higher on the horizon now, thin streaks slivered through the tall pine trees to the east in bright beams. Pfeiffer Cliffs was only a few miles down the road according to his map from the ranger station. If he got there before they opened, he might be able to get the drop on Avery. It all depended on whether or not Heath and Rori had found him yet, but Art had a feeling he was going to find Avery, and then all he had to do was set his trap.

Chapter Ten
Saturday, August 20, 1988
Heath

1

I woke up to an empty van, and my pulse instantly started to sprint. I fought through a painful aching in my ribs, legs, and arms and opened the sliding door to the van. The sun still hadn't quite peeked over the horizon yet, but my eyes still ached from the brightness outside the van. I quickly surveyed my wounds in the rearview mirror. It didn't feel like anything was broken, just bruised and swollen. My right eye was scabbed and puffy. I looked around for Rori.

The parking lot was nearly empty, and so was the beach. No Rori. An image from a dream I must have had the night before flashed in my mind. It was the psycho cowboy standing over Rori's lifeless body, a river flowing all around him. I looked on the roof and calmed down slightly because the surfboard was gone. Still, the image of the bounty hunter shook me. I took the .357 and tucked it into my waistline, pulled my sweater and beanie on, and started down the beach. In the distance, I could see a large lifeguard shack against the pink and blue silhouette of the rising sun to the east.

The time on the dash of the van had read 6:15 a.m. when I'd jolted awake, which meant we'd already been here a lot longer than I'd planned. I had no idea how far Rori thought she'd get with a cracked longboard and no wetsuit—the water here would give you hypothermia—and it bothered me that she would take off without waking me up. She was either in trouble, or she was being reckless.

The beach was on the north side of Monterey Bay and faced due south, so the sun, oddly, rose left of the shoreline, partially blocked out by the mountains beyond Watsonville. The angle of the sun caused the waves to glow green at their center and cast a monochrome shadow across the faces. The sight made me wish I'd grown up here instead of in the wasteland of farms, pesticides, crime, and religious fundamentalists. My feet dragged through the heavy sand, and it felt like the sun was trying hard to warm everything up. I had a deep chill I couldn't shake along with a sense of vulnerability that made me want to crawl back into the warm nest of clothes inside the van, clutching my .357.

Down the beach, I could see silhouettes of about a dozen people ambling around, and out on the smooth bay, a few surfers sat up on their boards, looking out toward Monterey and waiting for their sets to roll in. About midway down the beach, there were a couple of guys together on the shore talking, and when I got up to them, they puffed up and stared at me like I was some sort of feral animal. I stepped to them anyway, and they stopped waxing their surfboards and lifted their chins toward me, then glanced at each other like they were deciding if they should kick my ass or not.

"You guys see a girl with red hair and a cracked surfboard come through here?" I asked, trying to sound low-key.

"Fucking kook lost his girlfriend," the taller, dark-haired one said.

"And his board," the shorter, shaggy, blonde-haired one said, and they laughed.

Growing up the way I did, I could take a hit. Obviously. But these surfers also looked like they'd seen their fair share of action. Their wetsuits hung around their waists, keeping their toned upper bodies exposed, and their pecs and abs looked chiseled out of marble. The taller one had a tattoo of a wave across his ribs, and they both had scars on their chins and brow lines—fighting scars.

"I'm not here to surf or fuck with you guys. I just need to find the girl." I was still trying to be cool, but I slipped my hand under my sweater just in case I needed to teach these fuckers a lesson. I wasn't going to get rolled by coastal wannabes.

"That board look familiar?" the blonde one said, and pointed up the beach about thirty feet. Resting on the sand next to a couple of towels and a backpack sat the cracked surfboard, but it looked like the crack was gone. Someone had fixed it, and fast.

"Yes, that's hers. Jesus." I didn't realize how tense I was until the wave of relief hit, but where was she?

"You might want to check your girl, kook. She's learning from the best," the brown-haired one said, and pointed out toward the water. I looked out at the ocean, and the mercurial figures that had been bobbing suddenly began to paddle, and then I saw her. Rori paddled, and the other figure gave her board a slight push. She stood, wobbly, and a small wave crested, then started to peel and crash behind her while she planed across the face. She almost fell over and squatted low, as if she were learning to balance all over again. As she neared the shore, the wave turned into a foamy mass. I could hear Rori squeal with laughter. I smiled.

"Eric's got it under control, man. No worries," the shorter one said with a smirk.

"He's real gentle with the ladies," the other said, and they both laughed like this was all some big fucking joke, and I thought about pistol-whipping the taller one. But that would be stupid. After the old man, I felt like I should check my impulses. If not for the sake of my conscience, for the sake of staying under Burke's radar.

2

Rori surfed on the whitewash until the fin hit sand and stopped abruptly. She fell forward and jumped into the shallow water. A small wave rolled against her legs and nearly knocked her over. It all seemed like a dream with the sun now partially up and the shadows blacking out their faces. Eric coasted in behind her, cutting back and forth on a shortboard. When he got to her, he picked up both boards and held her arm so she could gain purchase on the shifting sand below her feet. They walked in together. I couldn't see anything except his silhouette and his hand on Rori.

When Rori spotted me, she smiled and began to sprint. She was cold and wet and kissed me hard on the mouth even though I winced from the pain. The surfers went back to waxing their boards. A moment later, Eric caught up.

"Did you see me?" Rori brimmed with excitement, and my fear and anger melted away. She was so goddamn beautiful. At least, to me she was. I pushed wet hair from her face. A streak of red dye streamed down her neck. She looked younger like this, with her pixie cut, so thin in the cutoff summer suit. But I could also still see that hardened twenty-something in the leather jacket I first met. It was a well-constructed act. I forced a smile to show her how excited I was—and I was, but these alpha males were stressing me out, and I wanted to get on the road.

"It was amazing. You surfed the whole way in," I said.

"That board should be ready to go by tomorrow," said Eric when he stepped into the oddly shaped circle our bodies created in the sand. Eric stood in front of me, and he was considerably taller and better built than the others. He pulled the top of his wetsuit down, revealing a hulking frame, and I thought he looked part bull, with thick brown hair pulled back by the water. "Your girl here is a natural." He extended his hand, and when I took it, I felt my knuckles pop under his strength.

"I'm Jared. We're just passing through," I said.

"Didn't she just call you Heath?" Eric said.

"I don't think so. It's Jared Smith. Or Smithy. That's my last name."

"Right. That's Pete and Thorin," Eric said, and the other two lifted their chins.

"Thor, god of thunder, bitch," the shorter one said. And they both laughed again at some sort of inside joke probably about surfing and storms and his nickname.

"Let's head out," I said, but Eric didn't appear done with our conversation and stepped into my path.

"Your girl was about to go out with that broken nose-rider when I caught up to her." It wasn't lost on me why he was being so fucking chivalrous, but he seemed to be respecting the situation now, so we were good as far as I was concerned.

"Thanks for the lesson. And the wetsuit rental," Rori said, and smiled.

"No worries. You can keep that if you want. It's my ex's anyway."

"No. Thank you. I'll hang it on the rail by the bus," she said, and pointed toward the parking lot.

"And thanks for fixing the nose-rider," I said, not knowing exactly what the term meant.

"I know that board," Eric said, and paused, and we all stayed silent. "That bus in the lot, too. Where'd you find it?" He carefully eyed me.

"The Volkswagen and the board are my best friend's. We were supposed to meet up with him up—"

"Wait, you know Avery?" Thorin said, and Eric held his hand up to silence him.

"I just need you to explain to me why you have Avery's van and board." Eric's face darkened, and I could sense the conversation heading in the wrong direction depending on my answer. I gripped the .357 under my sweater, and I was ready in case anyone flinched.

"I was supposed to go up to his camp, but I guess they got raided," I said.

"You were up at Hideaway? What's that under your shirt, Heath? You wearing a fucking wire?"

"He looks like a fucking pig, man," said Pete. He and Thorin stood, and I thought about drawing down and getting the fuck out of there, since it was three extremely fit assholes against me, but they seemed to know Avery, and I needed to know how. I moved my hand off the pistol and into my pocket.

"It's a card Avery left on his fridge. Those are my initials." I pulled the card from my pocket and handed it to Eric. After Rori had put it on the dash, I'd retrieved it. Eric took it and read it, still eyeing me. "Heath Walker."

He looked at the two guys whose frowns dissolved into smiles. "Son of a bitch. We've known that asshole for years. I can't believe he ditched his board though." Eric laughed now, and the tension between us drained almost completely away.

"We grew up together," I said, and forced a smile.

"I've never even heard of you," Eric said.

"I live in Central Valley, man. Shadow Valley."

"You fucking Valley kooks always coming out and crowding up my break," Thorin said, but it was in jest now, not a threat. The entire alpha-male, dick-showing contest was over, and I was cool, thanks to Avery.

"You know they all took off, right?" Pete said.

"Fucking cops and shit came down on them," Thorin said. He and Pete sat down, legs crossed, and started waxing their boards again. I wondered how much wax the fucking things needed.

"The surf community is small, Heath. And we take care of each other. Your brother, Avery, surfs with us. And we paddle for him when the shop comes in and drops. And we always deliver."

I wasn't sure exactly what he meant, but from the context, it sounded like they were part of Avery's network he'd been bragging about. I wanted to make sure they knew I was on the level. "Yeah, well, he sends me weed every couple weeks for my customers back home."

"So you're cool, then. That's good, man. You're probably right with that card. Pfeiffer Cliffs is a good spot to look for him," Eric said.

"Got it. I appreciate everything, but Rori and I really have to run. There's some crazy fuck from the Valley chasing us."

"Yeah, your girl mentioned that there might be a cowboy showing up. Anyone comes around here looking for you, we'll take them out for a little late-night shred session," Eric said, and they all three laughed.

"I'm going to go hit some more waves. Rori, you take care. Keep the suit, you'll need it. You're good." Eric turned and trotted back toward the ocean.

3

The sun was fully up now, and I finally felt like I was thawing. My insides felt as twisted up as my body did. I wanted to lead Rori to safety, but if I were being honest with myself, I had no fucking clue where to go that might truly be safe. It made me want to cry and tear the world apart in frustration. If only she had told me sooner about her dad being a cop. At least Mom would have been still alive. But then again, without Rori, Mom wouldn't have had those last luminous moments. None of that mattered; I needed to block it out and focus on survival. We were here, and we needed to go.

Pete and Thorin hopped up, pulled their wetsuits on, and jogged out to meet Eric. They expertly paddled out and sat on the break, waiting for the next set. Rori jogged up and grabbed the longboard, showing me the repairs Eric had made. We walked back to the van, where Rori changed into her jeans and sweater. She left the wetsuit hanging over a small sign in the parking lot. I started the van and headed toward the 1 south. Toward Big Sur.

Chapter Eleven
Saturday, August 20, 1988
Heath

1

Just before Castroville I spotted a Texaco station and pulled in to use the pay phone. I wanted to see if I could call ahead and check in with Avery at the campground. I parked and opened the door.

"Why are we stopping?" Rori asked, a now familiar tension in her voice.

"Going to see if I can reach Avery, see if it's even worth trying."

Rori nodded. "I'm starving."

"Me, too. I'll grab something."

We hadn't grabbed much in the way of food when we cleared out of Mom's house, and my stomach was still sour from the whiskey the night before, but I needed food. I went inside and poured two Styrofoam cups of coffee and grabbed a half dozen stale donuts from a plastic display case. Maple bars, an apple fritter, and some chocolate ones with sprinkles. I brought the coffee and the bag of donuts to Rori, and I pulled a maple bar from the bag. I tore a bite out of it, and it was intensely sweet and turned pasty, so I took a sip of coffee, and the bitterness of the coffee turned the mixture into a pleasurable and briny syrup. I swallowed it all down. When it hit my stomach, it warmed me. I dialed 411 on the pay phone right of the entrance, and the operator put me through to Pfeiffer Cliffs and Campground. The phone rang several times before a distracted man's voice picked up.

"Pfeiffer Cliffs," he said.

"Hi, my name is Jared Smith, and I was wondering if Avery Chastain was available," I said, trying to sound businesslike.

"Avery is off today. I can put you through to his room?"

"His room" meant that he was living there, which was good to confirm. "How much would it be to stay there tonight?"

"The cabins are forty-seven dollars per night, the campground is eight dollars. One car per space."

I reserved a campsite and asked to be put through to Avery's room.

"Avery here," a voice said. I smiled so hard, my eyes started to water.

"Avery, shit. It's me."

"Heath. Goddamn. It's good to hear your voice."

"You too. You have no idea all the fucking shit we've—"

"Hey. About that job, you know, with the camp. I wanted to call you and tell you it shut down, but I couldn't. It was too dangerous with the cops and shit." He paused a second, then said, "But I'd love to see you. I've got a studio cabin up here at Pfeiffer Cliffs. You're more than welcome to crash on the couch. You alone?"

"I've got a friend, we're on our way to you. Thought I'd call ahead and make sure it was all clear."

"It's uh, clear—yeah. Where are you, by the way?"

He sounded a little more formal than usual, but I figured he was worried about narcs or tapped lines after being raided up at Hideaway. "I'm down in Castroville, heading straight there."

"Cool, brother. I'll see you in about an hour, hour and half. Drive safe."

"Wait, there might be a guy—" The phone clicked silent, and I thought about putting another quarter into the phone, but I didn't want to get routed through the front desk again. I figured we could check in to a campsite and call Avery from the lobby or somewhere else on property. We'd be all right; we just had to be careful. Even though Rori was afraid of this cowboy, I was pretty sure he'd lost the trail by now. If he ever had one.

2

Coming off a little sand hill, the highway descended into Monterey. Rori and I both stared at the beautiful little peninsula that jutted out into the Pacific with its clusters of pine and cypress trees spread over the small hills in every direction like windswept statues carved by ocean breezes. After a brief traffic signal around Carmel, the road opened up into the most beautiful stretch of road in the world.

Starting low, with ambling cattle and large, green swaths of open fields, the highway rose up. The road gave way to quick turns, and a huge naval island appeared with a tall lighthouse blinking at its apex. The road rolled through the land, and the beach broke white and turquoise against brown, jagged rocks with thin lines in them like veins where the water pulled back toward the sea.

Then, very suddenly, the road diverged from the ocean and up an embankment. We traveled up the highway and disappeared into a little mountaintop valley that closed off our view on both sides with alpine mountains. We entered the rustic little town of Big Sur.

It wasn't much: a ragged little gas station, a coffee shop, and a few inns that looked more like cabins than the Motel 6s I was used to seeing in the valley. It was midday, but the whole town seemed to be asleep, as if it didn't realize that there was a bustling universe of people and surfers and traffic and economy just forty-five minutes the opposite direction.

"We almost there?" I asked.

Rori had been navigating with the map I'd taken. "Pfeiffer Cliffs and Campgrounds are about three miles up if we just got to the town of Big Sur," she said.

I watched the odometer closely while we drove. After another mile, the mountains to the right—on the ocean side— fell away, and we stared down at the Pacific Ocean churning deep and cobalt with white at the shoreline eight-hundred feet below. It was stunning, and I had to jerk the wheel to stay on the road. "How have we never heard about this place?" I asked.

"Valley kooks," Rori said, and laughed. "I don't think anyone in my family tree has ever been out of Shadow Valley."

"My mom hasn't left Shadow Valley in half a century." The thought of Mom stabbed at my heart in a sharp burst of pain. The urge to cry almost overwhelmed me, but I choked it back. The dust was settling on my initial shock from the day before, and the thing that stood out still, that ate at me, that destroyed me, was the image of Mom's body holding that shotgun. She had died to protect me, the miscreant lost boy who murdered two people when he was twelve. A woman who had stood by me until her last breath. Damned that thick-neck cop, and damn that fat fuck, Burke. I didn't even care about Rori lying to me anymore. I would have done the same thing. But for my mom, I wanted blood. Rori's dad would fucking die.

I tried to relax my tight grip on the steering wheel and clear the raging fear from my chest. I needed to be present, and dwelling on something I couldn't do anything about right now wouldn't help. Avery and Rori needed me. We drove a little farther, and another mountain passed between us and the ocean, and then finally a short wood sign emerged from a cleared patch of ferns that blanketed the forest floor.

"There," Rori said, excited by the discovery.

I turned up a steep road and followed switchbacks until we got to a massive clearing surrounded by dense forest. I parked, and we stood for a second to stretch before we approached a huge log cabin lodge nestled among the coastal pines: the Pfeiffer Cliffs Lodge.

3

The lobby was simple but clean and well-kept, and there was a gift shop, a bar, and a little restaurant tucked away near the back, situated right over the massive cliff. After I checked in, paying cash, I asked the front desk man, Ronald, to call my brother again. Nobody picked up. He gave me a receipt to put in my windshield and showed me a property map with a road that wound along the cliff edge to the far side of the property, where campsites were. He also showed me on the map where to find the employee housing.

Unlike the road leading to Big Sur, there was no guardrail, and it was sketchy when we had to pass an oncoming car. I had to edge closer to the cliff, the white water churning at the rocks nearly a thousand feet down, about a dozen times. After about a mile, I was relieved when the road veered back into the forest. The campsites were remote with only a dozen other campers and a few outhouses.

"Can I see the map?" I asked, and Rori handed it over. Avery's cabin was up the cliffside road about a half mile.

"Let's just drive straight over to Avery's," I said, and pointed to the circle on the map.

Rori looked at me intensely, and I knew she was thinking the same thing as I was. It was safe here, but it didn't feel right somehow. Maybe because Avery had gotten busted and never even gave us a heads-up about the job. Somewhere in my gut, my intuition told me to turn around and head for the border. But this was Avery, the closest thing to family I had left, and I couldn't leave here until I knew he was okay.

A half mile later we turned up a small hill. After a few hundred yards, a large three-story clapboard complex appeared tucked into the alpine trees. It was considerably less impressive than the lodge. There were a half dozen cars and a brown Chevy with park ranger decals on it. Everything looked quiet and peaceful, but my lungs felt tight. I got that vacant feeling in my lungs, breathless. I told myself it was the altitude, and parked.

4

It was hot out, so Rori and I stripped down to our jeans and T-shirts before we went up to Avery's room. We found number twenty-seven and knocked.

"Come in." When I heard Avery's muffled voice, I felt a surge of joy. Turning the brass handle, I slowly pushed the door open.

It was a small rectangular studio with a little fireplace at the back and a tiny round table near a kitchenette where Avery sat with his hands by his sides. Oddly, he didn't stand, but I was so excited to see him, I stepped over the threshold with Rori right behind me.

It was too late by the time I caught the quick movement to my right, blocked by the door. Standing with his back against the wall was a man dressed as a park ranger. His cool, avuncular face seemed disarming, even kind. But I knew in that moment that I should have trusted my gut—it was him. The cowboy bounty hunter, and he was fast.

"Run, Rori," I shouted, low and fierce.

Instead of running, Rori grabbed my arm and tried to yank me back though the doorway, away from danger, but the bounty hunter was already on me, a pistol aimed right at my heart.

I shook Rori off and raised my hands to protect her, and she still didn't turn and run. Art covered the distance between us in an instant, and the blow came from his left hand, where a thin, black steel object flashed just before it made contact with the right side of my face. Even though I rolled with the strike, I felt a sharp burst of pain, and the jarring thud of metal on bone. I dropped to my knees while the universe spun out of alignment, and could hear Avery sobbing. I had never gotten my ass kicked three days in a row, and I wondered how much more my goddamn body could take.

"You promised you wouldn't hurt him, you bastard!" Avery yelled.

Blood dripped off my nose and chin while I tried to regain my faculties. I dropped down on all fours and felt a hard kick to my gut that knocked the wind out of me. I rolled onto my side, and Rori stooped beside me, crying, and tried to help me up.

"Get out of here," I wheezed, but she wouldn't listen. Her eyes flashed green in the noon sun streaming through the open door; dust particles suspended in the air swirled in the beams between us.

"Stand up and put your hands behind your back," Art said to Rori. "The only way he lives is if you come with me."

She glowered at him, her brow furrowed, and if she had a brick, the motherfucker would be dead. I put pressure on my wound to stop the blood from trickling out and looked up at Art. He had the pistol trained on Rori. She turned and placed her hands behind her. Art walked toward her, and I tried to stand, but he used his boot to push me back down. I was so weak, so dizzy from the strike, I fell to my side and tried to stay conscious. Art zip-tied Rori's hands and walked her out to the brown Chevy.

Half conscious, I was hoisted over Art's surprisingly strong shoulders in a fireman's carry but was unable to move. After a few minutes, I started to see the world clearly again, and I was back in the Volkswagen. Art's face hovered over me.

"This is how it went down. I took off with the underage girl that you kidnapped, and in a rage, you tried to come after me. But being the drugged-up hippy you are, you dropped the keys, then flew right down the embankment, and, well, the cliff was right there. You should have been more careful, kid," Art said.

"You don't know what you're doing. You can't bring her back there," I managed to mumble, though the blood was steadily dripping from the cut on my head, and I felt like I was about to lose consciousness again. I tried to cover the wound and realized my hands were tied in my lap.

"Save it, kid. It's all over. You'll have a peaceful descent." He smiled, and his black and gray mustache curled in the corners, and I wished I had my gun.

He put the VW in neutral, then dropped the keys between my feet, and I tried to reach for them, but he caught me in the chin with a quick elbow. I saw cracks of light, and it felt like my jaw broke against the steering wheel. I was still awake but played dead. He reached over and released the emergency brake, and the van lunged forward about an inch and rested firmly against the park ranger truck in front of me. I heard the door slam, and I waited a second, then rolled my head and saw Art get into the brown Chevy. Beside him I could see Rori's red pixie cut in the passenger's seat.

Art started his truck and pulled down the driveway toward the cliffside road. The VW stayed put at first, and Art made a right turn back toward the lodge but stopped, put the truck in reverse, and pulled out of the way left of the intersection so he could watch what was about to happen. It looked like he had a camera out to document this.

The VW crawled slowly at first. Then it picked up speed, and I tried to move but couldn't. I watched in horror while the forest cleared, and I got closer to the cliff's edge, and then I saw her, Rori, tears streaming down her face, and I felt a surge of adrenaline. Art sat beside her, a professional calmness about it all, like this was something he did all the time, and it roiled under my skin like the turbulent waves crashing below. The cliffside grew closer, and I knew I had seconds before I careened off the cliff and watched the ocean rush toward my bleeding face.

I moved my hands from my lap, and they fell onto the keys. I grabbed them limply like a claw machine grasping for plush toys. Rolling faster now, the intersection was only about twenty feet away. I tried the brake with my feet, but they were soft and useless without the ignition on.

Clawing at the steering wheel, I tried to turn the van, but my grip was too weak to budge it. I pushed my bound hands through the steering wheel and gathered every ounce of self-preservation I could. I leaned hard on the wheel with my whole body weight. These old buses didn't have power steering, just an oversized wheel for leverage. It barely budged. I was a goner.

In a last desperate attempt, I gave the wheel one last jerk to the left with everything I had. To my surprise, the van slightly altered course. It wasn't much, but it was enough. Instead of heading straight off the cliff, I headed straight toward Art's truck. I could see the shock register on his face. He hadn't seen this coming. He had been so calculating and meticulous, so confident, he'd overestimated his plan.

I didn't want Rori to get hurt, but I had to stop this car and stop them from leaving. She couldn't go back to her father, not ever. This was the only way.

Art dropped the Polaroid camera and started the truck. He quickly tried to throw it into reverse, but it was too late. The left side of the Volkswagen clipped the right side of the Chevy, and all that weight, all that inertia, transferred to the ranger truck, and the bus stopped dead in the road, but the Chevy moved. The van pushed the truck just a few feet, stopping inches from the cliff's edge.

5

For a second nobody moved. Nothing happened. Then, very quietly, the Volkswagen pushed forward again, just a few more inches. I had to do something before Rori spilled over the side of the cliff. I pulled the keys from the mat and put them in the ignition. My limbs moved, barely, but they moved. I started the van; the engine was in the rear, so there was no damage to it, and I put the VW in park, and it stopped. The Chevy halted on the cliff's edge, teetering. Then, it slipped over the edge a few feet and stopped again, almost completely on its side. Caught on something but not secure. Rori's passenger's window had broken from the impact, and I could make her out just above the cliff line.

I hobbled over to the edge, clutching my head wound. Rori had her seat belt on and was being careful not to move. Art's window was busted, too, and he must not have been seat belted, because he was gone. Down at the bottom of the Pacific.

"Slip your hands behind your legs," I said. She roughly maneuvered her hands to her front. I anchored my legs around a big rock and reached down. Rori wrapped her bound wrists over my neck and shoulders while I pushed the red button on her seat belt. The seat belt snapped free, and at that moment, the truck slipped again and fell, bouncing off the cliff's edges until it plunged into the crashing Pacific Ocean. Rori climbed me like a human ladder and then helped me to my feet. When I stood, I put pressure on the wound above my right eye while she helped steady me. We looked over the edge and couldn't see the place where the truck landed. It had just disappeared, like Art, down into the depths.

"Are you okay?" Rori asked, and looked me up and down.

"I'll be fine, just lost some more blood," I said. "What did he do to Avery?"

"I don't know. He was still when he put you in the van."

I looked over the cliff again and couldn't see anything except the marks in the hillside where the truck had scraped it. I breathed a massive sigh, but my body was still shaking with nerves and adrenaline. My head throbbed, and that numb feeling was back. The shock of surviving again, still raw and unsettled. How the fuck did I keep making it out of these situations? More importantly, how did they keep finding me?

We surveyed the van. The right headlight was smashed, and the steel bumper was ripped off and tucked under. I grabbed the bumper and yanked it out, then pulled it up and felt the sheet metal bend. Placing it back where it should go, I kicked it hard, and it snapped awkwardly back into place. It was the best I could hope for until I found someone who could repair it. I reversed up the hill and parked. Rori helped me up to unit twenty-seven, and we tried the door. It was unlocked, and this time, when I swung the door open, it was just Avery inside. He was on his side, still tied to the chair, struggling against his restraints.

"You said you wouldn't hurt them! Goddamn it!" he screamed, and his face was red, and his eyes were puffy and blacked out from a bloody slash across the bridge of his nose. Art had given him a little parting gift, too.

"Avery, it's me. Bro, it's me."

"Oh my god. Fuck. Heath. I'm so sorry." He sobbed and stopped writhing against his restraints. Rori and I closed the door and walked over to him, helping him right his chair.

"You have a knife?" I asked.

"Drawer left of the sink."

I pulled a chef's knife from the drawer and carefully cut Rori's zip ties, and she cut mine. I cut the zip ties from Avery, and he stood, a little unsteady himself. We hugged, and it felt like we were kids again for a brief moment, back in that orchard after we'd told our deepest truths. Just before the murders.

"Who the fuck was that guy and where did he go?" Avery said.

"Long story," I said. "But he's a bounty hunter, and we have to keep moving."

"Is he dead?" Avery asked. "I thought the fucking cops tracked me when he first drew down."

"He's at the bottom of that cliff out there."

"Fucking gnarly," Avery said, then pushed from his eyes a blonde lock that was wet with blood from the cut on his nose. "But that makes me happy to hear. Fucking psycho posing as a ranger."

"I'm sorry about that guy. I have no fucking clue how he tracked us."

"I told you, Heath. He'll find us anywhere," Rori said, pain in her voice.

"Fuck, man, I'm just glad we're both alive, and I'm not in prison," Avery said. "You guys going to stay awhile?"

"I don't mean to be a dick, but Rori and I need to move. And we need all the money we can get."

"Holy hell. I wish I'd saved more." Avery went to his freezer, cracked ice cubes into paper towels, and handed me one. Then he pulled a first aid kit from under the sink, and Rori helped me clean and dress my wounds, again. Then she helped Avery with his nose.

"Yeah, fuck, man. That's why I never called you back. I don't have work for anybody right now."

"Shit," I said. And I could feel Rori tensing up. Our promised land was disappearing.

"Why don't you guys post up here in town for a while? Lay low?"

"I can't," I said. "These cops showed up to my house looking for her"—I nodded to Rori—"And my mom pulled a shotgun on them. She's fucking dead. And so is one of them."

"Shit, man. You killed a cop?"

"That bounty hunter worked for the one that survived. Her dad. The plan is to head to Mexico and hide in some small pueblo at the coast."

Avery perked up at the mention of Mexico. "A cop. Shit, you guys definitely need to get out of Dodge. Probably forever. Funny thing is, if you're going to Mexico, I might be able to help."

"We can use all the help we can get." Avery's connections reminded me of Pete and Thorin. "We met some surfers up in Santa Cruz earlier, they said they knew you," I said.

"Oh, hell yeah. Who was it?"

"Eric, Pete, Thorin, I think? They said they'd done some work for you."

"Yeah, I was expanding into some pretty heavy shit, man. There's a reason I'm cleaning toilets and living in the dorms down here in nowheresville. Goddamn cops came for me. Still can't figure out how they got the tip-off."

"Are you sure you're safe here? Why don't you come down with us?"

"Nah, man. I have some assets back in Santa Cruz I need to pick up when shit dies down. But I do have a little cash for you, for the road."

"Your call," I said.

"Look, one thing about Mexico is you can buy security pretty cheap, but you'll need more than a couple hundred. It happens that I know a guy, Jacques. Since you're going down there anyway, you should look him up."

Avery walked into the kitchenette and pulled a box of Wheaties from the cupboard. He opened it, unrolled the opaque plastic bag, revealing a coin purse with some cash in it, but it looked like it was running low. He pulled out a hundred-dollar bill and five twenties and handed them to me.

"I can't take this, man. I know you're in a tough spot." I tried to hand him the money back, but he wouldn't take it.

"Just keep it. You need it more than I do."

I slid the money into my pocket. "Who's Jacques and where would I find him?"

"Here's the deal. It's a little more than fucking trimming weed, brosef. But it pays better. Jacques sends a pleasure craft up the coast once a month—a fifty-foot yacht, actually. I contract the surfers that unload for him in Santa Cruz, and they make the drop in east Salinas. That's how I funded the property up in the mountains until the cops fucked it all up."

I hadn't realized that he owned the camp, and I felt a glimmer of hope that this crazy escape might pan out. It might just provide deep pockets and security from bounty hunters. I glanced at Rori, and she had the same excited look she had after smashing those biker guys up. She was all in.

"Thanks, brother. I won't forget this."

"Head down to Puerto Nuevo, or just past that. There's a little pink resort hotel called La Fonda. Jacques runs that place. I'll call ahead and let him know you're coming."

I stood, steadied myself, and hugged Avery. "We should go now, while we still have the sunlight."

"Damn. Just murder a dude and leave. I get it. Same old Heath." Avery smiled.

Rori stood, gave Avery a quick side hug, and followed me to the door.

"I don't know where I'll be when you get back, but if you guys killed a cop and now that ranger guy, I'm going to lay low somewhere else for a while, too. Somewhere not here, and not Mexico." He laughed.

"Yeah. Someone will come looking for the real forest ranger soon," I said.

"Later, guys. I'm going to grab my shit and head out, too."

We walked to the van, got in, and started her up. Avery watched from the doorway.

"Take care of her, I want her back someday. Preferably in one piece," he shouted over the whine of the engine. I waved and backed very carefully down the driveway

6

When we got to the T in the road, I turned right to edge along the cliff back toward the freeway. I saw movement in my rearview, and I checked it. A dark figure rolled out of the high grasses beside the road. He stood, favoring one leg. He leveled a gun at us. A sudden flood of fear spiked in me, and my chest tightened, my teeth set hard in my aching jaw.

My eyes darted to the narrow road ahead, the cliff off to my left side now, then back to the bounty hunter. At that moment, I saw the muzzle flash. The bastard fired three rounds at us, and the rear window exploded. I hit the gas and made the next turn so fast, the van almost slid off the cliff. The rubber caught, and we pulled away in a cloud of dust. We roared past the main lodge, the tires chirping when we hit the 1. Any relief that I had felt before was now gone. The bounty hunter was alive, which meant Rori and I would never be safe unless this drug runner could protect us. It also meant that I had failed Avery. He was fucked, and there was nothing I could do about it.

Chapter Twelve
Saturday, August 20, 1988
Art

Art clung to a cypress tree twenty feet below the cliff line, and he realized something. He was going to have to kill Avery. Avery had to go; it was too damaging to his reputation to let the fuck live, but first, he needed to know exactly where the kids were headed. The fact that he had managed to hang on to his Glock while falling through an open passenger's window was a miracle. Even though his left arm—his baton arm—was currently bleeding from multiple lacerations, he still had a gun.

It wasn't Art's modus operandi to kill innocents. In fact, he usually avoided killing anyone unless there was a paycheck attached. Why fuck someone's world up if there wasn't any money behind it? And more importantly, why risk getting caught? But there had been special circumstances in the past, like the clerk at the gas station. Mercy killing, plus a possible frame job for when he put a bullet in this Heath kid.

Art looked up to the cliff's edge and saw Heath peek down. He quickly ducked behind a rocky outcropping. He didn't need the kid taking potshots at him with rocks, or worse, a gun.

After waiting until it felt like his arm would snap, he looked back over the rocks, and the kid was gone. Art pulled with his right arm, gained a footing, and slipped; the roots of the little cypress tree crackled under his weight. He had that feeling of muscles about to give out—that tingling nervous sensation that shakes from adrenaline just before collapse. It was a sensation he didn't feel very often: a marathon he'd run in his thirties, a max-out set of bench press at the gym, and now, clinging to this fucking tree for his life. His left arm was numb, but he still held his grip on the gun. His right leg, however, was snapped at his calf, the bone sticking out against the fabric of the green pants that were darkened with blood. He realized this surge of energy would be his last, and he tensed up, shut his eyes, and heaved himself up onto the little rocky ledge, then rolled a few times for good measure. Looking up the steep embankment and back down, the cliff itself wasn't a straight drop—it was an undulating drop with multiple rocky ledges. If he'd fallen any farther, he wouldn't have been here with a bleeding and busted leg—he'd be dead.

Art clawed his way up the twenty feet to the road on his belly, using his good arm and good leg. He army crawled across the road toward Avery's apartment and rolled into the forest canopy, and then he heard it—the high whine of the Volkswagen exhaust. He poked his head above the scrub brush and watched the Volkswagen with both kids in it pull slowly down the driveway.

Looking around, Art found a stick. He snapped bushy pine needles free, shaping it into a makeshift crutch. He stood and winced at the pain and realized he'd have to hold the crutch with his shooting hand, but he could still aim okay with his right. The van turned toward the lodge, and Art stepped out onto the road and took a steady aim with his right hand and caught Heath's eyes in the rearview mirror just before he fired three quick shots. The rear window exploded, but he missed very slightly to the right. "*Fuck*." Goddamn right hand.

Art let his arm fall, and he took a long glance up the driveway to Avery's house. Maybe he wouldn't kill Avery after all. Maybe the kid could be useful in other ways.

The crutch bowed every time he put his weight on it, but he made it up the drive and stopped in front of Avery's door. He could hear soft music playing and Avery talking to someone on the phone. He tried to listen to see if it was the cops, but he couldn't make out the words. Breathing in deep and slowly exhaling, he pushed the pain away from his leg, arm, and shoulder. He needed exactly two things: a ride to his truck, and the location of the kids. He knocked on the door and knew the kid's ass puckered, considering what the kid had been through, but there was no way Avery knew what was waiting for him, the bounty hunter was dead, right? Over the cliff? Art smiled to himself when he heard the dead bolt slip away. The door slowly cracked open, and Avery's face dropped in terror when he saw Art just before the muzzle of the Glock flashed.

Part II

"Hunting is not a sport. In a sport, both sides should know they're in the game."

-Paul Rodriguez

Chapter Thirteen
Saturday, August 20, 1988
Heath

1

A few miles down the road, I spotted a restaurant called Nepenthe and carefully pulled over. We parked and found a bright red pay phone that looked like a replica from England.

"Watch the road," I said, "and hit the horn if you see anything."

"Why are we even stopping?" Rori looked scared and alert.

"It's probably too late, but I have to try Avery. Warn him."

Rori frowned, but she didn't say anything. She didn't have to, because there was no good way to handle this—I knew we needed to keep moving, and she was right. But I'd just thrown Avery to the wolves. Or, wolf.

I walked up a short Carmel stone stairway lined with ferns and fresh flowers, and stepped into the booth. I dialed the Pfeiffer Cliffs.

"Avery Chastain, please," I said, and the phone rang through. The phone continued to ring, and with every pause between them, my stomach soured. After fifteen rings Rori tapped the horn. I scanned the parking lot, but there was nobody there. She was right; somehow that crazy fuck cowboy was still alive, and we were burning our head start.

"No answer," I said when I got into the van.

"I'm sorry, Heath," she said, as if it meant we were already dead.

"Let's go," I said. I felt tired, terrified, and pissed. I tried to refocus on the task at hand. Mom was gone, Avery was a good as gone, and if I didn't want to join them, I had to keep going. "No more fucking around. Straight down to Mexico."

We pulled back onto the freeway and followed its tightly wound surface along the cliff line for what seemed like endless miles of pure beauty that I was too sick with nerves to enjoy.

After a while, Rori must have sensed my thoughts churning away on death and revenge scenarios, because she reached over and put her soft hand on my leg. I breathed away the tightness in my chest and put a hand over hers. At least we had each other. I would have to try to focus on that instead of the trail of destruction behind us.

"Tell me the rest of the story. About the hotel. I won't fall asleep this time."

I nodded and tried to remember where I had left off.

2

I fell asleep that night, feeling pretty safe next to Mouse and his new pet, shotgun. The next day was a blur since my mind was stuck on the plan the whole time. I sleepwalked through breakfast, taking a shift at the register in the market (an older kid named Scott Sanchez teaching me) and having dinner in the cafeteria. A few other kids introduced themselves, but I could hardly remember their names. I sat across from Mouse and tried eating a thick slice of pizza that tasted like cardboard, but I couldn't say a word. Mouse just smiled, his lips thin and pale, and pointed to a beat-up Casio watch on his wrist.

I got up and cleared my plate, and Mouse followed. We told the activity manager, who was the older kid from the register, Scott, that we were going to skip the movie in the quad and go straight to bed. Mouse showed me where the little library shelf was back of the store, and we checked out books on the honor system. Sal was at the register up front talking to some grotesquely overweight guy in overalls and a Bass Pro Shops trucker hat, and I shuddered thinking about what that guy would do to me or one of the other kids here if he got the chance. If Sal let him. If Sal, in his position of trust and authority, took money to let that man violate one of us. Not if, but when.

Mouse jerked his head toward the back door, and I followed him. We walked the hall toward our room, and he gestured for me to open it. I used my key, opened it, and stepped in. Flipping on the light, I left the door open and waited a second, but Mouse never came in. I popped my head back out and jumped. Sal stood behind Mouse with a tight grip on his shoulder. Mouse winced in pain.

"What the fuck. Let go," Mouse said.

"Martin Garcia, you broke the cardinal rule. You broke my trust."

"What the hell are you talking about? Let me go."

"I feed you. I clothe you. And yet you steal from me. Why? I would have given you the candy."

"Let me go or I'll—"

"You'll what?" Sal spun Mouse around with surprising strength. He yanked a Sugar Daddy from Mouse's pocket and held it up. "You want juvie? Is that what you want? Or you want to spend the night in the tank?"

"No. Please. God, no. Look, I'm sorry. I don't even know how that got there."

"A night in the tank will do you some good," Sal said. I knew that somehow this was part of Sal's sick game. There was no way Mouse had stolen the candy; I had been with him the whole time. Sal was obviously planting evidence as a way of picking an older victim. One that might put up more of a fight in the middle of the night.

"Not the suite," Mouse said. "Please, no." Sal dragged him away. Mouse's eyes were wet with fear. Sick with it. But he shifted his eyes toward our room. Toward the gun. And I felt the whole world fall away from my feet. I was floating alone, hovering. I should have gotten the gun right then and blasted Sal. I could put an end to this whole thing. But I was paralyzed by fear. By not knowing what to believe. That sick thought wormed its way in again. Did I believe this establishment was inherently good and Mouse was crazy? But it wasn't just Mouse; it was everyone. Sal had hurt Avery and Yessi too. But how was I supposed to help Mouse? I didn't know the way. And plus, I'd never shot anyone. If Mouse was going to the fuck shit suite, then I was the only person who could stop what was about to happen to him. That comfort I'd felt the night before, knowing Mouse would protect me with that shotgun, kill to save me—now I had to become that. For him.

It was 7:37 p.m. when Sal took Mouse, and I waited in my room until night fell and curfew started, 9:00 p.m., according to the chart on the wall. At 9:02 p.m. I slipped out of bed and used the blankets and pillows to make it look like I was still in there in case someone checked on me. I grabbed the duffel bag from under Mouse's bed and took the shotgun out. Pulling the pump action back, I loaded one more shell into the magazine and slipped one into the barrel, then closed the action. Stepping as carefully as I could, I went through the cabinet in the bathroom and came out in Avery's room. Avery was waiting for me.

"They got Mouse," I said.

"I heard," he said. "The fucker must have found out."

Avery gestured toward the bathroom, and I followed him. We went back to the shower, and he moved the rug aside. Carefully, he slipped through the floorboards. I followed him and replaced the planks and rug as best as I could. My heartbeat thumped so hard, all I could hear was the rush of blood in my ears. Still, I continued through the dank undercarriage of this infestation of a home. Overwhelmed. Confused. What the hell did I think I was doing? Pretending to be a grown-ass man? Going to kill men. I was a kid, wasn't I? What if Mouse had it wrong? What if I screwed up? Question after question plagued me. After nearly twenty minutes of dragging our bodies past rusted pipes, dead mice, and rotten wood, Avery stopped. He looked up and pointed.

"That's it. It leads to a closet inside the fuck shit suite," he whispered. "Are you really going to do it? Shoot him?" Avery's eyes looked kind, bewildered, and scared. He needed me to do this, too. It was all up to me.

"I've got this," I said.

He nodded again. "I'll be the eyes. If I wave, then you come up. Don't make a fucking sound though. They'll hear us."

I nodded.

"Are you loaded?"

"Five in the magazine, one in the chamber."

"Are you sure you can do this?"

I wasn't. My heart was thundering in my ears so loudly, I was afraid Sal could hear it above us. I nodded.

Avery turned and climbed using some rusty pipes and loose planks. When he got to the top, he pushed a square of floorboards up with his head, then peeked over the ledge. It must have been clear in the closet, because he pushed the planks fully up and moved them to the side. Then he shimmied through the small hole. I heard some voices, and Avery's face appeared over the hole.

"Run," he said, and shoved the planks back over the square.

I heard Sal's muffled voice shouting, "How the hell did you get in here? What am I going to do with you?" I heard Avery yelp, then go quiet, and I wondered if Sal was going to hurt him, gag him, or drug him. Or all three.

I waited, squatting there in the dank underground space until I heard the thunk of a door closing. What should I do? How long should I wait? I didn't want to get caught, too. Then we were all goners. But if I waited too long, Avery and Mouse would get hurt. Thinking about them getting hurt made me want to cry. I couldn't in good conscience wait a single second longer.

Standing up, I shook the numb feeling out of my legs. My hands were damp from the wet dirt, but I clutched the shotgun with my right hand and climbed the pipes and planks. Pushing the planks up, I could see the small closet, but the room beyond was silent. I set the boards aside and climbed into the space. There wasn't any time to bother with putting the floorboards back. I took the shotgun in both hands and tried to place the stock on my shoulder so I was ready for Sal. Only, my hands were damp still, and the duct-taped stock slipped out. I tried to catch the gun, but it was too late. The hard steel barrel hit first, a hard thud against the wood floor.

"What the goddamn hell?" I heard Sal say. Footsteps rushed toward the door. "Are you kids packed in here like rats?"

The door swung open, and I made eye contact with Sal. He looked relieved. Then his gaze fell to the shotgun on the ground. "New kid? What are you doing with that? What kind of bullshit did these kids fill your head with?"

"You need to stop what you're doing. Now," I said.

Sal made a quick movement toward the gun, but I dropped to my knees and had it up and trained on him fast. His hands shot up, and that wide, crooked clown smile spread over his face.

"What are you going to do, shoot me, kid? Why don't you just come with me into the other room and take a look for yourself. It's just the staff hall in here. We're watching a movie. That's it. Come take a look. There's popcorn."

My biggest fear in that moment was that I was wrong. That we were all wrong. What if they really were watching E.T. or something in there? Everyone having a good, safe time. All this a big misunderstanding. But I couldn't take that chance, could I?

Sal took a step toward me and dropped his hands. "That's it," he said softly. "You aren't a killer, are you? If you give me the gun, this won't even go on your permanent record, I'll make sure of that. Come have some popcorn."

I wanted this to be over, for Sal to be right. I wanted this to end peacefully. I didn't want to pull the trigger. I didn't want to be a killer. He took another step toward me, and I started to lower the gun. But just then, I heard another voice from inside the room.

"Sal, I thought we had a deal for the new kid?"

Heavy steps thundered toward the door, and then I saw his face. The fat trucker from the market earlier with his sweat-stained hat, scruffy beard, and sagging jowls. Sal lunged for the gun, but my finger was sitting on the trigger. And I pulled it. The blast was so powerful, it felt like my shoulder shattered, and I fell back on my ass. Through the burning smell and ringing in my ears, I saw the blood. Sal's leg suddenly shredded from the knee down, and he was screaming. Blood painted the wall behind Sal and the fat trucker.

"You're fucking dead, kid," the trucker said. He pulled a massive bowie knife from his hip and motioned like he was going to throw it at me. I pumped the action and fired again with his hand cocked behind his ear, about to release the knife. Buckshot ripped through the big man's chest. No massive hole, but fat red dots painted his embroidered Western shirt. Sal screamed more, but I left him where he was, and rounded the corner out of the closet.

The room was exactly as Mouse had described it. There was a camera set up pointed through a big window that had a view inside a bedroom that looked similar to the one that Mouse and I stayed in. Lying in the bed, handcuffed and unconscious, was Mouse. Avery was beside him on the floor. Their shirts were off, but that was it. I was glad that was as far as these monsters had gotten.

I found near the camera equipment the keys to the handcuffs. There was a door left of the window, and I opened it. Inside, I helped Mouse and Avery out of the handcuffs. Then they put their shirts back on. Avery was still so doped up, he could hardly walk. They must have given him something strong, but Mouse seemed to be sobering up a little. At least he could talk straight.

"Did you get them both?" he managed to say.

"The big guy is dead," I said, and the weight of the statement landed hard. Lead in my gut. Heavy. I was a murderer.

"Sal?"

"Shot his leg to shit. He's bleeding out."

"Good. Damn. Good job, Heath. Shit, somehow, I knew you could pull it off."

It felt good to hear that. I didn't believe it myself, but I had wanted to protect him, and Avery. And Yessi and all these kids like me. Because even though we were ditched by our parents, even though the world considered us leftovers, I was one of them. I belonged with them. It felt good to be a protector.

"But go back and finish Sal. He's gotta die," Mouse said.

"But it's over now. Yessi probably already called the cops."

"He can't live. I would do it myself, but I'm still weak from the drugs. Please. If he lives, he'll do this again. Perverts get, like, five or ten years, and when they get out, they start all over again."

I thought about that for only a second. He was right, and I couldn't let that happen. "Okay," I said.

I turned and went back into the camera room. Sal crawled along the wood floor on his stomach, army style. Tears streaming down his face. He was reaching for a phone. "You got me all wrong, kid. I was going to help you. Protect you."

I pumped the action on the shotgun again, stood with my legs squared up, and sighted the man down.

"Where's the popcorn, Sal." I pulled the trigger. This time, his head exploded into a mist. I dropped the gun and went back in with Avery and Mouse. I sat with them, huddled together on one of the beds in that room. That room of untold horrors. And we waited there with Avery until the police arrived.

3

When the police did finally get there, I asked for Officer Domino. They called him in from home. And after they taped off the crime scene and got everyone calmed down, he showed up and asked for me.

"You're a very lucky young man," Domino said. We were sitting in his cruiser with the doors open in front of Sal's Market. Ambulances, fire trucks, and cop cars everywhere. Lights still flashing.

"I don't feel very lucky," I said. I was still shaking like I had the chills from the flu.

"You took out two longtime criminal masterminds with a shotgun. And you're twelve. You're a survivor, kid."

I shrugged. I couldn't find the feeling inside of me to react. It felt as though the whole situation was stuck like a knife in my belly, and my body and brain still didn't register what had happened. I was numb, in shock, my mandatory therapist would later say.

"What you did in there, what you did for those other kids. Most people wouldn't be able to do that. I'm not saying that to scare you, or say something about you as a person, but this world needs people like you. People willing to risk their lives to help others. People who want justice."

"I just did what I knew Mouse would do. What he tried to do."

"I get it. I just want you to know that you shouldn't feel guilty. A lot of guys on the force feel guilty after using their weapons, even when the perp was straight evil. It changes a man."

"You think I'm going to be different now?"

"That's up to you. They'll get you a therapist and go through all of that. I just want you to know right now, you did the right thing. Do you understand? You did what had to be done."

I nodded, the numbness wearing off and the sharp edges of reality starting to sink in. My body went from jittery and cold to overheating. I felt like I might puke.

"You know, when you grow up, get through high school, you should consider joining the force. We need more of the good ones out there on the street. At the end of the long, hot summer night, when the criminals stay up late, it's nice to know there are at least a few good cops on the team fighting to protect the innocent. You could be that."

"I don't know what I want to do when I grow up. But I don't want to do that again." The image of that terrible room surfaced in my

mind, Sal's wicked smile. The fat trucker. I leaned out of the car and puked up my pizza on the sidewalk. "I'm sorry, Domino."

Domino's radio blared something unintelligible, and he responded into it in some sort of code. "You don't need to apologize, kid. You're a damn hero, and I never saw that. We've been making emergency calls all night to get you all a place to stay. And we have a nice family that will host you until we find you a home. I'll drive you. Go get your stuff, I'll wait."

Walking back into the hotel to get my things, the thought that struck me was that maybe Domino was right. The gun dropping, that split second I had to pull the trigger, my aim. It was all a blur, like I was awake but not in control of my body. Someone else had taken over. It all seemed so impossible now. Like I couldn't believe it was me who had done all of that.

When I got through the store and into the courtyard, all the other kids stood there in front of their rooms, watching me. Like I had just interrupted twenty-two people all talking about me. Avery, Mouse, and Yessi stood by my room. When I got there, they cried and wrapped me up in a hug that felt so pure and so warm, I wanted to stay inside of it forever. The only problem was, this was it. We were all getting moved tonight, and maybe that was why the hug was so bittersweet. I hated that feeling, that sadness of knowing I was losing the first people I'd ever felt at home with. We'd only known each other for two days, but it felt like years to me.

I hadn't just protected Mouse. Or Avery. I'd saved all of these other kids from that fucking monster. And something rang out inside of me, some truth I felt deep in my body, that this was just the beginning.

I got back to Domino's cruiser and closed the door. Domino drove us through the dark streets of Shadow Valley, wet with pre-morning dew.

"One more thing," he said. "You'll probably get asked a lot of questions after this. By the cops, lawyers, all that shit. They might even try to make it seem like this one act defines you. Brands you forever. But don't let it. Never be defined by your past. We get to live life from the present forward. You'll need to find a way to let it go."

"This moment forward," I said. I knew I could let it go in a way, like I knew what I had done was the right thing to do. I felt that in *my bones. But Domino had a point, and it scared the shit out of me. And that was what was coming next with all the cops, lawyers, and judges. "I'll remember to forget."*

"'Remember to forget.'" Domino looked at me and smiled. "I like that." He turned his eyes back to the road and didn't say anything else. We just drove with the static of his police radio going in sudden bursts and stops, and I watched Shadow Valley pass through my window, the reflection from the orange streetlights shimmering off the slick, dark city streets.

The court case made national headlines. All of our names were kept out of it, since we were minors. Especially with the nature of the case. I got bounced around a couple times during the trial, but an interesting thing happened. The family court judge, who was old enough to be my great-grandfather, was about to retire. His name was Robert Walker. And his wife, Linda Walker, was a social worker about to retire. They knew all about what had happened and knew nobody would want me anywhere near their families, so they took me in. They had a ranch in the countryside, twenty minutes outside Shadow Valley. All the other kids got scattered around, some to other counties. Luckily for Avery and me, we landed not too far apart. He was a few miles down the beat-up country road with the Angler family. And that's how I ended up a Walker. They adopted me. Which helped, since I still had the last name of the family that gave me back when I was four: Hastings. I was proud to be a Walker. They were good people. They took me in. And even though I appreciated it beyond words, I still fucked up some from time to time. I never did see Mouse again.

4

"Jesus, Heath," Rori said. Her eyes were trained on me, glassy with empathy for what I'd been through, with what I'd done.

"I thought I'd retired from killing people until I met you," I said. It sounded so much worse than I meant it. Her face wrinkled in disgust. "I didn't mean it like that."

"Jesus, Heath, I didn't mean for any of this to happen," she said, her voice tightening up, tears starting to fall. It was the elephant in the room, the conversation we had been avoiding. A land mine.

"Seriously, I didn't mean it like that. I made my decisions to help you in that bar. You helped bring my mom back from being a vegetable, and your dad killed her. Look, you're not your father. He abused you, too. You were just trying to save yourself. I get it."

"If I thought you and your mom were at risk, I never would have—" She stopped herself because that thought had obviously crossed her mind. "I never thought he would hurt her. I planned on leaving way sooner. But you—we were different. I wanted us to be together."

Her tears made my anger and fear drop away. The girl was in love with me. Not just pretending to get away from her dad, really actually in love with me.

"What's done is in the past," I said. "It can't be changed. Just know this and know it clear. I am going to kill that motherfucker, Art. And I am going to kill your father. Make peace with that, and don't try and stop me. Understand?"

She stayed quiet. The scene that played out at my mom's house replaying in our heads. She'd pulled me away from him when he had been lying there unconscious. "Time to go." The sirens. Even at his most sinister, she didn't want him actually dead. It reminded me of Mouse's story. How he wanted see his father even after the bastard had shot him. I couldn't imagine ever forgiving my parents for deserting me, but I never had the opportunity to. And never would.

"I know," Rori said.

5

She pulled her hand away and curled up in her seat, watching the cliff and the ocean out her window. We drove in silence for hours. I stayed the speed limit and stopped only for gas and food while we passed through San Simeon, Santa Barbara, Los Angeles, San Diego, and by midnight, the border came into view. It didn't occur to me how important it was to make it across the border.

Approaching the border, my palms went slick with sweat, and my mouth ran dry. A vast paranoia kicked in and started to run a million worst-case scenarios. We needed a strategy. I took the last off-ramp before the point of no return and pulled into a Shell station and parked at a pump.

"What if your dad put our names on a list or something?" I asked. "Can he do that in an unofficial way?"

"He sent his best bounty hunter instead of calling in for discretion. Do you think I should drive us in? Your face looks like you went through a wood chipper."

I checked my face in the mirror. The Sex Wax beanie covered up the forehead wound, and I was tired with my right eye swollen and discolored. "I have a license."

"I have a fake. How do you think I drank at the Blue Cue?"

"Can I see it?" I asked.

She pulled a small zipper wallet from the front pocket of her jeans and slipped a couple of cards and IDs free and shuffled them until she found it and handed me a California driver's license.

"Margret Rivera?" I asked. "Age twenty-six?"

She shrugged. "It's always worked for me."

"If it doesn't this time, we end up dead or in jail."

"If my dad did call anyone down here, then I should definitely drive us across with the fake, and you should hide in the back. I can tell them I got a haircut. Which is true."

"Can you drive stick?" I asked, realizing she hadn't driven since the Crown Vic.

"I have, a couple of times. I'll manage."

"Shit. We're at the border." This was do or die. Our whole plan for survival hinged on this one event. My hands slipped against the plastic steering wheel.

"It's the best option."

"Let me hold on to your other ID," I said.

"What for?"

"Just in case they look for it." I held out my hand, and she handed the zipper wallet over, and I pulled it out.

I glanced at the California ID that her father had probably gotten for her. It was a couple years old, but she seemed so much younger in it. A girl. Her face in it looked sullen and determined and possibly angry. Braces spanning a forced smile. I felt a momentary pang of guilt for what we'd done together that first night, but I had been tricked, hadn't I?

"Charity Aurora Burke. Born August 27, 1971."

"That *is* me."

"Shit—your birthday *is* tomorrow. Well, technically in a few hours." I pointed to the clock; it was after 8:00 p.m. "Happy almost eighteenth birthday."

"I haven't had a birthday, a real birthday since my mom passed." Rori pulled a loose strand of hair behind her ear, her face down, green eyes up. She seemed sad now, and vulnerable. This side of her broke my heart. "I can barely remember."

"You may have missed your sweet sixteen and your seventeenth, but you'll have an eighteenth in Mexico."

She flashed a half smile and put the fake ID back into her coin purse. "Bonnie-and-Clyde-themed birthday?"

"Sounds like a hell of a time."

"Get in the back," she said.

"Fine. But we're throwing you a party tomorrow."

"Just get me drunk and make love to me," she said. "That's all I need."

"Now that you're legal, you mean?" I said this with a little more ice than I had meant to.

"Ouch. Sorry about that," she said, her voice getting smaller.

I let her kiss me and slipped into the back of the van. The blankets were a little musty, but I pulled them over my head and leaned the surfboard over me so I blended in with the clutter. Rori started the van and ground the gears a little, slipping it into first.

"Try a double-clutch," I said through a crack in the blanket.

"Okay! I got it!" she shouted back, sounding frustrated.

Rori dropped the clutch and slipped the transmission into first and slowly released the clutch but didn't give it enough gas, and the van lunged but didn't stall out. We jerked a few times, and we were soon pulling back onto the highway, moving closer to the border. Almost free.

6

When Rori slowed up, I peeked over her shoulder and saw the border getting closer. She stopped behind a short line of cars.

"Are they checking IDs?" I asked.

Rori looked back and hissed, "Stay down. They see another person, and they're going to inspect our shit. Then we're fucked."

I covered back up and tried to remain still. Rori struggled with the smoothness of releasing the clutch, but she was doing surprisingly well for not owning a stick. Or having a real driver's license. We stopped, and I heard a voice with a slight accent.

"Hello, miss. What is your reason for traveling into Mexico?" asked the male voice.

"Hi there," Rori said in the most saccharine sweet voice she was probably capable of. "I'm just heading down to meet my boyfriend and a few of his friends for a surf trip."

"Do you have identification?" he asked, not taking the sweetness as bait.

"Absolutely," she said. And I waited and listened while she handed him something, and he was quiet while he scanned it.

"Rivera?" he asked, and his tone softened. "*Eres Mexicana?*"

"*Lo siento,*" Rori said. "Second-generation."

"Ah," he said. "You see that man over there? Please pull out and park in front of him," the man said, his tone formal. He apparently hadn't gotten the answer he desired. My pulse sprinted so hard, the rush of blood in my ears was all I could hear under the sticky, hot blankets.

Rori feathered the clutch, and we drove smoothly into Mexico, where she quickly pulled aside. I wished I could see what the fuck was going on. She slowed to a stop, and I heard another male speak sternly.

"Miss, please shut the engine off." Rori did, and he came closer to her window. "Is there anyone else inside the van with you?"

"No sir. I told the other guy that I'm meeting my boyfriend and his friends in Rosarito."

"Please take the keys out and place them on the dash," he said.

I clenched my teeth and tried to breathe under the stifling blankets. There were noises outside the van and a couple of distant barks, and I wondered if they had a drug dog. I wanted badly to ask Rori what was going on, but instead, I tried to control my breathing and stay calm. *"A bird came down the walk: / He did not know I saw."*

After a few minutes, the side door slid opened, and there was a change in the light, noticeable even underneath the blankets.

"We are going to do a search of the vehicle," the voice said.

"I'm just going down to meet my boyfriend. Is this necessary?"

"Stay there with your hands on the wheel," he said.

I felt something pushing at the pile of blankets and felt it jab my leg, then knew it was the barrel of a rifle. It pushed again hard, and it hurt, but I bit my tongue. Then the surfboard slipped away, and I felt exposed. The next jab came right at my solar plexus, and it was so hard and fast, I had to gasp for air.

"I think I found your boyfriend, *güera*," the man said, and he pulled the blanket from my face. "Good morning, *puto*."

I slowly sat up and raised my hands. The guard kept the barrel of what looked like an AK-47 pointed at my chest, and I remembered what Avery had told me about Mexico and paying for protection. These guys weren't looking to bust us; they were looking for money.

"*Tengo dinero*," I said, gagging slightly from the sharp ache in my stomach that moved up into my chest and down into my balls. I coughed and tried to catch my breath.

"I am an officer of the Mexican army, please do not offend me," he said. He was probably five nine, dark-complexioned with a jarhead haircut, green military fatigues, and had a young face that I pegged as closer to Rori's age. And yet, he seemed like a pro at this.

"Two hundred. American," I said.

"I was offered more than that by the American cops. We've been waiting for you two." He flashed a mug shot of me and a recent picture of Rori on a folded-up piece of paper that didn't exactly look official. Burke very clearly had connections off the record. "So, I'm sorry that I will have to turn you over to the authorities. Diego," he shouted, but not so loudly that someone might actually hear him.

"All right. Fuck," I said, doing the math on my cash supply. I had twenty bucks tucked into my sock, and the rest totaled about four hundred with the cash from Avery and the gas station. "I have four hundred, it's everything, man. I swear. The guy who wants us, he's going to kill us both."

The man stayed quiet a moment, then said, "I can't do that, you know. A deal is a deal."

"How much did he offer you?"

Someone shouted, and I heard a dog bark nearby. Several armed men ran toward another vehicle that was parked a few stalls back. His radio blared rapid-fire Spanish. "Shit. Fucking gringo with a gun. Give me the four hundred."

I pulled my wallet from my back pocket and counted out the cash and handed it to him, but he eyed it suspiciously.

"Thank you, *güero*. Enjoy Mexico. It is a beautiful country. Unlike in the United States, where everybody gets in *Dirty Harry* gunfights, we have rules. Stay away from trouble, and you will stay out of trouble." He lowered his gun, winked, and slid the door shut. I heard him slap the side of the van twice. "*Vamanos*, gringos."

I didn't bother covering up this time while Rori started the van, and when she released the clutch, it was smooth, and we swept forward and were finally on our way down now. Down into the belly of Baja, with its remote coastal towns, where there was world-famous surf. This was a place I'd wanted to go my whole life. If it weren't for the fact we'd just been stripped of our entire cash reserves, we could have survived for months. Not that it mattered. After the bounty hunter found us in Big Sur, I wasn't taking any chances. We would go to La Fonda, find Jacques, and get money and protection. Then Burke and his pit bull, Art, would be on *my* hit list.

Chapter Fourteen
Saturday, August 20, 1988
Art

1

Art felt faint when Avery finally pulled to a stop in front of the ranger station in the three-row golf cart. The kid didn't have a car, which had complicated Art's plan. After being rammed off a cliff, Art wanted blood, but scaring Avery into a state of shock and compliance was more beneficial. So, when he arrived at the kid's doorstep with a bone fragment sticking out of his leg, he fired his gun into the door beside Avery's head. He needed two things from the kid. A ride to his truck, and information on where Heath and Rori were headed. His Glock had gotten him both.

Art, with his gun inside his windbreaker, kept his Glock trained on Avery. They had commandeered the golf cart, and Avery had driven him along the highway five miles back to the station. The short trip had made Art start to appreciate the oddly secluded nature of Big Sur, since they hadn't passed a single car or roving batch of drugged-up hippies.

Avery parked the cart next to Art's F-150, and Art slipped the gun from beneath his jacket and pointed it at Avery's head.

"Over to the truck and put your hands on the tailgate," Art said.

With his arms limply above his head, Avery moved slowly to the truck. It was clear that between the blow Art had given him with the baton and the gunshot that had missed his head by a quarter inch, the kid was practically catatonic. Art stood on his makeshift crutch and limped over to Avery. He shoved him into the truck and zip-tied him to the steering wheel. Art gathered his folded clothes and boots together and removed a first aid kit from his luggage.

Limping toward Kate's apartment back of the station, Art checked the time on his Timex. He'd been gone four and a half hours. He hoped she was still passed out so he wouldn't have to deal with her any further. She could wake up an hour from now and not quite remember what had happened.

Inside, Kate was still stretched out across the bed in almost the identical position as when he'd left. Art hobbled toward her and checked her breathing, and it was shallow, but she was fine. He tapped her leg with the crutch, and she didn't react, so he carried on.

Kate's bathroom was small and smelled of cedarwood and spices. He located a plunger behind the toilet, unscrewed the wood handle, and tossed the rubber end, placing the dowel in the middle of the bathroom floor, then sat down on the toilet. Opening the first aid kit on the counter, he pulled a pair of scissors free and used them to cut down the right seam of his green uniform but stopped when a sharp pain made him wince.

The jagged tip of his fibula flashed white from a hole the size of a bullet on the right side of his shin. Breathing slowly, he closed his eyes, bit down, and cut gently around the wound, continuing to his ankle. He slipped the pants off and used the scissors to cut long strips from the green material. The leather of his right boot was tough, but he cut it down to his foot and gently pulled it free. A few ounces of blood had pooled inside. He placed it in the bathtub, then slipped his other boot off.

The linoleum was cold on his exposed thighs when he sat on the floor. Art tied his right ankle to the doorknob, leaving the bathroom door open about four inches. He lay back and planted his left foot on the center of the door and closed his eyes and counted to three. When he kicked the door shut, it felt like a thousand knives plunged into his leg, but the bone slipped back into his skin and pulled roughly into place. Art's belly clenched, and a gasp that sounded half sob, half animal scream escaped his lips.

After the initial pain had dissipated slightly, Art sat up and untied his ankle and guided his leg slowly to the ground. He reached up and found a bottle of rubbing alcohol, opened the cap, and poured it onto his leg and fought the urge to scream again. He taped a square of gauze over the hole, then felt around for the dowel. He placed the strip of wood under his leg and used the fabric he'd cut to tie it in place, making sure it wasn't so tight that it would cut off circulation.

Once he cleaned up, he limped out of the bathroom and over to Kate. He cut the zip ties from her wrists and hobbled to the door to leave. He heard the rustle of beading behind him, and he turned. Kate sat up, groggy looking, but aware.

"Your name's not really Doug, is it?" Kate whispered, rubbing creases from her cheek.

Art slowly reached for his Glock tucked into the small of his back. "Go back to sleep and convince yourself this was just a dream," Art said, and watched her for a reaction.

Her eyes were glassy and bloodshot but unflinching. Art realized that if she came after him, she could easily overpower him with his fucked-up leg. If she had a weapon hidden, she might even be able to get to it faster than he could draw his. That was when he noticed that Kate's left hand was tucked between the mattress and box spring. His fingers were on his Glock, but he waited and prayed she didn't pull that hand free; he didn't want to get shot, and he didn't want to kill her.

"Doug, don't come back to Big Sur," Kate said, and Art carefully watched while her hand slip free of the mattress. Empty. She let her head fall to the pillow but kept her half-cocked eyes trained on Art while he stepped outside and closed the door.

The sapling crutch bowed with each step while Art limped toward his truck. He opened the back and put the bloody ranger clothes into a plastic bag and put the first aid kit back in his luggage. Avery sat awkwardly in the front seat with his hands behind his back, and Art cut the tie connecting him to the steering wheel. He retied Avery to the oh-shit handle inside the passenger's door and started the truck. Using the left foot for the gas and brake, Art managed to relearn very quickly how to drive without so much as flexing his right leg, because when he did, it felt like electrified shards of glass shooting up through his nuts and abdomen.

2

While he drove south, a rolling fog drifted up the tall cliffs, across the highway, and up toward the lush mountaintops of Big Sur. Art barely saw the sign for Nepenthe and hit the brakes hard, Avery almost hitting the dash when he turned in. Squinting through the fog, he thought he could just make out the shape of a van that had pulled out at the far end of the same parking lot and turned southbound.

Art slowed to a stop along a tree line at the back of the dirt and gravel parking lot, away from the half dozen other vehicles. He stepped out, circled the truck, and pulled the door open, yanking Avery's attached hands with it. Avery stretched sideways, then slid to a standing position, where he wobbled, weakly. The kid was a lot taller than Art and still bleeding from his nose and mouth.

Art grabbed Avery's chin and stared into his pallid eyes that rolled back in his head, closed, then opened and refocused on him. "I don't have time to fuck around, kid. Tell me where they went, or I put a bullet in you."

Avery started to mumble something, and Art wondered if he should crack fresh smelling salts but decided against it. He pulled his hand away from Avery's chin and slapped him hard in the face, and it seemed to help.

"They're gone, you sick fuck," Avery said, and started to sob, his head falling forward, and long blonde hair, wet with blood, covered his damaged face. Art saw a trickle of blood drip from his right ear.

"Where. The. Fuck. Did they go?" Art said, realizing how it would look to Burke that after all these years when he always got his man within twenty-four hours, these bastard kids might get away.

Avery laughed in a lazy way, and Art fought the urge to club him with the butt of the gun. "They're going to Canada, man. I told you earlier. Fucking poutine or some shit."

Art gripped Avery by the throat and pushed him against the crook of the door. "I will shoot you and throw you over the edge of this fucking cliff. Do you understand? Where are they going?"

"French Canada, to be exact."

Art racked the slide on the Glock and held it against Avery's right hand. "You right-handed? You ever want to be able to jerk off again? Hold a pen? Caress a woman?" Art started to squeeze the trigger, slowly.

"Go ahead and fucking do it, man. If I tell you who they're going to see, I'm fucking dead anyway. So go ahead. Motherfucker. Just do it." Avery started to sob, his bloody blonde hair falling over his face.

Art laughed and released Avery from his grip. "Fucking Canada, huh? Well, if you're not going to tell me, I'll take you somewhere where you will talk. Understand?"

Avery's face tightened into sharp lines. "What does that mean? Where are you taking me?"

"Look, I don't know who you're so afraid of. But what I'm going to do to you is much, much worse."

"If I tell you where they're going, will you let me go? I'm fucking tired, man. I'm tired of being a goddamn slave to you people. To everyone. I can't do it anymore. I just want to go home."

Art didn't know exactly what the kid was talking about, but if he was this scared of someone, he knew Avery was in something deep. Really deep. And now Heath was involved. He needed to intercept them before they got to where they were going. Art cut the wrist ties and lowered the gun. "Tell me, and you walk."

"All right, man. Mexico. I don't know where, and I can't tell you who or I'm dead anyway. But that's where they're headed. Fucking Baja." Avery stumbled backwards and tripped.

"Thanks, kid. Now get the fuck in the truck."

Avery was talking, but he wasn't saying enough yet. But Art believed him, that the kids were heading south; he had a sense for when his victims were broken enough to tell the truth. He also knew if you beat them too badly, they would start making shit up. Art didn't want to get to that point.

"You, you promised."

"You're a goddamn moron. And the only person you have to worry about killing you is me." Art pulled the Glock up, spun it so he held the barrel, and cracked him again, not so hard this time, with the butt of the Glock. The kid was heavy, but Art loaded him back into the passenger's side and shut the door.

3

With Avery taking a little nap, Art navigated up a short set of Carmel stone stairs with ferns and begonias planted alongside, and located a red, English-style pay phone, then stepped inside and closed the door. Inside, he felt protected from the cold, circulating fog, like he was in a sort of submarine. He picked up the receiver and made his first call. It rang several times before she picked up.

"Shakers," Tyra said, her voice distant and hard.

"Tyra, it's Art. Is everything okay?"

"It's over. They shut us down."

"What the fuck do you mean?" Art said, his heart starting to beat harder against his ribs.

"Your friend Burke came down here this morning and—"

"And what?"

"He gave me a warning."

"Did he touch you?"

"Art, just get his kid back and maybe this will all go away." Her voice was thin now, and Art imagined Burke's temple collapsing with a quick blow from his baton.

Art hesitated, and he could hear Tyra breathing into the receiver. "I lost the kid. I need your help."

"What do you need?" Art caught the subtle hesitation in her voice. Art had asked her to help on a few cases in the past, and on one, in particular, she'd had to shoot the perp, and it had deeply affected her. She just wasn't a violent person— that was Art's domain—and she'd asked to stay out of bounty hunting forever, but they had no choice now.

"Burke's daughter and her boyfriend are headed for Mexico," Art said. "They have about an hour lead on me, and I've also picked up a witness. Take Puck and head down to the border. Pack some camping gear and have some car trouble just before the border. When you see a green and white Volkswagen van with a bent front bumper, follow them. Female, young, red pixie cut. Male, six two, two hundred, medium complexion, orange-blonde hair. Busted face."

"What car should I take?" Tyra asked. Art had a full-size van he used for surveillance, as well as a station wagon and a convertible he used, depending on who he needed to be.

"You guys need to blend in with the surfers and drifters down in Baja, so take the station wagon and dress casual. Bring bathing suits."

"What do we do when we find them?"

"Do not engage. And tell Puck the same thing. Do *not* engage. Find them, follow them, and call me with their location."

"Are they dangerous?"

"They are, and whoever they're meeting down there is more so."

"What about the club?"

"I'm calling Burke next. I'll sort it out, don't worry."

"I'll call you from Mexico," Tyra said, her voice soft and sad. She didn't believe him, and that wasn't acceptable. He was going to fix this.

"Call the club when you locate them. Leave a leave a message on my voicemail. I can check it from any pay phone."

"Be safe, Art."

"I've got the situation under control," he said. He used his finger to depress the steel flap and released it, catching a fresh dial tone. He dialed his next number.

"Shadow Valley Police Department," a male voice said.

"This is Art Dominguez. I need to speak with Police Chief Burke."

The phone clicked silent and rang a few times before Burke picked up, and Art imagined him consuming the whole chair cavity of his desk with his sheer girth.

"This is Burke," he said in a husky, detached voice.

"You told me you'd leave the club alone," Art said, failing to mask his contempt.

"Jimenez, get the fuck out of my office," Burke shouted, and Art could hear the door to his office slam shut. Art waited; Burke breathed heavily into the receiver, and when he grunted, Art imagined him sitting back down. "Where are you and where's Rori?"

"What the fuck did you do to Tyra?"

"I'm the one asking the fucking questions here, you little pissant fuck. Where the fuck is my daughter?"

Art felt his stomach tighten, and blood flushed his cheeks and ears, but he held back; he was keenly aware of what the guy was capable of, so he changed tack.

"I've got the kid's friend in custody. Avery Chastain," Art said, and let that sit for a second.

"You went to Santa Cruz to get my girl, and you come up with a goddamn bystander. What happened to you? You too old for this?"

"I may have underestimated the kid that she's with. They drove me off a thousand-foot cliff—but I'm alive."

"Christ—you've lost your edge. You used to run anybody down in twenty-four hours—what're you planning to do with the friend?"

"This kid your daughter's with isn't the typical ice head who stole his mother's jewelry and skipped bail—and I had her in my goddamn car. It was all set, but the little fucker—"

"I'm calling the Ramirez brothers. It's over. And your club is effectively closed as of today."

Art looked down at his bandaged leg and back at Avery in the car, his head resting against the window.

"You send those boys down to Mexico and they're dead."

"The Ramirez brothers have gotten in and out of Mexico for me in the past."

"According to the bystander I've got in my truck, they're not just hiding out down there. They've got protection, and if you send those assholes in, they're dead."

"You'll say just about anything, won't you? Jesus Christ, Art, it's over."

"You listen to me, you goddamn prick. I almost got myself killed picking your daughter up *off* the record. This kid knows where they went and more importantly who they're going to meet. I need him, and you need me."

Burke was silent, and Art knew he was weighing his options and probably wondering how much of what Art was saying was true or to save his ass. "What's your play?"

"I already made a call to have them followed into Mexico."

"And then what?"

"If Avery's telling the truth and they're under protection, we back off. Otherwise, I'll go in and get them."

"Fucking Christ. He's got to be lying. I'm calling the Ramirez brothers."

"And if Avery's telling the truth, they disappear down there, and you won't be any closer to getting her back."

"And what's your plan if they *are* protected?" Burke said. "If you want your club, I want Rori back and Heath in the ground."

"We set a trap using Avery here as bait, lure them back across."

Burke paused again and breathed into the receiver. "Fine. In the meantime, I want Avery brought to my safe house."

"Give me the address."

"Five-four-one West Goshen, just before the canal out there in the industrial section," Burke said. "Behind Swing Time Grille, knock on unit number one."

"What are you going to do with him?"

"Make him talk."

Art felt a chill run through him, and he wondered if it was from the fog, the blood loss, or the thought of giving this poor, dumb kid to this fat, sadistic prick on the other line. Art was ruthless, and somehow, Burke was much, much worse.

"I'll be there in three hours," Art said, and hung the phone up.

Back in the truck, Avery lay awkwardly against the door with his eyes closed, and Art felt for the first time like he was making the wrong call. He didn't want to bring Avery to Burke. But he had no choice, at least not now. Burke had him by the balls. Also, Burke was up to something; Art could feel it in the pit of his stomach. If he was, Art would find out what. Art always found information on people; it was a goddamn gift, and depending on what he found out, Burke would pay. One way or another.

Chapter Fifteen
Saturday, August 20th, 1988
Tyra

1

A semitruck blasted its air horn as it sailed by, going ninety in the slow lane, and Tyra gripped the wheel. When she looked over, Puck finally cracked open his sunken, tired eyes.

"Having trouble staying awake there?" Tyra said, trying to contain her annoyance.

"Fucker blasted that horn," Parker said, rubbing his eyes.

"Stay alert. They should be coming by any time now," Tyra said. She'd been parked on the road shoulder at the last on-ramp before the US-Mexican border for almost two hours, waiting for the bounties to chug by in their Volkswagen. So far nothing except Puck and his constant need for food and sleep. The moron didn't think she knew, but he'd eaten a goddamn pot brownie a few hours back and looked stoned out of his already diminished, little coconut shell of a head.

"Can we get something to eat soon?" Puck said, rubbing his soft, distended stomach.

"Shut up."

"You don't have to snap at me." Puck looked a cross between wounded and angry.

"We're waiting here until we see the van," she said.

"How do you even know this is the way they went?" said Puck. "There are other roads into Mexico."

"Shut up," Tyra said, keeping her eyes trained on the oncoming traffic. She had no clue why Art kept the kid around, but she guessed it was because he was large and kind of scary looking. Not in a rugged way, like Art, but in a young, neurotic way. Like behind his narrow, deep-set eyes and chubby, acne-scarred cheeks was a brain that wasn't firing quite right. She guessed, too, that it helped to have someone watching cameras who got excited when a customer got rough with the girls, because that's what you needed in this business: someone crazy enough to charge into violent skirmishes without a moment's hesitation.

In Puck's case, because he was stupid, and also probably nuts. Though, she was glad she didn't have to do this rundown alone. Even though Art had promised she wouldn't have to get involved again, how could she have said no? She'd been in love with the bastard for twenty-five years, but as Art said, it just had never lined up quite right. Art also sunk every dime into helping her turn Shakers and Shots into a profitable business. She owed him one more of these. But this was it. Even if they ever did finally manage to get together.

Another twenty minutes went by, and Parker looked like he'd dozed off again. Then without moving, he said, "If they don't come in the next hour, can we get something to eat?"

"Puck—" Tyra breathed away a surge of anger that made her want to push Puck onto the freeway and just drive home. "I told you to bring snacks. We can cook hot dogs when we stop. If we stop. We're on their agenda."

"What are their names again?"

She didn't want to repeat herself but decided it wasn't worth the effort to yell at him again. "Rori Burke and Heath Walker. Now watch the road. In silence."

"I thought you said Burke. I went to high school with a girl named Rori Burke," Puck said.

"Yeah. You know what she looks like?"

"I mean, it's been a few years. She was a freshman. But yeah. I think so. Real pretty, blonde. Kind of quiet even when you try and talk to her."

The high pink color in Puck's cheeks and the creepy way he stared off made Tyra more nervous than she already was. They were waiting for cop killers, and she was pretty sure that, given the opportunity, this little weirdo would snap, too.

"Keep your hands off the perps. That's Art's first rule. Don't fucking forget it," Tyra said.

Puck stayed quiet and stared out his window, toward the cement embankment instead of watching traffic. Within minutes, he was sleeping again.

2

It started to get late, and Tyra worried about her ability to spot the van after dark with just headlights coming out of the darkness. But about thirty minutes later, while the late afternoon sun cut orange across the freeway in long shadows, a faded green Volkswagen zipped past in the number one lane. It was hard to tell, but it looked like a female in a beanie driving and nobody in the passenger's seat. She wondered if it was just another faded green van, but with the damaged front end, it had to be her bounties. Puck snored loudly when Tyra started the station wagon, released the brake, turned off the emergency flashers, and pulled onto the freeway. She jerked the wheel slightly and watched Puck's head roll off the headrest and thump against the window. She chuckled. The big, dumb idiot. Puck sat up and laughed, too, like he had been in on the joke the whole time.

"That them?" he said, groggy still.

"That's them," Tyra said.

With the radio low, playing a spotty jazz station out of San Diego, she trailed them by a few car lengths until they got to the border crossing. When they got there, they slowed to a stop behind a line of cars. Most vehicles were ushered through and once in a while pulled aside. When the bounties pulled up, they took a longer time than the others talking to the border guard, and sure as hell, they were pulled aside, too.

"What the fuck do we do now?" asked Puck when they pulled up to the guard.

"Quiet," Tyra said.

She showed the guard both IDs, and he shone a flashlight into the back of the station wagon, where they'd stacked a couple of boogie boards and some camping supplies. He flicked the light off and waved them through.

"Shit," she said, driving past the Volkswagen. A guard stood outside it, holding an automatic rifle. "They get picked up, and we're cooked."

"What's the plan?" Puck said.

"If Art's right about these kids, they'll get out of this."

Rolling down the freeway slowly, Tyra surveyed the new country in the fading daylight. It was surprising to her how immediately different it looked. Different gas stations, banks, small ramshackle houses built into the hillsides. Tyra had been here before; the rural poor in Mexico lived in rough conditions, leading into the larger cities like Tijuana and Rosarito. Towns crowded with high-end real estate, including posh hotels and fine dining.

She pulled off the freeway a few miles south of the border and parked where she could see the road. She shut everything down, and darkness flooded around them. It was quiet; Parker gripped the baton that he'd taken from Art's office. Like she hadn't noticed. If anything went bump out here, she'd gladly let the kid take off after whatever it was.

"Are we safe out here?" Puck said, scanning the rural locale. Nothing but darkness, desert, and tumbleweeds.

"Probably not. But we don't have an option. Hopefully, they get that inspection done fast."

"My brother had his car stolen down here once. Did I tell you that?"

"Only seven times."

"He left it in front of a hotel in Rosarito. Came out after check-in, gone."

"Any dumbass who leaves his keys in the ignition would get his car stolen in Chicago, or Los Angeles, or any place in the world. You would have to be stupid *not* to steal a perfect setup like that," Tyra said.

Puck stayed quiet, listening to branches pop outside his window. Probably squirrels or foxes or something, but the kid looked jumpy, and it made Tyra smile. She didn't know why she loved to fuck with Puck so much, but she did. Maybe because he had a mean streak in him that reminded her of the bastard tweaker that had pistol-whipped her temple and ruptured her eye socket. Goddamn glass eye for life because of that meth-addled prick. The calm of this desert felt like a comfort compared to the days of Tyra's youth. And, as if Art hadn't done enough over the past twenty-five years, he'd also made that tweaker pay, with his life.

"They're here," Tyra said, noticing the single round headlight and the characteristic whine of the Volkswagen engine.

"Finally," Puck said, rolling up his window and shoving the baton back into his pants.

The green van buzzed past them with zero interest in stopping to help. She didn't blame them for that. They were in a rush to not get killed. Also, who would stop for anybody on a dark stretch of road? Not her.

Once again, Tyra merged in behind the bounties and followed them far enough back to not get noticed. They continued south past through Tijuana, back into the remote roads, then through Rosarito. Both towns seemed pretty modern, though architecturally different. Lots of hacienda-style hotels and myriad restaurants and shops. She kept behind them for miles, until finally the van slowed and made a turn into a small resort south of Puerto Nuevo called La Fonda. She wondered if this was where the kids were going to hole up. She let them have a good lead, then followed them in and parked at the opposite end of the parking lot. She watched the boy, who must be Heath, with orangish hair and a beanie, get out of the driver's side and walk into the resort. The girl stayed in the Volkswagen, so Tyra and Puck did, too. About fifteen minutes later the boy walked out, started the van, and drove out of the lot. Tyra gave them a lead, then followed.

Another ten minutes down the freeway, the van slowed and turned into a small dirt road. Giving them some time, Tyra followed, and they passed a small sign that said *Salsipuedes Campground*. They descended a long, rugged dirt road that bottomed out the station wagon twice. Once inside the grounds, Tyra parked a good distance from the van so that they could watch without having to interact. The van had its lights off, and nobody got out.

"Puck, set up your tent. If it looks like they're staying the night, I'll go call Art."

"What about dinner?" Puck said in a whimper.

"Christ, Puck. Eat the hot dogs."

When Puck opened the car door, the hot, briny scent of tropical ocean filled the car and warmed Tyra's chest. It felt nice, like a honeymoon or vacation, though there would be no relaxing. She reclined her seat and tucked a rolled sweater under her head as a pillow. She kept a clear visual on the kids.

Stepping back inside, Puck slammed the door and ripped open the pack of hot dogs. Tyra cracked her window. Over the sound of Puck slurping down hot dogs whole, and the white noise of the ocean, Tyra tried to listen for any distant conversation. But the van was dark, windows rolled up. So were the other few cars collected around the big dirt lot. It looked like the bounties were going to sleep, and Tyra was exhausted from the drive. She began to nod off from pure exhaustion. She needed a quick power nap; then she'd go call Art.

"Puck, keep an eye on the van. Wake me if they even take a piss."

"Ten-four," Puck said. The big dummy. She would have to leave him here alone to call Art. Hopefully, he didn't mess that up.

Chapter Sixteen
Saturday, August 20, 1988
Art

1

It was 8:11 p.m. when Art got back to Shadow Valley. It felt like broken glass was being churned around inside his entire calf, and blood dripped out of his cutoff boot onto the floor mat. He needed to stash Avery and get his leg in a proper cast, fast, because when the call came in, he needed to be ready. It was hard to fully trust Puck, which was why he had sent Tyra, too. He hadn't wanted to send her down at all, but after he got rammed off a cliff, she was his only real hope. They had to pull this off, or they were both sunk.

The sun settled in the west, and it cast long shadows over the valley, but it was still hot and dry when he took the Goshen Avenue exit off the 99 freeway. He headed east toward Shadow Valley, and just before he got to the Friant-Kern Canal, where he had made Armando swim for his life, the neon lights of the club came into view.

He stopped in front of the building, 541 Goshen. This was it. And these were the same neon lights he'd seen the day before, which felt like a week ago. The Swing Time Grille. Such an innocuous and clever name, Art thought. It was clearly a strip club, probably more, and the operators, Art imagined, were the ones trying to put him out of business. With Burke as their muscle. Or maybe it was Burke's club. Either way, the raid on Shakers and Shots finally made sense.

Not too far behind the Swing Time Grille sat an old motel with the rooms forming an L shape behind the club. Art pulled around and parked in a dirt lot out front. In the parking lot were a few old pickups and a newer Mercedes Benz.

Art killed the engine and shut off his headlights. A bulky figure emerged from the first unit and stared out. The building was a wood ranch style built in the late fifties and maintained just well enough not to fall over. It was off-white with a porch running the length of the structure. When he counted across, there were exactly fourteen rooms, two or three of which had lights on visible through a small, curtain-covered window.

"This is your last chance, kid," Art said, and Avery tried to look at him through a slight line of vision under his swollen left eye.

Avery started to cry and covered himself up as if Art were about to attack him. "I told you everything. Why are you doing this?"

"I'm going down to get Heath and Rori. I need to know where I'm going and what I'm up against. And don't fucking lie to me."

"Why would I help you if you're just going to kill me anyway?" Avery sobbed.

"First, my boss wants the girl, not your buddy, not you."

"I already told you, man. I don't know anything. They're gone. That's it." Avery was pissed off and sobbing at the same time.

"Okay," Art said. "Here's the deal. I've got a tail on your brother. We get them before they make it to Mexico, I let you go. If they disappear down there, then you're going to spend some quality time with me until we figure out how to get them out. So, for now, you're staying here. Get up. Let's go."

"Fuck you, man," Avery said, and Art reached for his baton, which made Avery flinch into a fetal position against the passenger's door.

Beyond the little motel were sprawling, darkened orchards. It was mostly peaceful this far out of town. But there was something familiar and ominous about this place. The dark figure in the yellow, humming halogen light shook a chill down Art's back. Art tried to remember if he'd been here before, but the memories of his cop days were a blur, especially toward the end when he was drunk nearly every day by noon. His memory and his brain had turned to mush. Getting sobor brought some of it back, but not much. At least he could think clearly most of the time.

Getting out of his truck, Art went around and opened Avery's door. A stir of moths and other insects buzzed around, bouncing into the light behind the man on the patio. Avery slid from the car and dangled from his zip-tied hands.

"You going to help me with any of this?" Art yelled to the guy, but he didn't budge.

"Bring him to me," the man said in accented English.

"Fuck you," Art said. Slipping a locking knife from his pocket, Art cut the zip ties. He then took Avery by the arm and half leaned on him while they shuffled toward the building.

Over the sound of their feet on the gravel, Art could hear the crickets churn their nighttime melody in stops and starts, and they seemed to stretch out into the infinite swath of farmland. The air smelled like baked clay and held a hint of moisture from the irrigation from the nearby orange orchards. Art rowed toward the figure with his crutch, and when he got to the small set of wooden stairs, he could see the man's face, but Art couldn't place it.

"Stop right there," the man said. The figure before him was on the verge of chubby and wore black, pleated slacks with a tucked-in, white tank top revealing an over-the-shoulder tribal dragon tattoo that wrapped around so that the head and tongue hissed from the man's neck. His head was shaved, and he wore a single, thin gold chain.

"Burke sent me. Here's the kid," Art said.

The man stepped forward, and Avery yelped when he grabbed him roughly by his right arm and shoved him into the small quarters. Inside the room, Avery tripped and fell onto his chest and sobbed. Art took a step forward, but the man raised his palm.

"Get back in the truck, old man. And don't come back."

The man had a Beretta shoved into the waistline of his slacks that his gut enveloped.

Art turned and hobbled toward his truck and stepped into the cab. The man turned and started to close the door when the orange light that poured from the room flashed over a young Chinese girl in a sheer robe who had stepped out of the bathroom. She walked slowly, dragging her feet like she was loaded on heroin, and the man pulled his gun, causing her to drop to the floor just when the stream of light disappeared. The door clicked shut.

"God-*fucking*-damn it," Art hissed to himself. His whole body ached from the exertion of getting Avery to the door, and now his stomach knotted in disgust.

Driving back over the Friant-Kern Canal, Art thought about Armando again—his body was probably still stuck in the drain, and he wondered how peaceful it would be to drown. He wondered if he would be better off joining him down there than enduring the trouble that lay ahead. One thing was certain, he was too tired for this shit.

2

When Art pulled up to Shakers and Shots, it was 2:11 a.m. and his leg was in a firm cast. The goddamn emergency room was chaos on a Friday night with gunshot victims from the Norteños on the north side and drunk driving accidents from the yuppies to the south.

It was Friday night, technically, and this should've been the time when drunk and satisfied guests were meandering out of his club after a busy night, but instead, the lot was empty and dark. Burke had shut him down fast, and at least now Art knew exactly why, and it made him sick. That Swing Time Grille was a cover for a prostitution ring, probably underage. Art had that feeling of certainty. That hunch. He just needed proof.

Driving around back, he parked and let himself in through the back entrance. He limped through the hallway and into his office and locked the door. Opening the top drawer of this desk, he pulled a flask of Maker's Mark free and popped the lid of the prescription hydrocodone he'd gotten from the hospital. He drank two pills down with the liquid and took a second to savor the burn that warmed his belly with the lingering scent of toasted coconut and vanilla. Anger welled up in him, and he wished someone were here that he could murder with his bare goddamn hands. The face that kept appearing was the fat, mustached face of Chief Burke.

Art sat down at his desk and propped his broken leg up on an ottoman. He pulled his Rolodex down from next to his typewriter and flipped it until he landed on Officer Tracy Jessman. Tracy was an old friend on the force, and when he needed intel on a perp or a case file, she always came through. Only this time, it was a very old case file. He wanted to take a closer look at the old Triad file that had gotten him kicked off the force. And he needed to find out more information on the Swing Time Grille. She could handle that, too. He'd pay her standard fee.

Art left her card near the phone and limped over to his couch to lie down. He swigged down the rest of the whiskey; a familiar wave of pleasure filled his brain, and a sedate smile swept over his face. He missed his old friend. He closed his eye, and a wave of exhaustion carried him off to a deep and dreamless sleep.

3

A flashing red light penetrated Art's consciousness while he slept, and it eventually pulled him from his darkness. He rubbed his eyes, and the aching sting of his broken leg resumed its torturous pulsing. He stood and limped directly back to his desk, where he promptly sat. Slipping two more pain pills into his mouth, he looked around for something to wash them down. His flask was empty, so he reached for his water cooler and cupped some water into his palm and swallowed, the pills sticking in his throat.

The clock on the wall read 9:14 a.m., and he rubbed his eyes to make sure he was seeing it correctly. He verified it with his Timex. *Fuck.* He'd slept far longer than he had intended. The flashing red light that had woken him glowed from his answering machine, so he pressed Play, hoping for good news.

"Art, it's Tyra. We found the kids and followed them to a little campground south of Rosarito. Get here quickly, they're all alone out here, but I think they are going to a hotel nearby next. I have Puck watching them. I'm calling from a gas station ten minutes north. Salsipuedes is the campground. Hurry."

Art rewound the tape and played it again. He wrote *Salsipuedes* down on a notepad and pulled a map from the bottom drawer of his desk. Art had been to Baja before and gotten out with his bounty clean. It was always tough getting back across the border with someone who didn't want to come with you though.

With the map he verified the distance. It was nearly four hundred miles to Salsipuedes, and Art figured that without stopping, he could be there by 5:00 p.m. Maybe just after, since he'd have to refuel.

Art placed a call to Tracy Jessman's personal line. She didn't answer, so he left her a message to call him back. He said that he needed her help again.

Inside his small bathroom, Art freshened up by washing out his armpits and balls with a hot, damp washcloth and applied deodorant. He changed into a fresh Western shirt and cut a fresh pair of jeans to fit over his cast. From his supply closet, he restocked on sedatives, smelling salts, and zip ties and noticed that his spare baton was missing. *Fucking Parker.* Locking the back door, Art hopped into his truck and started it. The drugs had kicked in, and the pain felt distant, and so did his mind when he took another long pull from his freshly refilled flask. He slipped it under his seat and hit the gas, causing his tires to chirp. He sped away—it was time to put this fucking thing to bed.

Chapter Seventeen
Saturday, August 20, 1988
Heath

The next morning, I tried to sleep in, but the light streaming through the windshield of the van was too bright. I stared up at the sagging headliner when someone started banging on the door, causing me to bolt upright. Rori sat up, too, and an uneasiness passed between us that was palpable. I moved the plaid curtain to the side, and a short Mexican lady stood outside with a couple of toddlers hiding behind her legs. I cracked the door and peeked out.

"*Diez pesos, señor. Por anoche*," she said, and turned up a pale palm.

My Spanish wasn't great, but I knew some. She was asking for money. I looked down the beach at her homemade-looking shack that sat at the far end of the camping area. A man stood there in front of a barbecue, stoking some logs, and another couple of kids roamed around. It appeared to be an informal camp host.

"*Sí. Sí,*" I said. I dug into my sock and furnished a twenty. "*No tengo pesos.*"

"*Esta bien,*" she said, and took the money. She handed me back nineteen dollars American, and I figured most of the people that came through probably paid in greenbacks. I also seriously questioned the legitimacy of the little family's operation—this wasn't exactly a state park—and their seemingly arbitrary fees, but it was cheap, and I had no idea how it worked, so I didn't complain.

"*Perdon,*" I said when she started to walk away. I handed her a dollar back. "*Dos noches, por favor.*" I realized my Spanish was embarrassingly bad, but she seemed to get it and appreciate the effort. I didn't want to be here for another night, but when I tried to ask for Jacques at La Fonda the night before, three serious-looking dudes with guns came out of nowhere and told me to come back on Sunday. So here we were. Stuck out in the open until tomorrow.

I closed the door and turned back to Rori, who smoothed out her cloud of red hair. I slid toward her and kissed her softly on the forehead. Leaning against the side of the bus, I rubbed my face and breathed. My entire body felt depleted from the stress of the last few days, and I had that raw feeling like my mind and soul had been cracked open in the night and exposed to some dark power, and I needed help to pull it all back together. Or maybe I just needed some coffee. Rori smiled and burrowed into the blankets. I grabbed my soft pack of Camels and a lighter and stepped into the sunshine.

The coastline in this part of Mexico had a presence, a quality of light, a vibe that made it seem like it was always warm and kind, and the surf perennially vibrant and teal. Heaven all the time. I scanned around and noticed a green station wagon a few spots down toward the entrance, and on the other side, there were a couple of RVs near each other with a fire pit between them. It seemed safe enough, and I enjoyed having the morning to myself. I could get used to this.

I lit the cigarette, inhaled deeply, then surveyed the area. The campground sat at the top of a hill, and I couldn't quite see the waves from this far back, but I could hear them. The crashing sound called to me.

As soon as we had some money and protection, I needed to learn to surf with Rori for real. Also, as much as we needed to lie low, I really wanted to celebrate her birthday. I had eighteen dollars left, which in California wouldn't be much, but down here it might stretch pretty far.

I lit a second cigarette off the other and heard Rori stirring inside the van.

"Heath, that you?" She must have dozed off.

"Want a smoke?" I asked.

"Yes, please."

I pulled the slider open, and she sat up with her elbows on her knees. I sat on the instep of the bus and lit her a cigarette. "Happy birthday, beautiful," I said, and stroked her knee.

"I guess I'm legal now. Does that mean anything down here?"

"Makes you an adult back home," I said. "Down here, you already were one."

"You can do anything you want here," she said.

"You can do anything you want anywhere. As long as you have money," I said.

"How long do we have to wait like this?"

"The guys at the hotel looked ex-military. They said to come back Sunday."

"After Big Sur, I just feel—"

"I know. Me too. Let's just be extra careful. First thing tomorrow morning we head over and meet Jacques. Then we're safe. We can at least get some good food and booze for tonight."

"With what money?" she said.

I unfolded the eighteen dollars I had left and showed it to her.

"Not sure I want to know where you had that hidden." She smiled.

"We're going to get through this."

Rori paused and looked like she might cry. "I'm—I'm so sorry about your mom," Rori said. Her gaze fell so she focused on the dirt between us. "This just got so fucked-up so fast."

I looked out at the ocean horizon. Mom would have loved a view like this. Her favorite thing to do was riding up into the foothills behind our house and watching the sunset over Central Valley. My heart felt raw and my throat dry from thinking about here. That image of her holding the shotgun flashed again. There was no use blaming Rori. In the end, it wasn't her fault.

"She had been sick for a long time," I said in hopes of alleviating some of Rori's obvious guilt.

"And Avery. God, I'm a curse." Rori dropped her face into her hands and cried softly. "This is my goddamn fault. My father. My blood. I should have just let him take me."

"Christ. Are you kidding me?" I turned to Rori and held her face gently in my hands so I could see her wet eyes. "I would rather be dead than let you go back to that. You were savagely abused by a maniac. You deserved better. We'll be stronger for this. We really will. And so will Avery, if he makes it out the other side. He made his choice to get involved with dangerous people, same as you and me. We made choices. I chose you."

"It wasn't his decision to have my dad's bounty hunter nearly take his face off."

"I just mean that he plays with fire, too. He's going to make it through. So will we."

"Will we? What do we do? Hang out in the van another night and just hope nobody murders us in our sleep?"

"I don't know what else to do," I said, gritting my teeth. It was frustrating not being able to get protection right away. But we had no money and no connections until tomorrow.

"Can't we just go back to the hotel and check in as guests? I can do it in case they remember you."

"You want me to go back to a place where three armed security guards just kicked me out after I asked for their drug lord boss?"

"Fuck. I don't know? Yes?" Her brow furrowed; she looked confused and angry.

I spun my father's ring on my finger and found it soothing. I was connected to something greater than myself. I had a biological family, a father, and even though he didn't want me, he could still be out there. *"Buffalo Bill's / Defunct."* Out loud, I said, "I've still got the .357, and we'll stay low-key. We'll make it to meet Jacques tomorrow. I promise."

She scooted toward me and leaned her head on my shoulder. We both looked out over the coastline; Rori sighed. "I just want to feel safe again."

"I know. Me too." I didn't want to mention it out loud, but I knew she was thinking the same thing. How safe were we going to be working for a drug runner?

Safer than not, I guessed.

"I'll go back to town and get you a piñata, some beer, and some mescal. We can barbecue and get drunk and forget about the bullshit for one night," I said.

"I trust you, Heath." And it was the worst thing she could have said, because a door opened to a car on the other side of the lot, and I got the breathless feeling again. I breathed slowly to contain it. *"He bit an Angle Worm in halves / And ate the fellow, raw."* I wouldn't let Rori out of my sight.

Chapter Eighteen
Saturday, August 20, 1988
Tyra

1

It was pitch-dark out when Tyra's eyes snapped open. The warm, salty breeze was blowing softly through her cracked window. Forgetting where she was for a moment, she shot up in a panic. Then Puck snored like a damn chain saw beside her in the passenger's seat, and she remembered. Looking out over the campsite, she could see the darkened silhouette of the Volkswagen. They were still there. She shoved Puck to wake him up. Twice. And he finally looked up at her.

"Christ. What is it?" he said.

"Set up a tent. Watch the van. I'm going to call Art."

He looked at the car clock. "It's three a.m. What the hell? They're not going anywhere."

"Puck, get out. And don't fall back to sleep until I get back."

Puck groaned again, then opened the door, nearly falling onto his ass. He humped around the back, opened the trunk, and pulled the tent and a sleeping bag out. Tyra started the engine but kept the lights off. Puck came around.

"How long are you going to be gone?" he said.

"I think there was a gas station a few miles back. I'm going to go call Art, and I'll be right back. Twenty minutes."

"Shit. Fine."

Tyra put the car in gear. "And Puck?"

"Yeah."

"Do not engage. Sit in the tent and watch."

"Ten-four, Mom."

"I'm not your mother, thank god."

She started to pull away, and Puck whisper yelled, "Wait!"

She stopped.

He shuffled up to the door. "Can I grab another pack of hot dogs?"

"Jee-sus. You going to eat everything we got?"

He looked mock sheepish and clawed his way into the trunk, opened the ice chest, and took another pack of hot dogs. She pulled away as slowly and quietly as she could. But in the dead of night and with just the cover of the distant ocean hiss, she felt like the station wagon was as loud as a freight train barreling through a nitroglycerine plant.

The 1D freeway was roughshod and dark. She realized that being in a rural area either here or back home was ill-advised for a single woman in the middle of the night. But she had to get in touch with Art. There were no gas stations before she got back to La Fonda, so she pulled in and drove around the very quiet parking lot. Little yellow streetlamps illuminating small circles of pavement.

Tyra saw the glowing symbol for a pay phone left of the main entrance, and she quietly walked over and, realizing she had no pesos, collect called Art. After some confusion in Spanish, then broken English, Art's phone rang. It went to voicemail, and the operator came back on asking for money. Instead of trying to shout over it, she hung up.

She started back toward her car and heard something behind her. She quickened her pace and glanced over her shoulder. A large man in a uniform holding an assault rifle stood by the pay phone where she had been. He stayed where he was, letting her know he was watching. She got in and started the car. Pulling away, it finally dawned on her. She had to let Art know that La Fonda was where the kids were going next. Why else would they have stopped here first? But why not check in? Why camp out in the open for two days? It didn't matter, she had to tell Art. She headed a few miles back toward the border until she spotted an all-night gas station. She bought a Coke inside, made change, and called Art. It went to his machine.

"Art, it's Tyra. We found the kids and followed them to a little campground south of Rosarito. Get here quickly, they're all alone out here, but I think they are going to a hotel nearby next. I have Puck watching them. I'm calling from a gas station ten minutes north. Salsipuedes is the campground. Hurry." Tyra hung up the phone and leaned her forehead against the silent receiver. "I'm scared. Please get here soon."

Tyra looked around at the dark, dry landscape. A couple of men lurked in the shadows beside the building, smoking. She didn't want to be here. She didn't feel safe. And worse yet, she had to go back and spend the night with Puck and these two bounties who she was pretty sure were murderers. If she made it out of this one, Art owed her, big. She wanted a real wedding. And a rock the size of Pennsylvania.

Chapter Nineteen
Sunday, August 21, 1988
Heath

1

With the sun overhead, the arid desert heat was no longer pleasurably tempered by the onshore ocean breeze, and I switched into shorts and T-shirt. I kept making scans of the campground to see who was coming and going and assess any threats. Everyone looked like college kids out for a surf weekend. Well, everyone except the station wagon across the way. The car that just drove off and left the big guy behind sitting in a folding chair in front of a small fire.

He was chubby and probably mid twenties and seemed like an odd match for the other outdoorsy types collected around the campground. The black lady he was with also looked too old to be his date for the weekend. But they didn't register as threats, necessarily. Just an oddity at a campsite that was otherwise peaceful and relatively safe. Safer than venturing out and taking the chance of running into the goddamn bounty hunter. At least here I could see it coming. There would be no more surprises if I could help it.

I made a gimlet with mescal and lime juice for Rori. A few more cars moved in and set up camp, and I noticed a light-blue Volkswagen Beetle bump into the lot. It parked in the next space over from us. A couple about our age got out. We'd gone back to the last little town about twenty minutes back, passing La Fonda on the way, to get supplies. And to assuage Rori's urgings to check in, I drove into the parking lot, where I immediately recognized one of the armed guards and turned right back around. They looked like people that might just shoot first and ask questions later if provoked. Rori agreed this time. When we returned with the alcohol and food, I parked the van so the slider opened up to the collection of rocks and wilderness opposite the campground to keep to ourselves.

Rori changed inside the van, putting on her hoodie and jeans, and I lit a fire. It was just after 3:00 p.m., and the day couldn't have been any more perfect. That is, until the big guy glanced up again from his bonfire, then started a slow trudge toward our campsite. I tucked the .357 into my waistline just when Rori stepped out of the sliding door.

"Bogey from across the way coming in hot," I said.

Rori tried not to look over her shoulder too obviously, though it was. "What the hell does he want?"

"I don't know. He's been looking over this way all day."

"Where's the lady he was with?"

"Took off again."

"What do we do?" she said.

"We either shoot him or hear what he has to say."

"Shoot him," Rori said with a nervous laugh. She was kidding, sort of.

"Just be ready to hit the road," I said. My lungs felt pressed in; I needed to draw breath. This guy wasn't what he appeared. When he got within earshot, I said, "Hey there, buddy. You need to borrow a cup of sugar?"

2

He was huffing a little, and even bigger up close. Probably my height, but closer to two fifty, two sixty. "Oh. Ha, ha. No, I was actually just coming over to see if I could bum a cigarette or two. My aunt left to get some more beer and took the whole pack."

"I've got a Camel nonfilter you can have," I said, stepping into his path so he didn't get any nearer our campsite.

"Oh, you saved the day. Thank you," he said. I handed him two and helped him light one. He took a drag and coughed slightly. Nonsmoker, and he had passed two other camps on the way over with people drinking and smoking.

"How are you and your girlfriend enjoying the surf?" I asked, and he looked down at his feet, scuffing the sand with the toe of his boot.

"Us? Me and my aunt? We're just camping a couple nights. On our way down to Ensenada," he said.

"What's your name?" Rori asked, stepping up beside me.

"Oh, I'm Par—Peter. West. My aunt is Nancy."

"We're taking a little vacation, too, man," I said. "After the surf and weather down here today, not sure we're ever going back, you know?"

"You guys wouldn't happen to have a beer I can bum, too? I can bring you one when my aunt gets back," he said.

Rori cracked a Pacifico and handed it to him. I kept my eyes trained on him the whole time. The deep-set brown eyes followed Rori the whole way and snapped back to me once the beer was in his hand. "The beer and smokes are yours," I said.

"Where you from?" Rori asked. Less like a friendly camper, and more like an investigator.

"Me. San Diego. Her too," he said, and gestured toward his campsite.

"San Diego, huh? You come down this way a lot?" Rori said.

"Oh yeah. All the time." He took a swig of the beer and nodded toward the mescal. "I hate to be a bother, but is that mescal any good?"

"Still has the worm in it," I said. I took a slug from it and handed it to Peter. Rori leaned into me with her thigh as if to say, "Easy on the booze." But, as she had said herself, I could handle my drink.

"You ever been out to Shadow Valley?" Rori asked while Peter took a slug from the bottle, some residual fluid dripping down his chin.

"No. Never."

"I think it's time for the cake," I said. "You need anything else, Peter?"

"What kind of cake did you get?" Peter said, either too stupid to catch the hint or blatantly refusing to. He was getting on my nerves.

"Pete, Rori and I are going to celebrate alone for the rest of the night, if you don't mind," I said.

Peter pretended like he didn't hear me and glanced over to our fire pit, where I had a set up a makeshift table out of a cardboard box and some wood planks.

"Is that Mexican pan? I could go for one of those."

"Peter, we're—you know what. Take the bread, but we really need our space, if that's okay."

Peter looked wounded, angry, confused. He stepped past us and picked up one of the pink, swirled sweets we'd found at the market. He started to walk past us but stopped when he neared my flank. "You've been too kind," he said in a low growl.

He strode forward another couple steps and turned quickly, his hand pulling from his own waistline. Extending from his hand was a baton just like the one the bounty hunter had used. It even had the same metallic snap when it opened. I instinctively ducked, and the swift right hand sailed over my head and smacked against the rear panel of the Volkswagen. Peter leapt forward with all his weight, and I tried to free the pistol from the small of my back, but the weight fell on me hard and fast.

When we hit the ground, I lost my grip on the gun. My breath was also gone for real this time. I heaved for breath and stared up at the mottled cheeks of my assailant, which now seemed sinister. He raised the baton, but I just smiled. Peter looked momentarily confused by the reaction. Then the bottle of mescal crushed against the side of Peter's head. Blood and booze ran into my mouth and eyes. Rori helped roll the unconscious Peter off me. I coughed, spit, and cleaned the blood off my face and neck.

"That's twice now, Heath," Rori said. She tried to smile, but it came out in a tight, thin-lipped line. She was trying not to cry.

"We need to move," I said, and kicked Peter in the stomach, making a slapping sound with my bare foot. "Before his aunt, or whoever she really is, comes back."

"We can't take this van. It's been blown," Rori said.

"You got any better ideas?" I asked. She did have one.

We quickly broke camp, doused the fire, and loaded into the van. I backed out of the slip and angled down the rough dirt road for about twenty yards. I stopped in front of the recently arrived couple with the blue Beetle. Moments later, we were back on the 1D freeway.

3

"You knew him, didn't you?" I said. "That's why you asked about Shadow Valley."

"I tried to nudge you. He went to Shadow Valley High. Real name's Parker. I only vaguely remember him," Rori said.

"You think he remembered you?" I asked.

"Probably. Him being here has my dad's fingerprints all over it."

"Or that bounty hunter's," I said.

"Where do we go now?" Rori asked.

"I'm not taking no for an answer. Maybe they'll just hold us hostage, I don't know. But somewhere safe from them."

Rori smiled. "God. It's terrible that something that fucked-up sounds good to me, right?"

"We're in the shit now," I said, feeling that familiar pulse of adrenaline spike in my chest, my palms slick yet again. "Let's try not to get broken too many more times before sixty, okay?"

"We just going to walk right in again?"

"Maybe we can park in the lot tonight and ask for Jacques first thing in the morning." I had no idea if that would keep the bounty hunter off us, but I figured with security carrying Kalashnikovs, it was better than the campground.

"Bounty hunter would have to be stupid to come after us there."

"Doesn't mean he won't," I said. We passed empty, sun-parched lots enshrouded with barbed wire. And abandoned adobe structures with no roofs. After a few miles, the station wagon zoomed past with an F-150 closely behind it. Driving that truck was Art, the bounty hunter. I hit the gas and gave it everything the old 1600cc engine could muster. It wasn't much, but within minutes we were pushing ninety.

"Heath?" Rori asked after a few seconds.

"Yeah?"

"That was them, wasn't it?"

"Yup."

Rori stayed quiet for another moment, then said, "Heath?"

"Yeah?"

"This thing go any faster?"

"Nope."

"If we don't make it to La Fonda, thanks for spending my eighteenth birthday with me."

I reached over and put my hand on her thigh. She grabbed my hand; it was damp like it had been on that roller coaster. We'll make it to your nineteenth together. I promise."

"Can we have a more limited guest list next time?"

"Sure. Next birthday, no sociopaths."

"Deal. Now let's lead the dumb fucks into the hornets' nest," Rori said.

I thought it was a good metaphor. We had a bleeding probable corpse back at camp behind us, and security guards with AKs ahead of us. It was hard to believe I was just hustling a small bar in a shitty, little, crime-filled town just a few days ago. It felt like years. And it also felt like Rori and I were becoming something else. More than just trauma victims finding each other in a bar. Something kind of terrible and amazing. I kind of liked it, but I also sensed that we were heading toward a point of no return, and I wasn't sure these past few days were how I'd want to be remembered. A trail of bodies, both dead and barely alive, scattered across two countries now. Who the hell was I?

Chapter Twenty
Sunday, August 21, 1988
Art

1

After stopping for gas in El Segundo in Los Angeles, Art merged into traffic dead-stopped four lanes across. It was 1:15 p.m., so he was fucked. It would add another two hours to his trip, which would put him at Salsipuedes Campground closer to 6:00 p.m. But if Tyra's message was correct, he knew where the kids were going next. If he couldn't surprise them at the campground, he'd wait for them at the hotel.

The late summer sun was so hot overhead, the freeway smelled of tar and melted rubber. Once he got past LAX, traffic flowed a little better, and the windshields of the oncoming cars created a continual pulse of monochrome and pastel yellow. Art took a shot from his flask. He couldn't wait for nightfall. It made it easier to surprise people. At 5:03 p.m. he arrived at the border and funneled through a single entrance behind a short lineup of cars.

The border agent checked his ID and glanced through his rear cab window, then rattled off the basic questions with disinterest. While he did, Art wondered at his odds at getting back through with a bounty. He'd gotten away with it a few years back by flashing his law enforcement credentials that he conveniently kept with him. Still, coming back through with a zip-tied body in the back might raise some suspicion at the US border. He would have to heavily sedate her. Hell, if it meant ending this feud with Burke, Art would hire a goddamn coyote—he needed to finish this.

2

Art scanned road signs while keeping an eye on his mileage. It was dusk, and the sun glinted in his eyes, making it difficult to see and read. About fifty minutes into Mexico, he slowed to twenty-five miles per hour. He passed a gas station and spotted a familiar green station wagon. He braked hard and reversed into the small adobe convenience store.

As if she had expected him any moment, Tyra emerged from the driver's seat and stood with the remote Mexican desert spreading behind her in shadows from the light of the falling sun. Taking a long pull from his flask, Art allowed a sense of relief to wash over him. He got out, and Tyra embraced him while a soft, warm breeze carried a small, lopsided tumbleweed past the pumps and into the road.

"God, it's good to see you," Tyra said.

"Are you okay? Puck do his job?"

"I'm fine. I just want to go home."

"I know. I'm sorry I dragged you down here. You did great. You really did."

"They're just down the road. Puck's watching them." She released her hug and looked up at Art. He held her gaze.

"You tell him not to try anything?" Art asked. All he could think about was how the kid leapt at every opportunity to get physical with a client, but he mostly obeyed orders, which was why Art hadn't fired him. There weren't too many people simple enough to sit and watch a goddamn screen all day.

"Of course. But it's Puck. We should get back," Tyra said.

"Let's stash my truck somewhere safe and take the station wagon."

"The hotel, or at the campground. Though the college kids might fuck with it."

"I'll park it near the camp entrance, and I'll jump in the car with you. Once we have them, you can take me back out."

"Okay—okay," Tyra said, and hesitated. "I can do this."

"You *can* do this," Art said. "And you will."

3

Art followed Tyra farther into Baja until she double-tapped her brakes. Art slowed and watched another car coming in the opposite direction. When it barreled past, he couldn't see inside with the glare from the sun, but it was them. It was the green Volkswagen bus that had rammed him off a cliff. Puck had certainly fucked up, and now they were on the move. Tyra pulled over and Art alongside her.

"That was them," Tyra said.

"I know. I'm sure they saw us, too. Get in," Art said.

"What about Puck?"

"I doubt there's anything left of him—we'll come back and check. After we have them."

Tyra got in, and Art flipped around and spun his tires until the stench of melted rubber filled the cab. They rattled down the road, and Art could see a faint silhouette of the Volkswagen in the distance.

"What if they go to the hotel? Should we just go home, then?"

"Back to fucking what?" Art snapped, and immediately softened his tone. "They're right in front of us." He recalibrated. "Look, if we can pick them up before they get to the hotel, we head home and get our club back along with a shitload of money."

"And if they make it to this hotel?"

"We'll grab them in the parking lot," Art said.

"Maybe you missed the memo on the guards with assault rifles. This isn't a normal hotel. I don't want to die down here. These kids are up to something bigger than you and I and Burke."

"We'll catch them."

4

The F-150 was faster than the Volkswagen, and Art was on their six by the time they reached La Fonda, only the bounties didn't turn in. They kept driving. Art stayed on them, and they didn't slow down until they were back at the convenience store where he'd met Tyra. They pulled in and parked at one of the little gas pumps. Reaching into his glove box, Art pulled his Glock free and racked the slide. He guessed it would go down right here, right now.

"Art—" Tyra started.

"Get the zip ties from behind the seat."

Art hit the gas just when the passenger's door of the Volkswagen opened, ramming it off its frame. The person inside jumped back inside the car. Slamming the brakes, Tyra and Art were parallel to the Volkswagen with a clear view of the occupants. Art's heart fell into his stomach. It wasn't them. A teenage couple with near-catatonic expressions glared back at them. One was a tall, thin man with long, sandy-blonde hair and a Rasta bandanna. And the girl had feathery brown hair tied around the top with a braid.

"Sorry, in a big hurry," Tyra said, and waved.

"Fucking hippies. Fuck!" Art hit the dash with his fist. He pointed his gun at the hippies, and they both probably shit themselves. "Where the fuck did you get this van?"

"At—at camp, man. I traded it."

"For what, goddamnit?"

"My Beetle," the girl stammered.

"What color?"

"B-blue," she said.

Art threw the truck in reverse until he got to the road and started back toward the campground.

"Puck fucked this up somehow, I know it." Art popped another pain pill and washed it down with the flask of Maker's.

"God, I hope he's not dead," Tyra said.

"If he's not, he will be."

"Art, come on. You still have the brother, right? We can still set some kind of trap?" Tyra said, repeating what they'd already talked about just to hear the words between them. Just to hang on to that glimmer of hope.

"Yeah. We still have the brother. But it could take weeks to dig them out now. Or months."

"You know these bounties, you think Puck's alive?"

"No, but we'll check."

When they got to La Fonda, Art pulled down the circular driveway, and sure enough, there was a powder blue Beetle parked at the check-in. He debated going right in after them, but, as Tyra pointed out, there were several armed guards around. This would not be a valid extraction point. He needed to rethink this.

Back on the 1D, he pulled into the campsite, and Tyra showed him where Heath and Rori had been parked. Limping on his crutch, he found the spot where Parker's body still lay. When he crouched beside him, his leg throbbed, but he held his finger under Parker's nose to feel for breath.

"He's still alive," Art said, and laid his palm over Parker's head where the blood congealed.

Tyra let out a slight sob. "I told him to watch. I told him what you said."

"Well, he obviously had his own agenda. The kid wasn't all there anyway. We have to get the fuck out of Mexico, and I have to get Avery out of Burke's safe house before these Triad fucks kill him."

Art limped to the truck and pulled the Glock from the glove box, aiming it at Parker.

"No, Art. Christ!" Tyra said. "We're over if you kill this boy."

"What do you want to do with a half-dead American in Mexico?" Art said.

"Let's just drop him at a hospital. I'll just tell them he fell surfing or something," Tyra pleaded.

Art put the Glock away and got back in his truck. "We'd better get him loaded up."

Tyra audibly sighed and climbed in as well. They pulled the station wagon around and loaded Parker in the front seat, leaning him against the window, where Tyra bandaged his head as best she could with a first aid kit from the trunk.

"What about the camping gear?" Tyra asked.

"Leave it," Art said. She took Art back down the road to his truck. He got out and leaned in close to her. "I'll go get Avery and meet you at the club."

Tyra nodded and started the station wagon again. "I'll drop him off at a hospital somewhere. I'll call you with the location."

"Go home and get some rest. I'll see you in a couple days," Art said. He got into his truck and started it.

Tyra followed him for a while, past La Fonda and toward the border. It would almost be morning when he got back to Shadow Valley, and he couldn't wait to lie down and rest his leg. He felt it pulsing with bright stabs of pain from all of the exertion. Rattling his pill bottle, he shook two more into his hand and washed them down with a long pull from the flask. He lowered his gaze and forced a smile. There were going to be more bodies hitting the floor before this was over. And it wouldn't be his.

Chapter Twenty-One
Sunday, August 21, 1988
Heath

1

The sun was half-submerged behind the horizon, past the peeling, turquoise waves and lines of white shore break along the private beach. Jet streams and clouds glowed pink and orange in faded pastels. A weathered lifeguard shack stood empty and stoic at the center of the beach.

On the restaurant veranda overlooking the beach, Rori and I were sitting at a square table with an umbrella through the center. Rori's last-minute idea to switch Volkswagens had worked, and we'd slipped right past the bounty hunter just in time. That savage who had attacked us ended up saving us. The couple had been more than willing to trade the van for the Beetle, even with the dinged-up front end. Hell, they could sleep in it.

We weren't exactly treated like royalty when we'd come back here. Jean-Pierre, the steroid junkie head of security, had held us at gunpoint in a dank cellar for hours, waiting for clearance from his boss, Jacques. Eventually, mentioning Avery got us cleared to check in. And the layers of guilt for leaving Avery back there in Big Sur still rose in my throat like bile nearly every hour. It was hard to look past. But here we were at the Cantina La Fonda, eating grilled lobster straight from Puerto Nuevo for about two bucks a plate. I really wished Avery would have just come with us. The fact that he wanted to stay still didn't make sense to me. He must have had a lot of money stashed away up at the Hideaway. Not that I was feeling safe yet, we still hadn't met Jacques, though he was due in at any minute.

Rori took a bite of lobster, and when she looked up, she chewed quickly and swallowed. Her voice shook slightly. "Umm. I think he's here."

"Okay, relax. We're good," I said. "We got this." Jean-Pierre, who had stood by while we checked in, had told us to come down to the veranda at 7:30 p.m. to meet Jacques. It was after 8:00 p.m.

I turned my head slightly, not wanting to be too obvious, and saw the new face scanning the veranda, Jean-Pierre beside him with his hand inside his jacket. They apparently didn't flash Kalashnikovs in front of the guests. I'd known that Jacques was also French-Canadian from something Avery had said, but Avery had failed to also mention that he was Black, and that his clothing style leaned toward the Caribbean: he had on a tweed suit and bowler hat.

When he got to our table, he leaned over, and I could see sweat rings around his pits and the handle of a nickel-plated nine-millimeter secured in a shoulder holster beneath his jacket. I moved to stand and shake his hand, but he held up his palm.

"Please do not stand up." He bared a brilliantly white set of veneers. "I understand from my colleague that you are the brother of Avery Walker." He flipped a chair around and sat down. Jean-Pierre stood at one entrance to the patio with his arms crossed. Having armed guards around didn't seem to concern any of the other guests, which seemed odd, because if we'd been sitting at the Marie Callender's in Shadow Valley, I'd have taken my fucking coconut cream pie to go.

"Did you bring us the money that he owes us?" he asked, and I felt the acid reflux again.

"Money? They took everything we had at the border. We're here to help," I said, though my mind immediately went to the money Avery had mentioned. The money holed up back at the Hideaway.

He looked around cautiously. "I need you, then, to tell me why my associate shouldn't kill you both right now. Please," he said.

"Whoa. Christ," I said, my voice elevating unintentionally. "I thought you needed help. That's why we're here."

"Tell me something. You are supposed to be Avery's best friend, or brother, as he says, and yet you do not know about the money that he owes me?"

Avery had failed to mention that the money he was waiting to collect back in Santa Cruz belonged to Jacques, and now it added up why Avery hadn't come down here with us. He was a dead man down here without the money.

"Avery didn't tell us anything about any money," Rori said, a desperation in her tone. I watched her hand discreetly slip a steak knife under the table.

"Look." I folded by hands over the table. "All we know is what he told us. That you were looking for some help, and that he'd been working with you for a while."

Jacques studied my face, then started to say something, but was interrupted by a tiny voice. We all shifted our gaze downward.

"Chiclets?" A five- or six-year-old girl that Rori and I had seen walking the beach earlier held a big tray of multicolored Chiclets. "*Un peso por dos. Dos pesos por cinco,*" she said, and revealed a tiny set of yellow and darkened baby teeth. Her black hair was frizzy and pulled back in a dirty green scrunchie, and she wore a tattered little sundress with pink sandals duct-taped on the heels.

"*No gracias, hija,*" Jacques said, and handed her a silver-and-gold coin. She smiled and walked two tables down to work the next couple. "You two did not come down here to pay off his debt, then?" He seemed to be thinking over what to do with us.

"Didn't he call and let you know we would be coming?" I asked.

"I think it is time to go somewhere a little quieter," Jacques said. "Jean-Pierre, escort our friends to their room."

2

I put my last two dollars down on the table, and we were escorted briskly down the narrow pathway to our little room that I still wasn't sure how we'd pay for. Jean-Pierre locked the dead bolt behind us and stayed at the door with the same emotionless routine, and I wondered if he ever got bored staring menacingly at people and let his mind wander. Like, maybe he was thinking about puppies and lilacs the whole time. Maybe it was like me with my poetry. It allowed my mind to go elsewhere just before shit hit the fan.

"Sit down, both of you," Jacques said, and gestured toward the kitchen.

We both sat at the small, round table at the center of the kitchenette without argument. This man could make us rich but could also make us dead. It was almost dark outside now with just a red sliver of light visible over the coastline. Jacques's man flipped on the overhead light.

"Look, I'm sorry if we've made a mistake coming here. I thought we could be business partners, like Avery," I said, trying to strike a conciliatory tone, though it felt like pleading.

"Yes, well, your presence has caused my colleagues a lot of concern. You were followed here, no? And also, your brother has not responded to our calls over the past few days. These things concern us, as you can understand."

"Avery's camp got raided," Rori said, and leaned forward in her chair, pressing her palms flat on the table. "You guys should at least know that much."

Jacques looked back at his man, then at us. "We talked to your brother before he was to go down to Big Sur. He tells us that the money is safe, then he calls us once to tell me you are coming, then he stops. The raid, the policeman chasing you here. We do not like sloppiness."

"That was *not* the police," Rori said.

"Then who the fuck was it?" Jacques said sharply, his jugular bulging on his neck.

"He looked like a cop," Jean-Pierre added from the doorway. "And the lady came to use the pay phone."

"I don't know who the fuck that was," I said. "I swear to god, man. That guy has been on us since we talked to Avery."

"I do not know this man," Jacques said. "And if he was following you, then maybe Avery has gotten more sloppy than we know."

"Could be the Sinaloa," Jean-Pierre said.

"Shut your fucking mouth," Jacques snapped, and turned to face Jean-Pierre. "Those fucking farmers and peasants make a move here, and we bury them."

Jean-Pierre shrugged as if to say it didn't matter, but he'd struck a nerve with the Sinaloa question, which made it sound like Jacques had his own set of problems down here.

"We saw Avery Friday," I said. "He was just going to lay low until he could go back and get the money in Santa Cruz."

"Yes, this is the story we have as well, but we called this place, the Pfeiffer Cliffs, and he is not there. He has disappeared."

I felt that bile surge up and tasted it, raw and hot. Avery wasn't safe, and who knew what the bounty hunter had done to him to get information. I restrained my emotion as best I could and cleared my throat. "We're telling you the truth, man. He told us to come down because you needed help. That's all we know."

"We know as much as you do about Avery," Rori said calmly. "We came here for work."

Jacques paused, leaned back in his chair, and crossed his arms. "I am not stupid, you know. People come to Mexico because they are running from something. They deny this, but it is always true. I know why Avery came to me. But you, why are you here?"

"We're here because we're broke. My parents are dead, and I lost my job after the recession. We're hungry. Avery told us you could help. Plain and simple." I prayed that the routine resolved any concerns about our past so he wouldn't look into it—having American law enforcement in the family wouldn't look good on our résumé. "That guy following us could be anybody," I said, remembering Jean-Pierre's comment.

Jacques unfolded his hands and leaned back in his chair. "If you hear from Avery before I do, you will tell me immediately. Do you swear this to me?"

"Yes, of course," I said, and nodded. Rori hesitated and nodded as well.

"Good. I hope that he surfaces and that he pays. If not, you will have to pay his share. Is that understood?"

I nodded again, feeling the fist in my stomach start to relax.

Rori said, "Something Avery never mentioned, what exactly will we be doing?"

Jacques smiled and leaned forward, glaring back and forth at us. "Have either of you any experience on the ocean?"

"We're from Central Valley," Rori said.

"But we're fast learners," I added quickly.

"Today is Sunday. On Wednesday I will have Jean-Pierre pick you up at six a.m. The trip will take three days. It is all by boat, so I hope you are both, as you say, fast learners."

"Can I ask how much this pays?" I asked.

"I will have Beto move you into my suite overlooking the ocean. You will stay there as long as you work for me. Also, Remy will come by your room to fit you for your wardrobes. You cannot look like transients on board the *California Dreamin'*."

Rori looked to be fighting a smile that crept into the corner of her thin, pursed lips and said, "But the pay, Jacques. And what *exactly* are we doing?"

"Ah, yes. You will learn in this business that the less you know, the better—do not worry, you will be paid very well for your troubles."

Rori opened her mouth to speak, but Jacques raised his hand, signaling that the conversation was over, and he stood. He extended his hand to her, and they shook. Then he shook mine, his hands soft but strong and slightly dry. They left, and when I closed the door, I slid the dead bolt shut.

3

Rori stood, and I met her in the middle of the room. She glared at me, then smiled, then burst into an excited grin. I took another step forward, but she leapt into my arms, wrapping her body around mine, and kissed me hard on the mouth. I kissed her back, and she bit my bottom lip until she nearly broke the skin. When she released, I tasted copper.

"Fuck me, we did it," Rori said, and slid down until her feet touched the floor. She pulled me toward the bed, and I fell on top of her. I kissed her again, and I felt her nails dig into my sides when someone knocked sharply on the door.

"Yeah," I said, Rori kissing my neck.

The knock sounded again, louder, and I got up and brushed my hair down and went to the door. I looked through the peephole, and standing there was a bellman, so I opened it.

"Señor Jacques has told us to bring you to the presidential suite. Please follow me." His name tag said *Beto*. He was about five four and wore a formal maroon suit and held an intensely erect posture. "Leave the bags, we will bring them."

We followed Beto down the pathway lined with ivy and bird of paradise each with parrot-shaped orange blossoms protruding from the grassy branches. After ascending an iron staircase, we arrived at a large, hand-carved wooden door, and Beto furnished an old brass key that he then handed it to me.

"Thank you, Beto," I said, and slipped him a couple of pesos. We now had zero currency.

Rori followed me in, and I closed the door. The room was covered in matte salmon tile with a huge dining room with a thick, carved wood table like the door. We walked in farther, and there was a full bar just in front of the wall of windows that offered a panoramic view of the entire private beach. At the back, through another set of doors, we stepped into a bedroom with the largest bed I'd ever seen with rows of white pillows and thick, downy blankets that we fell into and sunk deeply. She kissed me again in the billowy folds of the bedding.

Later, after Beto had brought our luggage, I poured Jack Daniel's into crystal tumblers from the bar, and Rori took hers and walked outside to light a cigarette. I stepped out and stared at the flickers from the bonfires dotting the length of the beach and heard an occasional hoot from the beach side. The scene warmed my chest, made me feel something I hadn't felt in a long time. If ever. I felt a tiny bit of joy bloom inside me. I sat next to Rori on a matching wooden Adirondack chair; the air had cooled. I took her hand, and she rested her head against my shoulder. I kissed it.

"This is pretty fucking amazing," she said.

"It is. I never dreamed it would be like this. Avery never told me anything. I guess he couldn't."

"It's just. Avery. If we had taken him and he didn't have the money, do you think Jacques would have—" She stopped.

"Yeah, Avery would be dead right now," I said, a numbness inside of me that hadn't yet brightened into pain, or fear, or sadness. Maybe because we hadn't heard from him, there was still a glimmer of hope that kept all the other emotions at bay.

"God, I hope he's okay. I know what my father's capable of. You know."

"So do I," I said, rubbing at my ribs and touching my slowly healing face.

"One thing that keeps bothering me, though," she said.

"What?"

"This guy would kill Avery if he could. Hell, if he even knew where to find him. What's he going to do to us?"

"Let's not double-cross him or lose any of his money," I said.

"Sure, but you never really hear stories about people walking away rich in these scenarios. Right?"

"Dead or in jail, you mean?" I said.

"Yeah. Sort of. But also, what does this make us? Even if we do make it out?"

"It makes us survivalists," I said. "But I know what you mean. How far can we go down this path before we're no better than your fucked-up father."

"Right. I mean, we're running from corruption and evil. What happens when we become that? Who do we run from then?"

"I guess that's when people run from us," I said.

"The type of people that chase down guys like my dad. And Art."

"I mean, isn't that what we want? Power to help the powerless and punish corruption?"

"Yes. That is exactly what I want. That's what you are, Heath. I know I never responded to your story you told me about that horrible place. That hotel. But what you did was right. You saved those kids. I feel like you're concerned that killing those guys made you evil, but it didn't. You did the right thing. You saved those kids. So maybe some people think you're a bad guy. Maybe we can be good bad guys?"

"I don't think good and bad are real. Morality is shapeless and subjective. What you and I are, doesn't matter. It matters that we survive and settle our scores. Once we have the money and the power, we wield it fairly. Right?" I felt my heart rate picking up and straightened in my chair.

"Jacques probably thinks he's fair, is all I'm saying." Rori shifted her body so she faced me. We locked eyes. "My father thinks he's fair."

"Well, then we take a few big scores, and we run. We buy a house somewhere low-key and disappear." I shrugged. She had a valid point, and I spun my father's ring on my finger.

"We have to go back to the Valley at some point. You know we have to," she said.

"I know. Eventually we will." Our conversation hard robbed me of the happiness I'd felt a moment ago, and I wanted to change the subject, focus on the present. "But Wednesday though, we set sail."

"You don't think Art will catch us on the US side?" she asked. "Or the Feds?"

"Jacques seems like he's got a pretty clever scheme going. Let's just go to work and see what happens. I think Art will back off now that he knows we're connected to something bigger."

Rori smiled. "I think so, too. It's the first time in my life that fucker can't get to me. I feel kind of trapped, but kind of free. If that makes sense."

I smiled too. This poor girl, finally eighteen and finally out from under her father's oppressive weight. "Let's pay attention, and if it gets dicey, we cut and run," I said.

"Deal," she said.

"Deal."

"And, Heath," she said. "I love you."

Her comment landed like a wrecking ball on my already tattered emotional chords. Because I had been trying to focus on survival to survive, but also because, before I found out she'd lied to me, she was the closest thing to love I'd ever felt. I was still trying to forgive her, but I realized in that moment that I couldn't help resenting her, too. I breathed the confusion away and kissed her.

We toasted with shots of Jack Daniel's and drank them down. We made love until we were sweaty and tired. I opened a window, and we let our naked bodies cool in the tepid breezes chased by the tides through and into our room. The night grew darker beyond our balcony, and the chatter of people around faraway bonfires slowly faded away into the night.

Chapter Twenty-Two
Monday, August 22, 1988
Art

1

Art struggled to keep his eyes open the whole way home. So when he pulled off the 99 toward Shadow Valley and boarded the 198 at 4:37 a.m., he sighed and took another shot. His eyes were as red as the devil and puffy with black rings. It was un-fucking-acceptable to return to Shadow Valley empty-handed a second time—he'd misjudged these kids in Big Sur, and he could let that one go. But now he'd been fucked over twice by the little shits.

When Art rounded the corner, up Mineral King, the club came into view. Thoughts of his failures raced through his mind, and the only thing that satiated him was the thought of Heath's body beaten to roadkill with his baton. He imagined their smug and smiling faces safe in their little room at La Fonda. He parked and breathed to collect his thoughts—he needed the file on Burke, and he needed Avery in his custody. He had a plan formulating to draw the bastards out of Mexico.

Art rowed into his office through the back door and locked himself inside. He didn't like being in the club at night. It seemed so dark and empty and depressing. These early morning hours made it feel possible for ghosts to lurk behind doors and in shadows. But the only monsters out there were people, and Art was the motherfucker that went bump in the night. He reminded himself of that whenever he felt any thought to the contrary sneak into his waking consciousness.

Art limped to his desk, where his answering machine blinked in the dim room. He reclined into his large leather chair and pressed Play, and Tyra's voice filled the air.

"Art, I dropped the package at the hospital in Rosarito. They started asking questions, and I just told them that I found him like that. I'm heading home. I need a few days' rest. Call me at the house if you need anything."

Art deleted the message, and another message played.

"Art, this is Jessman. It was good to hear from you. I pulled the file you mentioned after hours and made a copy. Meet me at our regular spot tomorrow. Well, Sunday at ten a.m. Don't forget the payment. And, Art, I hope you're okay."

The answering machine stopped, and Art deleted the message. Sitting on the couch against the far wall, he carefully kicked off his boots. His mind raced and his pulse kicked hard in his temple. He reached for the flask in his back pocket and slugged the rest down. When he closed his eyes, he could see the kids' faces burned into the inside of his eyelids. Their smirks, and Heath's face when he smashed into his truck at Pfeiffer. They thought they'd won, that this was all over. But Art always got his guy. If they were going to run drugs, that meant that they had to come back to California. Where else would they run them to? Americans with their obsessive need for mind alteration at any cost. His drinking disgusted him. He would quit again. When this was all over.

2

When Tracy Jessman stepped into the café the next morning, Art watched her scan the room for potential hostiles—or anyone that might balk at seeing them together. Noting that it was clear, she approached Art while he sipped his coffee at their usual booth at the right corner of the narrow restaurant.

The Sidecar Café was built out of an old railroad car and had a stainless-steel exterior, and inside, booths lined the walls like passenger's seats, the kitchen visible behind the counter at the center. Art slid the cream and ramekin of sugar across the table when she sat.

"Officer Dominguez," Tracy said, and pulled a cup of coffee closer, adding a dash of cream with a tablespoon of sugar. The spoon clinked inside the ceramic cup when she stirred.

She looked just like Art remembered her from her first day on the force twenty-five years ago—her hair pulled back in a ponytail, the trademark tortoiseshell glasses, the same small, round face and sleepy eyes—a look that made her the perfect covert insider. She appeared to be a person who lived by the book and acted like a person concerned with fastidious detail. The fact that she received extra scrutiny being one of the only women on the force back then made her even more vehement about a work ethic beyond reproach. And it had played, because she'd made detective after ten years and was able to draw information for Art undetected since.

"You said you found the file," Art said, skipping the pleasantries. He was tired, and his leg felt like a handful of thumbtacks had been dropped into his cast.

"I've got it—are you okay?"

"I got rammed off a cliff in Big Sur," Art said, and tapped his cast. Tracy leaned over slightly to view it. "Then I was run off by a cartel in Mexico. And meanwhile, my club's been shut down, and I can't figure out why exactly."

"Jesus, I'm sorry." Tracy opened a small leather satchel that she'd brought in, and pulled a manila envelope free, setting it on the table.

"That the file on Burke?"

"Look, I know you'll keep my name out of it if anything comes up, but this—" She glanced over her shoulder, then back at Art. "If you're planning something with Burke, you're going to get burned to the ground. He's chief now."

Art reached for the envelope, and she pulled it back.

"It's nothing. I'm simply clarifying some unfinished business," Art said. "It won't come back on you." Art took a legal envelope with five hundred cash from the pocket of his jeans and slid it toward her.

"More coffee, you two? Or are you ready to order?" said a heavyset waitress named Liz, jarring Art from their conversation.

"We're just having coffee," Art said, and the waitress didn't hide her look of resentment for them taking up a prime table and not ordering food. Art would tip her well for the inconvenience.

"Well then, let me know if you change your mind," Liz said, and took the menus with her while she strode away with surprising buoyancy.

Tracy took the envelope, and Art pulled the file from her, placing it beside him on the booth.

"Be careful," she said. "He's a sadist if you piss him off. And he's been on a tear since his daughter was taken."

"She wasn't taken against her will," Art said.

"Yeah, well, I don't doubt that. I'd run from the bastard too. But still, don't get caught in his cross hairs. Because he's a thirty-cal sniper rifle right now."

"I appreciate your concern. I'll be fine. And thank you." Art slid awkwardly out of the booth and leaned on his crutch to stand.

Tracy watched him, then slid out, too. She leaned toward him like she wanted to help but stopped herself. "Take care," she said.

"I'll call you if I need anything further. I appreciate this."

Tracy smiled and turned away, slipping quietly through the restaurant and out into the already warm August morning. Art had the file; now he needed the kid, as long as Burke's people hadn't killed him yet. Art would have to look carefully through the file, but he was certain he'd find the connection. That bar out on Goshen, with the neon lights, the little motel behind it. The young girl in the negligee. These Triad bastards were back, and Burke wasn't only running interference, he was part owner. Art just had to prove it. Or, maybe he didn't, as long as he proved it to himself.

Chapter Twenty-Three
Monday, August 22, 1988
Heath

1

The next morning, the sun sliced between a thin gap in the sheer curtains over the sliding doors to the balcony. The bedroom felt tacky with the brine of ocean and sweat. Sitting up in the oversized bed, I lit my second cigarette and brushed Rori's tangled red hair back while she slept. I inhaled deeply but coughed, my mouth parched. I slugged a shot of watered-down whiskey from a tumbler on my nightstand.

I stood and pulled on an embroidered terry cotton robe and moved toward the living room. The robe parted while I walked, and it lured me into a false sense of nobility, like a royal cape of some sort. At the bar, I filled my crystal tumbler with ice and some tomato juice.

According to a clock hanging above the bar, it was 10:30 a.m., which made me feel guilty for wasting such a perfect morning. I poured more tomato juice for Rori and mixed in some ice with a small silver spoon. I started to turn and noticed the light on the room phone blinking. I pressed the button, and a message played from room service that said our breakfast was ready and to call down. I hit the call button and they answered.

"Señor Walker, are you ready for your breakfast?"

"I didn't order any breakfast."

"Señor Jacques has arranged it. Would you like it now?"

"Sure, send it up," I said.

I walked back to the bedroom, and Rori stirred and sat up. "Who was that?"

"That was room service. Jacques sent up breakfast."

"Ugh, I drank too much." She sat up, lit a cigarette, and stared down at the beach through the harsh light. I sat beside her and stroked her knee.

"Should we go down and surf?" I asked.

"I wanted to go so bad in Salsipuedes," she said. I handed her the drink, and we clinked glasses. She took a tiny sip and set it down.

"It's settled, then," I said.

2

We'd just slipped into bathing suits when a knock on the door came. Beto pushed a large room service cart in and stopped near the wood table. He slowly removed shiny metal domes from about six plates that contained fresh fruit, scrambled eggs, carnitas, tortillas, salsa, and everything we needed to make the perfect breakfast burritos.

We stuffed a little bit of everything into tortillas, rolled the burritos, and ate quickly and quietly. After, we took a couple of Coronas from the bar, towels from the bathroom, and our sandals and stepped out of the suite. We found the Volkswagen Beetle in the parking lot and retrieved the longboard we'd strapped awkwardly to the roof. Then we traversed a steep trail etched in the sandy hillside from decades of foot traffic. The private beach was inviting, and we pranced over the hot sand until we set up under a palapa reserved for us by Jacques.

We sat on our towels and finished our beers while we watched the waves and studied the tides. The surf produced small swells that peeled from right to left in perfect lines rippling out to the deeper stretch of ocean like from a pebble in placid water.

"It's going to feel nice to surf without a wetsuit," Rori said.

"I still haven't surfed at all."

"It's not *that* hard, at least probably not on a board this big," Rori said.

"Chiclets, Chiclets, Chiclets?" A small girl that I recognized from the previous night at the restaurant stopped near our palapa. She had refilled the cardboard box, which hung around her neck with braided duct tape, and I had to admire how resourceful the poor were down here.

"*Aqui*," I said, and raised my hand. She scampered in her taped-up sandals and size-too-big clothes through the sand toward us, smiling so brightly, it made me feel sad in a way. "*No tengo dinero*," I said when she got to us, panting. Her little distended belly pushed in and out with each breath.

The little girl's face dropped, and she started to turn to go.

"*Como se llama?*" Rori said.

"*Me llama?*" she said, and looked confused, and I could tell she wasn't used to the tourists asking her name. "Erica." Then she rattled off several explosive sentences in Spanish that flew right past me, and even Rori looked confused.

"*Me llama es* Rori. And *el es* Heath," she said, and smiled, and strands of her red hair tangled around her eyes and mouth from the soft breeze. The pixie cut had been rushed, and her bangs were still long

"*Eso es por surfer? Que no?*" Erica said, and she jumped on the board and got low like a surfer. She'd probably seen plenty of surfers come through here. There were probably locals, too, but I doubted Jacques let any locals on this beach.

"You want to surf, little girl?" Rori said, and she jumped up and brushed the sand from her butt and picked up the surfboard. The little girl squealed and pushed her whole box of Chiclets onto my lap and followed Rori, who dragged the surfboard toward the water.

They waded out about twenty feet before Rori picked Erica up. She clung to Rori as if both terrified and excited by the waves. Her clothes were matted to her skin, and her thick hair curled in defiance of the water. Moments later a small, broken wave rolled toward them. Rori set Erica on the center of the board and pushed. The little girl beamed with excitement and seemed to have pretty good balance in her frog-like stance. She fell off when the board collided with land, and jumped in excitement until Rori came back in to claim her.

It didn't take long for Erica to feel more comfortable in the water. Rori seemed to sense this and paddled out into some slightly larger waves. They caught a shoulder together, Erica riding on the nose, legs crossed, and coasted into the shore, laughing.

3

They beckoned me out, and I got up and brushed myself off. It was finally my turn to try and surf. I waded past the breakers, holding the board until the water was waist-deep. I then lay on the board the way I'd seen it done on *The Endless Summer* and in Santa Cruz.

Paddling hard, I pushed past the breakers and paddled toward the largest swells. I turned around, and I could see Rori and Erica jumping and waving to me fifty yards back at the shore. A wave crested up behind me, and it looked like it was just about perfect, so I paddled hard and got out in front of it. Then the nose dropped, and the back pitched up, sending me nose-diving into the ocean. I flipped and got smashed and rolled by the turbulent wave. I stayed under for several seconds while I held my breath. Then, just before I blacked out, I gained a footing on the sand and thrust myself up for air.

I took a huge breath and held on to the board, and when I looked back toward the shore, Rori and Erica were laughing so hard, it looked like they were tearing up.

I smiled; then I started to laugh, and I continued to laugh while two more waves crashed over me, but I didn't care. I felt alive in a way that I never thought possible. In fact, I couldn't remember the last time I laughed this hard, or at all. I couldn't remember the last time I let myself enjoy something so simple and so beautiful as this moment. Shared with Rori and this brave little girl and this vast ocean. I was hooked and I wanted more of this. I wanted to surf forever.

Another wave crashed behind me, and I pushed off and caught the broken white water. Planing along on my belly for a second, I felt brave again and slowly stood. The board wobbled, but I stayed up, and I couldn't help but let out a whoop of excitement. I rode it into the shore, where Rori and

Erica were giddy now. I hugged Rori and felt a small, wet body and realized that Erica was holding on to Rori's leg, grinning up at us. She was a sweet kid, and I wondered if she had parents around, or if she was an orphan, like me.

At that moment, a stocky man with a Polaroid camera approached us. "*Un* photograph?" he said in a thick Spanglish accent.

"How much?" I asked.

"*Un dólar,*" he said, and I knew it was a ridiculous price, but it was hard to argue with people trying to scratch out a living down here.

"*No tengo mas dinero,*" I said.

"Room charge okay," he said.

"*Sí, por favor,*" I said, and held up two fingers.

The three of us posed, and the guy snapped two photos, then handed them to us. It was white and undeveloped.

I handed it to Rori and whispered, "We should probably burn that." She nodded.

"*Gracias, Heed,*" Erica said, trying my name on, having probably never heard it before today. The man leaned down and rattled off something in Spanish that I didn't get, and Erica hugged my leg, then Rori's, and ran up to grab her box of Chiclets. She sprinted off in the direction of a young boy selling oversized straw sombreros down the beach.

"What an adorable little child," Rori said while I dragged the board back up to our spot in the sand. Erica had left a small box of Chiclets on our towels.

"Looks like we have a lot of Chiclets to eat," I said, and tore the wrapping off one pack and popped a piece in my mouth. It was a cloyingly sweet spearmint flavor that I could do without, but I chewed it anyway and hoped the little girl would be back.

"You want to surf again?" Rori asked a while later.

I looked out at the perfect blue-green waves and wanted to be back inside of it all, feeling the slack and swell of the tides, but I knew why she was asking.

"You go. I'll go next," I said, and she kissed me, picked up the board, and ran straight out into the ocean with authority. I wished we had two boards. With a little bit of money, that shouldn't be a problem. And we'd have plenty of that soon.

4

Later that afternoon, while Rori and I were sleeping off our afternoon-in-the-sun hangover, the door sounded off again. I leapt up, my mouth completely dry and my heart beating in my chest. Also, my skin felt hot, like it was glowing, from the sun exposure. I'd also had too many Coronas, but I lit a cigarette and grabbed my crystal tumbler and poured a splash of soda water with ice and lime, then opened the door.

"*Buenos tardes,* señor Heath," Beto said. He was back, but he had with him another very well-dressed woman in a suit with a button-down blouse and short black heels.

"I'm Remy," she said, and smiled with thick lips that had heavily applied red lipstick. "I am here to take your sizes." She had an accent similar to Jacques, and she pulled a rolled-up measuring tape from her bag that had some other equipment in it.

"Come in, I'll wake up Rori," I said. And she entered, walked over to the table, and started to unpack some of her tools.

I went back into the bedroom and shook Rori awake. She sat up, and her eyes were bloodshot from the sun and salt water. "Room service again?" she asked.

"No, it's a seamstress, I think. She just needs to measure us."

"Measure us for what?"

I paused. "I don't know, but probably because Jacques doesn't want us wearing tied-dyed shirts and ball caps on the ship Wednesday."

She swung her legs out of bed, and the backs of her calves were slightly red from the sun. Then she stood and took a drink of water from the bedside. "So very kind of him."

We walked back out to the living room, and Remy smiled wider now, and I wondered how many more of these

French Canadians were down here in Baja? They didn't exactly blend in with the locals. But, she had an air of authority about clothing, so I was interested to see what she came up with.

After about twenty minutes, Remy had taken all of our measurements, and she instructed us to sit in the chairs. We both sat, and she opened another of her bags and pulled out item after item until we had damn near a whole department store spread over the table.

"Who's first?" she said. "You both look like you fell asleep at a carnival."

Rori volunteered first, and they tidied her pixie cut, keeping her bangs long, then bleaching and toning everything white blonde. She looked striking. And older, and rich. With mine, she trimmed it to a practical military cut and dyed it back to a respectable chestnut brown. Once we had our outfits, we'd be regular high society. Except, well, the money and etiquette.

Chapter Twenty-Four
Wednesday, August 24, 1988
Heath

1

"Hey, Jean-Pierre. We still haven't discussed details. Like, how much we're getting paid," I said. We'd been driving for about forty-five minutes in a brown, full-size van with tinted windows and large crucifixes branded on the side and hood.

"Talk to Jacques," Jean-Pierre said in his oddly soft and high-pitched voice for such a huge man. He wore a white robe with a black tunic like a Trappist monk, and his brown hair was shaved close to the scalp. Sitting behind him at an angle, I got a closer look at his neck tattoo: it was a fleur-de-lis with flames. It was fucking weird, but so was this whole situation, and I wondered again but wasn't dumb enough to ask, how the hell a group of French Canadians came to operate a monastery slash drug ring out of Baja. I had questions, but Jean-Pierre wasn't our guy.

"You don't say much, do you, Mr. Pierre?" Rori said, having a little fun.

Jean-Pierre glanced at Rori in the rearview mirror, then at me. "I do not make friends with mules. They tend to—disappear." He made a gesture with his right hand like a magician.

A second passed and Rori said, "Nice neck tattoo." She covered her smile with her hand, and I nudged her. She ignored me and pulled a cigarette from a softback wedged into her cutoffs, lit one, and inhaled deeply. We continued without talking while the Billboard Top 100 from the previous decade played old hits: "Livin' on a Prayer," "Walk like an Egyptian," "La Bamba."

We drove into Ensenada and angled along the narrow roads lined with aging stucco-and-adobe buildings into an industrial shipyard. The port bustled with cruise ships, two full bays of pleasure crafts, and a couple of cargo ships. We parked and followed Jean-Pierre down a floating dock and through a barbed wire–framed metal gate to a slip that held a forty- or fifty-foot power yacht. Jacques stood on the deck in a similar outfit as before, and I wondered if he had a closet full of tweed suits.

"Welcome to your new home," Jacques said, and stretched his arms wide, his brilliant smile flashing in the morning sunlight.

Another man emerged from the belly of the ship and stood beside Jacques. He was a slight Latino with a square, handsome face and shaved head, and the first non-Canadian I'd seen on Jacques's management team. He looked like a nautical brand had thrown up all over him with navy blue slacks, boat shoes, a button-down shirt, and a seersucker jacket.

"This is Juan DeMarco, he's your handler. He will also be the captain of the ship, for now. But you both will need to know every operation on this boat. Do everything he tells you, understand?" Jacques said.

"We're quick learners," Rori said.

Jacques glared at Rori; his eyes bulged slightly. "These voyages can be difficult. This, your first trip, it is short, but you will need to learn very much to prepare for the long trips."

"Especially if there are twenty-foot seas—and there usually are," Juan said, and hopped boyishly onto the dock, extending his hand. He had a charismatic air, and up close I could see that he had a strong brow line that had deep scars in it, and his nose was flattened in the middle and a little off-center. His accent fluctuated slightly like someone who had control of both English and Spanish so well that he slid into one or the other depending on the mood or the sentence.

"Heath," I said, slightly confused.

"You thought I would sound different, right? Born and raised in Cali, my man. Also, DeMarco's Italian." He grinned while that sunk in. "It's actually Jimenez. I changed it back when I thought I could go pro in boxing. Everyone loves an Italian boxer after Rocky fucking Balboa…" He smiled, trailing off as if wondering how it all went wrong and ended up here. Then he sniffed and rubbed at his nose, and I had an idea.

"This is Rori—"

"Juan DeMarco, *guapa*." He grabbed her hand and kissed it. He held it a second too long, and she pulled away. "Your wife is beautiful, uh…"

"Again, it's Heath. And we're just—"

"We're *just* married," Rori said. "And this is our honeymoon. So, take it easy around the corners." She winked and leaned into my shoulder.

"All right, enough with the shaking of the hands, let us go below deck so we can become on the same page," Jacques said, and motioned for us to follow.

2

We stepped onto the deck of the *California Dreamin'*, *San Diego, CA*. It was a good-sized boat, not huge, but big enough to have a metal crane on the roof that held a four-person dinghy. We boarded from the back and walked up one large step to the main deck that extended into the center of the boat. The middle held a full bar, couches, a coffee table, and at the very front, there was a small formal dining room. At center right, a small spiral staircase led up to the helm. Left of that, a staircase descended into the belly.

"Juan lives in San Diego, and so does the ship," Jacques explained while we walked. "You are supposed to check in with customs if you dock in another country or with another ship, but he leaves early, and you will get back to San Diego in the afternoon. This way it looks like you have just taken the boat out for the day." He stopped and looked at us. "If anyone is really paying attention, you know, it looks like a common day trip out in the ocean."

He continued, and we followed him downstairs into the hull, and there were four closed bedroom doors down a short hallway. "The room on the left is for Juan, and the room on the right is for you two. This is the shared bathroom, and at the back is the conference room," Jacques said, pointing at doors while he passed.

We stepped inside the conference room, and it was a small space and nearly empty except for a table at the center with nautical charts pinned to its surface. There were also some nautical instruments and a small liquor cabinet against the wall.

"We always drop at the same locations, but we make other stops to keep up the appearance of a pleasure cruise. There is never to be an unscheduled stop. Understood?" Jacques stared at Juan, who raised his hands.

"Got it, boss. No unscheduled stops."

"You two will be steering as well, so you will need to spend time up top with Juan, and he can show you how it all works. You will take shifts, so you need to be alert. Except in San Diego, we use moorings, so there is no chance of anyone boarding our ship." He paused and looked at Juan again. "*Nobody* is allowed on the ship."

Juan looked at us. "I let a girl in Santa Cruz on one time, and you would think I compromised everything," Juan said. Jacques reached into his jacket and patted his gun. "Never again, I promise," Juan quickly added.

"This works very simply. In case you are questioned by anyone, like the Coast Guard, you two are the spoiled rich kids who got this boat as a gift from your grandfather, a wedding present. No? You will use the names and IDs that I will provide for you, and let them know it was a recent purchase. I have the release paperwork filled out from the previous owner with no date so it looks like this is all true." Jacques touched some papers folded up inside a plastic sleeve.

"Doesn't the Coast Guard track boats coming down here and back?" I asked. "Like with radar?"

"This is a good question and the reason for my clever idea here. San Diego is such a busy port, there is no way they can track every single vessel in and out. So, they track suspicious ones. Usually foreign-owned ships. This is why I have three Americans and an American ship. It provides for less suspicion."

I nodded and pictured a bunch of Columbians crammed on a fishing boat headed for the States, and wondered if that was what he meant.

"Is our Volkswagen okay back at the resort?" I said.

"I had a man go and pick it up. It is safely at the monastery in Puerto Nuevo."

"One thing, Jacques, before we go. How much do we get paid for…all of this?" Rori said, making a sweeping motion with her hand.

Jacques smiled and nodded. "Yes, I have not gotten there. This short trip is a trial. I will pay you both ten thousand combined. The long trip, when you return with the money, you will receive three percent of the total."

"Three points? For taking all the risk?" she said.

Jacques side-sat against the table that looked to be bolted down. "You are taking none of the financial risk. And also, that is three percent of the total. Or twenty-five thousand each on average. If you do not like the pay, I will find somebody else." That was a shit-ton of money, although I didn't like the thinly veiled threat this early on.

"No, no, that's totally fair," I said. Twenty-five thousand each, fifty thousand total was enough to buy a goddamn villa somewhere. Rori was stunned into silence.

"Anything else? No? I didn't think so. Stay on the course, I will have eyes on you for safety along the way. The San Diego drops are very simple. You will go up and be there in a few hours, you will dock the boat in the slip and go and check in to your hotel. Have some drinks, makes some friends, be rich assholes. The cargo will be unloaded overnight the first night, and the second, the money will be placed. You get back to the boat at five a.m. and come straight back."

"I'm sure I'm not supposed to ask, but what is it we're dealing with?" Rori said. "We deserve to know that much, right?"

"You know, I am starting to like you." Jacques reached into his coat pocket, and I flinched. "Easy, Heath. It is this." He tossed a small baggie of dark blonde hash onto the nautical maps. "Do not smoke it if you are steering the ship."

"Hash," Juan said. "These Canucks are like the hash whisperers. This shit's the best I've ever had, hands down."

I picked it up, and it smelled dank and skunky and familiar. It was the hash that Avery had mailed me in that coffee can what seemed like a lifetime ago.

"For this trip, you will make five thousand each. It is not negotiable. You are successful and learn how to operate the boat, well, then you can graduate to the long trip with Juan as your captain. The long run is in three weeks."

"We do one run a week," Juan said.

"Yes, this is correct. This is as often as most people use their boats in San Diego. So if all are in agreement, then we can drink on it," Jacques said, and he walked to the small cabinet in the corner and removed an ornate crystal bottle. He poured some into a large snifter, swirled, and took a sip. He handed the glass to Rori, and she smelled it and pulled her head away.

"It smells like vomit and berries," she said.

"This is the finest cognac in the world, Louis the XIII. It is a blend between forty and one hundred years old."

Rori took a measured sip and coughed, cringing. She passed it to Juan, who took a sip, shrugged, then handed it to me. I swallowed down the rest, and it warmed me, but without the burn of whiskey. It had a velvety texture, a smoothness that tingled on my tongue. It was a nice touch; it made me aware of the wealth and sophistication of Jacques's operation.

Jacques returned the bottle and snifter to the cabinet and locked it. He checked his watch. "Let us go above deck and get your bags for your first trip."

"Wait, one more question. Don't we need a license for any of this? A boat this big?"

Jacques smiled, and a smug look spread over his face, making his wide-set eyes wrinkle in the corners. "Heath, this is why it is so clever. You don't need a license, and they are overwhelmed with pleasure craft in San Diego—they really cannot track our movements. It is the safest way to do this, I assure you. You need a license for commercial activity only."

Jacques turned, and we followed him back to the main level, and when we got to the rear of the ship, he shook my hand, then Rori's. "Good luck out there. This is an exciting new chapter for both of us." He paused and gestured toward two large, black luggage bags sitting on the back of this ship. "There is your luggage, now go unpack while we get under way."

3

Just out of earshot, Jacques and Juan had another short conversation. Rori and I walked to the back of the ship, where two brand-new luggage bags with our fake names embroidered on the tags had been placed. I picked them up and carried them through the boat and down the stairs. Rori followed.

The room was small inside with a round, full-size bed in the center and a tiny closet that sat empty. I set our bags down inside the closet, and Rori and I started to unpack a few of the outfits. Khakis, slacks, Topsiders, seersucker. Also, a pair of leather loafers with the fancy tassels I'd seen while shopping at the mall with Mom and Dad.

Rori opened hers and pulled out several wide-brimmed hats, bathing suits, and a number of designer-looking suits, slacks, some jewelry which had to be fake but was quality, and an array of pumps and sandals. She smiled, kissed me, and peeled off clothing while she strode to the door to lock it. When she turned back, she stared at me, her chin low, a few strands of hair falling over her eyes. The danger had excited her, and I was in her cross hairs. I was excited, too.

"Rori, we need to go topside and help this guy—"

She quickly closed the distance between us, and I stepped back, bumping the mattress. She grabbed my chin between her thumb and finger and gave my head a playful push, then traced her fingertips down the front of my slightly sweaty *Baja 1000* T-shirt. A gift shop purchase I had charged to the room. Her fingers wrapped around my belt, she violently tugged me closer.

"Heath, look at us now," she said, breathing into my ear and kissing my neck. "This is kind of hot." She bit my neck hard, and it stung when I pulled away.

"We should really—"

She slipped a hand down my cargo shorts and grabbed me firmly. I stiffened at her touch and that made her smile. When she released, she yanked my shorts past my hips, and they gathered around my ankles. She pushed my head slowly down, and I kissed her exposed belly. She tasted salty, and I licked a few small beads of sweat holding against her skin, her almost invisibly fine hairs. I pulled her tight jean shorts down and smelled her, and she pushed my head toward her. She moaned when I kissed her.

"Choke me until I come," she said. She fell back onto the bed and put my hands on her throat the way she had before. This time, I obliged her, though I was still not sure about it.

Lying in the circular bed, our new clothes were strewn around the room with our old ones. I stroked her shoulder and observed the contrast of my dark-tan skin against her chalky pallor. I kissed her head and pulled her toward me to rest. At that moment, there was a loud, sharp knock on the door, and we jumped. The ship, I realized now, was moving out to sea. But that didn't make sense, because all three of us were down here. Who was steering this thing?

Chapter Twenty-Five
Wednesday, August 24, 1988
Heath

1

"Open the fucking door, mules," Juan said through the locked stateroom door.

We put our clothes back on quickly, and I unlocked the door to find Juan glowering like we'd enacted some personal transgression against him.

"I thought you were joking with the honeymoon shit. I need both of you assholes topside *hasta pronto*," Juan said, gliding into a slight Latin accent.

"Just unpacking," I said.

"You guys couldn't even wait two fucking minutes?" He paused and smiled. "Come up so we can go over the controls. You two have to *sit* at the *helm* until one of you can take over."

"We got a little carried away," I said. "But this boat is pretty amazing."

"Yes, she is beautiful. But I am your handler. So, let's go topside *ahorra*. Okay?"

We followed Juan to the helm, where he stood behind an oversized steering wheel. He'd stuck a piece of steel through to keep the boat traveling straight ahead. Beyond the wheel was a complicated set of nautical instruments built into the dash.

"You expect us to learn all this today?" I asked.

"I will show you the important stuff first. Come closer," he said, and leaned on a tall stool.

The helm stood fifteen feet off the water and provided an unimpeded view of the coast rushing by the cobalt blue of deep ocean giving way to a glowing cerulean at the shore and turquoise churning in the wake behind us. On our right, the sun rolled higher in the late morning sky. It was hot out, and the air seemed to blend with the ocean like we were enveloped in its softest layer. It felt good and exciting, like the best part of my life was developing right before my eyes.

Juan continued, "Look, for what we're doing, it's pretty easy. I can get the controls set for now, and when we get there, do the docking and anchoring, but you guys just need to keep an eye out and stay on course. When we get to San Diego, you need to pay attention so you can run this on your own if needed. I keep hoping I'll get a fucking vacation and get to spend some of that goddamn money." He flashed a boyish smile and revealed a neat row of small teeth. There was a scar in his upper lip that hadn't healed perfectly straight. "While we're here together, we can review the start-up and shutdown procedures." He started touching instruments and flipping things on and off. "I'm not your boat boy, remember that."

Rori nudged me and I patted her back. "We got it," I said, and waved a hand in front of Juan's stare. The asshole did need a vacation.

"Good, now let's go over the controls. You need to be able to name the instruments and tell me what they do. If something happens to me, not that it will, you have to get this to the drop and back."

We paid close attention while he pulled from his seersucker coat pocket a steel device the size of a bullet that had a sort of glass nipple on it. He turned the device around its center, and some powder fell into the clear tip. He placed it under his nose and snorted hard, leaning his head back, and his eyes teared up.

"*Cristo Rey,*" he shouted, veins in his forehead bulging. He placed it back in his pocket and pulled out a silver cigarette case that he cracked open, pulled a Pall Mall free, then lit it. He offered one to each of us, and we took them even though they weren't our brand.

On the horizon, a large cruise ship chugged toward us, and Juan flipped a couple of dials and moved the wheel a half turn to the right. "You see these boats are always coming through here because we're in the shipping lane. There are rules to this, and you don't want to fuck up and get us capsized or get one of these assholes to call the Coast Guard."

"They don't have dogs or anything at the ports?" I asked.

Juan smiled. "Maybe if you check in with customs, but our storage chamber is below water and sealed along the top so in theory, they wouldn't smell anything. Also, except in San Diego, we use moorings, so we never get close to anybody. Small American pleasure craft disappears to Ensenada in the chaos of fishing boats and tankers and sailboats and comes back in the afternoon. On the long trips, we head up the coast from there, so even if anyone did track us, it just looks like leisure. I've never been stopped once. So, don't fucking jinx it."

He laughed and turned back to continue his maneuver around the cruise ship, and when we came across the huge boat's wake, our ship bounced and shook like a plastic toy in a tidal wave. He spent the next forty-five minutes going over each instrument and how to stay the course, and I gathered the basics, and I figured it wouldn't be that hard to keep the ship moving. But the start-up, docking, mooring, dropping anchor, refueling—I had no clue on.

2

"What happened to the last mules?" Rori asked. We'd been cruising for over an hour.

"We've had a few. Your brother Avery, until he went AWOL, for one. Jacques could recruit pretty much any surfer asshole he wants from up and down Baja or SoCal, it's not hard. But when Jacques saw you and Heath, that was the clincher. A couple who could appear like classy gringos. A woman. That's a little harder. And, probably the only reason you're still alive, *vato*." He nodded in my direction.

"I had nothing to do with the deal before," I said.

"I know. But, I hear things. You know, about your brother and his problems with the cops. Also, going missing with some of Jacques's money? He's killed a lot of people for less. But then he sees you, and you're this nice American couple." He stopped and looked at me. "You're not a gringo though, are you? Are you related to Avery?"

"He's not my brother. We just grew up together," I said.

"Well, a nice California couple in a big fancy boat cruising up and down the coast with their Latino captain. It looks pretty normal. Especially with the outfits Jacques picked out for you two."

Rori smiled. "When do we get to play dress-up?"

"Funny you should ask. You both need to change soon before we get to San Diego."

We both started for the staircase, and he yelled, "One at a time!" The veins in his neck stood out, and dry spit flew from his mouth, and I wondered if it was the cocaine or if he was a murderous sociopath that I needed to worry about. In this game, probably both.

"Go ahead," I said, and Rori descended the stairs.

3

We planed along, the sharp hull of the ship chopping at the massive ocean swells. Juan chain-smoked in silence while I watched him make minor adjustments here and there.

"What if they ask for paperwork or the title or whatever and check their files?" Rori said.

"If we get boarded, the paperwork checks out. There's an old guy in San Diego that'll tell anyone who asks that the boat was a gift to you and Rori. Jacques takes care of the details."

"So you *are* the boat boy, after all." I smiled, hoping to get the guy to lighten up. Instead, he turned and put his hand behind his back.

"I'm not fucking around about that. *Comprendes?*"

"Easy, man. We're on the same team."

He paused, then slowly turned back. "Where the hell is your girl anyway? Maybe I'll go check on her," Juan said.

"Probably just making sure everything fits," I said.

Juan turned his attention to another yacht about twenty feet larger than ours, and on it stood an older couple dressed like they were walking the red carpet in Hollywood, who waved from the upper deck as though we were both members in some sort of secret society.

"Eat shit, *putos*," Juan said, waving.

I waved at the couple, and they seemed satisfied and continued sipping their martinis on their way south. I heard footfalls on the metal staircase, and a second later Rori appeared. I tried to stifle a laugh.

"You want to keep your dick?" Rori asked.

"You look great, babe," I said, and smiled because she did. She had on a white and blue one-piece swimsuit with large rectangle patterns on it, and a white cape with shoulder pads that had captain tassels hanging from them. She also had on oversized *Breakfast at Tiffany's* sunglasses, and her hair was pulled back tight with a white and blue headband. "Is that cape from—"

"Goldie Hawn, *Overboard*. I know it," Rori said, and kept her brow furrowed, but cracked a smile like she was trying to stay in character, but failing.

Juan turned. "You look like someone who would own this boat. Very good. Appearances. All right, asshole, your turn," Juan said.

I brushed off his comment and started down the stairs, then stopped and waved Rori over. "You all right up here?" I asked quietly enough that Juan couldn't hear.

She pulled the robe open so I could see that she had wedged the steak knife from the Cantina La Fonda into a tag in the seam like a sheath. I nodded. Juan did seem nice, but I'd learned the hard way at the Hotel Dog Shit that appearances were deceiving.

I took a minute to better sort my luggage. I put away in the small dresser several pairs of pleated khakis, three button-down Oxfords in different shades of blue, a navy blue jacket with gold anchor buttons, and a white captain's hat. And the two pairs of shoes. I changed and adjusted the hat in the bathroom mirror. I looked rich, and it felt good. Taking a deep breath, I slipped on the tan Topsiders and returned to the upper deck. It was Rori's turn to laugh.

"Holy shit, my boyfriend is Hugh Hefner," she said.

I strode up to her and couldn't help but feel a sense of swagger. It felt good, overwhelmingly good. And I instantly pictured myself in this life forever. I realized why rich people were such assholes; having possessions like this was a drug. I wanted more.

"I thought you two were married?" Juan said.

"That's what I meant, husband. Still getting used to that," Rori said.

"Whatever, just sit in the back and make sure you get this. You never know when they're watching." He slipped his shades on and then pulled an extra pair from a cubbyhole inside the dash. He tossed them to me. "I almost forgot; those are for you."

4

I'd never been to San Diego, so when it came into view, I was stunned at its network of skyscrapers and hotels. A massive freeway stretched over the water and out to Coronado Island. Juan slowed the boat up and took another snort from his vial. With all the sailboats and tankers and cruise ships in the bay, I tried to pay attention to how he navigated in and how to find the slip that he eventually pulled into. He showed us how to back into the slip, then how to drop the rubber bumpers and tie off the boat with the lines and cleats along the side. The weirdest part about it all was that there was nobody around that seemed to even notice us. We just waded into a bustle of activity with two and a half million dollars' worth of drugs, and nobody would ever know.

"All right, mules, let's go to shore. We'll check in to our rooms and have drinks at the top of the Hyatt, and maybe some dinner. Grab a change of clothes and whatever else you will need." Juan pulled a small backpack over his shoulder.

5

The lobby of the Grand Hyatt was a dazzling and expansive display. The ceilings seemed at least a hundred feet high, and the marble lobby the size of a stadium and packed with thousands of people. We checked in, got our keys, and followed Juan to the elevator. Rori had changed into a white and gold evening gown that dropped a low V in the front, matching pumps, and a circular Gucci handbag with a gold knot holding all of zero dollars inside. But she looked like a few million. I kept my outfit on from earlier but slipped into a more formal blue blazer.

"Put your shit in the room and meet me at the rooftop bar," Juan said. "Twenty minutes."

6

At the rooftop bar, a waitress showed us to a table along the south-facing wall of windows, where we could see the marina. Two other massive hotels stood along the shore that spread down the horizon, toward Mexico.

"Jesus, Heath," Rori whispered, looking at a menu. "The shrimp cocktail is thirty dollars." A nice dinner out at the Walker Ranch was getting tortas from Dora's in town. From her reaction, this was the nicest place Rori had ever been to as well.

"Obviously, I got the tab," Juan said. "You guys just order what you want. Just, do it with some style, you know."

"Appearances," Rori said, and crossed her legs. Her blonde hair was pulled back in a gold headband, and she manufactured an imperious, high-chinned glare that had me and everyone else fooled. And staring.

"Exactly," Juan said, and leaned back, pulling out his silver cigarette case. He took a Pall Mall out, and an attentive server arrived with a silver butane lighter and lit it for him. "How about a round of your finest tequila," Juan said to her.

"Certainly. Anything else?" she said, and touched the sides of her plume of brown, permed hair. She wore what looked like the standard uniform at the restaurant: a short black skirt, black heels, and a white blouse unbuttoned enough to show some cleavage.

"Steak. Filet," I said. "Medium." I had never ordered a filet in my life, but everyone knew it was the best cut.

"Shrimp cocktail and a steak. And some lobster," Rori said.

"And some bread, for the table," I said.

Juan snorted and swallowed; the waitress waited for him to order.

"Nothing for me. Just the tequila. And a beer, Stella," Juan said, and the waitress started to walk away. "Hey there, wait up." She turned and came back. "Also, some wine to go with their steak, whatever you recommend."

"We have the Opus One. It's a Napa Valley Cabernet, sir. It's one of our best wines. Or a Châteauneuf-du-Pape if you prefer French?"

"Two bottles," Juan said. "One of each."

The waitress smiled, and the calculation of the tip sparkled her pale brown eyes. She turned and strode away; then Juan leaned in. "Also, this is for you." He slid an envelope from his jacket pocket toward us, and I took it. "This is your petty cash, for any unexpected expenses."

"How much is it?" Rori asked. I folded it and put it in my jacket pocket.

"A thousand or so." Juan smiled and puffed his cigarette. "Don't worry, it comes out of your end."

7

The shots came and we toasted and drank. Juan left to the bathroom every ten or fifteen minutes and came back invigorated, ready to take another shot. It wasn't long until he was talking loudly, and the veins in his forehead were standing out again. The bar eventually grew crowded, so our behavior didn't matter. Not that it mattered anyway. I was learning quickly that when you spend this kind of money, people would tolerate just about anything. And cater to it.

We stayed at the bar until after 11:00 p.m., and when they started closing up, we drifted back down the elevator and went to our rooms in the north tower on the thirty-sixth floor. The bank of windows drew me in like an insect to a bug zapper. The panoramic view was captivating but also filled my stomach with that weightless, butterfly feeling, like I might fall through it to my death at any moment.

Rori stood next to me, watching the sparkling lights of the city. "I want to go out into it. Be inside it," Rori said.

With a soft, excited buzz from the money and the wine, I felt it too. Rori and I rode down the elevator and strolled into the city while signs and lights and people streaked by in my periphery. We ended up in a region called the Gaslamp District and popped in and out of a few bars and clubs and kept drinking until the night started blending together in a seamless vision. We wandered farther until we were too tired to take another step. We retreated to our castle on the river and slept.

Chapter Twenty-Six
Thursday, August 25, 1988
Art

1

"Avery, we need to talk," Art said.

Avery whimpered from his fetal roll on the couch in Art's office inside the shuttered club. His eyes were still nearly swollen shut.

"I'll tell you anything, just please, Christ, please don't bring me back to that fucking place." Avery's tears trickled down with snot and blood from wounds on his face and nose—he was ten times worse than when Art had dropped him off at Burke's "safe house."

"I'm not going to touch you, kid. We're safe, back at my place. But you need to cooperate with me. Do you understand?"

"I don't even know where we are, man," Avery said.

"Do you know that man's name? The one who did this to you?"

"Fuck. Which one? I think they called one guy, in the wife-beater, Chow Boy."

"Could that be Derek Chow? Approximately forty-seven years old?"

"I don't know, man. I guess."

"Chow was a Triad member from the San Francisco Hop Sing Boys. Did you hear anything else or see anything out there?" Art had read through the file that Jessman had gotten him, and decided not to bother alerting Burke to his need for Avery. He'd cased the place for a couple days, parked in a dense orchard nearby, and learned the routine. When he saw his opportunity, he just walked in and grabbed the kid. He'd also seen how the operations were going down, and watching it had made him feel a certain kinship with the rotten, molding citrus carcasses that littered the rows around his surveillance van in those orchards.

"I don't know, man. I was blindfolded most of the time. Are you going to kill me? Is that why you're telling me this?"

"Christ, Avery." Art shook a painkiller from his prescription bottle and put one in Avery's hand, then handed him a flask. "Take that, you'll feel better in ten to fifteen minutes. Then we'll get you cleaned up."

"Where are you taking me?"

"We're getting you cleaned up. Then we're going to get your buddy Heath."

"Heath? You're not getting him out of Mexico, man. You shouldn't even try."

"That's not your decision. What you are going to do is call Heath, and you're going to tell him that you need to see him. And the girl. Concerning what, I don't care—something personal, between the two of you—do you understand?"

"Why the fuck would I help you if you're just going to kill us both anyway?" Avery whimpered.

"My boss wants the girl, not Heath. And nobody gives a shit about you. Or I could take you back to Chow Boy. Your choice."

"Fucking Christ. No. Please, god no. He's in Ensenada, I already told the other guys that. He's working for a drug runner named Jacques. I don't know his last name. The only way to get in touch with him is through the resort. La Fonda. Okay. I'll find out. Just please, don't send me back there." Avery sobbed, covering his face with his hands.

"Okay," Art said. "Then here's the deal. Call the fucking resort or die with Burke."

The door to his office opened, and Tyra stepped in wearing a purple tracksuit and her short, naturally curly hair picked out into a fine halo that shone in the half-light.

"Wasn't sure if I'd find you here," she said, and stepped aside.

"I'm glad you came by," Art said. "This kid needs first aid."

"Christ, Art. Did you do this?" she asked. She walked to his armoire, pulling the first aid kit free.

"No, Burke happened to him."

Tyra shrugged like it didn't matter. She helped Avery spread out on the couch. She opened the kit, removed the cotton swabs and rubbing alcohol, and began cleaning the dried blood from Avery's face.

"We out the game?" Tyra said, placing bandages over the cleaned and disinfected areas.

"Not in the least," Art said, and held the file he'd gotten from Jessman.

"Puck's nearly dead, this boy's nearly dead, and you got a file? Christ almighty."

"I know. God, I know. But I'm going to fix it, I promise. I just have to get these two kids out of Mexico, and that's what he's here for. This kid here is Heath's childhood friend."

"And you think this boy's going to help us?" Tyra said, and Avery hissed when she dabbed rubbing alcohol on his cracked knuckles.

"Yes, he is. It's a long story, but the Triad ring is back, if you remember. The one I lost my job trying to take down."

"Just don't get yourself killed. Money's not worth dying over."

"I'm not the one you should worry about," Art growled, and Tyra glanced at him.

"I don't doubt you. Not ever. But this guy, Burke, seems to have your number, that's all."

"I'll take my time on this rundown. I've got a plan."

"I'm sure you do," she said. "You always have a plan."

"You heard from Lacy since the shutdown?"

"She tore out of here when you took off with that ballplayer. I believe she's picking up shifts at the Black Stallion in Fresno."

"She won't be coming back. Neither is that ballplayer."

"You didn't—never mind. I don't want to know. Damnit, Art."

Art moved closer to Tyra. "When this is all done," he said. She looked up from dressing Avery's wounds. "You and I need to figure out what we're going to do."

"If you're talking about the club—"

"I'm not talking about the club, and you know that."

Tyra stood and looked Art in his eyes; she was close to an inch taller. "Don't you go and make empty promises now. We can *just* be business partners. It's worked this far."

Taking her hand in his, he lightly pulled her toward him. Decades of friendship that, at least in his mind, and he assumed in hers, wandered into terrain reserved for lovers. According to an article, Art read once, it was psychologically impossible not to develop feelings for someone you are in contact with on a daily basis. It hadn't worked out, but he felt that underneath it all, they would eventually find each other in a real and lasting way.

"I tend to do what I say I'm going to do. Unless something I can't control stops me," Art said.

"Being dead might stop you," she said, her eyes darting away, down to Avery.

Releasing her hand, Art walked back over to his desk. "I'm going to bring this one home. I promise."

"I'll be here waiting. Either to bury you or marry you. You know that. You always knew that."

2

Art felt his heart rate sprint, and for the first time in a long time, it wasn't because he was about to murder or maim someone. It was because he really loved this woman, and he wanted, more than for himself, to save their investment for her. And for their future together.

"Will you hand me the phone and dial the police station?" Art said, changing the subject before he looked too soft in front of her and the kid. She did have a point though; this was the case that brought him down years ago. And it was back, which excited him because it gave him a chance to square some unfinished business, but he wasn't in his youth anymore. Especially with his leg. He sat down and propped it up on his desk.

Tyra dialed and handed Art the receiver. It rang through, and Art was patched to Burke's office.

"Burke," the voice said, short and gravelly.

Art momentarily lost words, but he breathed softly, wheezing. He thought about that underage girl he'd seen when he had dropped Avery off, the operation he'd monitored, Chow Boy, and the case file. He had enough evidence to convince himself, and probably the world, that Chief Burke wasn't only running interference for this resurfaced sex ring, he was practically a member of the co-op board.

"That you, Art? Hell, you sound like you're dying."

"It's me," Art said.

"You get my girl?" Burke said.

"Short answer, no. Long answer, I have a plan, so I will."

"So you fucked up again?" Burke said.

"They are being protected by a small army with assault rifles. I can't just walk in and ask nicely."

"I knew I should have called the Ramirez brothers."

"My fee just went up to twenty grand. Also, you'll come down personally and apologize to Tyra and let her run her business free of harassment—forever."

Burke laughed. "I don't think you heard me. It's over."

"You send anyone down there, they're dead. I'm your only shot of ever seeing your daughter again, asshole. They're being protected by a goddamn cartel." Art felt his blood go hot, his fingers turning into a fist gripping the phone receiver.

"Yeah, that's what that idiot Avery kept saying, too. The drug runners, the drug runners. Doesn't look like you can do a damn thing."

"I'm not. They're going to come to me. The question is, do we still have a deal?"

"You're a goddamn fool."

"I said, do we have a fucking deal?"

"Your club's never coming back."

"I know you lost the kid. Snuck right out of your little operation over on Goshen."

"How the hell did you—I just got the call on that."

Art needed to throw Burke, keep him on the defensive. Keep him in need. "Yeah, well, maybe Heath came back to spring his buddy? Maybe the cartel got to him."

"Christ, Art. I don't know what you've got planned, but fix this. You have *two weeks*."

"My club comes back. And you apologize to Tyra. In person."

"Once you have my daughter, you call me and put her on a phone. Then we have a deal."

"Expect a call. Have the money and your apology ready," Art said, and hung up the phone. Art turned to Avery, who looked like the opioids had kicked in. Tyra still gently dressed his wounds.

3

"Avery, boy, I hope you're ready. As soon as I can take this cast off, we're finishing this thing." Art said.

Art watched a hopefulness return to Tyra's face, which seemed to smooth out some of the thin lines around her mouth and eyes.

"Avery, sit the fuck up and call your brother," Art said. "I don't care how you do it, but I need you to schedule a meeting with them here. In California. Get me a time, place, and date."

Tyra backed off a little and helped Avery sit up. His hair was bloody and greasy, and his face, which looked like it had been beautiful once, was smashed up.

"I have something he wants," Avery said, softly.

"Who? Your brother?" Art said.

"No. Jacques, the French Canadian. I owe him money from a drop. It's in Santa Cruz. I just need to go back and get it." Avery's speech was slightly slurred, but he seemed clear minded, which was good.

"How much money?" Art said.

"It's—no. You touch that money and we're all dead." He waved his limp hand. "If you fuck with Heath or Rori, they'll come for you. I don't think you know who you're dealing with—you don't want to fuck with these French Canadians, man. They bury motherfuckers."

"How much?" Art said.

"Two hundred and fifty thousand. It's hidden under my cabin, if nobody's gotten to it yet."

"Why are you being so helpful all of the sudden?" Art said.

Avery scoffed, then flinched like he thought Art would crack him again. Art felt sorry for the poor bastard.

"Look," Avery said, "I have to give that money back one way or another. If you want to take the risk of the drop, less of a chance I get murdered by those psychos."

Art dropped his leg, leaning forward on his desk, catching Avery's gaze. "Do you think this guy, Jacques, would trade for that money? Your brother and Rori for the money?"

"Don't involve Jacques, he'll send mercenaries. He'll take the money and kill us all. I'll call La Fonda, and if Heath's already working for Jacques, he'll be staying there."

"What are they doing for him, exactly?"

"He cultivates hash out of a monastery near Puerto Nuevo. He uses Americans as mules. He thinks he's a genius because he runs a fifty-foot yacht up the coast registered in San Diego and dresses Americans up like spoiled rich assholes—the kind law enforcement doesn't hassle. He's been doing it for years."

"Where exactly will they be going?"

"I'll have to find out when they leave, but they always do the same routes—Ensenada, San Diego, Santa Barbara, and Santa Cruz."

"How do you get ahold of this guy?"

"I leave a message for the cabana guy at La Fonda. But we shouldn't tip Jacques. I'll call and ask for Heath's room directly if they're checked in."

"Tyra, get this kid the phone," Art said, and Tyra pulled a corded phone from Art's desk and placed it on the couch next to Avery. Art thought for a second, then said, "Tell Heath that you need his help to clear your name. That you have Jacques's money, and you'll give it to Heath, and Heath alone. But it has to be covert. You'll meet him in Santa Cruz, so get that date."

"You promise you're not going to kill him?" Avery said.

"I'm not going to kill anyone," Art said.

"What about the girl?" Avery asked.

"The girl comes with me. That's the deal. Your brother can run the shipment back and hope that this Canadian doesn't come for anyone. Because if he comes here, we'll be ready."

Avery nodded and picked up the phone. He dialed a number from memory, and it rang, and a few seconds later he spoke. "*Bueno. Por favor, el cuarto de* Heath Walker."

Art could hear a tinny mumbling on the other end, and then it rang through. Adjusting himself, he felt his leg throb. After about seven rings, it went to a voicemail, and Avery looked at Art and shrugged.

"Leave a message. Tell him you made it somewhere safe and sound. To call you at this number," Art said, and he pulled a business card from his wallet and handed it to him. *Art Dominguez, Co-owner, Shakers and Shots, Shadow Valley, CA 564-9874.*

"Hey, Heath, it's your bro. Hey, give me a call at 564-9874. Good news, I got away clean back in Big Sur. Just laying low and had something I wanted to talk to you about." He hung up. "What now?"

"We'll try again tomorrow, and the next day, and the next day until we get through. Tyra, can you run to the store and get me a leg brace and some ACE bandages when you have a chance?" Art said.

"I will not help you take that cast off," Tyra said. "If that's what you think you're going to do."

"When this kid comes to Santa Cruz, we need to be ready to move," Art said, and put his leg back on the ottoman.

"Well then, you better hope he comes in six to eight weeks," Tyra said.

"When the time comes, the cast is coming off," Art said. Reaching, Art picked up the TV remote from a small table beside his chair and pressed the power button. A small, wall-mounted tube TV flickered to life beside the armoire, and Art flipped through the channels until a baseball game between the Houston Astros and the LA Dodgers came on.

"You a Dodgers fan, Avery?" Art said, and chuckled because the kid was trying to see through the little slit in his swollen right eye.

"They're going to win it this year," Avery said. "Almost had it last year."

"I'm more of a Giants fan," Art said, and smiled again when Avery sunk back down on the couch. Art thought sports rivalries were stupid, but the kid was easy to fuck with and was kind of growing on him. Not to mention the way he could take a beating and stay seemingly upbeat. Avery hissed in pain again when Tyra began to change the bandages on his hand where they'd almost cut a finger off. The kid was banged up, but Art reminded himself that Avery had gotten himself into this and turned informant to save his own ass, so he shouldn't care. Although maybe Avery was really smarter than he looked, and the whole thing was a big setup. The kid *was* a goddamn drug runner; he had to do something right. Art looked at Avery trying to watch the game and smiled to himself. Maybe he'd let the bastard live, after all.

Chapter Twenty-Seven
Thursday, August 25, 1988
Heath

1

The next morning, our wake-up call came through at 4:15 a.m., and neither of us moved. After a dozen rings, I picked the phone up and left it off the hook, then leaned over and kissed the back of Rori's head. We were supposed to meet Juan in the lobby at 4:30 a.m., and that wasn't going to happen at this rate.

Rori started a shower, and I gathered our things into our luggage. I heard Rori singing softly, so I slipped into the bathroom and pulled the curtain aside. Smiling, she pulled me closer and kissed me while water streamed over our faces. I stepped inside and let the hot water run over my tired body and felt the hangover and stale taste in my mouth wash away.

After, we changed into one of our fancy outfits, and at 4:45 a.m., the door erupted with the pounding of a fist that I was pretty sure belonged to Juan.

"You two are sloppy," Juan said when I opened the door. "Always late. I was down in the lobby for fifteen minutes waiting."

"Not everyone has powdered energy in their pocket," Rori said.

Juan scoffed. "*Boca grande*, how many times do I have to tell you? We have schedules for a reason, and we expect you to keep them. Jacques is going to have to hear about this."

"Yeah, couples like us pop up in Mexico every day, right?" Rori said.

"Actually, yes, you arrogant peasant. Tens of thousands just like you every day. And just about every single one of them can be persuaded to ride around in a yacht for twenty-five large. Now let's go," he said. "Pretend you're professionals."

2

To throw off anyone who might be paying attention, Juan first headed the ship out to Avalon, a little town on Catalina Island, before heading back to Mexico. At 12:22 p.m. we entered the marina in Ensenada. The sprawling industrial wharf with its flat, dated two-story buildings was such a contrast to the overgrowing industry of hotels, houses, and skyscrapers on the other side of the border. Juan pulled into the slip, and Rori and I helped with the docking procedures and walked to the bough, where we met Jacques.

"Leave the bags on the boat. Nacho and Miguel will take them," Jacques said. Rori and I stepped down from the boat, and Jacques shook our hands. "Do not worry about the little incident, go up and see Jean-Pierre, he will take you to the boathouse for debriefing."

Jean-Pierre stood by the van with two other men, all still in brown monk robes. The men hopped onto the deck and descended into the hull. Jean-Pierre guided us into the back seat of the van, and we watched through the window while Juan, Jacques, Nacho, and Miguel all emerged with two heavy bags each and moved up the ramp. They opened the back and loaded the bags while I scanned the surroundings. Everyone on the wharf seemed to be ignoring our activity, and in fact, I noticed a cop in the street literally looking the other direction. Probably on the payroll.

They did another trip to the boat and came back with more bags. Then everyone climbed in with Jacques sitting shotgun. Miguel sat next to me, sandwiching me between him and Rori; the other men climbed in behind us, and I had a feeling of vulnerability I didn't like. If these men wanted, they could kill us both, and I wouldn't even see it coming. We started driving, and Miguel, who I'd seen once before, glanced down at my hand, then up at my face.

"*De donde has sacado esto?*" Miguel said. I must have looked confused, because he added, "Nice ring. Where did you get this?"

The comment and the attention on the ring felt like an invasion into a private world that nobody was invited into. The narratives I'd been imagining about my father and mother since I was a kid—they weren't something I wanted to share with just anybody, certainly not with one of Jacques's henchmen.

"Thanks. I bought it at a pawnshop in Tijuana," I said.

He nodded and switched his attention to the road. Of Jacques's men, Miguel seemed the calmest and most calculating. A little older, he had short hair that was mostly gray but speckled with black. A scar down his right cheek gave me the impression he'd nearly been killed at some point in his life, but there was a weariness to him, too. Like he'd been happier at some point; he looked like he might have been handsome years ago.

3

After driving a short distance, we made a quick right into an industrial warehousing section with decaying sailboats up on trailers. We snaked through a bunch of equipment and drove directly up to a tall warehouse with rusted sheet metal framing. It looked to have swinging doors locked at the center, but Jacques tapped a button on the passenger's visor, and the whole front of the building tilted up like a garage door. It was a clever aluminum façade.

We pulled inside, and Jacques hit the button again, and the wedge of light streaming in grew narrower while the door came to a close. A series of bright overhead lights flipped on, and it took my eyes a second to adjust to the room. We seemed to be in a packing facility for Mexican exports: tomatoes, avocados, and a brand of tequila called El Camador. In front of us, a man and a woman were dressed in business suits and wore uneasy expressions. Behind them sat an armored car.

"You two stay in the car," Jacques said. "This will be fast."

Everyone got out of the van, and Jean-Pierre, Nacho, and Miguel opened the back, pulling two bags at a time and stacking them inside the open doors of the armored car. Jacques approached the man in the suit, who was shorter and had puffy cheeks with sparse black hair. Jacques put his arm around the man and whispered something. He led him away from the woman, toward the far side of the warehouse where the boxes stacked nearly to the ceiling.

The woman glanced around tentatively while the men finished loading. They slammed the rear doors of the armored car and got back in the van. The woman stood alone. There was a flash, and a muffled gunshot echoed through the steel rafters, and I felt Rori's body flinch beside me. Her hands gripped me hard on my arm; her eyes were wide with fear. My pulse raced.

A moment later Jacques strolled out from the boxes, unscrewing a silencer from his nickel-plated nine-millimeter, and stopped in front of the woman. She backpedaled with a terrified expression, and I thought she might cry.

He said something to her; then she got into the armored car that read *Banamex*. She started it and drove forward, waiting for the door to open. Jacques said something to Miguel, and he hurried over past the boxes and didn't return. Jacques got into the passenger's seat, pressed the button on the visor, and the door opened again. The woman drove through slowly, then pulled away. Jean-Pierre backed out; then the door closed and we drove on, toward the resort.

4

"That man was the manager of the local Banamex. Our last deposit didn't go as planned, and he needed to be taken care of. We should be okay now. Alice will be handling our account from now on. Much more carefully."

Nobody had anything else to add. Forty-five minutes later we pulled up to La Fonda. Jacques got out and opened the side door for us. We stepped out, and he walked us back to our suite.

"You two have done well. Is the job, you know, a good fit, do you think?" Jacques said while we walked. A nervous silence generated by what we'd just witnessed hung between us.

"It's a dream," Rori said finally.

"And you, Heath, is it what you expected?"

"I think we can do this forever," I said, knowing that we for sure had to get out sooner rather than later. Before a disagreement like with the bank, or with Avery, came between us.

"This is what I like to hear." Jacques stopped outside the carved door to our suite. "You two will have full use of the suite, and we will keep you well fed, dressed, and taken care of. This all comes out of your end, as you understand, but the costs are not that expensive down here as compared to back home."

"Do we get paid for the last drop?" Rori asked.

"Yes, of course." Jacques pulled an envelope from his jacket pocket. "The deal was for ten thousand, but after the charges, well, you will see. The rest is there."

Rori took the envelope, looked inside, and smiled.

"Thanks, Jacques," I said.

"The next shipment will be another to San Diego in one week. And then in two weeks, you will be going to Santa Cruz. You will need to know everything about the boat. It is a much harder journey."

"We're fast learners," Rori said.

"So you have said, this is good. However," Jacques said, leaning closer, "Juan has told me about your tardiness and that you have not been listening well. I cannot tolerate this. It is a business, so you have this one more chance to show me that you can be on time. Is that fair?"

"We'll be on time," I said.

"This is good to hear. I do not want any more incidents. The Coast Guard can get suspicious. Now, enjoy your week. The weather will be perfect, go get some sun. If you need anything at all, you can communicate through Beto. Okay. Just one more item."

"Sure. Anything," I said.

"Don't ever steal from me, and don't ever lie to me. You understand?"

"Of course," I said.

"We understand completely," Rori said.

"Never. Okay. Never. Now enjoy the evening."

Jacques promptly turned and walked with his usual swagger toward the parking lot, and I took the iron key from my pocket, opening the door to the suite. The sun was already balanced west, but it was still bright out. Rori slumped down onto a white, overstuffed armchair in the living room.

5

"Jesus Christ, what the hell have we gotten into?" she asked, letting out a deep sigh.

I wasn't sure how to respond. In many ways, we were safer. But we were also well-cared-for prisoners. One mistake, though, and we were in a worse way than before. Moving toward her to sit with her, I noticed the red light flashing on the room phone and went over to it.

"Hold on," I said. I went to pick up the phone, but before I could, it rang. I paused.

"Are you going to answer?" Rori said.

"Yeah, that was just a little spooky." I picked up the phone. "Hello?"

"Brother, man, how are you?" The voice was distant but distinctive. It was Avery, and I felt a burst of pure energy ignite up through my chest like a sunrise. I almost started to cry with joy.

"Avery, my god, are you okay?"

"I'm fine, man. Did you check your message?"

"Not yet, we just walked in the door from a trip."

"Got it. Glad you hooked up with you know who."

"Christ, I can't believe it's you. We've been worried sick. I literally can't stop thinking about it. That bounty hunter, somehow, he survived. He tried to fucking shoot us."

"Yeah, man, I was watching through the window. Split out the back way. Took a golf cart up to the main lodge and hid out in the wine cellar. That guy wasn't getting the drop on me twice."

"Good. So good," I said. "Rori, it's Avery. He snuck out the back after the psycho took a shot at us."

She stood and beamed a smile of satisfaction back at me. "Did you tell him we tried to call him?"

"Oh, shit. Yeah. We tried to call you down at some restaurant. Nepenthe, or something. A red English pay phone."

"Yeah, I was gone, man. Thanks for looking out. I would have bolted, too, if someone was firing off rounds at me."

"No hard feelings?" I asked.

"None at all. Actually, I kind of have a favor to ask."

"Sure, anything. Are you in a safe spot now?"

"Oh, yeah. I'm staying with a friend in Santa Cruz. We're hella down-low."

"God, I felt so guilty this whole time. Glad to hear that."

"Yeah. No worries. I just want to come out of hiding eventually, and that's kind of why I'm calling. That money back at the Hideaway, you probably know by now, it's not mine."

"Yeah, no shit. Jacques thought we were going to bring it to him. I thought he was going to bury us when we first got here. He said he's taking it out of our end if you don't get it to him."

"Well, I want to square that with both of you, then. You down to help?"

"What do you need me to do?"

"When do you guys go to Capitola?"

"Is that the same as Santa Cruz?" I asked.

"Right, same spot," he said.

"Two weeks, we leave on a Wednesday."

"Good, that would put you there on what, Friday the sixteenth? I'll meet you there with the money. I'll be at the Venetian hotel, it's right next to where Juan and Jacques always stay. I'll give it to you, but I want you to hold on to it until you're back in Baja. He can't know I'm there."

"All right, let's meet somewhere public, though. So we're both safe."

I kept trying to scan Avery's voice for tension. It was hard; he was always so easygoing. I wanted to trust Avery, but not mentioning that the money at Hideaway was Jacques's had nearly sunk us. Then again, he also had helped that bastard bounty hunter lure us in last time. Not that I wouldn't have done the same for Rori and me, but still. I needed to know this wasn't another trap. Although it sounded like we were going to the same spot, whether we liked it or not. It was on Jacques's itinerary. I had to help Avery clear his name with Jacques. I would just be extra careful this time. No more barging into rooms.

"There's a dive bar down the street from your hotel, it's called Salty's. I'll meet you there Friday at midnight."

"Okay, bro. I still can't believe you're okay. I was so goddamn worried that I'd brought you into my shit. I can't wait to see you again." I smiled, and my eyes felt heavy, my sinuses full, like tears might spill. I breathed.

"Peace and love, motherfucker," he said.

"Later," I said, but the line clicked silent, and I wasn't sure he even heard it.

"I'm so happy he's okay," Rori said after I hung up.

"He's alive, and he's going to meet us in Santa Cruz. He's got the money to clear his name with Jacques, and we won't have to pay it back out of our end. We just need to keep a lid on it. He said Jacques might come for him if he found out."

"We just told Jacques we weren't going to lie to him, like, ever," she said.

"We're not lying, technically. We're just not telling him. Also, we're getting *his* money back."

"I don't like it," she said, her excitement fading. "I'm over adding to the list of people who want us dead."

"It's Avery. We owe him for bringing your dad's bounty hunter to his doorstep."

"He owes *us* for sending us down here empty-handed."

I moved in closer and held her gently in my arms; she looked up at me.

"We can save him and us," I said.

"Yeah?" she said, softening again. "How?"

"'Whether it is your feet, arching at a primal touch of sound or breeze, or your ears, tiny spiral shells from the splendor of America's ocean,'" I said, quoting Pablo Neruda.

"You suck," she said, and kissed me. "Who was that?"

"I could just be making it up as I go."

"Yeah, right." She smiled.

"Neruda."

"I like Neruda," she said.

"Me too."

We uncorked a miniature champagne and poured a little into two flutes. Clinking glasses, we drank the liquid down, and it was cool, but the bubbles burned. We kissed lightly, and she tugged on my belt, jerking me toward her.

"Maybe we can forget about the drugs and the money for a little while?" she said. We kissed again and fell onto the couch in the living room, the ocean beyond us crashing softly in the background.

Chapter Twenty-Eight
Thursday, September 15, 1988
Heath

1

At 7:29 a.m. pounding erupted on our stateroom door, only this time, I was already up, smoking. Since we'd promised Jacques we'd be punctual, Juan had taken to banging on our door a half hour early. The previous mornings, I'd shoot out of bed, my heart hammering like a piston, and he'd get a good laugh.

"Get up, *pendejos*. You're late again," he said through the door.

"Tell Juan to eat shit," Rori said, and buried her face into my T-shirt. I lit another cigarette, and the door hammered again.

"Let's get moving," Juan said.

"We have twenty-nine minutes," I yelled. But I stepped into my wrinkled khakis and slipped on my boat shoes.

Once dressed, we stepped into the hallway, and Juan stood there leaning against the wall, glaring like a sociopath.

"*Vamos arriba, pendejos.* You two are doing all the procedures this morning," he said.

We trudged up the stairs and stopped near the bar to pour a cup of coffee that Juan had brewed. I sipped the coffee black, then lit two cigarettes and handed one to Rori. I took another long sip of the coffee, a big drag off the cigarette, and felt partially reanimated. We quickly ran through the start-up procedures and maneuvered out of the slip in San Diego, heading north.

After a few hours of steering, Juan came up and took over. He maneuvered us toward a small enclave that had more of an old-world Spanish vibe. He pulled close to the shore, and the architecture of the city became clearer, and I liked what I saw.

Instead of the industrial high-rises and fifty-story hotels of San Diego, this city was filled with shorter, two- and three-story hotels and one-story restaurants all beautifully articulated from the shore, up the small hills beyond. We stopped at a mooring, and Juan watched closely while I tossed the lasso over the ball and pulled it close so Rori could slip the lines through the eye, and we both tied them off to the cleats on either side of the stern.

"Good work. You *pendejos* learn quick. We'll show you how to drop anchor up in Santa Cruz. Now let's go back up top so we can lower the dinghy."

The operation on the dinghy was simple, and we were quickly on board and headed in. Nearing the shore, Juan picked up speed and pulled the outboard propeller up just when we hit land, and the dinghy slid up the embankment and came to a sudden stop in the wet sand.

"We're here, my masters." Juan smiled.

We helped him drag the dinghy and lock it to a railing.

"Follow me. The Four Seasons bar is where the *mujeres ricas* hang out. The dinghy heads back at ten."

"You can run that thing without us?" Rori asked.

"Just stick with me, all right?" Juan said.

2

We followed Juan over a red brick crosswalk that led to the hotel. On the other side of the street, the sidewalk continued up to a grand hacienda entrance with high stone archways lined with ivy and terra-cotta roof tiles. The circular driveway was filled with Mercedes, BMWs, and Rolls Royces, and we strolled past it all in our sophisticated yacht wear. All of the fancy, rich assholes strutting around didn't even seem to question our pedigree. We approached the entrance, and a valet rushed over and opened the front door.

"Are you checking in?" he asked, and I looked at his pressed slacks, black shoes, and little bell cap and wanted to laugh.

"We're here for dinner and drinks," Juan said, and I wondered at that moment, when Juan answered so authoritatively, why he would ever want a break from this. We were living a veritable dream. Maybe we should scrap the idea to cut and run. Just not fuck up.

"Right through the lobby on the left. Bella Vista is open until nine thirty."

Juan nodded and handed the guy five bucks. We passed into the grand lobby constructed out of hand-cut marble and dripping with simplistic elegance. The property gave the impression that no amount of money had been spared in its construction. It had been simply a matter of getting the best of everything.

"Table for three?" the hostess asked when we approached.

"Can we sit by the fire pit?" Juan asked. She nodded and showed us out to a large brick fire ring at the center of an ornate garden patio with tables, each with a white umbrella, set loosely around a large open space. The whole property, and town, was decorated with short, squat palm trees as well as tall, gently swaying palms.

"Here you are. Your server will be right with you," she said, and placed the menus on the border of the pit.

Another couple, sitting on the other side of the pit, looked up from their menus and frowned as if trying to read something without glasses. Their eyes were glassy, and I got the sensation they were interested in us and that we were going to know why, whether we liked it or not.

The man, who was wearing a five-piece suit and a silk bow tie when it was seventy-two degrees, leaned over to his wife and whispered loudly enough for us to hear very clearly, "Look, darling, they allow the help to sit with the guests here." I wasn't sure if he was referring to me or Juan.

His wife forced a smile and said, "Well, it *is* California." Like that explained everything that concerned them. "Dreadful place."

She wore a long evening gown, and they looked like they thought they were attending the fucking Met Gala. They both had their hair slicked back, and hers was dirty blonde with some sort of jeweled hair clip. His was brown and speckled with gray, and through some sort of East Coast blue-blooded inbreeding, they had the same arrogant jawline that pushed forward like a bulldog.

"You know, we can hear you both," Rori said, and I wanted to laugh but also didn't want to cause a scene.

Since I was sitting in the chair closest to the couple, I tried to mediate. "Nobody here is the help. My wife and I hired Captain DeMarco and his boat for a cruise up the coast," I said, trying to match their New York inflection of assumed superiority.

"Is that right? Did you travel on a raft?" The man snorted, and his head rolled back, and I didn't understand why anyone would fuck with us, but I guessed people like these didn't like to see new money, especially if it went to people that looked like Juan and me. They were also drunk.

"That yacht," Juan said, and pointed with his chin toward the bay, where it bobbed gracefully like a middle finger to these assholes. "Bought and paid for."

"I wouldn't dare ask what you did for that kind of money," the woman said, and took a sip from her martini, then retreated to her menu like they hadn't started this whole thing.

"You want to know what I do, lady? I'm a boxer. Thirty-three KOs in three countries. That's not counting the knockouts in bars when people insult me and my heritage."

"She wasn't insulting your heritage, I'm sure Mexico is a fine place," the man said.

"A fine place I can do without visiting," the woman added.

"Mexico? My family has been American citizens since the fucking Treaty of Guadalupe Hidalgo. Not that you incestuous fucks would even know what that is."

"Manhattan, actually. And I do know what it is. It's when the American government marched into Mexico City and destroyed their army."

"Then you should know that this was all Mexican land, from Tejas to Alta California. And you should also be informed that my great-great-grandfather was a wealthy rancher near the port of San Francisco. Then, the greedy fucks coming from the east wanted it all, after Mexico had already granted them land and was gracious to them."

"Yeah well, it's ours now, and they should shut the border down to stop the rest of you from flooding in," the woman said, and splashed her drink without noticing, her face flush with color.

Juan stood and his hand trembled slightly. The people around us stopped their conversations and stared. "My family was in Alta California over a hundred and fifty years ago, which makes me and my family more American than your ancestors, who probably snuck in with the Nazis in the forties. But if you'd like to talk more about it, we can step out to the parking lot, and I can make my knockout record thirty-five instead."

"He's an excitable little man, isn't he?" the woman said, slurring slightly.

"Waiter, check, please," the man said, and stood. "Boxing is a brutal sport for thugs and criminals. Enjoy your life in *Alta* California. I prefer the sophistication of the East. Even the well-off here dress like hobos and gypsies."

The man paid and helped his wife to her feet. They staggered at a brisk pace through the lobby and down one of the wings of the hotel. Hopefully to sleep off their embarrassment.

"I'm sorry if they were bothering you," the waitress said when she arrived. "They've been drinking all day and never ordered any food."

"It's all right," Juan said. "Just bring us a bottle of Dom and three glasses. And some appetizers to start. Chef's choice." She beamed and spun to place the orders. The three of us tightened our circle around the fire pit, and the afternoon sun started its descent, and the yellows and oranges filled in the cumulous etchings of the skyline.

3

"Was your family really part of that treaty?" Rori said after everyone on the patio stopped staring and started talking again. "I kind of remember that from school."

"We were. But my family lost their land in the treaty and moved to Mexico City. They were able to get dual citizenship, and my father was born in 1948 in Mexico, but because my grandfather was a citizen, so was he."

"And you were born here?" she said.

"I was born in Mexico City, but my parents were American citizens, so I got to keep it as well. But when my father was a student at the Polytechnic in Mexico City, he joined the CNH when the government took over the university system. He died in the Tlatelolco massacre in 1968. My mom was afraid for me, since I was only two at the time, so she came back to California, to Tulare, and began studying to be a nurse."

"It's hard to believe that Tulare is better than Mexico City," I said, knowing how abandoned by the world Shadow Valley felt to me, and Tulare being so close by.

"It's not, but it's in California, which means better money."

"You know a lot about this shit for a boxer," Rori said.

"My mother was studying political science when my father was killed in the massacre. She puts on the Mexican news and yells at the TV all the time. It's like her soap opera."

"You happen to know how Jacques got started in Mexico?" I asked.

"That's a good question. Jacques is a smart man. It's kind of a long story and started because of interest rates. Sounds stupid, but Mexico owes the US something like sixty billion, and they can't make the interest payments with the rates twenty-two percent, or whatever they are right now."

He paused to see if we were still paying attention, and I was curious, although I didn't know shit about Mexican government—I barely followed what was going on with ours. "How does that explain Jacques and the operation?"

"Two reasons. One was that President Madrid operated like a dictator and appointed all the heads of all the cartels in Mexico. It was good because he could tax them and control them. But now with the big election fraud, we have Salinas as president, and he's under pressure by the US to keep making payments. So Mexico is taking bailout money from the IMF, and they don't like heads of state managing criminal organizations, even though it's better for everyone that way."

"What the hell did we lend Mexico sixty billion for?" Rori asked.

"Didn't you know? Mexico is supposed to be the next big win for democracy and the spread of the middle class even though, spending my youth there, everybody I knew just wanted to be a narco. It's the real dream. So, to cater to the US and the IMF, Mexico is cutting the cartels loose to self-operate and also ending subsidies for farmers, again, because of US pressure. So right now, we have millions of small farmers going broke, no leadership in the cartels, and a big recruiting pool. Jacques sees all this coming and swoops in and buys up the abandoned monastery and starts making his hash with plenty of cheap labor, farmland, and perfect growing conditions. All because of interest rates."

"And it's good hash," Rori said.

"That's where Jean-Pierre comes in, he's an expert. They were up in Canada, growing in greenhouses, but they developed a hash recipe that uses a hybrid strain that makes the cleanest, happiest high on the planet. It's good but has a problem. It grows best outdoors in the heat. So, Mexico is the perfect place to start up while Mexico is in transition—we can smoke that shit Jacque gave us tonight on the boat."

The waitress returned with a bottle of Dom in a standing ice bucket and set it behind us. She ceremoniously uncorked the bottle into a napkin and poured three glasses. Then a food runner came out with some ceviche, peeled shrimp, and a large bowl of guacamole and chips.

"Thank you," Juan said. "Wait, what's your name again?" The waitress stooped so he could read her nametag. She had on a black dress that clung to her thin frame. She was tall and tan with black hair pulled back in a floral headband, and it was shiny and fell beautifully around her shoulders. Her narrow face held delicate features and a set of hazel eyes that had a striking contrast against her complexion.

"Rebecca," she said. "And you are?"

"My name is Juan DeMarco. What time does your shift end, Rebecca?"

"When we close at nine thirty," she said, their faces almost touching.

"Here's a hundred dollars. Can you keep the food and champagne coming until you close?" he said. "Then you can come back to the yacht with us, and we can have a real party."

"That's *not* yours," she said, casting her gaze toward the ocean.

"It is. And also, will you do me a favor and send a bottle of this Dom to that couple that was sitting here? Add a note that says, 'Viva Alta California.'"

"*Por supuesto*," she said, and giggled when she took the hundred Juan handed her. She disappeared into the restaurant again.

"Eat. Drink. Be merry. Jesus Cristo said that," Juan said.

"To Alta California," Rori said, and raised her glass to cheer.

"And to Canada," Juan said, and we clinked glasses and drank down the dry, acidic wine, and I wondered why the stuff cost eighty dollars a bottle, because it was terrible.

I took a peeled shrimp, dipped it in guacamole, and took a bite, and figured that Juan seemed to be in a pretty good mood. I could finally ask him another question I just remembered about this broken nose. "Why don't you box anymore?"

He sniffed and looked at me, then slugged down his champagne. "You know, if Jacques knew you were asking all of these questions, he wouldn't like it. Right?"

"You don't have to answer."

"It's fine, but you know if you ever do get caught, they'll find a way to kill you from the inside, too. So the less you know, the better. It makes you a liability, and they have to deal with liabilities, eventually."

"I don't plan on getting caught."

"Nobody does." He paused and looked around, then lowered his voice. "I'm still the best flyweight boxer in the country, but I got banned, *pendejo*. They said I was fixing a fight."

"Were you?" Rori asked.

"I owed somebody a lot of money. I'd been hanging out with some girls with—expensive taste. If I went down, I was supposed to be in the clear. But somehow the refs found out and called the fight. I got caught and banned. I ended up cage fighting in Mexico and lost to some fucking savage twice my size, and Jacques approached me after he'd lost money at the match in Tijuana. Told me there was a better way to make a living. Now I'm here."

"How about another toast? God knows this is better than living in Shadow Valley," I said.

"Amen," Rori said.

"Or Tulare," Juan said, and we toasted once more and downed the rest of our drinks.

A while later the waitress uncorked another bottle of the Dom, and she squatted by Juan, and he let her take a sip out of his glass. He picked her hand up and kissed it, and she said, "I have to clean my station, so I'll be ready at nine forty-five." She stood and walked back inside.

"The yacht is a powerful aphrodisiac," he said, and grinned.

"I thought Jacques said nobody on the boat," Rori said.

Juan leaned forward and his eyes narrowed. "Hey. I'm your handler. *Dar recuerdos*," he said, and leaned back in his chair. "She comes back with us unless, you know, you two want to join me in my stateroom?"

"Fuck you, Juan," Rori said, and I saw her hand resting over her jacket pocket, where I knew she had that steak knife from Cantina La Fonda.

Juan laughed. "Then tonight, we party on the boat."

We all looked out at the yacht and sipped our drinks. Our entrées came, and we ate in relative silence while the sun continued to inch closer to the oceanic horizon until the boat was a burning silhouette. Then, moments later, it was dark. Rebecca eventually emerged from the restaurant with her hair down and a light sweater on, and we all stood and made our way through the lobby and back down the red brick path that led to the beach. It was a warm and beautiful night, but going against Jacques's direct orders made me uncomfortable, and I wished I still had my .357, just in case.

Chapter Twenty-Nine
Friday, September 16, 1988
Art

1

"Tyra, hand me the saw," Art said, poking at the inside of his cast with a pen. He pulled it out and added to the line he'd been drawing down the side of the cast to avoid cutting into his skin when he sawed the plaster.

"Art, it's only been a couple weeks. Aren't you supposed to wait at leas—"

"You want the club to reopen?"

"The cops aren't going to let that happen. Sometimes you need to realize a bad investment and let it go."

"Saw," Art said, and held his hand out. "This is about a lot more than the club."

"Your ego?" she asked. She pulled a silver hacksaw from Art's armoire and handed it to him.

"Thank you." He began to saw along the line he had sketched. "I'm going to get Burke's kid, and I don't give a shit if I break my other femur. We're getting our club back."

Art grunted while he carefully sawed down the length of his leg. He nicked his skin around his kneecap but didn't slow down. When he got to the bottom, he gave the saw one last push, and the rest of the plaster clattered to the floor. His leg was free for the first time in weeks, and it looked thin and pale comparatively, so he wiggled his toes and dabbed at the fresh cut with a paper towel.

"Hand me the brace," Art said, and Tyra handed Art the leg brace and gauze he'd asked for. Art carefully wrapped his leg with gauze and then strapped the brace on tightly. He could just barely bend his knee. He stood and put a little bit of weight on it and winced when an electric pain pulsed down his leg and into his foot. "*Shit.*"

"I told you. It's not worth it. Just stay in and heal up," she said.

"You should listen to her, man. Your boss is crazy, my boss is crazy. Let's just lay low and keep watching baseball," Avery said. His face had healed up some except for a few short scars forming from scabs over his brow line. His right cheek was still bruised with yellow shadows, and his nose was off-center with a slight bulge on the side from where it'd been broken.

"Avery, shut the fuck up," Art said, and Avery looked wounded.

Art hadn't let Avery out of his sight in weeks, and the kid had started to grow on him. He was a little on the simple side, but good-natured and whooped with delight whenever the Dodgers won a game, or Oral Hershiser struck out an opponent, or Kirk Gibson hit a home run.

"I was just saying Tyra has a point."

"See? Two against one," Tyra said, and went around to the desk and sat down in the leather chair, staring back at him.

Art walked to the armoire, slipped off the pants he had on with the leg cut open for the cast, and pulled a fresh pair of dark jeans free. He slipped them on, being delicate when putting weight on his left leg. Then he pulled his Glock out and Velcroed it to his other ankle and smoothed his jeans over the gun. He pulled a black leather belt that hung on the door, and slipped it through the loops in his jeans from the right side first, then around and through the sheath for the collapsible steel baton and fastened it at the front. Removing his musty T-shirt, he exposed his graying chest hair and slightly diminished muscle tone from the weeks of being sedentary. He put on a coating of Old Spice, a white tank top, and a black and gray, embroidered Western button-down. Then he pulled his black felt cowboy hat from the top rack and slowly lowered it onto his head. Looking in a small, square mirror affixed to the inside leaf of the armoire, he grinned. He limped slowly over to the desk where Tyra sat, and worked to control his wincing while also trying to correct his gait so he didn't appear injured. Standing in front of her transformed, he smiled at her.

"We've got everything in place," Art said. "I just need the girl, and everything will go back to normal around here." Art gestured around at the shuttered establishment.

Tyra nodded, leaned forward, and rubbed her temples with her fingers. "I never could control you. Just—be safe."

"Avery, get in the truck. It's time to go back to that fucking hippy commune and get your money."

2

Art repacked his luggage bag of supplies from his armoire and pulled a uniform that he had vacuum sealed along with several others in a tidy stack. Avery walked out to the truck with him and got in—he didn't even protest his captivity anymore. In fact, the kid seemed to regard Art like a surrogate father, like he had some sort of bizarre Stockholm syndrome. But then again, Art couldn't imagine hurting the kid now and, he wanted nothing more than to let Avery go when this was all over. Hell, maybe he could replace Puck at the cameras down the line.

Pulling away from Shakers and Shots, he checked his rearview mirror. The parking lot was empty, and the lights were still off. Art pushed his gas pedal to the floor, and his tires chirped while he sped toward the 198—back toward Santa Cruz, where it all had started.

After winding through the coastal range and into Monterey Bay for the second time in just under a month on the same rundown, Art found the inkling of fall on the coast, which left a vibrant, warm sheen over all the tall coastal pine and cypress trees. It was a stark contrast to the rapid cooling that had made the valley feel like Halloween was imminent. Art took the exit up Graham Hill Road, and Avery showed him a back road that saved them a few minutes, but they emerged right at the base of Mount Hermon, just before the turn that led up to the abandoned commune, where he saw what remained of the gas station.

A shiver constricted Art's chest when he remembered the old man's split skull and that flash of fear right before he died—the police had wrapped the building and pumps with yellow tape. Art flexed his left leg to get rid of an ache from driving and instead felt a sharp pinch. He pulled a pill from his nearly empty prescription bottle and washed it down with his flask of Maker's Mark. A few minutes later they were in front of the old A-frame, and it was darker and even more run-down than Art remembered.

"Let's go," Art said, and Avery got out and moved toward the house so that Art could follow. Art did appreciate that he didn't have to threaten the kid anymore. They stepped into the house, and the carpet and wood sagged under their feet, and it was dark with shadows cast into the corners of the house like secrets.

They moved through the house and into a hallway at the back of the living room, and Art followed Avery into the master bedroom, where all the walls had patches of black mold growing along the baseboard. Avery slipped into a walk-in closet, and Art leaned down and unholstered his Glock, training it on the kid's back—he'd been doing this for long enough to know that there was always a weapon with the cash. Always.

Avery stepped to the back of the closet and reached into a cubbyhole on what appeared to be a shoe rack. Art heard the metallic click of a door opening. Avery pushed, and the entire back wall swung outward, revealing a crawl space in the floor that Avery descended into and disappeared. Art waited and watched his Timex, and after sixty seconds, he started to worry the kid had an escape route down there. He edged closer to peer into the abyss, but then he heard something rustling below, and then a black vinyl backpack surfaced inside the closet, and Avery was close behind it, looking dirty and covered in spider webs.

"Where the hell did you have that thing, kid?" Art said.

Without looking at Art, Avery gathered himself inside the closet, sat beside the bag, and unzipped it. Art felt a jolt and cocked the hammer on his Glock when he spotted it. Sitting right on top was a small .22. Avery's hands shot into the air in anticipation of Art's reaction. He slowly looked up with his eyes wide as shotgun holes. Art chuckled.

"Whoa," Avery said. "I thought we had a deal? What the hell, man?"

"Zip the bag up and toss it over," Art said.

"You can't take that money—he'll come for us both," Avery said, and then he zipped the bag and tossed it to Art.

Art opened the bag and slipped the .22 into his hip pocket. Then he flipped through the deep stacks of damp money.

"How much did you say was here?" Art said.

"Two hundred fifty K. But it belongs to the drug runners, man."

"Maybe I should have traded the kids for the cash," Art said.

"Probably wouldn't have taken that deal," Avery said.

"I bet he would if I threw you in with the cash."

"Ouch, man. That hurts."

Art smiled. He'd never seen this kind of cash all at once before. It was enough for Art to be clear of his troubles for good. It was enough to give up the club and do something else entirely. He could build a greenhouse and grow tulips, or something low stress. It was definitely enough to marry Tyra and run off somewhere. He'd leave the club if he didn't need the money. Zipping the backpack up, Art tossed it to Avery, who slumped against the door and breathed in quick, shallow breaths like he was recovering from a run.

"Let's get out of here," Art said, and helped Avery up. Avery stood, and they walked back toward the entrance. "How the fuck did you live here anyway?"

"It wasn't like this before the cops came in and trashed it, man. Besides, we mostly all slept out in the yurts," Avery said, and they stepped outside and back into the truck.

"Well, maybe you'll eventually be able to get this place back up and running," Art said, turning the ignition.

"That would be rad, man." Avery leaned back in his seat while Art pulled out and headed toward the 1—toward Capitola.

3

The Venetian hotel was situated right on the water, and it had its own secluded parking. Art maneuvered into the lot and parked. There were only a few other cars. The rooms looked like terra-cotta cottages straight out of a seventeenth-century Italian village. They were built so close to the beach that there was moisture on the cement berm in front of them from high tide waves spilling over.

"Let's go," Art said.

Avery got out, and they walked toward the street where a narrow walkway led them to the hotel check-in. The office was tight, and a tall, stooped older man checked them in and gave them keys. "We're slow this week from the storm coming in, so we put you up in the two-bedroom by the water—one fifteen. You'll love the view."

"What storm?" Art asked, leaning back toward the door to check the sky through a window.

"News is calling for some heavy rains this weekend." The man looked down at his register. "Have a great stay." He said this quickly, as if trying to get rid of them before they changed their mind about staying so close to the shore in a storm.

"Thanks," Art said.

They left and moved down the corridor, and Art watched the numbers on the doors. They had pictures of Italian inspiration carved into each one: boats, vineyard-lined countryside, the Leaning Tower, etc. The ocean- and riverfront rooms had doors facing the parking lot, and above each door was a painted clay scene that had two large dragons breathing fire into a chalice of greater fire, and Art wondered how that related to Italian heritage.

Each unit had a large window facing the parking lot, and Art could see inside. There was a dining room table and a small kitchen in each. They also all had a floor-to-ceiling glass slider that opened to a patio overlooking the ocean. He spotted 115, unlocked the door, and Art followed Avery inside. The room had a short entryway that opened up into a living room and dining room to the left, and a short hallway to the right with three doors for the two bedrooms and a shared bathroom.

"Sit down," Art said, and pointed to the round dining table, and Avery sat.

Art sat beside him and looked out over the ocean. The scene looked postapocalyptic, since not a single person walked the beach or the small wharf that extended from the far right side of the hotel. The water was brown, and the sea looked angry with jagged waves crashing against the rocky shore close enough to their room to send spindrift over the cement berm and onto their small balcony. It looked like, if the storm got worse, they might be underwater soon.

"Let's run the plan again," Art said, piercing the silence between them.

"They're already here," Avery said.

Art followed Avery's finger pointing out past the river mouth, and along a rocky outcropping meant for a beach break. Beyond it, a huge, off-white yacht bobbed in the heavy surf.

"That's the boat," Avery said.

"Good. Then this should be easy. Let's run the plan," Art said. Art hoped the kid would pull his weight. He wanted this plan to go down smoothly, though something almost always threw a wrench in the gears of the best plans. Like getting rammed off a cliff. But Art had done his homework, and these kids weren't like the other rundowns he'd done for Burke. He went after and killed hardened criminals, murderers, rapists, evil men. If anyone deserved to die today, it was Burke.

"I got this," Avery said, his brown eyes lighting up, and Art thought the kid was as affable as a puppy. "I meet Heath at the bar, Salty's, and I tell him the coast is clear. Then, while I'm with him, you are going to get the girl."

"Good. And as long as you don't tell him anything stupid, nobody has to get hurt."

"Right. I tell him I'm here alone and that the money's in my room."

"And you don't tell him about the girl."

"I won't tell him about the girl."

"Or else what?"

"Or else you have to kill us." The kid was so glib, Art wanted to laugh, but he knew the kid was serious. Avery just wanted this to be over as badly as Art did.

"Or else I have to kill you, cor—" Art's words got interrupted by the phone in the kitchenette ringing. They both stared at it for a second, then Art said, "Pick it up. Remember your part and everything will be fine."

Avery picked up the phone. "Avery," he said, and he flashed a smile and a thumbs-up. It was happening.

Chapter Thirty
Friday, September 16, 1988
Heath

1

Gray clouds swirled overhead, and the wind kicked up while we crested over small ocean swells, heading north out of Santa Barbara. We rounded Point Conception, where the seas tripled, and the pitch of the boat became unnerving. Survival became a matter of holding on to something stationary or getting pitched overboard. I watched a spot on the horizon, so I didn't vomit.

The previous night, between the alcohol, the cocaine, and the hash, I'd hit a high so pleasurable, so pure that I'd never thought possible. I paid for it now. Juan and Rori sat at a bench behind the captain's chair, gripping the partition, and didn't speak. They were about to puke, too.

"Only nine more hours of this," Juan said, and put his head in his hands.

"Fuck this," Rori said, and she lit a cigarette, then ping-ponged downstairs, tightly holding the railing.

2

The seas remained eight to ten feet for hours. We traveled through spots where a low ground fog settled and clung to the stubble on my chin, pierced my clothing, and soaked my bones with frigid moisture. We took turns at the helm three hours at a time, and Juan pointed out Moro Rock, then, later, the tall cliffs of Big Sur. We'd almost killed that bounty hunter somewhere around here, and I wished his body were still inside that truck, churning under the ocean's might.

Juan took over for the last leg. An hour later we passed a lighthouse on a golf course at Pacific Grove, and he turned toward Monterey Bay. We glided through the calmer waters of the bay just when the sun started to set. It was 8:26 p.m. when we finally slowed near the wharf at Capitola. We passed the little beach where Rori first surfed, and the memory felt distant, like a previous life. Juan maneuvered the yacht near a river mouth that emptied into the ocean. Left of the river was the Capitola pier with a restaurant at the end and a dock with a few sailboats. At the base of the pier sat a hotel that looked like an Italian village. It was the Venetian, where Avery was staying. He could already be there.

"You two haven't learned to drop an anchor yet, so pay close attention," Juan said. "You have to let the boat drift and give the anchor some room to catch and bury itself into the sand on the bottom. Pull here." Juan pointed to a lever with a ball at the tip.

Rori pulled the lever up, and a soft hum started somewhere in the ship. A chain clinked starboard while it unspooled into the scalloped sea. I lowered the dinghy and tethered it to a cleat at the rear of the ship. Once the boat was shut down and our anchor dragged until it held, we climbed into the raft, and I pull started the engine. It purred to life, and I navigated us to the shore, beaching it the way Juan had. We dragged the dinghy up the beach and chained it to a rock near a beach-access walkway.

"All right, listen. We need to check in to our hotel, and then we have a nine p.m. reservation at Shadowbrook. At eleven thirty we need to be back at the dinghy so we can meet the surfers at the ship to make the drop. They will take the product back to a little house off the cliff there." He pointed past the pier and toward Santa Cruz. "*Entiendes?*"

"I could use a beer," Rori said.

"I could use a shot," I said. My hands shook slightly, so I shoved them into my slacks. I wasn't sure why, but this whole operation gave me an empty sensation, like after a three-day bender with no sleep and your body had nothing left. If I were honest with myself, I was terrified I would fuck this up and have to answer to Jacques and his men.

"There's a little bar right here called Salty's," Juan said. "I need a tequila *tambien*."

"Where we staying anyway?" Rori asked.

"We always stay at the Capitola Plaza, across the street. *Siguime.* I'll show you."

3

Esplanade Street ran along the water and held a string of restaurants, bars, and hotels on either side. My legs were rubbery, and my equilibrium rocked like I was still on the boat. We passed by the parking lot where Rori and I had spent our first night on the road, and when I glanced over, she was looking there, too. Seemed like yesterday in some ways, and it seemed like a lifetime in others.

Salty's was a dive, and likely the only dive for miles. Inside it was hot with humanity, and the crowd was a mixture of people. Surfers, blue-collar workers, hippies, and a few well-dressed tourists. At the bar, Juan ordered three shots of Patrón and then disappeared to the restroom.

Rori and I took our shots and split Juan's, then ordered another round. I picked up my second shot when somebody bounced into me, and it spilled down my Oxford shirt. From the weight of the shove, I'd expected a guy, but it wasn't. I turned and observed a thin and pretty woman in her mid twenties with a spread of sun freckles across her nose. Without acknowledging me, she wedged up to the bar beside me. Her sense of ease reminded me somehow of surf culture. The almost arrogant sense of well-being developed by mastering the source material of the sea. Her skin was sun-kissed, and her brown hair had highlights from exposure to sun and salt water.

"If you're going to push people around, you might as well buy them a drink." She teased. She paused a moment, then made eye contact. A half smile formed, and her brown eyes gleamed liked she'd already had a few.

"Who's the asshole, Beth?" a stocky blonde guy approached from the side, and I could sense by the way he approached that he wouldn't hesitate to make a move. We exchanged glances and his eyes widened—a few lonely synapses in his brain made the connection that we'd met before. "Holy shit. I remember you guys. It's Avery's bro and Rori? Right? Beth, these are the guys I told you about."

Even though he was a brawny asshole, it was surprisingly good to see Eric, caustic swagger and all.

The girl put out her hand. "Beth. Good to meet you."

"And I'm Rori," Rori said, pushing past me and intercepting the handshake.

"Is this the chick that ditched my wetsuit in the parking lot, *Eric*?"

"Whoa there, she just borrowed it and—" Eric started.

"First, I didn't know it belonged to anyone. Second, Eric told me to keep it," Rori said, and inched closer to Beth.

"Hey, to be fair, I bought it for you when we were together," Eric said.

"It was a gift—wait, you tried to give it away?" Beth said, switching her attention to Eric.

Eric looked tongue-tied.

Beth turned to me and said, "Now, about that drink, uh—"

"Heath," I said. "Four shots of Patrón."

"No, five," said Juan, and wedged into the bar.

Beth and Eric exchanged worried looks.

"What the hell are you two doing here?" Juan said.

"Um—sorry, Juan. We were just getting loose for tonight—"

Juan raised his hand, leaned in, and whispered, "Our friends down south would not like us to be seen drinking together. Also, drink after. Okay? Be professionals for Christ's sake. Let's go." Juan placed a hundred down on the bar. We followed him outside and down Esplanade.

4

The weather had turned cold and the tacky; coastal fog loomed all around us, casting muted shadows across the damp sidewalk. Rori huddled closer for warmth, and it gave me a touch of nostalgia for that first night on the Boardwalk.

The Capitola Plaza was a surprisingly humble hotel compared to the properties in San Diego and Santa Barbara, but quaint and fit the architecture of the little town. It was a two-story stucco structure opposite the ocean side of Esplanade. A corrugated iron trellis with the gold lettering that spelled out *Capitola Plaza* at the entrance. A courtyard at the center of the property held a tiny café with tile tables and steel chairs. Vines grew through the sign and up the faux brick walls of the courtyard.

Our suite was on the second floor with a partially blocked ocean view, but we could also see the street, and down the way, the Venetian. The room was large and clean with a lot of off-white and sand colors—generic pictures of the beach hung from the walls.

"Not exactly the Four Seasons," Rori said.

"I was just thinking that, too. We've been ruined by luxury in less than a month," I said.

Rori laughed, and I walked to a courtyard window and looked down at the little café. My eyes drifted up to the opposite tower, and I startled. Juan stood at his window, staring in our direction. I gave a nervous wave and closed the blinds. Rori leapt onto my back and pushed her tongue into my ear. I laughed and fell backwards onto the bed. She rolled off, and we lay there giggling for a second. When the laughter wore off, a heaviness fell, deep and palpable between us.

"I'll call," I said.

"Venetian hotel, Capitola," I said after dialing zero. It rang several times before the receptionist picked up.

"Venetian," a woman's voice said.

"Yes, Avery Walker's room, please," I said.

"Hold, please." It clicked over, then rang again.

It rang several more times, and I imagined the worst. But then, it picked up.

"Avery," he said.

"Bro," I said. "God, it's good to hear your voice again. Are you okay?"

"Everything is copacetic, man," Avery said.

"What's the plan?"

"You dropping at midnight, right?" Avery said.

"Yeah."

"Okay, then let's meet me at Salty's at one a.m. I got it in a backpack."

"No traps this time?"

"No worries, brother. I'll see you then," he said, and hung up. I hung up the receiver and sat by Rori on the downy bed.

"He alone?" Rori said.

"I couldn't tell for sure. Seems that way. We're meeting at Salty's. You'll be safe here. I'll go and get the money alone."

"They try anything, I'll fucking cut their throats out," Rori said.

"I know. Stay alert tonight," I said. We hugged and the phone rang. We both jumped. I picked up the receiver. "Heath," I said.

"It's Juan. Cab is downstairs. Let's go."

"All right, we'll be down in five," I said.

"Just hurry up, *pendejos*." The line went dead.

"Freshen up quick," I said. "Car's downstairs."

"I can't tell if I like Juan or hate his guts," Rori said.

"I know, but we have to deal with him. For now, at least."

Rori nodded, stood, and went into the bathroom. I heard the water in the sink run, then splashing while she freshened up. I could use a splash of cold water, too, for sobriety's sake. We had to pull off two transactions tonight, and with Juan around, either one could turn ugly fast.

Chapter Thirty-One
Friday, September 16, 1988
Heath

1

Shadowbrook sat nestled near a riverbank that fed into the Capitola Bay. The water was brown with a rippling current. I had on my blue nautical suit jacket, and Rori, in mock refinement, had on an oversized folding hat and white pantsuit jumper with white stiletto heels. Living like this made me realize how many other people there were that lived well. It made me also realize how, a few weeks ago, we would have been run out of a restaurant like this. Treated like trash. But not in this moment. In this moment, we were king and queen of every place we stepped foot.

We rode down a slow gondola cart on railroad tracks that dropped us off at the entrance to the restaurant. Shadowbrook, according to a plaque outside the gondola, had been an institution in the Santa Cruz area since the late forties.

We were greeted by a well-dressed and professional staff and shown to a table overlooking the river, the bay visible in the distance. The place was about as pricy as the Four Seasons in Santa Barbara, but the fare was old-world and continental. Broiled steaks, grilled fish, and steamed vegetables with hollandaise sauce. Stuff like that. Rori and I ordered the steak and lobster paired with a five-hundred-dollar bottle of Bordeaux—we were just doing our jobs, after all.

We ate quickly, without savoring the experience like we should: our minds raced with what the evening had in store for us. We skipped the slow gondola on the way back and opted for the stairs. Back at our hotel, we fell onto the cloud of a mattress, and I felt full and sleepy.

I wanted to nap, but Juan knocked, and we let him in. Without asking, he took a hand mirror from the bathroom and lined it with cocaine. We all did a bump but were only slightly rejuvenated. We'd gone so hard at sea, that the floor seemed to move out from under me with every step. I had, as Juan called it, my sea legs. We needed a solid night of deep rest to recuperate. But that wasn't going to happen, not tonight.

Juan instructed us to be at the dinghy at 11:45 p.m. and left. I watched through a crack in our blinds and saw his lights turn on; then his silhouette appeared. He began stalking back and forth behind the sheer curtain. We tried to sober up by drinking water and doing small bumps. I didn't want to drown out there tonight.

2

At 11:32 p.m. I took another bump and chugged more water. The room felt unsteady still. I stood over the dresser, looking out at the darkened avenue. It was empty, and since we'd gotten back from dinner, the weather had taken a violent turn. In the distance, the seas were getting higher and crashed hard against the shore and the cliffs. I hoped we could even get out past the breakers in the dinghy without flipping over. Rori lay across the bed in her jeans and sweater, ready for the mission.

"It's time," I said.

She let her feet slowly slide to the floor. "This isn't my favorite part of the job," she said.

"Especially not in this weather," I said.

I arranged two little bumps on the mirror and took one. The burning jab of pain deep in my sinuses quickly diminished and transformed into a noxious drip that tasted of diesel fuel. A moment later, a soothing numbness took over that reminded me of the dentist. The sluggish drunk sensation and rocking in my head was diminished enough now; I was as ready as I could be.

Rori took the dollar bill and snorted a line, furrowing her brow and looking up toward the ceiling for a second while the pain seemed to pass. She pressed against me, kissing me hard on the mouth. It felt wet and numb and exciting.

"Let's get this over with," she said. She pulled away, wiping her mouth.

We unwrapped rain ponchos supplied to us in our luggage. I wondered what we were supposed to do if the storm didn't clear. If we were expected to navigate back to Mexico in a squall.

Outside, a fine mist collected on our ponchos. A strong wind whipped through the corridors in sudden, unexpected gusts that felt like it would blow us over. When we got to the shore, the waves ranged from five to seven feet tall and crashed in all directions with no predicable seams. Although—from my limited surfing, I'd gained an understanding of how currents worked—there had to be a riptide that would pull us safely into the bay. Still, we would get very wet.

3

Juan was already working to unchain the dinghy when we stepped down the beach access. The violent surf pushed up the beach and sucked around his ankles. We helped him steady the craft, remove the chain, then push it into the shallow water.

"Let's angle along the rocks here," I said, shouting above the ocean's white roar.

"I don't think it matters, Heath. Look out there," Rori said.

To most people, the ocean looked like one solid, writhing mass, but it wasn't; there was a riptide, a seam that ran along the inside of the rock jetty, so I pushed the boat down the beach, and he followed.

"Get in," I said once we got to the jetty.

Juan and Rori jumped into the boat just behind the rocks where the water pooled. I pushed the craft until I stood waist-deep, then pulled myself into the dinghy. I started the engine, and it chugged but didn't start. I pulled it again, and I smelled gas, which meant that I had flooded the stupid two-stroke. I engaged the choke and pulled four more times, hard, then switched the choke off and pulled once more, and it purred to life. I sat idling for a second, and Juan glared at me, his face crinkled in disgust. I watched the waves; they were wind swell, but even wind swell had breaks. Just like traffic on a freeway—sometimes you had to just wait for the opening.

A few more waves came through, and I saw it, a slight lull in the crashing. I cranked the throttle, and the boat took off, almost sending Rori and Juan overboard. Keeping us along the jagged rocks, we missed most of the crashing waves. At the end of the jetty though, the swells got bigger and white capped. I angled toward the yacht when an overhead swell crested in front of us. I tried to maneuver directly into the wave so if it crashed on us, it wouldn't capsize us.

I had the tiny outboard redlined, and it sounded like it would bust a gasket. I gripped a handle on the boat; Juan closed his eyes. We moved up the face and the top when the wave started to crumble. It crashed over us at its peak; white water fell over the nose of the boat, but we broke free. Then we were airborne, the prop spinning in open space like a launch ramp into the darkness. We splashed hard into the ocean, and the spray covered our bodies. We were free of the breakers and motored much more easily to the rear deck of the yacht.

Juan boarded and we followed him. He told us to stay on deck and disappeared into the hull. When he came back, he held the key to the little bar where Jacques kept the cognac. He handed it to me.

"Your turn to unload," he said. He then handed me a rock-climbing harness. "Put it on."

I climbed into the harness and fastened it. Juan clipped a rope to my carabiner, then tied me off to a cleat.

"Jump over," Juan said. "Starboard side."

"Where does the key go?"

"There is a hole, just below the waterline. Unlock it, pop the handle, and open the hatch. It slides inward on guides. Remove the bags, and we pull you back up."

"What about the bags?"

"Just leave them, they float."

"Shouldn't we wait until the storm clears?"

"This isn't a fair-weather sport, Heath," Juan said.

I looked down at the gnashing water and felt a stiff shove. I cartwheeled over the bow line and splashed, face-first, into the freezing water. I hoped, for Juan's sake, that Rori hadn't seen him push me.

My hands felt instantly numb, and I fumbled with the key, probing below the waterline for the hole. I couldn't feel anything, and after several minutes of frantically searching the hull, I looked up to find Juan watching me. Smiling.

"*Abajo, guero.* It's lower, follow the crease in the hull."

I found the crease, and I followed it with my palm, and finally, six inches below the surface, I felt a small bulge. The key slipped in, and I twisted it, exposing a handle. I turned the handle, and a small, circular section of the boat popped just above the water level. Some water rushed in when I pulled the top portion of the panel, the lower section pushing inward. I reached into the cavity and felt sheet plastic. Yanking hard, I pulled the first sealed duffel bag free. It was connected by a rope to a dozen other bags just like it, so I continued to pull until all the bags were free and floating around me. I clicked the panel shut and snapped the handle back.

"All right. Juan," I shouted. There was nobody there.

My body began to tremble from the cold, which meant I was close to hypothermic.

"Hey! Fucker!" I shouted. Juan's small face appeared. Still no Rori.

"You think I can pull you up, fucker? Swim around back," he said, and untied the rope from the cleat, dropping it on my head.

4

I tried to swim, but my limbs felt leaden like they no longer belonged to me. I tried the backstroke, but the harness pulled me downward. I needed to swim forty feet, but my energy had been spent. My heart racing like hummingbird wings. I faltered; a flash of fear ignited inside my chest like a thunderclap. There was no way I could survive this. I was going to drown out here.

Using the burst of adrenaline to my advantage, I fought the urge to free-fall—I aggressively swam toward the rear deck, but the current was against me. I pushed harder, and a wave crashed over my face and stung. Then I was underwater, where it was quiet and peaceful. I surfaced and breathed. I tried swimming again, and a larger wave hit me over the head. I was underwater again. I thought I surfaced, but when I inhaled, it was heavy and briny. I choked and inhaled more water; a burning pain ripped through my lungs. I fell into a blanket of warmth and serenity, and I was only vaguely aware that I was sinking.

Then I suddenly began to race toward the surface. My body felt cold again, and when my head popped out of the water, I inhaled, coughed, and puked up ocean. I was dragged from the water onto a small boat. I coughed up more water and tried to breathe.

When I finally glanced up to see who had saved me, I was again surprised to see her. It was Beth, the surfer. I held on while she paddled hard toward the back of the ship. Around us, also in kayaks, were Eric, Pete, and Thorin. They had the sealed duffel bags stacked on their boats.

"Holy shit, the fucking kook is back," Thorin said.

"You guys know each other?" Beth yelled above the rain, wind, and seas.

"Just dump him on the back, and let's get the fuck out," Eric said.

Beth used her double-sided oar and paddled until we were touching the back of the yacht. "What the fuck happened to your lifeline, bro?" Beth said while she tried to steady the kayak.

"That fucker—he cut me loose," I said. I rolled onto the rear deck and stood clutching the railing.

"Juan's a shifty little fuck, bro. Be safe. We'll catch you out here same time tomorrow," she said. All four of them paddled toward the cliffs. I wondered how they were going to get to shore without capsizing the boats in this storm. But then again, they were practically amphibious.

I fell to my knees and breathed, fighting the urge to vomit again. When I could stand, I moved unsteadily toward the main galley. When I saw Juan's face, I wanted to crush his windpipe.

"What the fuck was that, you sick fu—" I coughed again.

"Easy, *vato*," Juan said, and smiled. "I saw the surfer fuckers. I knew they were going to grab you. Did you lock it up?"

"Yeah—I fucking locked it up."

"All right. Let's get back to shore. We're all done with business until tomorrow, and then we can all head home and see Jacques a little richer."

"Fuck you," Rori said, and tugged against handcuffs holding her to a galley chair.

"Sorry, I couldn't have you messing with the drop, you understand," Juan said. He had apparently handcuffed her there before sending me over the edge of the ship. "Now get back in the dinghy." He uncuffed her and she rubbed her wrists.

Sitting in the dinghy, the hypothermia seized my body, and I couldn't move my limbs. Juan took over and followed the same line that I'd shown him. We landed on the beach, and Rori helped chain the dinghy to the same rock. We trudged, soaking wet, up the railing and back to our hotel.

5

Inside our room, Rori helped me tear my wet clothes off. I turned the shower on and let it steam before plugging the bath drain. We got in and kissed, but I still shook so hard, I nearly went into convulsions. Rori wrapped her thin, tan arms around me. Her small breasts pressed against my chest while the hot water poured over my numb limbs, which began to tingle.

By the time we were out of the shower and I could move again, it was five minutes to 1:00 a.m. I dressed in decidedly warmer clothes and kissed Rori before I left to meet Avery. I looked across the courtyard and could see Juan's silhouette sitting in a chair at a desk. Probably doing more coke.

6

Walking into Salty's, I felt surprised that it was still at capacity. It was apparently the place to be for people who weren't the silicon-lined nouveau riche hanging out at places like Shadowbrook. The music was loud, and the voices fought for prominence in the low, wood-ceilinged room. I saw a waving arm across the bar and maneuvered through the crowd toward it. When I got closer and the crowd parted, I finally saw him. Avery looked like the same beautiful man as before, but with some street sense kicked into him with the nose of a boxer.

"Goddamn, it's good to see you," Avery said, and we embraced. He squeezed harder than normal.

"You, too, brother. Christ, it feels like it's been a decade. You look ten years older," I said, and we both laughed even though it wasn't funny.

"Did you guys drop? Did Eric pick up?"

"Yeah. We dropped at midnight. Everything went down right. Eric and the others grabbed the bags and paddled off. Juan cut me loose in the goddamn water, and I almost drowned though."

"Juan. Yeah, I never really worked with him. Jacques was captain when I ran—is he, you know, pissed about the money?"

"He said we'd have to pay him back if you didn't come through, so I'm glad you called. I'll get it to him, and you'll be square. Right? No harm?"

"Right, no harm," Avery said.

"Where is the money anyway? And where *was* it?"

"I had it stashed at the A-frame. It's in my hotel room. I didn't want to carry all that cash here." He motioned to the bar.

"Hey, I'm sorry about that crazy fucker in Big Sur, man," I said.

"That dude is fucking crazy. He had a gun to my head, but he promised he wouldn't hurt you guys," Avery said.

I let the comment go; I'd squared that in my mind. We fucked him, he fucked us. Now, we were doing each other a solid. "Where have you been hiding out?"

"Over in the east side of Santa Cruz. Near downtown," Avery said.

"You okay otherwise? Need anything?"

"I'll be good once this debt is squared with Jacques. I'll be able to live again, you know. Maybe reopen the Hideaway someday."

"That would be righteous," I said.

"You ready to go get that money? I need to get the hell out of Capitola before any of Jacques's guys see me."

"How about a drink first, man. This has been a good gig for us. We've been making good money thanks to you. Bartender, can we get two tequilas and two beers?"

"One drink. Then we get over there," Avery said. And when the bartender brought the drinks, we clinked glasses and drank them down. The warmth from the alcohol rid my body of the last shiver from the chill Pacific waters that had almost consumed me.

Chapter Thirty-Two
Friday, September 16, 1988
Art

1

There was one other car in the parking lot of the Venetian hotel, which Art decided had to be the front desk guy's car. Everyone must have checked out because of the storm, which was good. They were alone. A quick gust whipped rain across his face while he walked. When he got to his truck, he looked up at the clouds, brooding and dark. The storm blocked out all but the faintest glow from the moon and stars.

In the back seat of his truck, Art located the vacuum-sealed bag and pulled a blue janitorial jumpsuit free. He opened a hard plastic case beside it and assembled a silenced tranquilizer pistol. Within the foam of the case, he slipped a narrow, custom dart free. The darts were made from animal tranquilizers. It was filled with tranquilizer, liquid methaqualone, and a touch of morphine. Art figured if his marks were going down, at least they would be comfortable. The gun only held one dart at a time.

Art pulled the uniform over his clothes, tucked the pistol into the jumpsuit pocket, closed the door, and pulled a dolly and large rubber trash can from the truck bed. Art moved down the street, staying close to the restaurant façades to shield himself from the wind and caught a glimpse of Avery's yellow parka just when he slipped into the bar's front door. Art checked his Timex: it was12:45 p.m. He took a right toward the beach and found a small alcove near some dumpsters. Hidden, he watched the front door of the bar.

At exactly 1:00 a.m. Art finally saw Heath leave the Capitola Plaza and walk briskly to the bar. Once the kid was inside, Art got closer. Through the window, he watched Heath work his way toward Avery, and then they embraced in the crowded space. Now was his chance.

2

Art went straight through the Plaza courtyard and to the receptionist's desk. A sign taped to the counter gave an after-hours number to call. A light shone from a back office, and Art checked, but it was empty. People in small, low-crime towns seemed to feel safe all the time, and that kind of confused him. That was the best kind of place to hit.

Art left the dolly and trash can in the lobby, then moved behind the desk. He stooped down and pulled drawers until he found tabs for files on each of the twelve rooms. The folders were all empty except for eleven and twelve. The names were bullshit, but one had two registered guests, the other a single occupancy. Across from the desk, a pegboard was attached to the wall, and he pulled the spare key for room eleven, the double occupancy, and grabbed his dolly and trash can from the lobby.

The numbers counted up when he neared the window. At the end of the short hallway, a square window looked down at the street below. Shadows on the asphalt shimmered like broken glass. Art tried the handle softly. It was locked. He put his ear to the door to listen.

A toilet flushed inside, and Art heard footfalls on the hardwood floor coming out of the bathroom. A TV set snapped on, and he could hear the tube warm up for a second. Then the encapsulated voices of an old sixties rerun came on. The bed squeaked. Art needed to make his move fast. He knocked on the door.

"Yes, hello. Room service?" Art said, masking his voice. "You need a towel?"

Art held the pistol under a towel from the front desk. He kept his head down so if she looked through the peephole, all she would see was the uniform and the top of his head.

"I don't need a fucking towel," came Rori's voice from a direction that sounded like the bed. He gently slipped the key into the door and turned it slowly, trying not to rattle the knob.

"So sorry, miss. I leave by door," Art said, and he knelt, took a deep breath, and shouldered into the door. Dropping to his knee, he rolled to his right while aiming the dart gun at the bed. She wasn't there.

Art quickly scanned the room, and he knew where she was. But it was too late. She jumped at him from behind the door just when he turned. A wood-handled steak knife glinted in the glow from the television. She took a steady aim at Art's throat—she meant to kill. What caught Art off guard more than anything was that she had zero hesitation, like she'd been trained for this. People always hesitated; this was new.

Art blocked the blade with his left arm, the tip lashed deeply into the meat of his forearm. Trying to suppress a scream, he emitted a guttural growl. He fell to his back and kicked at her to gain some space which backed her up. She wrapped both hands around the handle and came down toward his chest like a samurai. But he'd had enough time to aim. He fired, and the dart pelted her in the soft tissue of her belly. She stalled, stunned by the sensation of being shot. Her hands fell, confused, and probed at the dart. She pulled it free. Blood bloomed in her white cotton shirt; the dart clattered to the floor.

"You piece of shit. You can't bring me back to him. I can pay you…you dumb fuck," Rori said.

She stumbled toward the bed, where she sat, clutching her wound. The drugs hadn't kicked in yet, but she seemed to realize there was no escape at this point, which was good because it meant there would be less collateral damage. "You have no idea what he's going to do to me."

Art cringed when she said that. It was no big surprise why the girl had run away; he was certain Burke had beat the hell out of this kid for years. But he needed her to finish this.

"You're feeling the morphine right now. The tranquilizer will knock you unconscious in ten to fifteen minutes. You're going back to Shadow Valley."

Art stood and pulled the jumpsuit sleeve up to expose the stab wound. The cut was about two inches deep and an inch wide. She'd ripped into the muscle, but it wasn't bleeding much, so no arteries were nicked. Using his teeth and a pocketknife, he cut a strip from the towel and tied it around his arm.

"I don't know what he's paying you, but I've got fifty—we've got fifty thousand," she said, bending forward with her elbows on her knees. "And there's more. We can get more."

"It's not about the money. Where's the phone?" Art asked. And this was only partially true. Burke was a special case; he had far too much power, but Art intended to turn the tables. Tonight.

Rori glanced beside the bed, and Art walked over, then dialed Burke's home phone number. It was almost one thirty in the morning. The phone rang eleven times, and a groggy Burke finally picked up.

"It's Art."

"Put her on," Burke said.

Art handed the phone to Rori.

Her voice turned high and girlish, and she smiled wickedly at Art. "Hi, Daddy. Apparently, I'm coming home. Just like you wanted." The whole scene shook a chill like ice down his back.

Art pulled the phone away. "There she is. I've got Tyra reopening the club tomorrow. Do I have your word that she's going to be able to do that hassle-free?"

"Bring her to me. Bring her back, or I'll shoot your stupid whore partner."

Art tried to control his breathing. A mixture of anxiety, fear, and raw panicked anger rushed into his stomach. He didn't know any better ten years ago on the force, but he'd known better this time. But somehow Burke killing Tyra had never occurred to him. "If you've even bruised Tyra, I'll fucking burn you to the ground." Art said.

"Don't you threaten me, you ingrate. Get my daughter home tonight, or Tyra's a goddamn missing person," Burke said.

"Don't fucking touch Tyra…I'll bring her."

"Safe house in three hours," Burke said. "And bring the kid—Heath—or you're not getting paid either."

"I thought you wanted him dead and buried. I'll need an extra hour," Art said.

"Make it six a.m. Goshen. And bring the kid alive." Then the phone clicked silent.

Rori had slumped to her side, her eyes fluttering. Art set the phone on the receiver. "He's screwing you over, isn't he?" she asked. She was still smiling.

"You should be awake in four hours with the dose I gave you. We're going to give your father exactly what he wants. Go to sleep," Art said.

"Heath. Is Heath okay?" she said, her eyes closed now.

Art walked to the window and glanced down at Salty's to the left, the Venetian off to the right, and the empty street in between. Two men came out of the bar, one with a yellow raincoat. Art hid behind the curtains and watched. The brothers laughed and walked slowly past the Capitola Plaza. When they got to the Venetian, they turned left and disappeared into the corridor. Art started to close the curtain when he saw another figure slip from the courtyard below him. The smaller man glanced around, then stepped out. Art could just make out a small object that the man pulled from his waistline. The man followed the same path down the corridor, moments after Heath and Avery.

3

Art arranged Rori into a comfortable position on the bed and checked her breathing. It was heavy but consistent. When he started for the door, he noticed the cocaine. He pushed it back into the small baggie and placed it into his change pocket. Stepping out, he pulled the dolly and garbage can inside with Rori, then closed the door and went downstairs. His leg ached like the hands of God were crushing it through his brace.

Art stepped quietly past the carved wooden doors of the Venetian. He stopped at the inside edge of the corridor. The small figure stood in a raincoat, watching the brothers through the window. It was a gun held in his right hand—he screwed a silencer onto it. Art ducked low and waded into the parking lot, hiding behind the attendant's car. This guy had to be with the Canadian Cartel, and there was no way to close the distance without getting shot. He wished he'd brought his Glock, or another dart. All he could do was wait.

A moment later, the guy kicked in the front door to Art and Avery's room, splintering the doorjamb. It swung inward and he went inside. Art limped as fast as he could toward the room and snapped open his collapsible baton.

Through the window, Art could see Avery and Heath jump when the man burst into the room. Based on his dealings, Art assumed there would be a negotiation. That would give him some time. The gunman made one short statement.

"Avery, long time. Jacques said to tell you good-bye. Nobody steals from him."

Art finally made it to the window, and at that moment, he heard Avery scream, "No!" Then Avery's chest burst open. Three large, quick bullet holes the size of fists punched into him. A fine mist of blood sprayed the wall and window beyond. A pain heaved in Art's chest, a leaden sadness he'd never felt before on a hunt. This fuck would pay. Art shimmied along the windowsill and hid behind a strip of stucco between the window and the door. He could hear footfalls coming, and beyond that, Heath weeping for his fallen friend.

"Why the fuck did you kill him? He has your money!" Heath screamed.

"That money was skimmed over time. Think about that for a moment. Meet me back at the hotel when you're ready."

Art stood statue-still and waited. As soon as the man's foot crossed the threshold, Art's swift left hand was in motion. The man jumped when he saw Art blindsiding him. But it was too late. The rigid steel baton connected with his temple. He didn't even get a chance to fire off another round.

The man's body snapped like a matchstick. His left eye bulged and popped free of its socket. The body crumpled straight down. Art raised the baton again and swung repeatedly.

He watched, somewhat detached, while the man's skull cracked and blood sprung from the ears and mouth. When he straightened, he realized he had been crying.

Wiping his face, he cleaned blood from his hand and baton on the man's clothing, then stepped into his room. Beside Avery's slumped body, Heath sat, sobbing. When he saw Art, he froze. His eyes widened and glowed like a feral animal caught in a flash of unexpected headlights. He scooted toward the window as if to escape, but there was nowhere to go. Art had him now.

"I have Rori, so stand up. You and I are taking a little trip," Art said, and pulled his tranquilizer gun from his pocket and trained it on Heath, even though it was spent. "You're coming with me one way or another."

"Fuck you, man. My mom's dead because of your boss. And now my best friend is dead." He sobbed again. "I could have done something. I tried to save him. I wanted to save them all."

"Avery is dead because your employer ordered it." Art paused and looked out the door—he needed to move these bodies, fast. "Plus, he set you up twice. Think about that. How much is he worth to you?" The words stabbed at Art; he missed the kid already, too. Even though Avery had been a terrible criminal and a shitty friend, Art had already begun to believe he could shape him into something working at the club.

"And what the fuck are you going to do? Kill me and take Rori back to that lunatic? Fuck you," Heath said, and spit. He continued to sob.

"Nobody else needs to die." Art paused. "Rori mentioned that you two have fifty thousand dollars," Art said, still holding the gun on him.

"Fuck—we will after this drop, but you killed Juan, and the storm—and I can't pilot that thing without her." The kid seemed to be wising up to the situation, which was good.

"When do you have to leave here to get back in time?"

"We leave tomorrow at midnight, after we get the money from the surfers," Heath said.

"Listen. I've got a plan to save you both and take down Burke. But first, I'm taking fifty thousand from Avery's money. Second, you need to help me get these bodies in the truck. Third, you and Rori are coming back to Central Valley. We've got an appointment with Chief Burke." Art smiled. Heath stood.

"What about Avery, man? He's fucking dead."

"You can't help him now. You can only help yourself and Rori. We need to get rid of these bodies and keep this quiet."

Heath nodded.

"Let's move," Art said.

"Can you at least tell me what you have planned?" Heath asked.

"I'll tell you on the way. It's a long story."

Heath nodded and helped Art drag the gunman to the bed of the pickup. They moved Avery, and Art covered the bodies with a new tarp, tucked it under, then flipped the gate up. Art handed Heath the spray bottle of bleach and a roll of paper towels.

"Go clean up as much of the blood as you can. Spray anything that looks red. I'll be back in ten minutes." Art paused. "And when you do get back to Mexico, you tell your employer that Avery took that little fucker out. They killed each other."

Heath nodded again, and Art got into his truck and drove the block or so to Capitola Plaza. Stopped in the loading zone with his hazards flashing and engine running, he got out. There was still nobody on the street, and Art carefully pulled the sleeping Rori into the plastic tub and moved the trash can onto the dolly, then wheeled it to the elevator.

When he got to the truck, a couple stumbled out of Salty's a block down and moved in his direction. He leaned on the trash can and waved. They turned up a side street, and Art got back to work. Slipping his hands under Rori's armpits, he lifted her into the back seat of the truck and closed the door.

Back at the Venetian, Heath sat in front of the darkened room with his head in his hands. He stood, clutching the duffel bag of money that the gunman had tried to take. He got in.

"We going to kill this fucker?" Heath asked. "For fifty grand?"

"I hope so. But we need to get to his safe house before he does," Art said, and looked at his Timex. It was 2:47 a.m. If he could get there in three hours, he'd have thirteen minutes to pull it all together. "Count out fifty thousand and put it in the glove compartment. The rest goes back to Mexico with you." Heath counted while Art drove with rain sheeting across the dark windshield and gusts of wind shoving the vehicle side to side up over the coastal range, back toward Central Valley.

Chapter Thirty-Three
Saturday, September 17, 1988
Heath

1

The soft pre-glow of the morning sun peeked over the Sierra Nevada mountains to the east when we pulled off the freeway. It was clear here, which meant we'd outrun the storm, but it would probably make it here eventually.

I hadn't been this close to the bounty hunter before, and after three hours of watching him drive without his disguises, he looked pretty normal. Not just normal, but friendly and familiar. I'd seen him before; I just couldn't place when or where, because, well, I didn't usually end up on the business end of a bounty.

The bounty hunter pulled off the freeway just before the main exit to Shadow Valley and turned down Goshen Avenue. We were way out in the industrial warehouse region. I hadn't been out here in years, and my gut started to tighten like it were being squeezed by the hands of God.

"Where are we going, exactly?" I asked him.

"Burke wants us to meet him at his club, Swing Time Grille. Why, you been here?"

We passed a set of roll-up warehouse spaces, an industrial-sized self-storage, and then the neighborhood began to take shape from my memories. It was different in some ways, but the same in others. New traffic lights, fresh paint, but this was the old neighborhood.

The bounty hunter slowed almost to a stop in front of a bar. The neon lights spelled out *Swing Time Grille* with a martini glass at the end. It wasn't open, so the lights looked dull in the dim moonlight. The fist in my stomach gripped harder, and I thought I would be sick.

He took his next right, and behind the storage facility, there it was. A different color paint, but the same ratty, evil fucking place I had stayed at two years ago. It was Hotel Dog Shit.

"What the fuck are we doing here?" I said. I wanted to run, I wanted to fight, I wanted to kill again. This place pulsed through me with so many mismatched urges and emotions, I couldn't separate them. I just knew it made me sick.

"This is Burke's drop spot." The bounty hunter looked at me and paused. "You look like you fucked a ghost."

I tried to respond, but my mouth went dry. I cleared my throat and tried again. "I lived here," I said. "This was Sal's. Sal's Market. This was a group home."

The bounty hunter turned back to the building, and he clenched his eyes shut, then reopened them. "Jesus Christ, kid. Holy fucking Christ, kid. I just got chills."

The moment he said it, my arms and back burst with goose bumps too. My skin crawled because I came to the same realization that the bounty hunter did.

"Art Dominguez. My god. You're him—you're Domino. Aren't you?"

He turned to me, his hazel eyes watery with tears. "It can't be," he said, his breathing turning ragged. "You're the fucking kid. The one that iced those goddamn perverts. I'd buried that memory with a decade of alcohol with all that shit from the force. But it's back, and you're him."

"I am. I changed my last name. But that was me. *Is* me."

"God. I'm so sorry, kid. For everything. I can't—"

"It's done. We just have to finish this. And destroy this place," I said.

"Once this is over, we burn this hellscape to the ground," Art said.

"Tonight," I said. "It should never have reopened." I wondered if a physical space could attract evil. If so, this place did.

"We don't have a lot of time, kid. Take this," Art said. The baton he gave me was heavier than expected. "Burke will be here in twenty minutes. I need you to wake her up." He opened the glove box and pulled an ammonia inhalant from a small box and cracked it. The sharp smell filled the car with its chemical sting. He handed it to me, then pulled a small baggie of cocaine from his pocket and set it on the dash. "In case that doesn't work."

I got out and pushed the seat forward, then slipped into the back seat and set Rori's head on my lap, gently wafting the inhalant under her nose. She stirred slightly, so I did it again. Seeing her like this made my eyes fill with tears again; she wasn't safe. Not yet. But we were so close.

Art pulled a Glock from his ankle holster, limped to the first door, and knocked. A second later a short, dark-haired man in a tank top and a necklace appeared in the doorway. Art fired two rounds into his chest, and the man fell back. Art went into the dark room, and I could make out a few more muzzle flashes. Then Art emerged, closing the door behind him.

I waved the inhalant under her nose again, and Rori's eyes flickered open. I lined up some of the cocaine on my finger and helped her into a sitting position.

"Where the hell are we?" she asked, blinking heavily.

"We're in Shadow Valley with the bounty hunter. He's helping us. Your dad's on his way," I said, hoping I could get it through to her, through the drug haze. I also wondered, just like Mouse and the others back in the day, if she really wanted to be free of her dad. I mean, I knew she did, but also, there had to be a part of her that loved him. He was her dad, after all.

I held my finger under her nose, and she snorted the coke. Leaning her head back, she gagged slightly. She rolled her head in a circle, and I could tell she was getting that kick from the postnasal drip. "*Is* he helping us?" she asked.

"I'm a thousand percent," I said. She nodded.

Art came back to the truck and opened the driver's side door. "Hurry up, let's go," he said, and we got out, and he walked us to the farthest room in the line, room twelve.

2

Inside, the room was bare except for a full-size bed to the left and a chair in the corner. The layout had changed over the years, but I still felt like a demon was clawing at my guts. Art gave us a specific set of instructions and then unscrewed all the bulbs in the room except a night-light in the corner at the bottom of the bed. He left, closed the door, and we got into position and waited.

I sat in the chair with a rope tied tightly around my chest. Rori lay in the bed under the covers with just her head sticking out, and she curled into a near fetal position. After about ten minutes, her breathing turned heavy, and I wished I had more coke to give her, but we were out—she'd fallen asleep.

We waited, and all I could hear in the near darkness was my heart buzzing inside my chest fast and hard. Finally, I heard a car roaring down the street, tires chirping around the corner. The engine grew closer, and I heard the distinctive sound of tires treading across loose gravel. The engine shut off and a door opened, and I could just barely make out the voices. It was Burke, his savage rumble of a voice, and Art was telling him that it was done, that we were in room twelve waiting for him.

I heard the boots fall across the wood on the deck. The girl's old man, the person who had slaughtered my mother, the crooked bastard who had sent Art after us with a license to kill, sauntered toward us, and the sensation of evil grew inside of me, from my stomach, spreading out through my chest and arms. An angel. The footsteps stopped at the door, and I could see his boot shadows below the doorframe. A tentative knock followed, which confused me unless this was some sick cat-and-mouse game he liked to play.

The door opened, and the old hinges creaked like a bad horror film. He stepped in, and the smell of whiskey and halitosis filled the room. He tried the lights, but they were out. I kept my head down and listened to Rori breathing heavily. Through my half-closed eyes, I watched Burke, in his off-duty, Western clothes. Wranglers, and cowboy hat, and boots. He stopped at my feet and took a pistol from his hip holster, placing it under my chin. He lifted my head, and I pretended it was dead weight. Reaching back with his free hand, the bastard pelted me with a vicious backhand that nearly knocked me out of the chair. It took everything in my power to stay quiet.

"You worthless little prick. I'm going to gut you slow, you little kidnapping son of a bitch," he said. He spit on my face, and I felt the hot saliva burn, and it smelled like Copenhagen tobacco. He reached back to hit me again but stopped when he heard Rori's voice.

"Daddy," she said. "Daddy, why are you in my room?" Her voice was soft and low, and I felt another chill course through my entire body.

"It's okay, sweetie. Daddy's here," he said, and Rori sat up in bed with the covers wrapped around her so only her head and cloud of messy hair showed.

"Leave him alone, Daddy," Rori said, and her voice sharpened slightly.

Burke turned to face her but kept his gun trained on me. "This man is a criminal, sweetie. You know what I do to criminals," he said.

"I'm sorry, Daddy," Rori said, her voice cold and sharp now.

"I know, but we can put it behind us now, can't we? We can go home and make everything all better again, right, sweetie?"

"I'm sorry we didn't have time to finish you back at the ranch."

At that moment, the blanket fell from Rori's arms and exposed her hands that firmly held Art's Glock. She aimed it steadily, and the barrel flashed bright, burning my retinas like staring at the sun. The smell of cordite stung my nostrils, and I was disoriented, but I stood and shrugged off the ropes that had been mock tied by Art.

Trying to refocus and clear my eyes and ears, I saw Rori move toward me until she was close. She pulled the ropes completely off me, and I rubbed my eyes. It took a second, but I could finally see again, and there we were, side by side, standing over the writhing body of Police Chief Burke. She reached down and grabbed Burke's off-duty pistol from his limp hand.

"Take this, Heath," she said, and handed me her father's .38 pistol, retaining Art's Glock.

"You little *bitch*," Burke said, coughing. "I'll send you both down to county and let the warden know you're cop killers. You know what the guards will do to you in there?"

Burke coughed and tried to stand, but I pushed my foot down on his chest where the bullet had slammed into his off-duty vest, the way he'd stepped on my back at the ranch. At such a close range he'd probably broken half his ribs. I leaned on him with all my weight, and he screamed. Tucking his .38 into my waistline in front, I put Art's baton under Burke's chin and pushed his head back. The tables had officially turned, and I wondered if he could appreciate the irony.

"That fucking little Mexican." He coughed and winced at the pain. "Twirl your little baton, criminal. All three of you are going to fucking burn for this when my boys get here."

"You know, it is actually a pretty effective weapon." It was Art speaking. Looking up, I saw Art, a dark silhouette in the doorway. "It's silent, it's compact, and when it comes from a southpaw, nobody ever expects it," Art said.

Burke's eyes rolled over to Art, and he spit on the wood floor. "Fuck you, Art. You double-crossed me. Your whore is as good as dead."

"No, Chow Boy is dead. Tyra is very much alive."

"You have no idea what you're doing, you moron. You know who he works for?"

Art walked over and stood at Burke's feet. "Nobody's ever going to find out what happened here tonight, Burke. Kid, show the police chief here how effective that baton—"

He didn't have a chance to finish that sentence, because Burke shoved my leg aside and reached for the pistol in my waistline. I moved and reached back with the baton, coming down on him with everything I had. Burke partially ducked, but the baton slashed across his forehead and did plenty of damage. A gash opened, and a trickle of blood spilled down his face. He scooted back against the wall in a sitting position.

"Goddamn it. *Look*, what do you want, Art? More money?" Burke's voice had gone from cocky venom to pleading.

Art took the baton from me, folded it down, and slipped it into its sheath. He then took the Glock from Rori and put it in his ankle holster. "Let's get him in the truck," Art said. "But tie his hands first."

I zip-tied his hands, and it took all three of us to lug Burke's body into the back of the pickup, where we tossed him over top the other bodies. He kicked and strained unsuccessfully against the rope. Art went back into the first room and came out with a bewildered Black woman who was tall and frail and had on a crooked, red wig. He tossed me something, and I caught it. It was a set of keys to the Mercedes.

"You'll follow me first before you head back to Santa Cruz," Art said.

He walked the short deck and unlocked every door, going inside each room. A moment later, several young, wan, and bewildered Asian girls emerged from each room, looking sleepy and scared. Once the rooms were cleared, a small, orange glow flickered up inside several of the rooms, which grew brighter while smoke began to pour from the open doors.

"Tyra, wait here with the girls. I'll be back in twenty minutes," Art said to the tall woman while the girls gathered around her. They all stood together and watched the flames slowly lick up the walls and engulf the structure. "Let's go," Art said to us.

3

A distant warmth preceded the light blue that appeared over the Sierra Nevada mountains at sunrise. We all stood on a small stretch of riverbank on the Friant-Kern Canal. The bounty hunter pulled the bodies one at a time from his truck bed and tossed them in the canal. They floated peacefully just behind the blue tarp. I wondered where the hell he thought the canal would take them. From the ground, he reached over and cut Burke's zip ties.

The truck shimmied when Burke tried to get onto his knees. He fell, slipping on the blood generated by his face and the other bodies. Gaining purchase, he stood. When he stretched to his full height, his dim shadow lengthened out over the dark, placid water. To the west, it looked like the storm had followed us here with dark clouds along the eastern skyline.

"What the fuck is this, Art? Some kind of game? Those two are *cop* killers. You want more money? What?" Burke nearly fell out of the truck bed, but Art pulled his Glock and held it on him. Burke steadied himself. I started to feel my stomach knot again, not in fear this time, though. But because I wanted Art to gut this motherfucker, and he still hadn't. What if he changed his mind?

"It's not a game, Burke. I know you ratted on me back in our beat cop days. I dug up the file. You were on the Triad payroll then, and you still are," Art said, and the statement clarified for me, finally, what Art was doing and why. Burke was much, much worse than I even knew.

Art continued, "I also know you abused your own daughter and murdered Heath's mother. So, here are your options. You can confess on the record, or you can swim for it. If you make it across the canal, you're free."

Burke scanned Art's face like this was a joke of some sort. I felt my pulse sprint. No way he would let this asshole walk. Burke's eyes fell on the canal with its calm waters. The tarp and the bodies were moving so slowly, they almost looked like they were floating in place. "What kind of sick shit is this?"

"It's not a joke. It's a simple wager. Confess, or swim for it."

Rori grew restless beside me, and I looked at her. She eyed her father's pistol I had tucked in my pants. "Only if we have to," I whispered. I couldn't tell what, but Art had a plan.

"You're a goddamn fool," Burke said. He stepped carefully to the tongue of the truck. "I swim across, you're going to shoot me in the goddamn back."

"You make it across, you're free," Art said.

"Yeah, well fuck you," Burke said.

He jumped and splashed hard into the water, thrashing toward the far side of the canal. A sliver of the sun emerged, and it glowed and danced over the water. Orange and purple obsidian glinted off the surface. Burke made it to the other side, but he was noticeably winded and clung to the cement with desperation creeping in. He tried to crawl up the wall, but he slipped off the embankment and floated a little farther. Swimming hard, he flattened against the cement again and seemed to get some traction. He crawled halfway out of the water, started to slide, and lunged for the edge of the canal, but his grip gave out. This time, Rori relaxed.

Burke, a few seconds later, swam toward the ladder on the far side of the valve. Just before he got there, the tarp ahead of him slipped under the surface and disappeared, followed by the two bodies. Now Burke panicked and howled in disgust, but it came out in gurgled cries. The current tugged him down, deep, and his head finally dipped below the surface. And just like that, they were all gone—the bodies, the tarp, and Burke. The river returned to its calm, silent flow. Beautiful, with the sun pushing off its now soft, yellow surface.

It was only then, when I knew my mother's murderer was gone forever, and I could see the flames in the distance from Hotel Dog Shit, that the fist in my stomach started to release. A sense of calm passed between Rori and me, and she leaned into me, her arm around my waist. The fear was gone.

4

We followed Art back to the burning hotel, where he parked across the street, where the women all huddled. He got out the bag of Avery's money and handed it to us through the window. "You kids make your delivery. If you ever need my services, you'll find me at Shakers and Shots."

He turned and helped Tyra and the girls into his truck, some of them piling into the bed. I backed out of the space while the building was consumed by flames. When we pulled back onto Goshen, I noticed that the bar was on fire too—that was where Sal's Market once stood. When we drove away, the glow from the structure fires blended in with the orange sun burning behind it, and it was as if we were on a race to get out of Central Valley all over again, only this time the only thing chasing us were the long shadows that grew and stretched all the way back to Santa Cruz, and Ensenada, and into the storm.

Part III

*"I wanna take your misery, replace it with happiness,
but I need your faith in me."*

-Tupac Shakur

Chapter Thirty-Four
Saturday, September 17, 1988
Heath

1

The trip back to Santa Cruz, picking up the money from the surfers, and splashing back down the coast on the yacht played out like a nightmare scenario. The storm raged, and we were tossed through squalls and treacherous waves like tiny, broken toys. But we still did our part as best we could. We dressed up, drank fancy wines, and ate like queens and kings. But I was numb. There was no pleasure in it. Everyone I knew and loved was dead except Rori. I couldn't stop thinking about Avery's body riddled with bullets. I had never seen it coming, or at least I hadn't expected it to be Juan.

It meant that Jacques and I had unfinished business. Avery had been a good guy; he had planned to pay his debts, and Jacques had ordered him killed anyway. I wasn't sure that this was the line of work for me. Or for anyone, really. I was pretty good at staying alive, it seemed, but at what cost? Even if I survived this, worked my way into Jacques's good graces, then what? What would I become? Juan? Did I aspire to be Juan DeMarco? He was dead. Could I kill someone if Jacques ordered it?

Still, we drank Dom at the fire pits of the Four Seasons and smoked our cigarettes, getting eyed by everyone, but we didn't care. We had each other and that was all. Back on the ship that night, I tried to sleep, but Rori tossed and somersaulted.

When we got to San Diego, the weather cleared, which was a nice change of pace. We docked and tried to unwrinkle our clothes by splashing water on them. We checked in and sent a change of clothes up to be laundered, then went up to the fortieth floor. We drank and ordered our steak and lobster and picked at it and smoked but called it an early night. We went to our suite overlooking that massive industrial bay and slept poorly, if at all. We were both numb still, I thought. How could we not be after all that death?

2

The next morning, we had the ship out in the bay and chugging toward Ensenada a little earlier than the last time, and we pulled into the port of Ensenada ahead of schedule. Jacques stood on the dock with Jean-Pierre and the unloading crew—Nacho and Miguel—ready for our arrival. I tried to back the ship in and nearly took out part of the dock, but eventually got us angled right with just a few scratches on the hull and splintered two-by-fours.

Jacques, Nacho, and Miguel came on to unload the ship, and nobody said a word. The whole process was unnerving because we were missing Juan, and Jacques just treated us like we weren't quite there. When we got to the van, Jean-Pierre searched us and took the .38 I still had from Burke, and the steak knife Rori had. We sat and watched while the bags were loaded. We pulled into the warehouse with the false garage door, and once again, the lights flipped on and the same armored car and woman in business attire stood off to the left, and I wondered who was getting shot.

"You two, out of the van, please," Jacques said.

"After you, Jacques," Rori said.

"Please just step out so we do not have to force you out," Jacques said, and I couldn't help but feel like a conversation had taken place with decisions made behind our backs.

"Come on," I said, and patted her hand. Jean-Pierre opened the rear door, and we stepped out, but he stayed behind us and walked us beyond the towering stacks of boxes. In the clearing behind them, plastic sheeting had been spread across the floor with two chairs at the center. My mouth ran dry as chalk.

"Sit down and stay quiet." He crossed his arms.

Rori looked at me, and I sat first; then she followed suit. We could hear the armored car get loaded, start, and the door creak open again while she pulled away. Once the door closed again, Jacques appeared in front of us in the clearing and stood beside Jean-Pierre.

"There was one thing that I asked of you when we agreed to our business. Do you remember what this is?" Jacques said, and pulled his jacket open so we could see the unsnapped handle of this nickel-plated gun.

"Jacques, we were getting the money *back* for you," I said.

"I asked you never to lie to me," he said, and paused.

"*Why* did you have to kill Avery?" Rori asked, and a pink color rose in her cheeks.

"Ah yes, the loud Americans. We have missed you here in Mexico. Would you like me to have Jean-Pierre teach you to keep that mouth shut, or are you going to listen?"

Rori stayed quiet, and Jacques continued. "You did not tell me about this phone call from Avery, and perhaps it is because you did not know. But that money was stolen from a series of shipments, and that is why we had to kill him. You see, we do not allow this to occur. This…skimming."

"He planned to give it back to you before the local cops raided him," I said.

"No, that was when I found out about the skimming. But yes, he also got very sloppy. And, he sent you two here as a peace offering. So, your beloved childhood friend set you up. How does that make you feel, Heath. Rori? Huh? Are you still angry that he is dead?"

"You're lying," Rori shouted, and this time Jacques nodded.

Jean-Pierre slapped her hard on the cheek, nearly knocking her out of the chair. She looked up at him through strands of stray hair and dabbed at the blood in the corner of her mouth.

"Your friend had to go, but my question is, what happened to Juan? He was supposed to call when you left Santa Cruz, and when he did not, I became worried. My contacts did not see him in Santa Barbara, or San Diego, and voilà, he is not here."

"Avery killed him," I said.

"Was it Avery? Because you know I research my employees, and it turns out that Rori here has a family in law enforcement. No, her father is the chief of police. So, this is another lie that you told me."

"Look," Rori said. "My father is dead. Nobody's looking for me."

"So, if you disappear, then there will be no questions?" Jacques asked. A brilliant smile spread across his face, and his sophisticated French accent sounded, for the first time, menacing.

"We've got one person who knows we're here, and he'll fucking come for us," Rori said.

"Your father's bounty hunter, Art Dominguez? He is a threat that we could very easily neutralize. However, I don't think that it will come down to this. I am going to let you live, but there is a condition. With the weather changing for the fall and winter, the ocean gets too rough. I cannot risk a sinking ship. So we are going to try a new method of delivery for some products, and I think you will like it. One of you will drive the product up through the border to the delivery site, and the other will stay behind. If you do not return, the other is dead." He smiled at this like he was some sort of mastermind. "You will leave in a week and a half. You can decide who goes and who stays."

"What do you mean we drive?" Rori asked. "I thought the whole safety of the operation was about the open ocean and lack of checkpoints? The border is crawling with drug dogs and security."

Jacques watched me for a reaction, I stared back without flinching. Then he switched his attention back to Rori. "We have a new, very clever plan. Do not worry. You and Heath actually helped us to devise it. It is with surfboards." Jacques smiled.

I already knew where he was going with this. "You're going to hide the drugs in surfboards," I said.

"Yes, that is correct. We have hollow surfboards coming out of a bonded facility in Puerto Vallarta. They come here, we load them with product and ship them over. And one of you gets to be our test rabbit." Jacques's wicked smile returned. "The Volkswagen with five longboards inside. This will be twenty kilos of product. A good test run, right? And if anything goes wrong, the car is registered to you, and you go down. It is perfect."

Rori tensed up, and I knew she wanted to kill Jacques with her bare hands, because I wanted to as well. I could rip his throat out and wouldn't need a single therapy session, because I would never regret it.

I placed my hand on Rori's shoulder, and she shrugged me off. Then she calmed slightly. He did have a fucking gun to our heads, after all. I gritted my teeth but spoke as evenly as I could. "What will we do in the meantime, while the shipment is prepared?"

"You will go back to La Fonda and eat and surf and be yourselves. Also, we have a small gift for you. We have switched your little Volkswagen for a VW van. It will have surfboards already loaded with product. You are still the happy American couple on vacation, so cheer up. Jean-Pierre will take you back to the suite now."

"When can we go home?" Rori asked, and Jacques stopped and turned back.

"This is your home now. The dream you always wanted, no? A permanent life of freedom and happiness and all the money you could want. You're welcome," Jacques said, then winked and walked over to a long seventies Cadillac, got in, and drove away while the garage door opened again. Jean-Pierre walked us slowly to the van, and we got in. Nacho and Miguel got in behind us, and we drove away, back to La Fonda resort. Our new life, and full-time prison.

Chapter Thirty-Five
Monday, September 19, 1988
Heath

1

The next morning, I woke up with a slight hangover and a vehement desire for cocaine. Juan had ruined us with his abundant supply. I pulled my robe on and walked into the living area, opening the curtains. The sky was gray with a marine layer blending in with the horizon of ocean. The crowds below had thinned from their peak in August, but there were still some tourists out and the same number of vendors strolling the beach, and I even saw little Erica walking in the sand with her Chiclet box.

I made some coffee and grabbed some Sun-Maid raisins and Cool Ranch Doritos from the minibar and brought them to Rori, who was sitting up in bed and staring at the window even though the blinds were closed. I opened them a crack, and she squinted and shielded her eyes. She sipped the coffee and lit a cigarette and pulled her knees to her chest with her arms around them.

"We need to end this now," Rori said, as if we were picking up from a previous conversation thread, which, maybe we were from the last one-sided conversation we had with Jacques.

I sat on the bed and rubbed one of her feet, but she drew it back and set the coffee down.

"We can still make money and disappear," I said. "Plan it right and get lost on one of the voyages."

"You heard him—we're going one at a time now. And driving across. And we have no option—we're not exactly free to leave." She gestured around the room, and I thought about whether or not someone was listening. I moved to the side of the bed and turned the alarm clock radio to a station playing some mariachi music, turned it up, and moved beside her.

"Just in case," I whispered, and she seemed on edge but played along.

"I can't do this another year, two years, three years. I just can't." Rori's head fell to her hands, her blonde hair falling through her fingers.

"Maybe, if we do these car drops, Jacques will trust us again to do the boat runs in the spring."

"I can't—I'm not coming back from this mission," she whispered. "I'm not going from one hostage situation to the fucking next."

I wanted to debate her, but she had a fair point, and I wanted that for her, too. That was what this was supposed to all be about. It was why we had come down here. I would have died fighting those bikers in that bar, and I would stay here and let her go home. I would die here.

"You go, then," I said. "You go, you make the drop, keep the drugs, whatever. I'll stay here and deal with Jacques."

"Fuck you, Heath," she still whispered, but it came out harsh. "We need to stick together. Forever."

"What are we supposed to do, steal the yacht?"

She laughed, then looked up at me, her eyes puffy and red. But she looked serious. "If it meant we went together," she said.

"There's no way we'll get away with that."

"How about this? I'll take this mission. I'll be alone in the van, and I'll lose the fucking follow, and I'll come back for you. Then we go to Art and get protection. He can protect us," she said.

"Art can't stop what's coming if we skip out on Jacques. They'll never stop until we're dead. Avery is proof," I said.

"Then we can keep running. Forever," she said. "But we need to get out of here. This can't be our life." She started to cry again. "This can't be all we'll ever know until we die at the age of twenty-six."

"Then we escape. We at least have to try," I said.

"I'm sure they will follow me to the border. Do you think I could lose them and come back for you? Then we drive for the border together?"

I thought for a second, then said, "The kill switch. If this van has one like Avery's did. Once you get on the road, you can use the kill switch and pull over. Make your follow come take a look under the hood. They'll never expect anything from you. Their egos won't allow it."

"Then what?"

"Then, start it up and run them the fuck over. Maybe I can have one of the vendors down on the beach get us some Mace, and you can just blind them. Or a butterfly knife."

"Where would I pick you up? I can't come back here."

"I'll go surfing like I always do. I'll paddle around the jetty and head to the beach just south of here. We'll pretend we're playing along with them, right?"

She nodded. "Sure, we'll pretend."

"When your follow comes over to help, get them to lift the hood in back, and kill them. Knife, rock, something."

Rori smiled. "How about a brick?"

I laughed. "Perfect. If you can, come back and get me. If not, just run for the border," I said, and stood. "If it ever feels too risky, just make the drop in the States and don't come back."

I walked to the hotel safe in the closet and opened it. I removed the cash Jacques had given us from our first drop. It was well under ten grand, but it didn't matter. The rest of our money was, Jacques liked to say, in the big bank. Which meant he owed us money that we were never going to get. I emptied the Doritos from the bag I'd opened, and dumped them on the nightstand. I slipped the money inside.

"What are you doing with that?" she said.

I leaned in close to her ear and whispered, "You're not going to need this, and neither will I. You'll have two million, and I'll be dead."

Rori's face ignited with color, and she slapped me hard in the face, and it stung. I backed away and felt my pulse there, in the reddening tissue, and she looked like she might stand but decided not to. She puffed nervously on her cigarette. "I'm coming back for you. No matter what. You fucking understand?" She somehow screamed this in a whisper.

"I want that too," I said, rubbing the sting away. "I'm going surfing." I grabbed the longboard leaning against the wood dining table.

2

I took a towel, the cash, and the board and walked down the path to the beach. When I got there, Erica saw me and the surfboard and started trying to run with the weight of the Chiclets and her duct-taped sandals catching in the sand. I wanted to laugh and cry at the same time. When she got to me, she threw her box to the side and grabbed onto my leg, and I patted her back. I glanced around to see if this was causing a disturbance with her parents or her handler or however this beach kitsch game worked. I didn't want her to get in trouble.

"*Donde esta* Rori?" she said, and Rori sounded like *worry*.

"In the *cuarto*," I said, and pointed up to the room.

"*Vamos a* surf," she said, and grabbed my finger, pulling me toward the water.

I laughed and set the bag of money down under my towel. She helped me drag the board to the water's edge. The waves were small and breaking softly beyond the shoreline, so I perched her on the surfboard, and we pushed out into the water. I paddled out to where the swell was unbroken, and we turned around. We surfed a dozen waves, and she screeched with excitement every time, with her distended belly poking out of her wet, threadbare street clothes that consisted of jean shorts and a pink onesie with frills around the neck. We rode a final wave in on my belly and her sitting on my back, then beached the surfboard. I dragged it up to my towel and I handed her the Doritos bag.

"*Para los Padres*," I said slowly, and she nodded and didn't even look in the bag. She knew it was something important.

She took up the Chiclets and shoved the box into the hands of the heavyset man who sold the Polaroids. The way she looked at the bag, it was as if she had anticipated something like this and knew exactly what to do with it. Maybe some kind guests had given her larger bills before. She seemed to know that she needed to get this to her parents before someone else took it from her, and I hoped when I saw her little frame getting smaller down the beach, that the gesture brought more good in her little life than it had for me. I decided that she would be fine, that her parents would keep the money safe, and that I would paddle out again and catch as many waves as I could until Rori and I had our next, and our last, delivery.

Chapter Thirty-Six
Wednesday, September 28, 1988
Heath

1

I sat up on my surfboard and bobbed with the small waves and let the current carry me farther south down the beach. The line of sight between my bodyguard, Nacho, and me disappeared. It was funny to watch him scramble down the beach and wave his arms at me. I flipped him the bird and paddled farther beyond the rocky peninsula that created the small private beach the hotel was built at the center of.

For a good several hundred yards, I paddled hard and it stayed rocky. Then, finally, the next beach opened up. This beach, instead of a single resort, had a tidy row of beachfront houses that were probably mostly vacant vacation homes. It would take Nacho twenty minutes to sprint up to his van, drive out to the 1D freeway, and take the private drive down to the beach to find me.

The surf was a heavy fall swell with ten-foot faces and out of my league, but it felt good to be out in the water, and I was starting to understand the solace of the ocean. It was a different world out here, better and calmer in many ways. The culture and ritual around surfing made sense to me now, because once you let wave riding become part of your life, it left an indelible imprint on your soul. I scanned the shore for the three-story blue house and found it. Sure enough, a freshly painted gray and white Volkswagen pulled down the drive and parked—I felt an exhilarated thrill in my chest that our plan had worked.

I waited for the perfect wave and patted the steak knife that I'd stolen from Cantina La Fonda as Rori had done. I'd rigged it with some neoprene from a torn-up wetsuit into a makeshift dive knife and bound it high on my thigh so my board shorts partially covered it.

The set swelled just behind me, and I adjusted my position again and angled toward the shore to start paddling just when my body and board rose high off the water, and I could see the coastline more clearly from up here. The Volkswagen looked almost new, but I was certain Jacques's crew had reinforced it in more than one way and probably beefed up the engine. I wished it were Avery's van, though I also hoped the hippies I'd traded it with had made it to where they were going after Art assuredly tracked them down.

Rori honked, and the wave broke to my left, so I took off down the steep face, a good ten feet, then turned hard to the right—it was the biggest wave I'd ever been on, and I didn't want to get rolled. The wave curled into a small barrel behind me and looked like it would close out ahead, so I tucked low on the board and pushed through a cloud of white water and then opened my eyes and was in a different world. The wave sheeted over me, and the water looked fluorescent and cyan in the early morning sun shimmering through.

When the wave crumbled, I dropped to my belly to ride the wave into the beach. I should have felt excited, happy, but I didn't. That hollow breathless suck ripped the air from my lungs. Something was wrong. Paddling hard toward the shore, I started to see the van a little better. There were two figures inside—Rori wasn't alone.

I dragged the board up the beach, tucking the steak knife into the small of my back. We'd told Jacques that I would stay behind, so it had fallen on Rori to make the delivery of the new product into Corpus Christi. My job had been to draw the sentries away from their posts and then to meet Rori here at this house at 9:00 a.m.

I felt an acid rush of anxiety and fear when I finally saw through the windshield. Jacques sat in the driver's seat, and Rori was bound, gagged, and blindfolded in the passenger's seat. I tried to run toward the bus through the sand, but it felt like a dream where your legs just wouldn't work. My feet sticking in the wet sand.

2

Ten yards from them, I could see Rori's face, and she was bleeding from her forehead and nose. Jacques rolled the window down partway, and I calculated the time it would take me to close the distance before he pulled the trigger of the nickel-plated gun aimed at Rori's temple. The odds weren't good, so I stopped about a few feet from him and spread my arms wide, showing I was unarmed.

"Heath, you and your girlfriend had a little plan, no?" Jacques shouted through his partially rolled-down window.

"I went surfing. What the fuck did you do to her?"

"Do not lie to me. This is bad idea for you both."

"I wish I knew what the fuck you were talking about. Look around, man," I said.

"Miguel, *dar me la niña*," Jacques said, his Spanish accent clear and focused.

The rear door opened, and Miguel got out wearing the white-and-black monastic robes, and he pulled a little girl from inside. My chest felt waterlogged and heavy. I wanted to scream and lunge for his throat but couldn't. It was Erica, and her tiny hands were bound with string, her mouth gagged, and she was crying.

"What the *fuck* are you doing? Let her go. She's got nothing to do with this," I yelled, and didn't care if it pissed him off.

"You see, you and Rori have a big plan. I already suspected it, but then you gave your money away to the little girl," Jacques said, and he tossed the Dorito bag onto the dashboard. I slipped the knife from the small of my back and held it flat against my right wrist, The serrated edge of the knife dug into my wrist, and a few warm drops of blood pooled into my cupped fingers. I was a fucking idiot for thinking I could help, that this tainted money could do any good in the world. I was an idiot for thinking I could get away from this man.

"Fuck you," I said, cold and flat.

Jacques smiled, and his white teeth flashed in the morning light. "See, the problem with you Americans is, you think that everyone else is stupid. All people are stupid except for you."

"Look, we'll go through with the plan. There's no need to overreact."

"I do not overact, Heath. But I do react."

"Okay, good. Then, just please—let Erica go."

"Miguel, *esta bien*," Jacques said.

Miguel cut the strings from Erica's red, puffy wrists, and he let her go. She pulled off the blindfold and saw me crouched twenty feet away and burst into tears, sprinting toward me.

"Señor Heath," she sobbed.

"Miguel, *matarla!*" Jacques shouted. But Miguel, standing with his hand tucked behind his waist, didn't budge.

The girl continued sprinting toward me. Jacques cursed Miguel, then took his nine-millimeter off Rori and aimed it at Erica, not more than six feet from me now. An involuntary, guttural scream escaped my throat. I tried to lunge and block the shot, but I couldn't reach her in time. But I didn't have to. Miguel, more quickly than I'd ever seen someone move, pulled his arm from the small of his back, freeing a Beretta of his own, fired three quick shots, all of which hit their mark. Three dots appeared on Jacques's forehead. Blood and broken glass sprayed behind it. His body immediately slumped forward, over the driver's side window. Rori, blindfolded, screamed and sobbed.

I stayed crouched, holding Erica against my chest while she, too, cried.

"Why…did you just get us all killed?" I asked, watching Miguel. I couldn't calculate something. It didn't add up, and it was because I couldn't think straight, or I didn't have the right data.

"Stand up. Help your girlfriend," Miguel said. He had a calm and practiced air about him. Like this was a normal part of his day. Walking over, he picked the little girl up and held her for a moment. Then he whispered something to her, and she scampered off down the beach. She must have known how to get back from here.

3

Walking around to the passenger's side, I opened the door, and Rori flinched. I gently peeled off her blindfold and cut her ropes free with the steak knife. She fell into my arms, her tears felt hot against my bare chest.

"What the hell just happened? Why aren't we dead?" Rori asked, and looked at me, then at Miguel.

"Come on, let's get out of here," I said, and helped her down from the seat.

"I didn't say you were free to go," Miguel said. He stood at the rear of the bus with the Beretta now trained on Rori and me. With his sharp jawline, broad shoulders, and black and gray hair, he looked distinguished and menacing all at once.

"Why the hell did you save us if you weren't letting us go?" I asked.

"I saved the little girl. No children. That has always been a rule of mine. I lost my own son once. Over twenty years ago," Miguel said.

"How—how did you lose him?" Rori asked, though my next question was more concerned with what his plans were for us.

"I had a son and a wife, and they were taken from me because I did bad things for bad men and bad governments. Jacques wasn't the worst."

"Then why do you still work for these people?" Rori asked. "Like Jacques?"

"I have no choice now. It is all I know. And I don't work for Jacques. I never did. I work for a much stronger organization. A new organization out of Sinaloa. I was brought in to take Jacques out of the picture. We have accomplished part of that today."

"Christ. So you meant to kill Jacques this whole time? Were we some sort of bait?"

"You two are very unpredictable. You have been fun for me to watch. But no. You were not bait. He went too far with Erica. And I could not let him kill you, either."

"If you work for another cartel, why would you protect us? Aren't you supposed to kill us all?" Rori asked.

"What are you going to do to us?" I asked. His gun was still on us.

"I have to answer to my bosses. Yes, the men who hired me. They are going to want these operations over here to be taken over smoothly. They want to take over, not destroy it all. In fact, it will look better on my résumé if this delivery still gets made."

"You want us to deliver the surfboards still?" Rori asked.

"If you don't, it will make my job a lot harder."

"But Jacques is dead. Can't you make something up for your bosses?"

"I cannot. I—"

"I'm pregnant," Rori blurted. She held her hands over her stomach, tears sliding down her blood-mottled cheeks. "I know I am. I don't know when it happened, but I was late. I took a test back at the hotel."

Miguel paused and looked out toward the ocean like a distant memory flickered somewhere behind his cool demeanor. "I guess congratulations are in order for you two."

I looked at Rori in her green eyes, the gold flecks shining in the sunlight. All this death, evilness, and destruction, and here she was, Rori, bringing new life into it all. The timing was goddamn shit, but the thought of being a father made my chest fill with an odd, comforting warmth. I kissed her knuckles and held her tighter in the opened doorway of the Volkswagen.

"What's going to happen, Miguel?" Rori asked.

"Well. As soon as I give the word, the monastery and the resort here will be cleared of all of Jacques's personnel. The ones who are not killed, those who surrender, will be offered employment with the new Sinaloa Cartel. Including his mules."

"What about us?" I asked.

"Well, I don't know. You lied to me, Heath."

My heart dropped into my stomach, and my mind raced, thinking through our limited conversations. I wanted in no way to piss this man off. "I did? When?"

"I asked you where you got that ring. Why did you lie to me?"

Having this man stand in front of me and confront me like this rocked me in a way that was hard to describe. Like I couldn't lie to him again, because he knew something I didn't. Or maybe a lot that I didn't. He had a timeworn, battle-hardened calmness to him that gave me the impression he knew what I was thinking. "I got it from my mom when she died."

"It looks a lot like this one," Miguel said. He lowered the gun and pulled a necklace from under his shirt. On the end was a ring. He pulled the necklace free and handed it to me.

Examining it closely, it looked almost identical to the one I had on with the dark center stone and engraving. I still didn't understand the inscription. I looked back up at him, and the realization of who I was looking at sent a cold chill down my back, and my heart felt like it would explode with pain and joy. He was my father.

"Where—how?"

"I left that ring on my son's neck twenty years ago in Panama. We had to get him out as enemies were approaching. I was supposed to connect with him in America, but the family he stayed with passed away. He got lost in the foster care system. We couldn't find him again."

My entire body tingled and felt weightless. My brain spun through twenty years of memories, fears, dreams, and imaginations at what this moment would be like. And here it was, here he was, and I couldn't hate him. Maybe Mouse was right. When you actually had a chance to see this person, your biological parent, you wanted them to love you. Even though it made no sense, the hate flew right out of your heart.

"You're my—" I felt my sinuses swell, my eyes burned. I fought it back. My first impression from my biological father shouldn't be of my tears. Though, I guessed it wasn't. He'd watched me this whole time, though I had no idea who he was.

"What does it mean?" I held the rings side by side, and now the tears splashed down on them, and I was ashamed to look up. I tried not to sound like I was crying. "The letters? Are they your real name?"

"My real name, son, is Hector Montoya." He moved a step closer, his voice clear and strong and showing no emotion. "So is yours. Your mother and I named you after myself."

The mention of my mother sent another surge of excitement, fear, and sadness through my body. It was all too much, and the numbness of shock felt like it might take over soon.

Rori looked down at the rings, running her finger over the engravings. "What is 'AO'?"

"That is an Old English *D*. The ring is the name given to me by the people who hired me a long time ago. They called me the Angel of Death."

Miguel, Hector, my father, took another step closer so we stood face-to-face. I was about an inch taller than him, but I felt like I was looking into a mirror twenty years from now. The face, cheekbones, shoulders—they were all mine. He turned his palm up, and I placed the ring back in his hand. He took the ring and slid it onto his ring finger. He was close, too close, and I remembered that he was, truly and absolutely, more of a stranger than anything else. I tried to recalibrate, shake off the emotion of being overwhelmed.

Taking a step back, I asked, "What happened to my mom?"

"She worked for the CIA and went AWOL when we got pregnant with you. When we lost you, it tore us apart." Hector's face fell, a crack in his stoic persona. Now his eyes pooled, and for the first time, I could see that he wasn't just a war machine. He was a person. "We didn't last another month together after they burned the house. And then we couldn't find you. So I went back to this, the thing I do best. Killing. And not dying. You seem to have a knack for surviving, too."

"Is she alive?" I asked, a glimmer of hope flickering deep inside of me, that I'd buried so many times over all those years in foster care. Could I really have a mom and dad again? Could we really be some sort of fucked-up family that was really good at killing bad people? Together?

"Your mother. Oh yes. At least, last time I checked she was. I can tell you where to find her. God, I wish I could see her face when you tell her who you are." Hector smiled now, the thin lines around his eyes spreading into something resembling joy. "Wear that ring."

"So, what now?" I asked. "What should we do? Will I see you again?"

"Well," Hector said, his face returning to its hardened scowl. "Now I am supposed to kill you both or convert you to our side."

"Christ. I'm *pregnant*." Rori said, letting out a soft cry.

"This is true. With my grandchild, too. But it is either that, or they kill me." He smiled, lines gathering at the corner of his eyes again. He was fucking with us with some wicked brand of vigilante humor. "If they can."

"You have a plan for us, Hector?" I wanted to call him Dad, but I also didn't. He wasn't my real father; he was my biological father. My father was the man who raised me. And every second we stood there, my brain did micro calculations about all the similarities between us. Hairline, posture, mannerisms. I couldn't help it. Now that I knew he existed, I couldn't undo that. And I wanted to know him, and there was something I had to say or regret it forever. "Is there any way we can go together? Just leave this all behind?"

"You know there is not. If I leave, they will find me. And if they don't find me, they will find you. I was foolish enough to believe we could be together once, and it almost killed us all. I will never risk that again."

"Even if it means I won't see you for another twenty years."

He looked into my eyes, and he softened. "I would die to be with you, son. But I would not let you die. Not ever."

More tears streamed down my face, but I refused to sound choked up. "So what next, then? How do we get out alive?"

He wiped moisture from his eyes with the palm of his hand, and his face turned rigid again. All business. Death and survival. My dad was gone, and Hector had returned.

"The best thing that you can do is get down to Ensenada and get to Jacques's boat." He moved around to the driver's seat and took the keys from Jacques's pocket. "Jacques planned to leave it here for the winter for repairs and upgrades."

"How do we get there?" I asked.

A church van came winding down the hill toward us, and Hector saw it and tensed up. "Those could be Jacques's men. I need to make the call and take care of these guys."

"Should we take the Volkswagen?" I asked.

"No, Jacques's men are going to scatter. It may take a little while to track them all down, and the Volkswagen will be too obvious. Plus, the windshield and blood. Take the surfboards and paddle down the coast. Take some cash and barter transportation from a local. Be careful. Trust no one. I will square things with the cartel once it is all done. They will not come after you."

I stepped closer to Hector, and he looked up at me, since I was slightly taller. "You turned out to be a beautiful man, son. My god," Hector said. His voice wavered now, and a few tears dropped down his cheek. "I loved that little child I held in my arms twenty years ago. I wanted to give it all up for him. For you." He placed his rough hand on my cheek. "We tried to give it all up. To have a family."

His hand on my cheek felt like an electric shock. It was hard to explain, even to myself, but this destructive man, this mercenary—I could feel in that moment that he must have loved me. At least, he had a long time ago, before I was ripped from his arms. We moved toward each other and embraced. He was wiry-strong and fit. He pushed away.

"You need to go. Take Jacques's two guns with you. I will take care of these men. Go down the beach. Get to the boat. Your mother lives in Kauai. On the North Shore. The name she goes by is Martha Helen. Now go!"

I wanted to ask him when I would see him again. But I knew it was a stupid question to ask. I already knew what the answer was. Never.

4

Helping Rori out of the van, I wiped some blood from her cheek. Other than the small abrasions to her face, she seemed fine. We took Jacques's two nickel-plated nine-millimeters, and each slipped one into the small of our backs. Taking a board from the van, and mine from the beach, we sprinted down to the water.

The shore break crashed against our knees, but we pushed the boards onto the water and leapt onto our bellies. Side by side, we paddled hard and fast into the ten-foot seas. Behind us, I could hear shouting; then gunfire erupted. When I looked back, the surf was too heavy, and I couldn't see the parking lot clearly anymore. But the sudden rush from my lungs made me wonder. I hoped he lived. I hoped he wiped them all out. Based on his profession, I assumed he fared just fine. He deserved a real life and would never get one. But thanks to him, Rori and I would have that. The family that he never got, and he'd sacrificed himself, his reputation so that we could have a clean slate. It was more than I could ask for from a stranger who had given me life so many years ago. A stranger that still wore the same ring.

Chapter Thirty-Seven
Wednesday, September 28, 1988
Heath

1

The water was cold, and although Rori had also become a strong swimmer, the swells were huge, and we were nearly a half mile from the shore. We weren't exactly safe. While we paddled in the direction of Ensenada, a thick layer of fog rolled in, and now we could barely see land. Which also meant that nobody could see us out here. Which was good.

"How long do we paddle? I'm freezing," Rori said.

The fall chill, with the blanket of wet fog, made the normally tropical climate feel cold. "If Jacques's men are on the run and they find us, we're as good as dead."

"Well, we can't paddle all the way to the boat. We'll drown or die of hypothermia."

She was right, but I wanted to be encouraging. "Let's just paddle until we can find something secluded. Something quiet."

She quietly paddled at a slow, rhythmic pace, and the fog created an odd sound barrier that muffled all other noise. Just the soft splashing of our hands in the cool water.

After nearly a half hour, my arms burned, and Rori was using one arm at a time and falling behind. "Let's get closer," I said.

We paddled closer to shore and saw an empty, rocky shore break. We turned back toward Ensenada and paddled for another fifteen minutes. My arms felt dead, but then I saw it. In the murky distance, I could just make out the frame of a little fishing shack with a makeshift dock. At the end of which was a small, aluminum fishing boat with an outboard motor.

"Let's go," I said. Rori followed.

We slipped in behind the boat softly and quietly. Sitting up on my board, I shimmied along the dock and untied the little boat. I wrapped the rope around my ankle and paddled back out to sea, towing the boat. I could hear Rori giggle in the muted fog. It probably looked ridiculous, me towing the fishing boat. But it was easy to do, mostly.

Once we got a couple hundred yards out, I tied our boards to the cleats on the back of the dinghy with their leashes. I climbed onto the boat, then helped Rori in. I choked, then pull started the little motor, and it purred to life, coughing up black swirls of exhaust. I covered Rori in some blankets that were used to cover the seats while I twisted the handle and rode the little fishing boat as fast as she could go toward Ensenada.

2

It took us three hours of thrashing over six-foot seas, threading between the swells so we didn't capsize, but we made it. The usually bustling little port of Ensenada seemed subdued today, probably because summer was over. We towed our surfboards around and navigated to Jacques's boat, the *California Dreamin'*. She looked beautiful in her slip, and I realized I felt a little homesick for the ship. Even though most of the adventures we'd had on her so far had been running drugs, maybe that could change.

"You think we can just sneak on it and take off?" Rori asked.

"I don't know. Let's get a closer look. If it looks clear, we get her out to sea."

I throttled down to the lowest speed the little motor could handle without dying and snuck into a slip a few over from *California Dreamin'*.

"Stay here," I said.

Jumping onto the dock, I walked slowly down the creaky planks and poked my head around the commercial fishing boat nearest *California Dreamin'*. I half expected to see Jacques and the loading van from the monastery. But no one was there. I waved to Rori; then I heard voices. I flattened against the ship and motioned for Rori to stay.

Watching closely, Nacho moved quickly down the dock toward the ship, holding a large duffel bag in each hand. Jean-Pierre followed him with two more. They disappeared into the ship, then a couple minutes later, jumped onto the dock and walked briskly back to the parking lot. Around the corner, a black SUV was parked with the back opened up.

"Stay here," I mouthed to Rori.

I sprinted around the fishing boat and jumped onto *California Dreamin'*. Crouching low, I climbed behind the wall of the kitchenette. From here, I could easily get the drop on them—put two bullets in each of them before they even realized who it was. I touched my ring. The name Hector Montoya repeated in my head like a cymbal crash. Finding out Miguel, Hector, was my father had rocked me hard. Cut me in half, only my body and mind still hadn't caught up yet. They would, I knew that. I could feel that, and once things calmed down, it would hit hard. I thought of Domino; he had been right all those years ago. I was lucky, in a very bad way. Death and destruction followed in my wake, and I, so far, always made it to the other side.

Just like my dad.

Miguel. Hector. My name was *Hector Montoya*. For god's sake, I had a name since birth. Only, that wasn't me. I wasn't my father. I killed, yes. But Mom and Dad, back on the ranch, they had also taught me that I was what my actions were. They had loved me, made me work, and shown me through their own actions the value of hard work, of sacrifice, and of doing the right thing.

They had taught me daily to focus my rage, and most importantly, every lesson—I was realizing now—was that quick actions that came with anger, they could haunt you. Forever. They taught me, with the poetry, the martial arts, the breathing exercises, and counseling, that you couldn't take back those quick actions. Death was forever. I finally understood, holding Jacques's nickel-plated nine, waiting for Jean-Pierre to come back, that what my parents had been trying to do all those years wasn't to stop me from defending myself. Mom died defending us with a shotgun in her hands. No, what they were trying to teach me was that in the moment, I needed to slow down and act with purpose. And to use extreme force, to kill, only when absolutely necessary. I couldn't let the anger, or the fear, drive my actions.

I wanted to kill these men for what they had done to Rori and me and countless others. But then I would be no different from them. From my father. I had been raised differently, and if I were going to do anything to honor Mom's memory, this would be it. Kill as a last resort. I didn't need the gun to get the drop on Nacho and Jean-Pierre. I just needed them off this ship.

I remembered the steel bar Juan had used to lock the steering wheel. I threw the gun overboard and retrieved the steel bar. I held it in my hand, and it felt roughly the same as Art's little baton had. The two men approached fast with two more duffel bags each. They were taking everything and taking their time doing it. How much did they need? They both jumped on the boat and quickly descended into the hull of the ship.

Hiding, crouched behind the stairwell, I waited for the two men to come up. I let Nacho lead, hop off the boat. A second later, Jean-Pierre came up, and I recited, "'Who used to ride a watersmooth-silver stallion.'" He turned, eyes narrowed, and he reached for his gun. I pounced, and with a vicious right-hand strike, I crushed every finger in his trigger hand. He howled in agony, and Nacho looked back. But I'd already closed the ten feet between us, so when he went for his gun, I cracked him hard in the elbow with the steel bar, likely shattering it. I took his gun and dropped it in the water, then shoved him on board.

"*Penche guero, pendejo,*" he yelled. We were attracting attention. I needed to end this quickly.

Behind me, Jean-Pierre reached for his gun with his good arm, but by the time he had it, I was already standing over him. *"Jesus / he was a handsome man."*

"You good for nothing mule. You are supposed to be dead," Jean-Pierre said.

I kicked the gun away and leveled the bar at his jawline to show him how easy it would be to end his life. "'How do you like your blue-eyed boy, Mister Death,'" I said.

"Fuck you!" he said, and spit.

I left him sitting here, holding his busted hand, and took some rope from the extra stock. I tied both men up tightly, back-to-back. I called Rori over, and she motored to the back of *California Dreamin'*. She helped me load both men into the aluminum fishing boat, and I tied them to a cleat on an empty slip near our boat. I took one of the duffel bags out and put it in the boat with them. Then I took the surfboards and loaded them into the ship. Rori and I went through the start-up procedure quickly and just in time. Sirens blared in the distance, and unmarked black cars pulled quickly into the parking lot of the marina. An explosion burst in the distance. Right around where Jacques's warehouse had been. But it didn't matter. Rori and I were already heading out to sea. Into the thick fog. And at full speed, I wasn't stopping until we hit Kauai.

Chapter Thirty-Eight
Saturday, December 15, 1990
Heath

1

"Dadda, burger," Linda said, pointing to a picture on the oversized menu at the Happy Tiki Restaurant. Our table on the second-floor lanai overlooked Hanalei Bay, its tall, majestic cliffs rising from the perfectly turquoise waters in the distance.

"We should really get her to eat something healthier," Mom said. Well, my biological mother, who for ongoing purposes, still went by the moniker of Martha Helen.

"You can try. But she smacks my hand away when I get anything green within three feet of her," Rori said.

"I'll just give her some of my burger and fries," I said. And it seemed to settle it. Baby Linda screeched, and I handed her a crayon, which she bit instead of drawing with. Rori took it and handed her a plush toy she could put her mouth on. We'd named the baby after my mom, Linda Walker. It had been Rori's idea, a way for her memory to live on in our hearts and lives. She had been a good woman, and I think she would have loved to meet our little girl. In fact, I knew she would. The Walker's would have made her waffles every weekend.

"My god, I never thought I would see you in this lifetime," Mom said. She said this every time she drank a couple of mai tais since we'd made it to North Shore and tracked her down. Which hadn't been all that hard with a local population of less than fifteen thousand on the entire island. She was tall, medium build, and beautiful. Allowing her gray hair to nearly take over her streaks of blonde. She wore light, simple summer dresses and kept a shiny red manicure with an array of necklaces purchased from the farmers' market. It had been so strange meeting her, and I almost felt guilty for allowing her to come and be such a large part of our lives, but I had to let all the anger and resentment go. They had done what they did to protect me. Hell, I wouldn't even be here if they hadn't handed me off all those years ago. "And my beautiful granddaughter. I'm just so thankful."

"Still no word?" I asked. We met for dinner at this restaurant once a week since Rori and I had made it to the island on *California Dreamin'*. Thankfully, not only had the boat been pre-loaded with all the money we would ever need, but it had also been supplied with food and beverage for wherever Jean-Pierre and Nacho had planned on taking it. Not to mention the paperwork filled out for ownership. All we had to do was complete it, and it was ours.

"Still no word. He has a way of reaching me though. If he wants to."

If he's alive, I wanted to say, and she must have read it on my face.

"Nobody can kill that man. He'll surface, when it's safe," Mom said.

The waitress came to our table with a bottle of champagne and three glasses.

"We didn't order that," Rori said.

"It was sent to you by a guest." She gestured to the bar.

Even though it was probably bad form, we all turned at once. Sitting there in a Hawaiian shirt, shorts, his graying hair cut short was Art Dominguez. Domino. Beside him was Tyra, his old partner at the club. I guessed they had gotten my postcard. It had been from the lobby of this restaurant, so it wasn't exactly magic that they were here. But it was, in a way. They had gone to great lengths to find this place. I waved them over and they approached.

"I hope you guys are enjoying your dinner," Art said. "Apologies. My name is Art Dominguez. This is my wife, Tyra."

"This is Martha Helen, our realtor. And this is our daughter, Linda," Rori said to finish up introductions. They shook hands, and Tyra cooed at baby Linda.

"Did the server say that you're staying here?" I asked.

"Yes. Well, yes. Sort of. Tyra and I sold our club in Shadow Valley and got the hell out. We bought a condo here and run a little food truck down in Hanalei Bay."

Tyra rephrased for him. "We got your postcard from here and decided to come out on our honeymoon last year. We went back, sold the club and all of our earthly possessions, and now we're here full-time. We love it."

"It's growing on Rori and me, too," I said.

I'd sent Art the postcard hoping he would come out, knowing that this was the kind of change he needed. Knowing that if you didn't get out, Shadow Valley consumed you like a sinking ship. The seclusion of the island was both freeing from our pasts and confining to a certain extent. But much less confining with a boat.

Art and Tyra pulled up some chairs and joined our table.

"We've been here since we left Mexico. Came in by boat," I said, and pointed out to *California Dreamin'* that was moored in the harbor, but it blended in with the other ships.

"Took that ship all the way here. Sounds like a lot," Tyra said.

"What are you doing now for work? Do you need a job?" Art asked, smirking.

Rori and I exchanged smiles.

"We made some investments in a few technology companies. Microsoft, Apple. We're set for a while at least. Maybe we can help if you want to turn that food truck into a chain," I said.

"I do have a couple of other business ideas in mind," Art said. Tyra elbowed him gently. "Maybe for another time."

"Well, we're not going anywhere," Rori said, and gestured around us. To the island that contained and delighted us. Everybody laughed.

"Christ. We went through a lot back then. Can we let all that go? Put it behind us?" Art asked.

"You did try to kill us," Rori said.

"Just Heath," Art said with a mock sheepish lilt to his voice. We chuckled, but it wasn't funny. "*Heath* almost killed *me* as well. I still walk with a limp."

"He does. But he's strong and agile," Tyra said, and ruffled the back of his head.

"Everything is forgiven," I said. "We start fresh. Friends on an island, with a really fucked-up past."

"*Heath*," Mom said. She nodded toward the baby. "She's a sponge." Linda threw a crayon on the floor. Being a father was such a stark contrast from our life two years ago, it made Baja seem like a different universe altogether.

"Hey, one thing I always wanted to ask," Rori said.

"Yeah. Anything," Art said.

"That Volkswagen bus. Did you catch up to those poor hippies we traded?"

Art laughed.

Tyra's face tightened into a frown. "Good lord, you should have seen the looks on those two."

Art laughed harder, and I started to chuckle.

"I followed them," Art said, "and nearly ran the boy over. Took the door off when they stopped to get gas and tried to get out."

"He scared the piss out of the boy at the very least. Left them both very high, and very confused," Tyra said.

"They were fine. God, I'm glad those days are behind us," Art said. "You two, you are the only bounties I never finished the job on."

"Well, cheers to that," I said. I wanted to change the subject while it was still lighthearted, before we had to think about Avery, and Mom, and Burke. Before the darkness permeated the conversation. It only took one person to say the wrong thing.

"Wonderful idea," Tyra said.

Tyra popped the champagne and filled up our glasses. Then filled two more from the bar. We clinked and sipped the cool, acidic drink down. While we sipped and smiled, it was funny to think that every one of us, Martha included, was on this island for a reason. To start over. We had run from something and found our paradise. I certainly found mine, and judging from the smile on Martha's face, and on Art's and Tyra's, we were home. And we certainly made a very dysfunctional family. One I sure as hell would never want to cross.

The End

Gratitude

First and foremost, thank you, dear reader, for taking the time to read this story that took me five years to write. Your time is valuable, and I appreciate you. If you loved this book, I would be forever grateful for an honest review on Goodreads, Amazon, and anywhere else you love to post reviews. The Goodreads page is found here. The amazon page is found here.

Thank you again.

-Nik Xandir Wolf

Acknowledgments

This book took me five years to write. And in the preceding five years, I wrote two other novels that are in a digital trunk somewhere. And if I had known it would take me ten years of really, truly working hard in this creative process to finally publish a book that I believed in, I probably still would have done it. Although with a slightly different mindset. I would have felt less rushed to get something published and just enjoyed the ride, because I love the process. And the greatest thing about writing fiction, for me, is that it is infinitely fun, complex, and challenging, and there will always be boundless room for growth.

That said, there are so very many people to thank for their help and contributions along the way. First and foremost, I would like to the man who ripped my grad school thesis to shreds and started me on course for this novel five years ago, Tod Goldberg. Thank you, too, for believing in me. You are one of the kindest and most generous humans I have ever had the pleasure of knowing.

I would also have to thank Stephen King, and especially his book *Billy Summers*, for finally giving me the courage to put the truth into this story that I felt the whole time but was afraid to write.

Also, a huge thank-you to my beta readers and editors. Gina Frangello, the best developmental editor a guy could hope for. Ashley Santana for helping me find those little beats where the audience wanted more from me as a writer. Maria Duarte, Mark Haskell Smith, Chih Wang, Tom Provost, and Rob Roberge for being awesome readers and helping guide this story through its many evolutions. Also, Chih Wang again as my incredible copyeditor.

A huge thank-you to all of my friends, teachers, and fellow students at UC Riverside at Palm Desert. You are my literary family and I love you. And, of course, a big thanks to the Stanford creative writing community, who got the ball rolling and helped me along the way. Especially the OWC Novel Writing Program. I learned a lot about craft.

Lastly, I would like to thank my family for sticking by me during this crazy process that at times, was all I could think about, and at others, I wanted to burn it to the ground. Your steadfast belief in me makes all the difference in the world.

About the Author

Nik Xandir Wolf is a Monterey, California based writer and surfer. He attended Stanford's OWC program in novel writing and holds an MFA from UC Riverside-Palm Desert. His debut chapbook was published in February 2022 by <u>Kelp Books.</u> His essays, fiction, and poetry have appeared in various publications. *Shadow Valley* is his first novel.

www.ingramcontent.com/pod-product-compliance
Lightning Source LLC
Chambersburg PA
CBHW011317310726
48973CB00011B/2962

9 781964 880020